Will You Always Love Me?

and Other Stories

Will You Always Love Me?
and Other Stories

JOYCE CAROL OATES

A WILLIAM ABRAHAMS BOOK

A DUTTON BOOK

DUTTON
Published by the Penguin Group
Penguin Books USA Inc., 375 Hudson Street,
New York, New York 10014, U.S.A.
Penguin Books Ltd, 27 Wrights Lane,
London W8 5TZ, England
Penguin Books Australia Ltd, Ringwood,
Victoria, Australia
Penguin Books Canada Ltd, 10 Alcorn Avenue,
Toronto, Ontario, Canada M4V 3B2
Penguin Books (N.Z.) Ltd, 182–190 Wairau Road,
Auckland 10, New Zealand

Penguin Books Ltd, Registered Offices:
Harmondsworth, Middlesex, England

First published by Dutton, an imprint of Dutton Signet, a division of Penguin Books USA Inc.
Distributed in Canada by McClelland & Stewart Inc.

First Printing, February, 1996
10 9 8 7 6 5 4 3 2 1

 REGISTERED TRADEMARK—MARCA REGISTRADA

Library of Congress Cataloging-in-Publication Data:

Oates, Joyce Carol
    Will you always love me? and other stories / Joyce Carol Oates.
        p.   cm.
    "A William Abrahams book."
    ISBN 0-525-93972-5
    1. United States—Social life and customs—20th century—Fiction.
    I. Title.
    PS3565.A8W53   1996
    813'.54—dc20   94-43865
                                                        CIP

Printed in the United States of America
Set in Garamond Light
Designed by Leonard Telesca

for Greg Johnson

Contents

I

Act of Solitude

It had been an accident, of that he was convinced.

If he hadn't driven himself. If he'd gone in a company car.

If, driving, he'd taken another route through the city, avoiding that stretch of lower Decatur Avenue. If he'd left his home in sub-urban Willow Lake five minutes earlier, or later—nothing would have happened.

Or, assuming something *must* happen, it would not have been what had happened. It would have been . . . another story.

Another ending, another set of consequences.

And his truest self unaltered. Undefiled.

If he'd had a witness, another presence.

Someone in the passenger's seat beside him. A pair of eyes, a voice. To say, "No!" Or, "Don't!" Or, "You'll have to stop— please *stop.*"

If one of his children, Katie for instance, she'd have cried, "Daddy, no! Don't!"

If his wife Diane . . . but was there any story he could tell him-self that might plausibly include Diane, seated beside him on that trip through the city, an hour's drive to a routine business meet-ing in a Hyatt Regency on the far side of the river?—for only lovers new to each other, in a common fever of desire and pos-sessiveness, would accompany each other on such a drive, to no purpose other than being together. And he and Diane were not lovers, and they were not new to each other.

If one of his colleagues, one of the junior staff who admired him, yes, certainly.

If his father, if his mother. Yes?

If a witness, virtually any witness, someone who knew *him*, none of it would have happened.

Not the part of it that was, he was convinced, purely an accident, his reflex-panic, hitting the accelerator as he had, not that, nor the rest of it, the guilty response, the fleeing-the-scene-of-the-accident—*that*, that seemed to him the true criminal act, would never have happened.

He'd examined his car afterward, casually, in the Hyatt Regency parking lot. The left front fender, the driver's door, seeing, yes, yes there *was* a mark, or marks . . . an indentation in the metallic-green metal . . . so shallow, you would have to know what you were looking for, to discover it. Certainly you would have to know what you were looking for to identify it.

This most mysterious point, which Diane would raise: *Why* had he driven to the meeting in his own car?

It was customary for him to be driven to such meetings in a company limousine. The company owned six limousines of which two were stretch limousines, with smoky-dark rear windows, opaque from the outside. He was a busy man, a very busy man, why drive his own car, why subject himself to traffic on I-75, then Route 16 through the inner core of the city, why waste an hour's precious time, *why.*

Recalling now, when the children were very young, he'd made it a point to spend at least twenty minutes exclusively with them each weekday evening, reading them to sleep, he'd been so young a father when Rick was born he'd seemed even to himself a boy, comically ill-suited for such a responsibility and for such a privilege, seated at the bedside of a drowsy child, turning the stiff, elegantly illustrated pages of a new edition of *Mother Goose*, trying to keep his impatience from showing in his voice . . . for though he loved his babies, little Rick, little Katie, he'd been a very busy young man in a notoriously competitive profession, of sixty newly hired men (quite literally, this was 1967, they were all men, and Caucasian) only three or four would survive to be promoted up through the company, and Chester Jensen was determined he would be one of them . . . so he tried not to think of spending these twenty pleasurable minutes with his children as a waste of precious time. As his mother had said, the time when children are really *children* is so brief.

Ordinarily, on such a trip, a routine sort of trip, he'd have been oblivious of his surroundings, chauffeur-driven in one of the company cars, protected from any insult on the street, any danger. Seated comfortably in the deep-cushioned rear of the limousine, shielded from the glare of the daylight and from the occasional rude stares of strangers by the dark glass, he would have scanned the *Wall Street Journal,* always provided for passengers in the company's cars, and then he would have concentrated on his work, scarcely aware of traffic, of the deferential driver, of even the luxurious vehicle in which he was being transported.

Why had he wanted to drive himself, well he'd wanted to, no special reason. Just to be alone, maybe. Was that it?—the rare solitude of an hour's drive? No special reason.

He would say to Diane, if she asked, if, upset, as surely she would be if he told her, Look, please: I don't like to be interrogated.

You know that.

It had been a wet-glistening day. Early April. A glare to the sky and the pavement like pewter.

He'd left the house in Willow Lake at eight o'clock, the meeting was scheduled to begin at nine-thirty, he had plenty of time and was in no hurry, pleasurably alert, appreciative of the way his car (a recently purchased Acura) held the road, navigable as a small yacht in placid waters, amused to think that, yes, he enjoyed driving a car, simply driving, to no purpose save driving, an overgrown American boy, and why not: behind the wheel of a car there comes into being an indefinable yet unmistakable *self* that exists nowhere else.

If, at least, the driver is alone. Not distracted by conversation, the presence of others.

He'd been driving on Decatur, which Route 16 became, in the city, the shabby warehouse district near the Stevenson Memorial Bridge, where once his father and his uncle had owned property . . . leased to van companies, storage companies, Cziffra & Sons Bookbinding. (There, at the corner of Decatur and Seventh Street, was the aged red-brick building in which Cziffra's had been located, now tenantless. The name "Cziffra" had fascinated him as a boy.) It made him feel somewhat melancholy, to see how derelict the neighborhood had become: potholes in the streets, gutters and sidewalks littered with debris, including broken glass; shut-down stores; burnt-out and abandoned buildings; panhandlers and winos on the streets even at this early hour, and pitiful human shapes huddled in doorways or stretched out (sleeping? comatose? dead?) on filthy sidewalks, in the wet. Five miles to the south, Decatur Avenue was a respectable commercial street; beyond that, past the city limits in the suburb of Elm Ridge, its name changed, it was a leafy residential street, quite attractive.

Mr. Jensen, Chester's father, and his uncle, now deceased, had hastily sold their urban property after a plummet in prices, in the late 1960s. They'd lost a good deal of money, but not so much, they insisted, as if they'd stayed.

Mr. Jensen was still "active," as he liked to say, in business. And, though seriously handicapped by arthritis, he continued to live in the old house, in a section of the city called Woodside Park.

Mrs. Jensen, of whom, for some reason, Chester frequently thought, when he had a period of interrupted solitude to himself, had died seven years ago.

Three blocks from the bridge, his attention was drawn to a small group of men, vagrants, winos, homeless people, what was the proper term?—a contentious little group standing on a corner, quarreling. One shoved another, who stumbled backward, colliding with a third. They were black men and white men, little distinction between them . . . all rag-clad, bareheaded in the rain. Then he had to abruptly brake for a hefty red-haired woman with an ulcerated leg pushing a shopping cart across Decatur, in a benign sort of daze, oblivious of traffic. Then, his attention was drawn to a straggly line of ragged figures, mysterious at first until he saw that they were waiting to enter a storefront with the sign ST. ANTHONY MISSION overhead, a soup kitchen on Third Street.

"Life unworthy of life."

He thought these words, then said them aloud, "Life unworthy of life." A phrase that seemed to have slipped into his mind: from what source, he didn't know.

The way song lyrics drift through our minds, skeins of words, snatches of old conversations, memories, dreams.

In the next block, he saw a traffic light turn from green to amber; he was aware of vehicles on either side of him speeding up, to make the light; but he wasn't to be hurried, he continued at his own speed, though aware of, while not quite registering the significance of, several ragged men standing in the intersection.

Yes he might have sped through the intersection, blameless as the amber light turned to red.

Yes this is how accidents happen: what's called "fate."

Or, in another idiom, "destiny."

No I don't know why, there is no *why*.

He stopped for the red light, first in line in the outermost lane. Decatur and Second Street.

And one of the ragged men came immediately to his car, a light-skinned black man with a face that looked boiled, inflamed puffy eyes, wild Brillo hair, a raw gash of a mouth like something torn in meat. A wino, by the look of him. Yes and a beggar—an extortionist. Leaning aggressively over the windshield of Chester Jensen's car and before Chester could wave him away making swiping motions with a filthy rag as if to clean the glass.

Chester rapped on the windshield, shaking his head, calling, "No—*no*," and, when the black man paid no attention, "Hey, you—get away, goddamn it!"

Sitting there astonished and helpless behind the wheel of his newly purchased metallic-green Acura sedan, trapped at a red light while a beggar-extortionist befouled his windshield, in the pretense of cleaning it.

Chester rolled down his window and leaned out and said,

loudly, not threateningly but forcibly, "I said *stop*! You! Are you deaf? Get away from this car!"

Still, the black man ignored him. There was a sullen pride in his expression, a doggedness in his manner, that suggested deliberation; unmistakable aggression.

Life unworthy of life.

A nonhuman creature in human form. Ah, repulsive!

Chester, furious, sounded his horn; rapped again on the windshield; shouted for the black man to stop. But the black man coolly persisted with his malicious circling motions on the glass, his rag leaving oily smears. Chester leaned out the window and shouted, "Goddamn you! I'll get the police! I'm not paying you a dime!"

At this, the black man paused. He stared at Chester with his inflamed eyes. He wasn't an old man, no older than Chester, his nappy hair threaded with gray, one of his ears puffy and misshapen. He screwed up his face in a grimace, or a grin, and muttered something mocking and guttural resembling "Ngggghhh you, man"—then leaned close to the windshield and spat on it.

Afterward, Chester recalled that, in that instant, he'd lost all control.

And he'd been blind, momentarily.

He pressed his foot down on the accelerator, hard, not knowing or caring if the intersection was clear of traffic, and the car leapt forward, and there was a muffled outcry, and the heavy thud of the black man's body against the fender, then against the door, and the tires skidded on the wet pavement, and squealed, but held; and next thing he knew, Chester was a half-block away, seeing, blurred, in the rearview mirror, the black man's body sprawled motionless in the street.

He kept going, he didn't look back.

He provoked me, I lost control.

He taunted me. Rubbing that filthy rag in my face.

The police don't protect us, they've abrogated all responsibility.

I didn't realize he was standing so close.

I didn't realize I would hit him.

I didn't realize I was actually . . . pressing down on the accelerator.

I warned him, I made myself perfectly clear.

I won't be extorted in my own car, in daylight.

I'm not a coward, to be extorted, in my own car, in daylight.

I'm not a racist. I had no awareness of the color of his skin.

I didn't mean to hurt him, if I hurt him.

My windshield. My car.

Nothing like that has ever happened to me before.

I've never had an accident in any car I've driven, I've rarely been ticketed for speeding, or parking . . . probably not more than four or five tickets in my life.

I'm a law-abiding citizen. I realize that sounds . . . the way it sounds. But it happens to be true.

Of course I pitied him, yes I might have given him a handful of change, a dollar, yes, why not, if I had it to do again yes maybe that's what I'd do, just toss the money onto the pavement and he'd stoop to get it and forget about my windshield and that would have been the end of it, yes I'd do that now, but now's too late.

I'm sure he wasn't killed, I didn't hit him head-on, and I accelerated from zero miles per hour. I'm sure.

I have never raised a hand against anyone in my life.

I swear, it was not a matter of race. I never saw the color of his skin.

I mean, it was something else I saw: his face, his eyes.

Accusing, and mocking. Like death.

For their own good. Institutionalized—in homes, in psychiatric hospitals, prisons, wherever.

Tax money. No end to it.

You're a civilized person, you must protect yourself.

Of course, they need our help.

Of course, it isn't their fault.

What if we all let ourselves go. Alcohol, drugs . . .

I didn't realize I would hit him.

I didn't realize he was standing so close.

It wasn't an accident in the sense of a traffic accident, I mean I didn't hit a man in the street with my moving car, my car was stationary, stopped at a red light.

It *was* an accident, my bad luck, ironic bad luck. Having kept within the speed limit, obeyed the law. Missed the light.

No police. No one followed.

No witnesses.

Were there?

Driving over the Stevenson Memorial Bridge he'd felt his heart beat so violently he believed he would die. But he maintained perfect control of his car, he kept in lane, he was going to be all right, he *was* all right.

Switching on his windshield spray, and the wipers. So the gob of mucus-saliva dribbling down the windshield, and the oily smears, the mockery, were washed away.

A very long time afterward, though, in fact, only that evening, Diane was asking how the meeting had gone, and he was telling her it had gone precisely as he'd planned. Meaning, very well.

Politely, he asked Diane how her day had gone, and she told him.

They were eating dinner in the breakfast room, adjoining the kitchen. A bower of oyster-white and pale yellow, Laura Ashley floral curtains, spidery hanging plants. Rarely did they use the formal dining room, just the two of them. The house was uncomfortably large now both the children were gone.

Frequently, Chester lifted his head. Expecting to hear footsteps upstairs. A door slamming. Muffled laughter. Echoes.

As his mother had remarked, years ago, bemused, melancholy. After Chester and his elder brother Herman had left home and there remained only Mr. and Mrs. Jensen in the spacious old English Tudor house in Woodside Park. The elegant old neighborhood now bordered, on two sides, neat as a right-angled incision, by "transitional" neighborhoods.

Diane was smiling patiently. That smile that signaled impatience.

"Are you listening, Ches?—I said, he called again. This morning."

Chester nodded, to show he'd been listening. "He did? Again?"

"So I think we hadn't better miss another Sunday. I'll take a pork roast."

"Wasn't that what we'd planned?"

"Was it?"

Diane stared at him, the corners of her eyes whitely pinched, in perplexity.

His wife of twenty-seven years. His old best friend, sister-rival, mirror-twin. They were so close it seemed to no purpose, to observe each other, still less to judge. Any lie Chester told Diane became, in the telling, in her absorbing of it, truth.

"*Was* it?" Diane had gone into the kitchen for the salad, was calling back to him, a brooding thinking-aloud manner, as if she were alone. He heard her open the refrigerator door, and close it.

He swallowed a mouthful of red wine.

"Diane. I think I killed a man today."

He heard her at the sink. A faucet on, a faucet off.

From the radio on the windowsill, the local university station, classics by the hour, no commercials. A harpsichord piece of startling brilliance, almost painful clarity, like splinters of broken glass—Chester listened closely, willing himself to be struck, *moved*. Sometimes, unbidden flashes of beauty had the power to bring tears to his eyes.

When Diane returned to the table, setting down the handsome wooden salad bowl, Chester smiled, and said, "Bach, d'you think?"

The piece ended. The radio voice identified it as having been by Scarlatti.

Since returning home, Chester had showered and shaved for the second time that day, and he'd been able to eat most of the meal Diane had prepared, and he judged himself all right.

A certain constriction in his chest, that was all. A shortness of breath. As if, in his own house, in this prettily-appointed breakfast room, he was apprehensive, waiting.

A loud rap at the door, a ringing telephone.

But the telephone rarely rang this late in the evening now that Katie was gone, living in Washington, and it had not rung since they'd sat down to eat.

Diane had her own story to tell, her story-of-her-day, and she told it in a voice of womanly concern, solicitude. Her gray eyes with their perpetually damp lustre were fixed frankly on his eyes as if daring him to look away.

She was an attractive woman in her late forties, past the bloom of her odd wry beauty. An intelligent face, though narrow, angular: her chaste Unitarian face, he'd used to tease. And her lips so thin it seemed as if, brooding, she were sucking them in.

She was a good woman, but goodness is not enough.

Yes and he was a little fearful of her, the fineness of her perceptions now that their sexual life, never very vigorous to begin with, had subsided; become, you might say, chaste. The fineness of her perceptions, the *pryingness* of her moral sense.

". . . Almost as soon as you'd left this morning. At first I could hardly hear him, he has this new habit of lowering the receiver as he speaks, maybe lifting his arm tires him? so I have to say, 'Yes? What? I can't hear you,' and since his hearing is impaired he's saying, 'Yes? What? I can't hear you.'" Diane paused so that Chester could wince, and laugh. "Of course, he's lonely and he's frightened in that house and there's this sort of, I think it's anger, resentment, I don't know why, *you* know, your brother with all his success is the same way, well he misses your mother I suppose, he blames her for leaving him . . . well, anyway, after we'd been talking a few minutes, and he'd asked about you, and Rick, and Katie, and I told him more or less what I'd told him on Tuesday, I think then he realized he'd just called . . . but he had to bluff it out, you know how he is."

Chester laughed, rising from the table. He'd heard a car quietly pull up at the curb. Not in the driveway, but at the curb.

It was nine-forty by the kitchen clock. He glanced at his watch, to confirm.

He was puzzling Diane, walking out of the kitchen like this, and their intimate little meal not finished. Smiling, vague, he said over his shoulder, "Oh yes—*I* know."

But there seemed to be no one outside, no one he could see.

The grassy lawn in front of their house was large, and sloping, and strategically placed with trees and shrubs to form a natural barrier, shielding the house from the street. A single street lamp glowed, that muted suburban-rural light. Had no car driven up? Was no one there?

He waited, until Diane came to fetch him. The sensation in his chest increasing with the deliberation of a clock's ticking.

*   *   *

And time passed, days, weeks. And there were no consequences, in a public, legal sense.

For, out of an act of such solitude, and no witnesses who knew him, *what* might the consequences realistically be?

Chester knew, there had been several other vehicles at the intersection, beside and behind him. Out of the corner of his eye, even in the exigency of his distress, he'd been aware of other drivers being harassed by the rag-wielding beggars. And these other drivers had surely seen Chester's car start up, bronco-like, and the black man knocked to the street, they'd watched the metallic-green Acura driven through the red light and along Decatur and out of sight and no looking back yet, apparently, no one had taken down his license plate number, no one had reported the incident to the police.

The truest witness, the black man, would not have reported it, Chester knew he could count on that. Even if the man had not been killed, or seriously injured.

He wouldn't want any trouble, Chester thought—any more than I do.

Yet, in a way, he *did* want trouble. So oddly.

Mentioning, to a friend, over drinks, that he'd had an "incident" in his car, in the city, a dangerous-looking black man approaching his car as if to wash the windshield, demanding money, but Chester hadn't given him any, had refused.

"And then?" his friend asked, expectantly.

Chester saw the man's nostrils widen, just slightly; the pupils of his eyes contract. A vicarious rush of adrenaline. But Chester had to disappoint him. Lifting his hands, spreading his fingers in a gesture of noncommittal. "And then—nothing. I drove away."

"You didn't give him any money?"

"I didn't give him a dime."

Another time, at a dinner party, the subject had shifted to cosmetic surgery, of the kind sometimes required after traffic accidents—one of the guests was in fact a cosmetic surgeon—and there was talk of facial disfigurement, and ugliness, and the horror it evoked, out of all proportion to its danger to anyone; and Chester, who'd been sitting preoccupied for most of the evening, seemed to wake, and said, thoughtfully, "Is there a gene, or something in the brain, some neuron or such, that registers 'disfigurement'?—the familiar gone wrong? Apart from rational understanding, I mean, just a quick gut reaction, say you see a human being who isn't fully 'human,' missing an eye, a nose, or deformed, or whatever—is the instinct to recoil in disgust? I mean," Chester said awkwardly, wondering why he'd plunged so urgently into this, "quite apart from a rational understanding of the situation?"

The cosmetic surgeon replied at some length, as if pleased that the question had been asked. Yes, he said, there seems to be a physiological expectation, located in the part of the brain that recognizes faces; only by practice, that's to say by an act of will, can medical students learn to overcome it—"To substitute rational understanding for instinct."

Leaning forward on his elbows in order to see the surgeon better, Chester said, "The expression 'Life unworthy of life'— where does it come from?"

There was a moment's silence. Then the surgeon, whose name was Weissmann said, with a wry downturning of his mouth, "The Nazis. The 'purification of the race.' Genocide."

He made out a check for $2,000, for the St. Anthony Mission.

If Diane was astonished at this gesture, she gave no sign; she seemed most sympathetic. She said, "What most upsets me are the babies. The crack babies, the AIDS babies. They are so *innocent.*"

"Well," said Chester, smiling, vague, in this new vagueness of his that was disconcerting to those who knew him, "—they don't know, then."

Diane said, frowning, "Don't know what?"

Chester said, as if this were an answer, "What we know."

By the time a handwritten note from the director of the Mission came, to thank him for the donation, Chester had nearly forgotten it. He crumpled up the note and let it fall.

A curious ghost-pain played about his body, like the pain of a phantom limb.

*　　*　　*

Recalling that *thud!* of the black man's body against the fender of
the Acura. The swift shadowy somehow birdlike shape. His own
adrenaline pang, that wild thrill, elation.

And none of it deliberate, but only accidental.

A warm, humid Sunday in early summer but Chester's father, in a
gray cardigan sweater buttoned across his slightly concave chest,
complains of a draft from the French doors. So the doors are kept
closed.

Outside, green shimmers damply in the sunshine, like a mirage.

It's early in the day for a drink potent as bourbon but Chester
seems to have accepted—there's a drink in his hand. It would be
discourteous to decline his father's offer, and cruel, since, to Mr.
Jensen, the first alcoholic drink of the day marks the formal beginning of the day's conclusion.

And there's a sense of profound relief, in knowing that the
day, any day, is under control, and moving swiftly toward its
conclusion.

Chester is sitting in his father's study, listening to his father
talk, talk . . . perhaps it is more accurate to say that he is listening
to his father's voice, murmurous and ceaseless as a brook and interrupted now and then by spasms of mirthless near-soundless
laughter. He is concerned that his father looks so drawn, so pale,
so peevish, so . . . old. Yet, Mr. Jensen is almost eighty, what can
one realistically expect? He seems to have shrunk, there is something turtle-like about the way he holds his head, as if prepared
to retract it, yes and the loose wattled skin at his throat, quivering
as he speaks. What is he saying? What is he urging Chester?
Chester nods, smiles, sits with one leg crossed over the other,
foot wagging. His nervousness in Mr. Jensen's presence manifests
itself as boyish restlessness.

Chester is thinking that he loves his elderly father, but there is
a desperation in his love that must be disguised.

A middle-aged man's love for his father: what *is* it, precisely?

In the old days, Mr. Jensen spent most of his time, including
Saturdays and Sundays, at his office; when he was home, he hid
away in his study, this very room. Chester associates this room

with privacy and secrecy and being unwelcome. He sees that very little has been changed in this room. The enormous rolltop desk with its numberless drawers and shelves, complex as a honeycomb; the smell of dust, mildew; the leather chairs, in which both men are sitting, worn very thin, the leather cracked in places like broken veins. Dark walnut paneling on the walls that puts him in mind of a coffin, upright.

Chester's hand shakes, but he does not spill his drink.

Mrs. Jensen is in the kitchen preparing dinner—she is a wonderful cook, fussy and nervous but wonderful, compliments make her blush as if in annoyance but, yes, she is a wonderful cook, and Chester's mouth waters as he smells roasting meat, roasting potatoes, suddenly he is helpless in the grip of appetite.

He thinks, If I don't have guilt for a guilty act I don't have anything. I *do* have appetite.

He's a good man, but goodness is not strength.

He wants to tell Mr. Jensen that, to the very end, so long as one's body holds, there is solace in food, and in appetite.

He wants to tell Mr. Jensen that faith in food and in appetite is the last faith to go.

Yet: is Mr. Jensen telling *him* this? Has this been what the old man has been telling him, these many minutes?

Yet: if Chester is here in his father's study, a welcome guest in his father's study, if he is a man of fifty years of age, then, he realizes suddenly, with embarrassment, it must be the case that the woman in the kitchen preparing Sunday dinner is not Mrs. Jensen but Chester's wife Diane.

Of course, Diane.

It's a custom. Visiting Mr. Jensen. In the big old house, in Woodside Park. Every inch of the property protected by electronic surveillance. Alarms that ring both on the property and in the closest police station. Expensive, yes. But worth it.

For the same reason that the woman in the kitchen must be Diane, and not Mrs. Jensen, the French doors must be kept tightly shut. The squares of glass rebuff vision, like aged, wavy glass, since Mrs. Jensen's rose garden, once clearly visible beyond the windows, no longer exists.

Two or three summers ago, Mr. Jensen ordered the gardener to dig the remaining plants up. Scrawny, diseased. People who don't know roses are surprised how rose bushes wear out, and quickly.

Chester thinks, sipping from his bourbon, I am dreaming, aren't I.

Chester thinks, smiling, sly, If I am dreaming, I can end this any time I want.

Abruptly, rather impishly, as if he has been following Chester's thoughts all along, Mr. Jensen says, "Son, how *are* you?—you can tell me."

Chester thinks, He has forgotten my name!

Chester says, smiling, "Father, I told you didn't I: I'm fine."

Mr. Jensen regards him, benign, knowing, his pouched eyes narrowed, turtle-head wagging. "Yes, son, but how *are* you: you can tell me."

Making a dismissive gesture in the direction of the kitchen, as if to say, You can tell *me, she* can't overhear.

Chester says, smiling, "Father, I told you didn't I: I'm fine."

Mr. Jensen winks, and says, "*You* are fine? *You?*" He laughs his harsh sibilant mirthless laugh, rocking in his chair. "*You*—you are a happy man?"

Chester says, smiling harder, wagging his foot harder, "Father, I told you didn't I: I am fine, and I am happy, and I am the happiest man on earth."

Mr. Jensen nods, and laughs, his shoulders hunched as if he's about to fall forward out of his chair. He says, "*I'm* the happiest man on earth."

The men laugh together.

Chester says, "I thought you were dead. I'm sorry."

Mr. Jensen says, wiping at his eyes, "I'm dead, I'm dust and dead. I'm nothing."

Chester says, "*I'm* dead, I'm dust and dead, I'm nothing."

By now the men are laughing loudly together. They are in each other's arms, tight, tight, a suffocating embrace.

Their laughter is such a happy sound, someone jealous will interfere.

*   *   *

Diane had turned on the bedside lamp, and she was sitting on the edge of the bed, stroking his forehead, smoothing down his spiky hair. She said, "Are you going to tell me about it, Ches?"

At first her face was blurred, as if seen, grudgingly, through aged wavy glass.

He'd wakened her, again. Another of his dreams, squirming and kicking at the bedclothes, sweating like a pig. Groaning and laughing in his sleep.

It must have been bad, this time. He'd moved out of their bedroom to sleep in an adjoining room, the old nursery; meaning to spare her such episodes as this.

He said, "Oh God, I'm sorry. I'm embarrassed, and I'm sorry."

Diane continued stroking his head, smoothing his hair. She was clearly frightened. But calm. Wanting him to know how calm she was. How truly she was not in terror of this strange new seemingly unstoppable thing that was happening to him, and to her.

Chester was sitting up in bed, he'd swung his legs around, placed his feet on the floor. Squarely on the floor.

You're less of a fool, and less weak-headed, with your bare feet square on the floor.

As if to demonstrate masculine prerogative, though he was feeling very shaky, Chester slipped an arm around Diane's shoulders; squeezed her tight against him. He apologized for waking her. He apologized for being so susceptible to—whatever it was.

He'd use the bathroom, he said. Wash up a little, and go back to bed. It was only four-thirty, too early to get up. He was certain, now, he'd be all right.

Diane was holding herself stiff, tense. He'd frightened his wife to the very marrow of her being and she wasn't going to let him off lightly. She said, in that quiet, trembling voice, "Are you going to tell me about it, Ches? Please?" and he saw her eyes shining with tears, and said, "Tell you about what, Diane?" and she said, "You know what," and he said, his tongue a bit thick with sleep, "The dream, you mean?—just now?" and she said, "You could start with that," and he said, "What do you mean, 'start' with it?" and when she didn't reply, he said, "It was nothing—I can't remember. Primarily, I guess," and here he paused, as if sincerity urged pausing at this point, "—visceral, physical. As if

I'd gotten tangled in something. Bedclothes, I suppose," and he laughed, a little too insistently, and Diane said, as if she hadn't been listening, "This time, when I began to hear you, I just lay there for a while not knowing if I could make myself come here, I was afraid of what I might find, and when I opened the door you seemed to be talking to someone, or arguing, the only word I could make out was 'happy,' you were making a laughing noise and grinding your teeth and saying 'happy'—'happy'—and I was reminded of your father, for some reason, I don't know why," and Chester said, guiltily, "My father?" and Diane said, "Yes. But I don't know why."

Chester said, as evenly as he could manage, "Look, my father is not to blame. I'm not the kind of man who blames his father for—his life."

There was a startled pause, he knew he'd baffled her, very likely he'd frightened her further. The varieties of domestic assault.

Diane was holding him, and she was crying now, which he didn't like to see, and her nose was running, which she didn't seem to notice. Normally so fastidious a woman, yes, and unfailingly civil, courteous, loving, forgiving. He saw that he would lose her if he didn't speak.

She was saying, anger in her voice, "What for God's sake has happened to you, Ches, these past few months?" and he said quickly, "What do you mean?" and she said, "Not just the dreams but the rest of it, the way you *are*—are you in love with another woman?" and he broke from her, overcome with a terrible urge to laugh, as if, even now, seeing a man so dazed in his life, like a steer on its way to the slaughterhouse stunned by a mallet's blow, Diane could imagine desire in him: even the memory of, the anticipation of, desire.

"I'm not in love with anyone. You know that."

The week before, he'd driven back to Decatur Avenue. Out of curiosity. And dread.

And a hope of doing penance?

Carrying $5, $10, $20 bills loose in his pocket. For quick access.

He'd cruised a bit, caught sight of several black men he believed might be the black man he'd hit with his car, each time very excited but each time frustrated, for it was impossible to know, and impossible to make inquiries. What could he say: Excuse me, are you the man I tried to kill . . . ? He stopped at a red light at that same intersection, a wave of déjà vu powerful as homesickness swept over him as two ragged men shuffled out to clean his windshield, one of them black . . . but certainly smaller, older, grayer than the other. His windshield was left a smear of rainbow-iridescence, but he handed both men $10 bills as if they'd serviced him perfectly, as he deserved. One of the men pocketed his bill without glancing at it, and the other, the black man, grinned broadly, no doubt mockingly, and said, "Man!—ain't *you* the one!" and moved off, laughing.

When Chester returned to his bed, having washed his face in cold water, having made an effort to regain what he told himself was control, he was surprised, yes and guilty, to see Diane still sitting on the edge of the bed, waiting. In the lamplight her face was damp, pale, unlined. Of course he loved her.

She lifted her arms to him, she smiled bravely. "Oh Ches," she said, as if teasing. In their style of years ago. "Hey. Please?"

Chester knelt suddenly in front of her, head in her lap, arms gripping her hips.

He said, quietly, "I don't know how to begin, Diane."

She was stroking his hair. She said, "Oh yes you do."

You Petted Me, and I Followed You Home

This thing that happened to them, the little lost dog, it was like nothing that'd ever happened to them before.

They'd been at their friends' place, drinking. Got there at nine and left at maybe one-thirty in the morning. Which was early, for Vic, for a weekend night, but now that they were married, and Dawn still recovering from her four days in the hospital, they kept different hours.

And just their luck it was the first snow of the season, a gritty windblown snow, and only October. And Dawn lightly dressed. And no car. And it was too far to walk home. Vic was out in the street looking for a taxi, stiff head and back, angry eyes, they were "between cars" now that the five-year-old Mercury had broken down, a piece of shit as Vic called it, he was a man not used to not having his own car so maybe it wasn't the right thing for Dawn to ask, touching his arm, the only way you could talk to Vic sometimes, by touching him first, "Honey, why don't we go back upstairs, maybe somebody can drive us home? Frank, maybe?" But Vic didn't hear. Ignored her. She guessed he hadn't told his friends about the Mercury, he'd only be able to tell them when it had become a joke, something he could laugh at, but that wasn't yet. Dawn said, pushing it, "Do you have enough for a cab?—I mean, a tip, too? I didn't bring along my wallet."

Vic turned, and pushed her a little, not hard but so she'd know she'd been pushed, toward the curb. "Wait up there," he said.

"Those shoes—!" Meaning Dawn's spike heels, soft black leather with spaghetti-thin straps through which her textured black stockings shone like her own skin, translucent. Shoes impractical for walking a block let alone miles but Vic liked them, didn't he? Liked Dawn's sexy shoes, clothes?

Sure he did.

Dawn went to stand, not very steadily, in the arched brownstone doorway of the building they'd just left. Shivering in the damp wind that smelled of the river, a metallic-rot taste. That smell that, when it washes over you, reminds you of all the other times—winter, the wind, swirling-drunken snow, your eyes tearing so you're half blind—you've endured it, and getting older doesn't make it any easier. Dawn was hoping that none of their friends would leave the party just now, and see them. For sure, then, they'd be driven home, but Vic wouldn't like it, and she'd have to deal with his mood, at home. It wasn't Dawn but Vic who felt it: not having their own car, even if it was temporary. (The Mercury was so shot, Vic couldn't get a decent trade-in. So he'd have to borrow from—who? His brother maybe. His father. Dawn didn't inquire, and Vic didn't say.) And not only not having a car, but the prospect of other people knowing. It was humiliating. For him, not her. But, if for him, for her too. If for the man, for the woman too. They were married now.

It was Dawn's mother who'd said that. *If for the man, for the woman too.* What the hell it meant, why she'd said it, and when, Dawn didn't know.

And there it was, as if it'd been waiting for them: a little lost dog.

A little lost dog, out of nowhere suddenly, on the sidewalk. Shivering in the wind, peering up anxiously at Dawn. Panting—its breath steaming. Its brown fur was curly, matted, wet. Dawn saw how it was blinking, rapidly, snowflakes melting against its eyes.

"Aren't you—darling! Darling little doggie," Dawn cooed. It was her party manner, meant to be overheard. Girlish, good-hearted. Flirty. Dawn wouldn't know she'd been drinking until she exclaimed like this, over some small or silly or sentimental thing. "Oh—are you *lost?*"

The dog was a mongrel, Dawn guessed, small, wiry, ribs

prominent through its fur. Part cocker spaniel, with a spaniel's long loose ears, a stubby battered tail, mournful eyes—eyes that stared right into her own. Dawn murmured, baby-cooing sounds, stooped to pet the poor thing and it licked her gloved hands eagerly, and its malnourished body quivered with excitement. "Oh, oh! Not so fast! Oh, you're getting me all wet—" She was laughing, she wasn't scolding, but the dog cringed a little, then continued licking her hands, then Vic came over, and petted the dog too, more roughly, scratching it behind the ears like they were old buddies so the dog whimpered and squirmed with a pleasure almost too intense, like sex almost, Dawn laughed to see. It licked Vic's bare hands urgently, hungrily, its bony hindquarters thrashing from side to side. Vic laughed, Vic liked dogs, he'd had dogs as a kid, growing up. His banter was rapid-fire, good-natured, "Hey boy, hiya boy, poor little bastard you lost?—no collar?" To Dawn he said, in disgust, "Somebody must've dumped him. See, the fur's worn on his neck, from a collar. They took the collar *off*. Sonuvabitch."

Dawn said uncertainly, "Oh, let's take it home!"

"Yeah, that's all we need," Vic said. He was rubbing the dog's head with his knuckles and the dog was making flurried, flailing gestures with its front paws, as if about to leap up against Vic's legs, simultaneously restraining itself, a dog that has been kicked often, and has grown wise.

A cab came by, and Vic ran out into the street to stop it, and he and Dawn climbed inside, and the dog followed them as far as the gutter, the last glimpse Dawn had was of its sad searching eyes. A dog's eyes, but wise.

A ten-minute drive to their apartment on the west side. The young Hispanic driver kept missing lights, braking on the wet pavement for the yellow, you couldn't have said he did it deliberately but Vic was tense watching the meter, Dawn tried not to notice.

He surprised her then by gripping her hand. As, before they were married, when the emotions between them were quick-shifting and unpredictable as a wind-tattered cloudy sky, he'd often surprised her, scaring her a little, teasing. A man like Vic, you never knew. You prepared yourself for being hurt, thrown off balance, but he'd smile, he'd gaze at her sidelong, his eyes hooded, suggestive, like now. Like he knew something about her she didn't know, herself. Saying, "You were having a good time tonight, eh?—like I haven't seen you in a while."

Dawn felt a stirring, a quick stab in the pit of her belly. That quick sexual ache. Not knowing if this man was serious, or maybe was he testing her, hoping to get a rise out of her. She said, "I still don't feel they *like* me, those friends of yours, it's like they're always judging me, you know?" Vic said, "Shit, no. They think you're terrific." Dawn said, leaning against Vic, kissing his cheek that was damp from the snow, "I don't care what they think, just what you think." A thought crossed her mind, quick and fleeting as a shadow. "That poor darling little dog—we should've brought it home with us."

Vic laughed, in irony. "Yeah. Sure."

This was when they were living in the cramped, ground-floor apartment in the rust-colored brownstone building on Water Street. It was a neighborhood of aging apartment buildings and auto parts stores and, a short block away, van line warehouses. Two blocks farther, though not visible from any of their windows, was the broad choppy river the color, most days, of steel filings. The apartment was *just temporary*, and furnished with things Dawn hadn't exactly chosen, most given to them by relatives.

When the taxi pulled up in front of the building, Dawn got out and carefully, weaving on her high heels, walked away. She'd heard Vic with taxi drivers in the past, heard exchanges she'd wished she hadn't heard. She never looked at the meter.

Sometimes Vic tipped, and sometimes he didn't. When he worked, he worked damned hard; he had a union job, and it hadn't been easy to come by. It was his reasoning that not everybody, not just everybody doing their fucking job, deserved a tip.

Dawn, who'd waitressed off and on since the age of seventeen, did not agree with that philosophy, but didn't care to argue.

However it worked out tonight, Dawn wouldn't know. When Vic joined her, his face was tight but neutral. He was just putting his wallet back into his pocket.

Dawn cried, incredulous, "Oh, Vic! Look!"

She was pointing at the little lost dog, trotting breathless in the street. All those blocks, two miles at least—was it possible?

Vic whistled through his teeth. "Christ!"

Dawn said uncertainly, "It *is* the same dog isn't it?"

The little mongrel spaniel with the ragged ears, panting from its ordeal. The stubby tail wagging hesitantly. Those eyes. As they stared in amazement, the little dog sidled up to them at an angle, wary of being kicked. It seemed to be favoring its left back leg.

Dawn murmured guiltily, "Oh, poor thing!—you're all wet, all cold. What if your fur freezes?" Swaying in her ridiculous shoes she stooped awkwardly to pet the dog, guessing it was probably a mistake, and the dog threw itself desperately against her legs and nearly knocked her down. "No, no! No—*stop.*" Dawn was laughing, a little agitated. When she had too much to drink, she was susceptible to sudden laughing jags that could sound like sobs. "Vic, should we feed it something?—we can't just let it go, it's starving."

Vic said quickly, "Hell, no."

"It's so skinny, poor thing must be starving. Look at those eyes!"

"No."

"Oh, please!"

"He'll get the wrong goddamn idea."

"But it—he—he's starving."

Vic turned impatiently away, reaching for his keys. Dawn stared stricken at the little dog, its cold damp nose nudging against her knees. Flesh, living flesh, touching flesh. And those eyes. Dawn felt snowflakes melting against her warm skin, into her glossy black hair that had grown back to almost its original lushness, fanned out on her shoulders like a young girl's. A sound escaped her that was just raw noise—a sob, a moan of protest.

Vic was up the steps, keys in hand. He said, grudging, "He can't stay, though. Just feed him, and that's that, you got it?"

Dawn said, biting her lip, "Of course."

So at one-thirty in the morning, in her spike-heeled shoes and a headache coming on, there was Dawn feeding a little lost dog outside, on the pavement. She'd wanted to feed it inside the vestibule at least, but Vic said no, absolutely not. So she was feeding it in a part-sheltered space beside the front stoop, on sheets of newspaper, lardy stew scraps from the refrigerator, and some pieces of stale bread, and a bowl of water. God, how the dog gobbled its food! It even growled, tremulously, deep in its throat; its stubby tail went stiff. There was something absurd about the dog, yet so sad, Dawn couldn't help her eyes filling with tears. How old was it, she wondered. The muzzle wasn't gray, which meant it wasn't an old dog, but it didn't look like a puppy, either. And was it male, or female?

Within a minute, the food Dawn had given the dog was gone. And part of the newspaper devoured. And the dog was looking up anxiously at Dawn, and whimpering. Vic, of course, was nowhere in sight. He'd gone inside, leaving her to her folly.

You want to do it, do it. But don't come bellyaching to me afterward.

She wasn't sure which one of them had said that, or even when. Might've been years ago when she'd first met Vic, and so crazy for him.

The dog was begging for more, and Dawn didn't know what to do. Her temples began to ache as if something was tightening them from the inside. Her eyes and her skin felt seared, parched. She'd wanted to leave the party by midnight but Vic hadn't responded to her cues, he was having too good a time with his friends and she hadn't wanted to push it. So she'd let herself be talked into drinking too much, you'd think she would know better by now, not seventeen but thirty-one years old drinking beer on top of red wine, that bitter mouth-aching red wine the guys liked, then, later, two "jello shots"—new to her, vodka sweetened with grape-flavored gelatin. A woman's drink they called it, and Jesus it *was*, delicious and deadly. She might've expected her own husband to warn her but he hadn't.

The little lost dog was nuzzling its nose up beneath her skirt, tickling her. Christ, those eyes!

"Okay, sweetie. A little more, then that's it."

In the apartment, Dawn heard Vic running water in the bathroom, good he was out of the way, wouldn't know what she was doing. She found a few more scraps in the refrigerator, greasy pan-fried potatoes with bits of bacon, and some slices of cheese, fairly fresh slices she shouldn't be giving to a dog but there wasn't much else unless she opened a can of soup or something, Campbell's beef barley was Vic's favorite, but she hadn't better. When she went out into the vestibule, there was a surprise—the dog had gotten in somehow, inside the front door, though she'd have sworn she'd shut the door, carefully. "Sweetie, what? What are you doing in here? Bad dog—" She had to lead it back outside, back into the cold, the damned wind, awkwardly luring it out with the promise of the food, giving it a gentle nudge with her foot. It had begun to whine anxiously. "No, baby!—quiet! You'll wake the building."

Their upstairs neighbors were hostile to Vic and her. An older couple, the man a retired teacher. Complaining to the landlord of "noise and commotion"—when Vic got a little loud, raising his voice sometimes. Dawn kept out of it, as best as she could.

She was having trouble maneuvering the dog out of the vestibule, it wanted so desperately to come inside. *It knows the difference between outside and in,* Dawn thought. *The difference between living and—the other.* She'd taken off her gloves, and the dog's tongue on her hands was unnerving, thrilling—oddly cool, soft as chamois cloth—made her shiver. "That's enough. Enough!" she cried. Finally she was able to divert the dog's attention to the potatoes and cheese slices scraped onto what remained of the newspaper, and it began eating frantically again, its body quivering as if with electric current. So hungry! So—physical!—without a mind. You thought you could never be like that, just a body, just appetite, so raw, so not-human, but it happens.

Dawn stared down at the dog, feeling a sense of loss, terrible and final and irrevocable loss, not to be named.

Oh God. The pain glimmering in her head.

Saying lightly, as if the dog was one of those who had to be shielded from her truest deepest thoughts, "Now that's *all*. It really *is*. You'll have to go away, now."

She climbed back up the steps quickly, hoping the dog wouldn't follow. It paused in its eating to peer up at her, eyes stricken, quizzical. Muzzle damp with saliva and grease. Dawn shuddered, hardened her heart and went inside.

Making sure this time that the outer door, and the vestibule door, were both shut tight, and locked.

Instead of being in the bedroom, or in bed, as Dawn hoped he'd be, there was Vic in the kitchen, drinking from a can of Coors. Not a good time for drinking but Dawn wasn't going to say anything, nor even suggest by a frown what she was thinking. Vic asked her about the dog, irritated, bemused, her concern for the poor damned thing, wasn't that just like her, just like a woman, and at such a time. Wiry dark hairs bristled on Vic's chest, which was a compact, muscular chest, pushing through the thin cotton fabric of his undershirt, thick under his arms and on his forearms. In the early months of them being lovers, just the look of Vic's arms, like that, made Dawn's mouth go dry. She was saying, "God, I'm glad to be home." But in a way signaling there was something unsaid.

Vic shrugged. Acknowledging he'd heard her, but whatever she'd said, or hinted at saying, didn't call for a reply.

Dawn was feeling reckless, risky. Her cheeks flushed from the cold. She kicked off the damned spike heels, her ankles aching, now standing in her stocking feet on the cold linoleum floor. Vic was looking at her, steady, level—that look of his, in this mood like they'd been quarreling, almost, and tense, excited with their awareness of each other; that look that cut through her like a razor. When they'd first started going together and she'd see him look at her like that, his eyes narrowed, she'd felt the shock of it, of him, his wanting her, in the pit of her belly, leaving her weak, faint. Like she could not have said even her name, who she was. Now, since the pregnancy, that's to say the miscarriage, Dawn saw that look in Vic's eyes less frequently, and then only when he was drunk. And she was drunk. And the anger, the bafflement, beneath.

"Nightcap?" Vic asked, and Dawn said, "No thanks!" but when he held out the Coors, smiling at her, she couldn't resist, steadying his hand and tilting the can so she could take a sip. Cold, sour-malt taste, a trickle down her chin. She saw him watching her closely. His forearm grazing her breast.

In her stocking feet Dawn felt unprotected, vulnerable. And

heavier: her jersey dress tight across her hips. She'd gained maybe fifteen pounds these past few months, eating alone, odd hours of the afternoon, so hungry her hands trembled. Other times, sitting with Vic, she hadn't any appetite at all.

At the time of the miscarriage she'd been six months pregnant, and big. All the women in our family get big, Dawn's mother had said. Then she'd lost it, and lost weight, steadily, for weeks. How sick she'd been exactly she didn't want to know and no one, especially not Vic, was going to tell her. Don't look back, she instructed herself, don't dwell on what's lost, gone. *Here-and-now* is all there is. Right? It's useless to make yourself sick, crying, grieving when your truest personality isn't like that at all—it's a *happy personality*. Basically. Dawn's own mother had lost patience with her, finally. When Dawn was calling her two, three times a day crying over the phone. You can't let yourself go like that, Dawn's mother had said. Once you start, you can't stop. So *stop*. Dawn's mother had sounded actually scared of her, she'd started hanging up the phone when Dawn bawled. Hanging up! On her own daughter! Thank God, Vic hadn't known. Hadn't known any of it, and never would.

Now she'd gained back weight but it was just *fatty flesh*, nothing growing inside, pushing her belly out. It was just—*her*. Soft flesh at her waist she'd knead unconsciously, wanting to pinch it off. And her belly that had been so swollen from the inside, the skin so incredibly tight, and so luminous white: Vic was touching her there now, teasing, but a little rough, squeezing. He liked her, he'd said, with a little more weight than she'd had, when they'd first met; getting a grip on her hips, her buttocks; though never, when they made love, did he speak of such things, or speak much at all. How great she was, he might say. How beautiful. *Oh baby!—beautiful*.

All that passed between them, or had passed, how many times uncounted, too profound to be recalled—there were no words, no adequate words.

Dawn laughed and pushed Vic's hand away. He'd been backing her half-consciously against the kitchen table and, damn it, it *hurt*.

They were headed for bed, Vic's arm around Dawn's shoulders, and heavy, when suddenly there was a sharp scratching noise, close by. A dog's claws against the apartment door?—a dog's forlorn, high-pitched whining? Vic turned, his smile fading. How was it possible, the dog had gotten back inside the building?

Vic cursed, and went to the door and opened it—and there was the little lost dog, barking in quick begging yelps, pawing at his legs. In the half-light its fur looked coarse and whorled, the drab dun camouflage-color of deer in winter. It tried to scramble inside but Vic blocked its way with his foot. Vic said, furious, to Dawn, "How the hell did he get in here?—you must've left the front door open."

Dawn said, weakly, "But I didn't."

"You must've. How else?"

"Vic, I *didn't*."

"Fuck it, I told you—it's a mistake to feed a stray dog."

"It isn't a stray, it's *lost*."

Vic pushed the dog back out into the hall, with his foot. The vestibule door was wide open: the hall was freezing: someone must have come inside just now and forgotten to close it. Dawn said, "*I* didn't do it." Tears were smarting her eyes, she pulled at Vic's arm saying, "Why's it so important?—whether the dog is inside, or what?"

Vic said, "Look, you're drunk. Go to bed."

"I mean, my God, it could sleep in our place, couldn't it? Our kitchen where it's warm? Why not?"

"Are you crazy?"

"It's freezing out—"

"Dawn, for Christ's sake. Go on inside. I'll take care of the poor bastard."

Vic pushed Dawn, not really hard but Dawn's head struck the doorframe, it was like her headache exploded and she ran clumsily back inside, ran into the darkened bedroom, hands pressed against her ears. She heard Vic cursing the dog, and the dog's squeals. Thumping, thudding sounds. The front door slamming shut.

Dawn felt sick, faint. *It knows us,* she thought.

Out of nowhere such a weird, wild thought, of course she was drunk as Vic said, not in control, yet, still, bending now like an old woman, gripping her stomach in sudden cramping pains, it came to her again, unmistakable.

It knows us, that's why.

Dawn undressed with numbed vague fingers, slipped her nylon nightgown over her head and stood at the bedroom window, staring out, not knowing what she was looking for at first—she couldn't see much of Water Street, mainly the narrow alley, garbage cans, the brownstone building next door. Even by day the bedroom had a dim undersea look.

Snow was falling thicker now, not melting on the pavement.

Dawn said, not accusingly so much as wonderingly, "How could you do it! Put that poor little dog out in this cold."

Bedsprings creaked like derisive laughter as Vic settled into bed. She knew without looking at him that he was lying with his hands behind his head, watching her, his eyes narrowed. She'd seen Vic look at other men like that, calculating how to hurt them. If it was worth it, for him. But she wasn't going to turn.

Vic said, "C'mon to bed, honey. Forget it."

Dawn pressed her forehead against the windowpane. She wondered if she had a temperature, her skin was so dry, parched. Her eyeballs ached in their sockets.

"Hey," said Vic. "I love you."

"Well," said Dawn, not turning, "I don't love you."

"Yeah? You don't?"

"Because you're cruel."

"Yeah?"

"Cruel, and selfish. You don't give a damn."

"Sweetheart, I told you not to feed that dog. What'd you expect, he'd eat what you gave him, then go away?"

"What was I supposed to do, let him starve?"

"What's it to you? There are a million strays in the city."

"He wasn't a stray, he was *lost.*"

Dawn now pressed the back of her hands, which were cool, against her forehead and cheeks. Christ, she *was* hot: a hot-skinned woman: especially when she'd had a few drinks, and people looked at her, men looked at her, that kind of attention she'd first drawn as a girl of maybe twelve, basking in it, but scared, too. Because you can't turn it off when you want to. Because it isn't yours to control.

Thinking of the little dog now as *he*. But why?

For sure, it could be *she*.

Dawn saw nothing, no one on the street, a blur of passing headlights. She turned on her way to the bathroom and Vic grabbed her around the hips and pulled her down onto the bed. Meant maybe to be playful, just kidding around but Dawn gave a little scream and began fighting him, elbows, knees, fingernails, and Vic cursed her, and forced his weight on her, pinioning her against the quavering bed with his fingers closed hard around her wrists, her arms flung up beside her head. They struggled, panting. Dawn strained to bring her knee up against him but he blocked her, grinning angrily down at her, the color up in his face, cursing, as she cursed him, sobbing, "Damn you! Goddamn you to hell! You—" Vic yanked her nightgown up past her waist. Uncovering her breasts. His face was dark with blood, his skin burning. Jaws clenched tight. A man she didn't know, didn't love, a man she'd never seen before, veins livid on his forehead, in his throat. He wanted to hurt her, he knew how to hurt her. He nudged her knees apart, wrestled her down where she'd almost slipped from the bed, kept her thrashing hips in place on the violently creaking bed and Dawn heard herself say, "You! when you can't do anything else you fuck, that's all you can do isn't it, fuck, just fuck, fuck, fuck like you aren't even a—a mind! You make me sick."

Vic froze, in the very act of entering her, forcing himself into her, he froze, just like that: like he'd been struck a blow to the head. Staring down at her like he'd never seen her before.

Then he was off her, off the bed. Slamming out of the room. Dawn heard him in the kitchen, slamming around there. She was scared what he might do—break something, dishes, a window? Throw a chair against a wall? What fury in him, you wouldn't want to laugh at him, a naked man, careening, dangerous in his kitchen at almost two o'clock in the morning. But there came the sound of the refrigerator door being opened, and slammed shut, hard. Another Coors popped.

Make me sick. I hate you. Dawn lay in the tangled bedclothes, crying. Cupped her breasts in her hands, where they ached. No milk, never any milk but they'd ached. Upstairs, their neighbors were wide awake, and listening. Oh Christ. It left you so ashamed.

What time Vic came back to bed, after three o'clock probably, Dawn didn't want to know. Wasn't going to acknowledge even being awake though she'd gotten up to straighten the bedclothes, tuck the sheets in neatly, adjust the pillows. Lying then stiff and straight beneath the covers waiting for him, and not waiting.

He crawled in beside her. Not a word. After one of their fights they could lie like this for hours, now stone cold sober, both of them sober, Dawn on her side of the bed and Vic on his, sprawled on his back, perspiring. He'd had how many beers she didn't know and didn't give a damn. His skin gave off a humid heat. His breathing was harsh, irregular, like something was caught in his throat. Toward dawn he might begin to snore, thinly at first, then louder. Then Dawn might nudge him, but they wouldn't speak. And she might fall asleep, too. By degrees. That thin headachey sleep like the hospital sleep, sedation like someone squatting on your chest so you can't breathe.

After a while, Vic would reach out to touch her—tentative, groping. Not a word. The last time, a few weeks ago, they'd lain like this, stiff and furious, mutually wounded, he'd so slowly slipped his fingers through hers it was like a boy slipping his fingers through a girl's—shy, but pushy, knowing what he wanted. And finally gripping Dawn's hand tight so it almost hurt and still he didn't say a word, nor did she, why should she, unless he did? Fuck him!

So. They were lying in bed, in full wakefulness, each bitterly aware of the other, but ignoring the other, when suddenly there came a scratching sound, loud enough to be in the room with them, and Vic sat up at once, saying, "Who's there?"—and Dawn sat up beside him, her heart knocking in her chest, staring into the dark, toward the window.

It was the little lost dog: not in the room with them, but at the window, outside, scratching its toenails frantically against the pane. It was yipping, not loudly, but rapidly, scarcely pausing for breath, as if it were in pain. Dawn knew that sound, that terrible sound that cuts you to the bone marrow. Somehow, the little dog had managed to leap up onto the windowsill outside, which was at least five feet above the alley; it had managed to climb over the iron bars that curved over the lower half of the window, and to wedge itself inside, and squirm and wriggle down, head first, where, now, it was struggling to right itself, to wrench its head around and stand on its hind legs, muzzle smearing the glass, nails desperately clawing, peering in.

Good to Know You

How the subject came up no one would recall afterward.

They were at the Chinese restaurant where they often went, Friday evenings. Two couples, neither married. Both the women had been married before and one of the men but the marriages were history by this time and even the divorces had faded. From the perspective of your late thirties, if you've lived fairly swiftly, much has become history.

The subject was childbirth. Both the women had had babies, and the older of the men had fathered babies, during the time of those marriages now history. Only the women were speaking, laughing and animated like girls across the sticky Formica-topped booth table.

When I had my first baby, Constance said, everybody was doing natural childbirth. My mother was appalled but kept out of it—I figured, she belonged to an older unenlightened generation. I was prepared for a delivery that never happened. What did happen was the contractions started coming immediately every four minutes—not twenty minutes, then quicker—and I was scared to death and my husband almost couldn't see to drive to the hospital, he seemed to be having trouble with his eyes focusing—then I had thirty-six hours of labor and no anesthetic and in the end I was so worn out, my heart was beating arrhythmically, I couldn't push worth a damn and I was this howling animal and my husband had passed out twice, so they gave me a C-section anyway—exactly what I believed I would avoid. God, was I a mess!

Maryanne said, Yes, but you wind up with a baby.

You wind up with a baby. Right!

Maryanne said, My first delivery was fairly rough, too. The labor wasn't as long as yours but I'd been sick so much, the early months especially, depressed and scared, I'd have liked to do natural childbirth but it wasn't recommended. So I was out of it. It was a forceps delivery—you know what that's like. Ugh! Then, when I came to, in this dazed state, somebody gave me this baby I thought was *myself*—my mind was sort of shattered and not-right, I'd gotten mixed up in time and I thought this was *me*.

Oh, I know what you mean, Constance said. With my daughter it was the same way with me. Not seriously, I mean—just a fantasy.

Those fantasies are *weird*.

Well, they pass. You're so damned busy!

And learning to nurse. *That's* a trip.

The women laughed together like girls. The men had been listening respectfully if a bit stiffly. One of them, Murphy, who in fact had been married twice and divorced twice and had several children the oldest of whom was eighteen, asked both women, The crucial question is, would you do it over again? Knowing there's so much pain?

The women looked at him blankly. Constance, who was his lover, said, So much *pain*? Murph, who's talking about *pain*?

Maryanne, who of the two women fell into the role of being the more reasonable, said, Admittedly there's pain. But pain isn't the point.

You'd do it all over again?

Is that a serious question? Of course I'd do it all over again. I love my kids. Don't you love yours?

Murphy turned to Constance. *You'd* do it all over again?

Constance said, annoyed, This is getting insulting. Of course.

Why's it insulting, I'm just asking. I mean it abstractly.

What's abstract about it? We're talking about my actual daughter and my actual son. Whom you know and I thought you liked. Who exist.

I know they exist, Murphy said. They're terrific kids. But—

—but to get them, what you had to go through, the other man, Ted, intervened, that's what he means.

Both the women began to speak at once. Constance prevailed.

Look, of course you experience pain, it's like your entire body is being twisted in half, of course it's terrifying, and each time is different so you can't exactly be prepared, but in the end, you have a *baby*. Get it?

You have a *baby*, Maryanne said. Not a kidney stone.

Murphy had had a kidney stone episode a few months before. He'd been taken to the university hospital by ambulance, directly from his office, carried out on a stretcher writhing and ashen-faced and his features so distorted his own colleagues, happening to see him, had not recognized him. So it was cruel now to laugh but the women laughed and so did Ted and after a moment Murphy.

The women's laughter was bright and scintillating like flashing blades. By this time the waiter had brought the check and a plate of orange slices and fortune cookies and the other tables in the restaurant were empty. The spotty neon HOUSE OF WONG out front had long since been turned off for the night.

The subject might have been dropped as they opened their fortune cookies but Murphy, who never let anything go, said to Ted, How they do it, how women do it, it's a mystery to me. Frankly, I'd never have the guts.

I'd never have the guts, for sure, Ted said, with an affable shrug of his shoulders. Of the four, he was the youngest, younger than Maryanne by several years. He said, grinning, Brrrr!—just hearing you two talk about it gives me the chills.

Murphy said, When I was in high school, this English teacher of ours had a miscarriage practically in front of the class. Everybody joked about it afterward—guys, I mean—nervous half-assed joking—but I almost keeled over. I made up my mind then. I mean—I realized right then, aged sixteen, *I* could never go through it, what my own mother went through to have *me*.

The women looked at the men with alert, startled eyes. They were eating orange slices, sucking at the rinds. It was awkward eating, juice ran down their chins.

The men conferred over the check and took out their wallets. Ted said, shaking his head, If it was up to me—to have a baby out of my own *body*—hell, the future of the human race would be very doubtful.

Murphy said, winking at the women, I'm afraid if it was up to *me*, Homo sapiens would be extinct already. A kidney stone is enough.

Ted was taking bills out of his wallet and dropping them like playing cards on the table. It's a terrible admission to make, I guess, isn't it? he said. I mean, I love life. I think the world is a beautiful place, essentially.

Murphy said, as if protesting, *I* love my kids. And, well—lots of kids.

It was then both men started laughing. Something in Murphy's voice, or in his expression, triggered Ted, and Ted triggered Murphy, and suddenly the men were laughing like kids. They laughed, laughed. The lone waiter came silently to take their money and went away unnoticed. The women were sitting stiffly, not looking at the men, or at each other, their faces tight and drawn as masks.

The Revenge
of the Foot, 1970

Is a foot male or female? they were asking. One of them had
smuggled a human foot out of the medical school dissection lab
and they were tossing it about in the kitchen amid rowdy male
laughter and incredulous female squeals. "Look sharp, Yank! You
bugger, look sharp!" The ox-faced red-haired Prewitt from North
Bay tossed the foot, a frosty-luminous blur, an object at which
you could not not look, at Wingate, or Wheelhell, whatever his
name the draft-defector from Minneapolis, who dumbly fumbled
it, cursed and snatched it up from the linoleum floor where it had
fallen heavy and solid as a foot made of concrete—the foot was
frozen, they'd been keeping it in the freezer of the squat little
Pullman refrigerator in the corner—and in turn tossed it at another of his suite-mates and so an impromptu game of touch football started, the big, beefy boys stampeding and crashing through
the rooms, and Elinor who had been brought uninvited to this
party celebrating the end of final exams at the medical school, Elinor who knew not a single one of the five or six medical students
who lived in this pigsty fifth-floor flat on Halifax Street, blinked in
amazement and may even have laughed. A foot? A human *foot*?
She had not expected such a diversion on this desperate Saturday
night. She was holding a lukewarm Molsen's in her hand which
she did not recall having been given nor did she recall having
known where her friends, casual acquaintances from the Arts College graduate school, in truth virtual strangers to her, were taking

her, gathered up like a squirmy, willing fish in a wide net. Every weekend there were parties, often midweek there were parties, celebrating the completion of something or a farewell or an arrival or a birthday or a loss so terrible it could not be endured without beer and deafening rock music and the close, sweaty companionship of others, it was an era in which you began in a place known to you and progressed joltingly through the night, on foot or in cars driven by strangers, to places not known to you; wild improbable places that afterward, years afterward, you would remember with the eerie clarity of a waking dream as if these places had been permanent after all in a way that their inhabitants, including you, were not.

Elinor, unlike the other female guests at the party, several of whom had gone ghastly white at the sight of the flying foot, stared fascinated as the burly beer-flushed boys (you would have to call them *boys*, despite their size, not *men*) stumbled, careened, collided and crashed about the living room tossing the foot to one another amid shouts of "You sod!" and "Bugger!" A tubular floor lamp was violently overturned, empty beer bottles clattered rolling across the carpet which was so filthy it appeared, to the eye's cursory glance, to be an earthen floor. The air was a bluish haze of cigarette smoke and there was a trenchant odor of spilled beer and stopped-up drains and food (pizza crusts, the remains of Chinese take-out, Kentucky Fried Chicken bones and gristle) and urine. It was as if, celebrating the end of exams, the medical students were determined to wreck their living quarters. They were healthy, gregarious, not only Prewitt but the others muscular and randy as young oxen—their blunt names Nailles, Steadman, McMaster, Schnorr, Wingate, or Wheelhell. "Pass!" they screamed at one another. "Score!" The foot, flying, looked too small to be significant and it was wrongly, awkwardly shaped.

Elinor, from a doorway, blinked through the haze of cigarette smoke and the frantic tilting lights thinking if she'd been in love with one of these prize masculine specimens she would be eager and hopeful and vulnerable to hurt, she would be obsessed with her appearance, my God how she would smile and smile, how she would *try*. The effort of making another love you in proportion to your love for him.

Yes it was hell. As much as, in these secular times, one might guess of hell.

But Elinor was in love with no one in this pigsty-festive place. If there was a drunken happiness here, a frenzy of animal spirits and sexual innuendo, she, a stranger, knew nothing of it and would know nothing for that was the point of having come here tonight. Elinor was in love with someone else.

Recovering from love, with someone else. Yes?

The other female guests, several of whom were surely in love with Prewitt, Nailles, Steadman, McMaster, Schnorr, Wingate, or Wheelhell had recovered sufficiently from their shock at the sight of the foot to be crying now with flirty reproach, "Oh, how can you!" and "Aren't you awful!" and "What kind of doctors are you going to be?" and "What if that foot belonged to somebody you loved?"—this last shrill question made the boys laugh so hard tears ran hotly down their flushed cheeks and Prewitt with his coarse cherubic face took up the theme in a grieving falsetto, "Oh! what if this foot is somebody you love, you insensitive sods?" He waved the foot above his head as if he were about to fling it out boomerang-style. Gales of helpless laughter swept before him. "What if this frigging foot is *somebody you love?*"

Soon the game, which required much physical exertion, bored the boys, the thawing foot was tossed into the kitchen sink and seemingly forgotten except for Elinor who slipped into the kitchen to observe it while out of amplified speakers in the living room Mick Jagger was mock-crooning *time is on my side*. The Stones' percussion was so loud so vibrating as to be, to Elinor, inaudible. She was drunk enough to think it likely that, if you're encased in deafening noise, you are also invisible. With a trembling forefinger shyly reaching out to touch the foot—of course, it was clammy-cold.

This was spring 1970, the Americans were still fighting their bloody war in Vietnam. Cast the blame there?

Was the foot male or female? Elinor thought it crucial to know yet could not determine from examining it. Probably female for it was of only moderate size looking so wan and battered-humble there amid bottle caps and Styrofoam food containers in the greasy sink. An adult foot, in any case. Long, narrow, bony and waxy-white. Where it had been skillfully sawed off from its ankle there was exposed white bone and cartilage and a frosty glittering like mica. Though the foot was longer than her own (which took a size seven shoe) by as much as two inches it did not appear to be much wider. Each of the big toes curved strangely inward and was disproportionately large in relation to the other toes; the nails of the big toes were thick as horn and yellowish while those of the other toes were small, thin, a transparent bluish color. Where veins and arteries had been there were now flattened wormlike striations of the hue too of bruises for of course all blood, thus the pressure of blood, had drained out of the foot.

Whose foot had it been, and when had she died, and where, and how, and why, now, out of all places in the universe, was the foot *here*. And why, what could it mean, what coincidence, what design, on this gusty spring night cold as winter, was Elinor *here*.

She would learn a few days later that this notorious party had lasted through the night and that more and more guests, invited and uninvited, had continued to arrive, pounding up the flights of stairs eager to celebrate, some bringing six-packs of beer, ale, some bringing dope, drinking and smoking and passing out and late Sunday morning rousing themselves to continue the celebration with a fresh influx of guests hauling a case of wine from somebody's family vineyard in Ontario but by then Elinor was long vanished, slipped away unnoticed shortly after midnight.

Descending the dimly lit stairs, heart pounding with risk, daring, rectitude. She had stolen the foot out of the sink, by stealth wrapping it in double folds of aluminum foil still warm and smelling of the Kentucky Fried chicken it had covered, with obsessive neatness then she'd wrapped the object in some pages of the *Globe and Mail* and slipped it into her shoulder bag, and was gone without saying goodbye even to the bushy-bearded young man from her Old English seminar who had brought her here.

Outside in the deserted street a bone-freezing drizzle blew upward in her face but Elinor told herself sternly that climate is a state of mind.

She told herself, I am immune from harm, now. Her foot is my talisman.

And she was instantly sober—that was the first good thing. The drunken vertigo was left behind in the medical students' flat with the smells, the cigarette smoke, the *boys.*

She began walking east on Halifax without hesitation. She did not know that she would walk to his house until she began, and once started in that direction she could not turn back. Her own apartment which she shared with two other girls was in the opposite direction but she was not thinking of that now. However many miles to her lover's house on Sullivan Street she would walk them, would not have taken a taxi even if she could afford a taxi, Elinor was the kind of person, rural-reared, frugal, who resisted even taking a bus if her destination was within reasonable walking distance and to such persons most destinations are within reasonable walking distance in the city. She would make her way alert and vigilant at this late, dangerous Saturday hour and in this scruffy "mixed" neighborhood south of the university hospital and the discipline would clear her thoughts. I am immune, who can hurt me?—walking quickly avoiding both curbs and doorways, darting like a furtive wild creature against the bright-lit trafficked intersections of Dominion and Simcoe, of course she was safe. The foot wrapped in aluminum foil and newspaper in her bag, the foot entrusted to her out of all the universe. For there was no one else.

If Elinor's family knew where Elinor was alone at this rowdy hour, in this city of which they disapproved, what desperation coursing through her veins, yes but they did not know and could not have guessed for Elinor S. was like all the girls of her generation whom she'd known in college and now graduate school, determined to shield her family from hurtful knowledge of her personal life. A daughterly obligation. A task that brought anxiety but also a sense of vindication, high worth. Elinor was from a farming community west of Simcoe, Ontario, twenty-two years old completing her first year of graduate school at the University of Toronto in preparation for a teaching career in English literature even as her life was crumbling from within like an aged stone wall in an upheaval of the earth—except, and this was the crucial thing, this the weight in her bag thumping rhythmically against her thigh asserted as she made her way to 71 Sullivan

Street, it was not crumbling so long as she could hold it together. And she was not pregnant.

Thinking, From now on I am immune.

How do I know?—I know.

It was 12:48 A.M. when Elinor turned up Sullivan Street. Until this time she'd been invisible but now nearing her lover's house, which was a modestly restored brownstone in a row of part-derelict part-restored brownstones of the 1920s, she felt herself, like a materializing Polaroid image, becoming visible. A petite, slender young woman with olive-sallow skin, round wire-rimmed glasses and a defiant schoolgirl look, her hair a pale straight blond spilling shimmering over the shoulders of her khaki jacket. So plain, she believed, as to appear in the eyes of willful perverse men like her lover, beautiful. She saw herself through others' eyes exclusively and through her lover's critical eyes obsessively for what other vision of Elinor S. mattered?—none, really. Elinor S. knew herself thoroughly, she believed, and she was proud of her intelligence and her acuity and her accomplishments thus far though they were entirely academic accomplishments, she was secretly rather vain: yet no other vision except her lover's mattered to her, really. If he ceased loving her she would die because she would not wish to live, so simple was it.

Which was why, approaching 71 Sullivan Street, seeing the upstairs bedroom window lit, the downstairs darkened, she began to be frightened. He had said his wife was away for the weekend—frequently, these past several months, his wife was often "away"—but Elinor had not spoken with him for a day and a half and perhaps the wife had returned unexpected? Perhaps her lover had summoned his wife back?

You did not know. You knew, you guessed, but you did not know, really. And better not to know.

Nonetheless Elinor could not turn back. Clutching the bag, her eyes stark in her pale face, daring to ring the doorbell *as if she had the right.* Panting as if she'd run the many blocks from Halifax to this spot composing her terrified features into a smile, for you must always smile, you must *try.* Not thinking, Why am I here, what am I doing to myself, and to this man? Yet she could not turn back, this was the sole certainty.

Elinor heard footsteps on the stairs inside. She knew those interior stairs, she'd ascended them many times. And now a light came on illuminating from within the blind of the front window, and another light above the door, and cautiously at first the man who was her lover unlocked the door, unbolted and opened it and the shock of seeing her showed in his face yet in the next instant of course he was smiling, gripping her shoulders, passionate, half-angry, "Elinor, thank God!—where have you been, I've been calling and calling for you—" and he pulled her inside and firmly the door was locked and bolted again behind her and they were holding each other, and kissing eager and blind as always at such moments, and Elinor felt her antagonism against this man melt away as if it had never been, if indeed it had been antagonism and not instead apprehension and wonder and vertigo for *after all he did love her, what further proof?* It was that simple.

The wife must be gone away, then. He'd been about to go to bed, upstairs watching television, sipping red wine. Yes and lonely for her, and a little hurt, and angry, at Elinor's behavior.

Yes but I can't help myself, I am in love, no don't blame me I am innocent, look into my eyes. As I look into yours.

The wife absent, and Elinor would not think of her, would refuse.

Nor even to inquire, hesitantly, are they separated?—for the marriage, according to oblique remarks made by Elinor's lover, and by stray rumors that had come to Elinor's attention, was not a happy one.

Elinor had known the man who was her lover, who had been, her first semester in graduate school, her linguistics professor, since the previous September and they had been intimate for all but five weeks of that period of time and Elinor believed she had come to know the man thoroughly and at the same time she believed she did not know him, of course she did not know him, nor could she trust him. Nor he, her. Yet when they were alone together, clutching at each other, and kissing—how easy, how unambiguous, like the sun shining out of an empty blue sky.

How do I know?—I know.

The shabby book bag Elinor toted everywhere with her—her lover took no more notice of it than he ever did as, half-sobbing in his embrace, she lowered it to the floor.

They would make love of course. He was not angry with her for frightening him with her willful refusal to see him these past several days and she was not angry with him for whatever reason, she could not now in fact remember, she'd believed herself to be angry with him and had so wanted to die. But not now. They were trembling, shivering with the need to make love. To be naked together, upstairs in his bed, which was a bed he shared with another woman as he shared years of intimacy with this other woman but of that you don't think, you refuse to think. For why otherwise had Elinor S. come to 71 Sullivan Street at this hour of a Sunday morning, what other purpose?

The wife *was* gone—obviously.

It was an era in which wives were the enemy. You were the predator prowling for love yet you were also the prey. You pursued the man, and then you waited.

Elinor would use the downstairs bathroom as often she had in the past while her lover hurried upstairs. (For what purpose? To use a bathroom there? to hastily tidy up the bedroom? The first time he had brought Elinor here, the two of them reeling with desire, breathless and excited as if they were walking a high tightrope, Elinor had happened to notice through the bedroom doorway a disheveled bed and clothes including a woman's blouse lying across a bureau but when she'd returned a few minutes later the room had been chastely tidied up. All signs of the absent wife missing.) So Elinor went to use the bathroom noting that her face was drained of blood, the eyes sallow and triumphant. Her hands, her ridiculous hands, were shaking badly. She used the toilet urinating with difficulty and afterward wiped herself daring to glance squinting at the crotch of her panties. Which portion of a female's clothing could betray so much.

For eleven days the previous month Elinor had tortured herself with the unthinkable *Am I pregnant?* but the terror had proved false. Rather, the terror had been real enough, but its cause false. For at last, grudgingly, achingly, she'd begun to bleed. The profound weeping relief and the gut-sick sensation, *Is this happiness, now? am I saved, now?* she'd been too ashamed to share with the man who had—who had *not*—impregnated her. For what after all could Elinor have said that would not strike the masculine ear as crude, sad, embarrassing, ridiculous?

That was the horror, Elinor suddenly realized: the foot tossed about by the medical students, the thawing-meat foot, was ridiculous.

On her way from the bathroom Elinor slipped into the darkened kitchen. She'd been in this kitchen only once or twice, to make coffee and to hunt up food, they'd both been ravenous once, several hours of lovemaking. Quietly she opened the freezer door of the refrigerator and saw to her relief that there was space enough: her lover's wife was a conscientious homemaker however unhappy or neurotic or otherwise disappointing as a wife, she had not let frost accumulate in the freezer nor were frozen items haphazardly stored. Blue plastic ice cube trays in a row on the top shelf; two-thirds of a loaf of bread from the Whole Earth Co-Op, to which Elinor also belonged; a quart of marshmallow-chocolate ice cream; a package of Bird's Eye frozen halibut and a package of chicken breasts. Elinor removed the foot from her bag, calmly unwrapped the newspaper pages and discarded them in a wastebasket beneath the sink, then pushed the aluminum-wrapped foot into the freezer snugly between the loaf of bread and the halibut, a dull-glimmering object no larger than the loaf of bread and inconspicuous there in the freezer where her lover's wife would discover it within a week.

When she hurried to her lover he was on the stairs waiting for her. He'd removed his shirt and his chest, leanly muscular beneath matted frizzy graying-brown hairs, gleamed with perspiration. Elinor lifted her arms to him. His eyes shone with greedy love for her or what in those years Elinor believed to be love. Breathless she embraced him, her cheeks were damp with tears as he drew her swiftly upstairs and into the bedroom she'd memorized without knowing she had done so, one of those places, those settings, stark and vividly lit, that would outlive their inhabitants. "Why are you trembling so, Elinor?" he whispered. "You know I would never hurt you, darling. You know I love you, don't you?" Elinor pressed herself into the man's arms, his body was warm and enveloping and protecting and she held him as if for very life, "I know, I know," she whispered, tears blinding her vision so the bedside lamp seemed to melt, blur, and expand like flame, "—oh God, I know."

Politics

She was a cheerful good-natured girl, not a whiner or complainer; everyone liked her for that. On her purple quilted jacket she wore a sunny yellow Happy Face button: "Hi!"

Her new job was salesgirl at The Gap at Sky Hills Mall. She wore all their clothes except those long tunic sweaters where you really had to be skinny or it showed.

Parked off the highway she studied the surface of the compact mirror in which like something floating teasing in a dream her blurred face showed. Particles of powder made it seem shiny, distorted. The skin around the eyes like bruised fruit, the lid of the left eye swollen like an insect had bitten it and red as if she'd been crying which she had not. Not once that morning.

She hadn't gone to the store that morning, she'd driven to the mall and sat in her car for a while. Then she'd driven back home and called in sick. Maybe they believed her, maybe not.

It made her a little crazy to be in the apartment waiting for the telephone to ring, it was a whole lot better to go out again even to drive with no place in mind then, when you come back, you can see if any calls came in on the answering machine, and how many. One time last spring, Memorial Day weekend she'd been away and when she came back she saw there were seven calls. *Seven.*

She would not call him this time. This time, *no.*

He'd warned her never to call him at work which she'd done

once, a stupid thing to do but she'd been desperate. If she called his home number there'd been the answering machine, his taped voice clicking on like a stranger's and she couldn't deal with that.

When she was there sometimes the phone'd ring and the tape would click on and whoever was calling, one time it was another girl, an ex-girlfriend, would have to speak and they'd lain there laughing together. She couldn't deal with that.

She was a Sagittarius. She'd cut out her horoscope for June from *Self*. *Your high ideals and romantic heart make you vulnerable. Don't ignore good advice at the office. Don't be overly possessive! Ask: Am I doing all I can for myself? Expect HIGHS and LOWS with the man in your life. Avoid the temptation to control. Exciting times ahead!*

She held the compact mirror up close to her face. This *was* her face—wasn't it? Her neck was stiff. Shoulders and upper back in a shape like a T all glimmering pain. Swallowing aspirin, with black coffee. She was twenty-eight years old and that scared her but she looked five, six years younger, she really did. Even a time like now.

Was there something in her face that invited hurt. Her eyes that were brown, and warm. Her mouth that smiled almost without her knowing it. That look of sympathy of wanting to hear, maybe the word was "vulnerable," that was the word. Once an older guy she'd met at Friday's told her she had a face like a flower, she felt he had singled her out for it. But she didn't remember his name, probably he hadn't told her his real name anyway.

The man she was with now she loved so her heart could break—talk like that embarrassed him. Nor did he kid around, much. If she was a girl for him to marry and have kids with it had to be serious, even solemn like.

Times of hurt, she found herself thinking of: being cut from the cheerleading try-outs, the finals, sophomore year of high school. You never forget.

The girls on the varsity squad liked her really well, the captain surely did, and Marcy Myers the girls' gym coach, they were all encouraging then impatient, she was better than just about anybody but so nervous and scared so shaky that gets on other people's nerves so she tried to make herself vomit ahead of time but it didn't work and she fucked up and all those hours of practice in the basement at home all that hope and prayer they cut her from the finals picking four out of twelve and her name not spoken so she ran blind from the gym and in a toilet stall cried and cried and after a while she did vomit.

You never forget.

Let him get it out of his system, was what she'd heard off and on, growing up.

So sweet at first, calling her *Doll Baby.* Fitting her snug in the crook of his arm and in his pull-out bed, the thin lumpy mattress smelling of sweat and aftershave. *Love my Doll Baby, my sweet Doll Baby, you're the only one.* Yes and he'd meant it, too.

When he was feeling down, in one of his moods, it was never her fault and in the beginning, at these times, he'd make love to her more tenderly than ever and how and why it changed she would never know. There were other guys like that going back to high school but she didn't want to think it was a pattern or something. That would be just too depressing.

A while back he'd lost it, squeezing her breasts till she cried, digging his fingers up inside her and she'd gnawed the pillow to keep from screaming thinking *Let him get it out of his system.* And it had seemed to work, that time.

Through May, it seemed she couldn't do or say anything right, he'd actually said he felt sorry for her. But Christ she got on his nerves weepy and apologetic and needing to be told all the time he loved her which for sure he did but, Christ. And don't ever call me at work again. Even the married guys, the guys with kids, hated to be called at work.

That time he'd slapped her and her nose started to bleed and the look on his face when he saw the blood!—it'd been worth it, almost.

Oh Jesus honey what'd I do, hey look I didn't mean it honey, you know I wouldn't hurt you for the world and they were both crying saying after we're married and living together things would be different.

Yes. Oh yes.

Expect HIGHS and LOWS with the man in your life.

And: *Don't be overly possessive.*

Last night, when it'd happened so fast she couldn't exactly remember what had happened, she sort of sensed what set him off.
After work he'd gone over to his parents' and something must've
happened there or got said, not that he'd say what it was or
maybe even know himself, that was why he was so quiet so she
should have been more cautious trying to cheer him up. At the
store the other girls enjoyed her clowning around like she did
sometimes, but that was different, it's always different with your
girlfriends. She knew that.

Like she had to respect his privacy, not call him too much.
Like she couldn't lapse ever, be too familiar like his sister-in-law
with his brother, that disgusted him.

Lucky she'd just bought these new sunglasses. Chic white
plastic frames and lenses dark as ski lenses, almost black, the guy
at the gas station stared at her but couldn't see her bruised eyes.

Hung around while the tank was filling. Asked how she liked
that make of car, did she get it new or secondhand, where did
she live, yeah okay, he sort of remembered her, he'd graduated
from Central and she'd graduated from Valley and he'd been on
the Central varsity basketball team, hadn't she been a cheerleader?

Maybe yes maybe no. That's all she said.

Later, in the Sky Hills lot, parking her car thinking, It's a weird
fact of life how guys are drawn to you even if black eyes don't show.

Opening the compact, rubbing at the mirror with her thumb to
get it clean, seeing her face with tenderness and forgiveness: "Hi!"

The Missing Person

His name was Robert, and he was not the sort of man you'd feel comfortable calling Bob, still less Bobbie, or Rob. He was tall, not large-boned but densely, solidly built, an athlete in school, now years ago, but retaining his athlete's sense of himself as a distinct physical presence; the kind of man who, shaking your hand, looks you directly in the eye as if he's already your friend—or hopes to be. In his own mind, he moved through the world—now easily, now combatively—as if he had no name, no definition, at all.

He'd fallen in love with the woman before he learned her name, and even after he learned her name, and they'd become in fact lovers, he couldn't deceive himself that he knew her, really. And sometimes this made him very angry, and sometimes it did not.

He was thirty-six years old, which is not young. He'd been married, and a father, and divorced, by the time he was twenty-nine.

He told himself, I can wait.

One April evening, when Ursula had been away for nearly two weeks, without having told Robert where she was going, or even that she was going away, he turned onto her street, driving aimlessly, and he saw, passing the small woodframe house she rented, that she was back: lights were burning upstairs and down, her car was in the drive. It had been raining lightly most of the day, and there was a gauzy, dreamy, scrimlike texture to the air. Robert told himself, It's all right, of course it's all right, behave like any friend since you *are* the woman's friend, and not an adversary. He was shaky, but he wasn't upset, and he didn't believe he was angry. That phase of his life—being possessive of a woman, intruding where, for all his manly attractiveness, he wasn't always welcome—was forever ended.

So she was home, and she hadn't so much as told him she was going to be away, but he was in love with her, so it was all right, what she did had to be all right since he loved her—wasn't there logic here? And, if not logic, simple common sense?

The important thing was, she *was* back; in that house. And, so far as Robert could judge—he could see her moving about, through the carelessly drawn venetian blinds at her front windows—she was alone.

So he parked his car, walked unhesitatingly up to the door, rang the doorbell, smiling, seemingly at ease, rehearsing a few words to take the edge off his anxiety (just happened to be driving by, saw your lights), and, when Ursula opened the door, throwing it back in that characteristic way of hers in which she did most things, with an air of welcome, of curiosity, of abandon, of recklessness, yet also of resignation, and he saw her face, he saw her eyes, what shone startled and unfeigned in her eyes, he thought, She *is* the one.

Not long afterward, upstairs, in her bedroom, in her bed, Ursula said accusingly, though also teasingly, "Hey. I know you."

"Yes?"

"You're the one who wants me to love you. So that you won't have to love *me*."

Robert laughed uneasily. "What's that—a riddle?"

It was the first time the word, that word, *love*, had passed between them.

Ursula laughed too. "You heard me, darling."

She slipped her arm across his chest, his midriff, and pressed her heated face into his neck, as if into forgetfulness, or oblivion. Robert marveled how with such seeming ease the woman could elude him even as she was pressed, naked, the full length of her lovely naked body, against him.

He had sighted Ursula at least twice before he'd been introduced to her, once at a jazz evening, very sparsely attended, at a local Hyatt Regency, another time at a large cocktail reception at Squibb headquarters, where, striking, self-composed, she'd been in the company of a Squibb executive whom Robert knew slightly, and did not like. That woman, that's the one, Robert thought, brooding, yet half seriously, for, though his appearance suggested otherwise, he had a romantic, even wayward heart; his habit of irony, and occasional sarcasm, didn't, he was certain, express *him*—as he expected women to sense, and was hurt, disappointed, and annoyed when they did not.

Eventually, they met. He was struck by her name, Ursula, an unusual name, not exotic so much as brusquely melodic, even masculine. It suited her, he thought—her large green-almond eyes, her ashy-blond-brown hair in thick wings framing her oval, fine-boned face. She had presence; she had a distinct style; not a tall woman, but, moving as she did, with a dancer's measured precision, she looked tall. Her habit of staring openly and calculatingly wasn't defiant, nor meant to be rude, but had to do, Robert eventually saw, with her interest in others; her hope of extracting information from them. She was a medical-science journalist and a writer associated, on what seemed to be a freelance basis, with such prominent area companies as Squibb, Bell Labs, Johnson & Johnson. She said of this work-for-hire that it was "impersonal—neutral—what I do, and I usually do it well, while I'm doing it."

So Robert understood, and was touched by the thought that, like him, or like him as he'd been in his early thirties, Ursula was in readiness for her truer life to begin.

And what truer life that might be, what ideal employment of the woman's obvious intelligence, imagination, energy, wit, that might be, Robert did not know, and had too much tact to ask. Ursula was only a few years younger than he, maybe she'd catch up.

*   *   *

It wasn't the bedroom upstairs, which he'd rarely glimpsed by
daylight, nor even the living room with its crowded bookshelves
and spare furniture, but the kitchen of Ursula's rented house with
which Robert was most familiar. Ursula liked preparing meals,
and she liked company while she prepared them; several times
they'd eaten together in the kitchen, at a mahogany dining room
table, oddly incongruous in this setting, set in a rectangular al-
cove at the rear, in what had been a porch, now closed-in, with a
bay window. By day, there was a view, green, snarled, somehow
foreshortened by steepness, of an untended rear yard sloping up
to a weedy railroad embankment; there were tall, elegantly skeletal poplars scattered amid more common trees; there was vestigial
evidence of farming, and a badly rotted tarpaper-roofed shanty
that had been a chicken coop years ago. The neighborhood in
which Ursula lived was semirural but the houses, one- and two-
storey bungalows, were owned by working-class people; Ursula
liked her neighbors very much, but scarcely knew their names.
She'd rented the house because it was so reasonably priced, she'd
said. And because she hadn't meant to stay long—just to catch
her breath, to see what was coming next.

That was five years ago. Ursula hadn't gotten around to buying
curtains for the windows, nor had she taped over the name of the
previous tenant, which was on her mailbox. Each spring she
meant to have a plot in the backyard plowed, so that she could
plant a vegetable garden; but the seasons plunged by, and she
hadn't had a garden yet. Just as there'd been no specific reason
for moving into the house, so there was no reason to move out.

Robert, who'd been living for the past several years in a condominium village, so-called, backing onto the New Jersey Turn-
pike, thought of Ursula's house, for all its air of being only
temporarily inhabited, as a home. He liked it, he felt comfortable
in it, he told Ursula, though he couldn't envision her remaining
there forever.

Ursula's eyelids flickered, so very subtly, as if to express dis-
taste. She said, "Forever is a long time."

Robert laughed, and said, unexpected, "Yes, but doesn't it
sometimes seem to you, we've already been living forever?—but
forgetting, almost at once, as we live?"

Ursula had stared at him, her eyes resembling cracked marbles, a tawny light-fractured sheen, unnervingly beautiful, as in a moment of extreme intimacy. Though she'd made no reply Robert had sensed her surprise; her compliance; yet in that very instant, her denial.

As if, so unexpectedly, she'd been forced to reassess him.

In the kitchen, a can of cold beer in hand, Robert looked about as if curious whether things had changed in his absence. The tips of leaves on the hanging plants in the bay window were curled and browning; the soil, beneath his fingertips, was dry. On a counter, carried in from Ursula's car and set down untidily, were issues of *The New England Journal of Medicine* and *Scientific American* and several large sheets of construction paper with a child's primitive yet fussy drawings on them, in crayon. Robert glanced at the top two or three drawings, then turned quickly away.

He said to Ursula, who was at the sink, her back to him, "Why not let me take you out, Ursula?—it's been a while."

Ursula said, "God, Robert, I couldn't get into a car again today. I was nine hours in my own."

"Nine hours! Coming from where?"

Vaguely Ursula said, "Upstate New York."

Robert said, smiling, at her back, "Yes, but you like being alone, don't you. You like to drive your car, don't you, alone."

Ursula, picking up the edge in Robert's voice, did not reply.

Robert was feeling good, yes feeling very good, after love a man feels good, the burden of physicality eased for the time being; no problem to him, or to others.

He was feeling good, and he was feeling happy, as, he had to acknowledge, he hadn't felt happy, in some time.

And how close he'd come to driving away from Ursula's house—seeing the lights, the car in the drive, seeing, yes, she was back, she was home, it would be up to her to call him, since he'd called so many times in her absence.

A few years ago, he'd have driven away. Now, he was shrewd with patience.

Thinking, I can wait.

For love, for revenge?—for love, surely.

In any case Robert had risked embarrassment, he'd walked

briskly up to the door and rung the doorbell, and Ursula had thrown open the door, a lack of guardedness in the gesture that would trouble him, later, when he thought of it, but she'd been happy to see him, genuinely happy, crying, "Oh God, Robert— *you.*" And she'd stepped into his arms, and hugged him, hard. As if he'd come by her invitation. As if she hadn't disappeared for two weeks without telling him where she'd gone, or why. As if this embrace, and the feeling with which they kissed, signaled the end of a story of which, until that moment, Robert had scarcely been aware.

Ursula was breaking eggs for an omelet; her can of beer was set on a narrow counter beside the stove. Robert came to slide his arms around her, tight around her rib cage, beneath her breasts, and said, "Don't you want help with anything?" and Ursula laughed, and said, "My mother used to say, when I was a girl, and I'd wander into the kitchen and ask, 'Do you want me to help you with anything,' that, if I meant it seriously, I wouldn't say 'anything,' I'd be specific." She paused, methodically breaking eggs, scooping out the liquidy, spermy whites with the tip of a forefinger. Robert wasn't sure how to interpret her words.

He said, exerting a subtle pressure with his arm, feeling her rapid heartbeat, "Well, I did mean it seriously."

Ursula said, "Oh I know you did, Robert."

He said, "I'm not the kind of person to play games."

Ursula said, laughing, "Oh, I know *that.*"

He'd forgotten how Ursula's laughter sometimes grated at his nerves, like sand between his teeth.

In fact, there wasn't much for him to do: he set out plates and cutlery on the table, and floral-printed paper napkins; he opened a bottle of California red wine he'd brought Ursula, upon another occasion, months before; he switched on the radio, to a station playing jazz, old-time mainstream jazz, the kind of music he'd cultivated in his thirties as a reaction against the popular rock music with which, like all of his generation, he'd grown up . . . that heavy hypnotic brain-numbing beat, narcotic as a drug in the bloodstream. While Ursula prepared the omelet, Robert rummaged through the refrigerator, and laid out butter, bread, several wedges of cheese, dill pickles. He was reminded, not unhappily, of the slapdash companionable meals he and his former wife had thrown together, those evenings they'd returned home exhausted from work.

In such cooperative domestic actions, as in action generally, Robert believed himself most himself. It was in repose, in brooding, and willful aloneness, that another less hospitable self emerged.

As she was about to sit down at the table, Ursula replaced the paper napkins with cloth napkins; napkins her mother had given her. Robert said, "A needless luxury, but very nice," and Ursula said, smiling, "That's the point of luxury, it's needless."

They ate, they were both very hungry, and grateful, it suddenly seemed, for the activity of eating; like lovemaking, it was so physical, and as necessary, momentum buoyed them forward. But Robert asked, "Your mother—where exactly does she live?" and Ursula hesitated, her look going inward, and he felt a stab of his old irritation, that, in the midst of their ease with each other, that very ease was revealed as merely surface, superficial. He added, in a tone not at all ironic, "You don't have to tell me if you'd rather not."

Ursula said, slowly, "My mother and I are estranged. I mean, we've been estranged. Much of my life."

Robert said, "That's too bad."

"Yes, it's too bad." Then, after a pause, "It was too bad."

"Things are better now?"

"Things are—" Ursula hesitated, frowning, "—better now."

Robert laid a hand over Ursula's; both to comfort her, and to still her nervous mannerism—she'd begun crumbling a piece of bread. Her hand went immediately dead. She said, with a harsh sort of flirtatiousness, "*Was* it too bad? What does 'too bad' mean? We're the people we are because we've turned out as we are; if things had been otherwise in our lives, we wouldn't be the people we are. So what kind of a judgment is that on me—'too bad'?"

Robert said, joking, but squeezing her hand rather hard, "Since you've turned out to be perfect, Ursula, obviously it's an ignorant judgment."

Ursula laughed, and withdrew her hand, and poured the remainder of the wine into their glasses. Her eyes had that sharp, glazed look that Robert had come to associate with intimacy; with their moments of intense physical intimacy. She said, "You've turned out to be perfect too. But you know that."

Seen from an aerial perspective the desert landscape is an arid, desolate, yet extraordinarily beautiful terrain in which narrow trails lead off tentatively into the wilderness, continue for some miles, then end abruptly. Whoever travels these roads comes to a dead end and has to turn back. . . . If he proceeds into the wilderness, he will be entering uncharted territory.

Their relationship is such a landscape, seen from above, Robert was thinking wryly. The wine had gone to his head, he was feeling close to understanding something crucial. In such a terrain you followed a trail for a while, it came to an end, you had to retreat, you tried another.

In such a way, years might pass.

Yes. Well. They were the children of their time, weren't they, this was how, as adults, they lived, so it's to be assumed that this is how they wanted to live. Isn't it?

Half-past midnight, and Robert supposed he should be going home, or did Ursula expect him to stay, the matter seemed undecided. Ursula, grown quiet and preoccupied, was drinking more than usual; her face had taken on a heated, winey flush, its contours softened. Before coming downstairs she'd carelessly pulled on a cotton-knit sweater with a low neckline that stretching had loosened, and Robert could see the tops of her breasts, waxy-pale, conical-shaped, with dark nipples, and he could smell that sleepy-perfumy smell lifting from her, and he was thinking, yes, why not stay, he loved her and he didn't want to leave her and it didn't matter that he was angry with her too; that (this was a truth the wine and the late hour allowed him) he'd have liked, just once, to see the woman cry.

He said, "What did you mean, before—I want you to love me so that I won't have to love you?"

Ursula smiled, and creased her forehead, and shook her head, as if she'd never heard of such a thing. "Is that a riddle?"

"*Is* it?"

"I don't remember saying it, if I did."

"You said it upstairs. You know—when I first got here."

Still, Ursula shook her head. With seeming sincerity, innocence. Forcing her eyes open wide.

They'd opened another bottle of wine, a good rich dark French wine Robert had located at the rear of Ursula's cupboard. He had not asked if this bottle too had been a gift.

Ursula rubbed the palms of her hands against her eyes and said, with a shy dip in her voice, "I'm drunk, how can I remember what I said." She giggled. "Or didn't say."

"Do you want me to go home? Or do you want me to stay?"

There was a brief pause. Ursula continued rubbing her eyes, she was hiding from him that way, as a child might. Robert let the moment pass.

He said, softly, "Tell me about your mother? And you."

Ursula said quickly, "I can't."

"Can't? Why not?"

"I *can't.*"

She was trembling. Robert felt both sympathy and impatience for her. Thinking, why didn't she trust *him*. Why, sitting close beside him, wouldn't she look at *him*.

Robert's former wife, whom, for years, he'd loved very much, had too often and too carelessly opened herself up to him. Like a sea creature whose tight, clenched shell, once pried open, can never be shut again.

He said, "That's all right, then, Ursula. Never mind."

"If I thought that it was important, that it mattered to . . . us," Ursula said, choosing her words with care, "I would."

"I'd better go home. Yes?"

"You'll never meet her, probably."

"Probably, no."

"My father's dead."

"I'm sorry to hear that."

"So, you won't meet *him.*"

Ursula laughed, and hid her face. A crimson flush, as if she'd been slapped, rose from her throat into her face.

Robert was stroking the inside of her arm, the faint delicate bluish tracery of veins. Her skin was heated, he could feel the pulse, he was feeling aroused, excited. Yet subtly resentful too.

He said, a little louder than he'd intended, "So. It's late. I'd better go home. And call you tomorrow."

"All right," Ursula said, then, without a pause, "—wait."

"Yes?"

"I didn't say 'love,' before. I'm sure I didn't. You must have misunderstood."

"I'm sure I did."

"I was very tired from driving. I hadn't expected you."

"I could see that."

"You don't have to call me tomorrow, if you don't want to."

When Robert, stiffening, didn't reply, Ursula said, "Unless you want to."

Robert got to his feet, draining the last of his wine as he rose. His face felt like a tomato, heated, close to bursting.

He laughed, and said, "How'm I going to tell the difference?"

Robert's present job was a good job, busy, distracting, kept his mind off himself and what he considered "negative" thoughts; the kind of job that propels you into motion and keeps you there, Monday mornings until Friday afternoons, a roller coaster. He liked even his title: Manager, Computer Disaster Division, AT&T, what a flair it had, what style, a bit of glamor. When he explained his work—his clients were primarily area banks who, when their computer equipment was down, hooked onto an emergency unit at AT&T, to continue business as best they could—he saw that people were interested, and they listened. Most of the people he met in this phase of his life were associated with businesses that used computers extensively, or worked with computers themselves, and the subject of computer disaster riveted their attention.

You lived in dread of computer disaster but you wanted it too. Something so very satisfying in the idea.

Ursula told Robert, medical technology has developed to such an extent, there are now entire communities of men, women, and children, electronically linked, oblivious of one another, whose lives depend upon systems continuing as programmed, without error; one day, the earth's total population might be so linked. Yet people persist in imagining they are independent and autonomous; they boast of shunning computers, despising technology. "As if," Ursula said, "there is a kind of virtue in that."

Robert said, thoughtfully, "Well. People need these stories about themselves, I guess. Believing that, when things were different, years ago, they were different. Life was different."

Ursula laughed. "It had a more human meaning."

"It had *meaning*."

"Not like now."

"God, no. Not like *now*."

And they'd laughed, as if to declare themselves otherwise.

A final number before the jazz program, the very radio station itself, signed off for the night: Art Tatum, Lionel Hampton, Buddy Rich, "Love for Sale," recorded 1955.

Robert listened reverently. He was holding Ursula's cool hand, fingers gripping fingers. Listening to such music, you felt that, at any moment, you were about to turn a corner; about to see things with absolute clarity; on the tremulous brink of changing your life.

What happens of course is that the music ends, and other sounds intervene.

Ursula said suddenly to Robert, "I saw you looking at them, before. Those drawings."

At first Robert had no idea what she meant. "Drawings?"

"These." Ursula brought the child's cartoon-drawings to show him. Her hands were trembling, there was a sort of impassioned dread in her voice. Guardedly Robert said, "They're very— interesting," and Ursula laughed, embarrassed, and said, "No, they're just what they are. A young child's attempts at 'art.' "

The sheets of construction paper, measuring about twelve inches by ten, were dog-eared and torn. There were strands of cobweb on them, dust. Robert, smiling uneasily, knew he was expected to inquire whose child it was who had done the drawings; what the child was to Ursula; no doubt, they'd end up talking about the father. But he couldn't bring himself to speak.

Of course these stick figures in red crayon, these impossibly sky-skimming trees, clumsy floating clouds, reminded Robert of his own child, his son Barry, now ten years old and very distant from him; reminded him most painfully; for how could they not. He'd been drinking for hours but he was hardly anesthetized. It had been years since Barry had done such drawings, kneeling on the living room floor, and years since Robert had thought of them. (Did he have any stored away for safekeeping?—mementos of his son's early childhood? He doubted it, closet space in his condominium was so limited.) Barry lived in Berkeley with Robert's ex-wife, who was now remarried, very happily she claimed; coincidentally, her husband was a computer specialist at IBM. Robert had last seen Barry at Christmas, five months ago; before that, he hadn't seen the boy since April. Nor did they speak very often on the phone—with the passage of time, as Robert figured less and less in his son's life, these conversations had become increasingly strained.

Robert was looking at the first of the child's drawings. In what was meant to be a grassy space, amid tall pencil-thin trees, a sharply-steepled house in the background, there were two stick-figures: a stick-man, wearing trousers; a stick-woman, with hair lifting in snake-like tufts, wearing a skirt. In the lower right-hand corner, as if sliding off the paper, was what appeared to be a baby, in a rectangular container that was presumably a buggy or a crib, yet, awkwardly drawn as it was, it could as easily have been a shoebox, or a mailbox, or a miniature coffin. The adult figures had round blank faces with neutral slit-mouths and Os for eyes; the baby had no face at all.

After a moment Ursula said, with that breathy embarrassed laugh, "They're mine. I mean—my own. I drew them when I was two or three years old. My mother says."

Robert glanced up at Ursula, genuinely surprised. He'd expected her to say that the drawings belonged to a child of her own, unknown to Robert until now. "*You* did these—?"

"I don't remember. My mother says I did."

Robert could see now, obviously, the drawings were very old; the stiff construction paper discolored with age.

Now Ursula began explaining, speaking rapidly, in the mildly bemused yet insistent tone she used when recounting complex anecdotes that for some reason needed to be told, however disagreeable or boring. "My mother has finally sold the house, she's moving into a 'retirement' home, and I was up there helping her, she'd called me, asked me . . . it's unusual for my mother to ask anything of me and I suppose I've been the kind of daughter who may have been difficult, growing up, to ask favors of. So there's been a certain distance between us, for years. And a number of misunderstandings. I won't go into details," Ursula said, quickly, as if anticipating a lack of interest on Robert's part (in fact, Robert was listening to her attentively), "—you can imagine. But now Mother is aging, and not well, and frightened of what's to come . . . and I drove up to Schuylersville, where I vowed, after the last visit a few years ago, I'd never go again, and I helped her with the house-cleaning, helped her pack . . . and up in the attic there were trunks and boxes of things, old clothes mainly, the accumulation of decades, and when I was going through them I came upon these drawings, and old report cards of mine, old schoolwork, I was going to throw everything away without so much as glancing at it but Mother was upset, she said, 'No! Wait!' She'd come up into the attic with me, she hardly let me out of her sight the entire time I was in the house . . . this woman from whom I've been estranged for more than fifteen years. I asked her why on earth she'd kept such silly things, and she looked at me as if I'd slapped her, and said, 'But you're my only daughter, Ursula!' This is the woman, Robert, who failed to show up at my college graduation, where I'd waited and waited for her, claiming, afterward, that I hadn't invited her; this is the woman who complained bitterly to everyone who would listen that I neglected her, never called or visited, when I was in my twenties and living in New York, and, once, when I drove up to visit, having made arrangements with her, she simply wasn't home when I got there—wasn't *there*. Nor had she left any message for me." Ursula began to laugh, more harshly now. Robert could hear an undercurrent of hysteria. "So we were looking at these drawings, this one on top first, and Mother told me approximately when I'd done it, and I said, 'My God, that long ago!—of course *I* don't remember it, I don't remember drawing at all, and I was pretty bad at it wasn't I,' and Mother protested, 'No, you were talented for such a small child, you can see you were talented,' and I laughed and said, 'Mother, I can see I was *not* talented, here's evidence, my God.' Then I asked her what is this down in the corner"—Ursula pointed at the baby in the box—"and Mother said, 'I guess that must be your baby sister Alice, who died,' and I stared at her, I couldn't believe what she'd said, I said, 'Baby sister? Alice? What are you talking about?' and Mother said, her voice shaking, 'You had a little baby sister, she died when she was eight months old, her heart was defective,' and I just stared at her, 'A baby sister? I had a baby sister? What are you saying?' and Mother said, 'Don't you remember, you must remember, you were two years old, we never talked about it much when you were growing up but you must remember,' and she started to cry, so I had to hold her, she's frail, she's so much shorter than she used to be, I felt as if I'd been kicked in the head, I was thinking, Is this possible? how can this be possible? is she losing her mind? is she lying? but would she lie about such a thing?—it was so unreal, Robert, but not as a dream is unreal, no dream of mine, it was no dream I would ever have had, I swear." Ursula paused, and ran the back of her hand roughly across her eyes, and said, "You know, darling, I think I need a drink, something good and strong, will you join me?—just one?" and she brought down a bottle of expensive scotch from the rear of the cupboard, and poured them both drinks, straight, no ice, no ceremony, in fruit juice glasses; and she resumed her story, telling it in the same bemused ironic tone. "So, Mother and I, we were looking through these drawings, and I asked her if that was supposed to be my baby sister Alice, there, in that box, or whatever it is, and Mother said yes she supposed so, and I said, 'And here's you, Mother, obviously, and here's Father, but where am I?—because, in all the drawings, there is just the baby, and no other child. And Mother said in this plaintive mewing voice, defensively, as if she thought I might be blaming her, 'Well I don't know, Ursula, I just don't know where you are,' and I was laughing, God knows why I was laughing, I said, '*I* don't know where I am either, and I don't remember a thing about this.' And later, before I left, Mother showed me the dead baby's birth certificate, she'd found it in a strong box, but she couldn't find the death certificate, and I said, 'Thank you, Mother, that isn't necessary.'" Ursula was laughing, rocking back on her heels, the glass of scotch raised to her grinning mouth. " 'Thank you, Mother,' " I said, "—'that isn't necessary.' "

Then she put her glass down abruptly, and walked out of the kitchen.

Robert followed her into the living room, where a single lamp was burning. She was laughing softly, fists in her eyes, turned from him at the waist, or was she crying?—he went quickly to her, and put his arms around her, and comforted her, and though, initially, unthinking as if it were a child's reflex, she pushed against him, he was able to grip her tight; to prevent hysteria from taking over her; he knew the symptoms of hysteria; he was an expert.

They stood like that for a while, and Ursula wept, and tried to talk, and then Robert drew her down onto the sofa and they sat there, on the sofa, for some time, in the shadowy room with the carelessly drawn venetian blinds. Robert was deeply moved but in control, he was saying, stroking the woman's hair, feeling her warm desperate breath on his face, "Ursula, darling, Ursula, no, it's all right, you're going to be all right, I'm here, aren't I? *I'm* here, aren't I? Darling?"

And they held each other tight, to make it true.

Will You Always Love Me?

"Why do I like to act?—because I feel comforted by the stage."

She spoke with a curious bright impersonality, this strange young woman, as if she were speaking of another person. Her deep-socketed eyes, which seemed to him unnerving in their intensity, took on a tawny light, the dark irises rimmed with hazel as she looked up at him. She was a petite woman even in her sleek fashionable high-heeled shoes, and Harry Steinhart was tall, so she had to crane her neck to look up at him—which he liked. Within minutes of their shaking hands, exchanging names, she began to speak, in reply to a question of his, making a confession as if spontaneously, as night came rapidly up beyond the building's paneled glass walls.

"I played Irina a few years ago, in Chekhov's *Three Sisters*. Irina is the youngest of the sisters, the most naive and the most hopeful. I'm too old for Irina now—I'd like to play Masha now. I feel so protected by the stage. And, of course, I'm only an amateur, there's nothing really at stake. But I have an ease and a grace and a purposefulness on stage that I don't have anywhere else. Here, for instance"—indicating the crowded reception, in the ground-floor atrium of Mercury House, "—I haven't any real idea who I'm supposed to be, or why I'm here. I'm an 'employee'—an 'editor'—and I'm reasonably well paid—but the job is interchangeable with a thousand other jobs, I feel no special commitment to it, and the company has no special commitment to me. But when I'm acting, I'm in someone else's head and not in my own. I execute a script, with others. We're never alone. We're embarked upon an adventure, like a journey up the Amazon. On stage, my emotions aren't silly or excessive or inappropriate—they're justified. They're necessary. I can't shrink away in embarrassment, or shame; I can't say—" and here suddenly she began to act, with exaggerated feminine mannerisms, to make her listener smile—" 'Look, please, I'm not this important, that any of you should pay attention to me!—this is ridiculous!' No, I'm an integral part of the production. It's a family, and I'm a member. Without me, there's no family. Whatever a play *is*, it's a family."

She spoke so insistently, her eyes so intense, Harry was quick to agree. Though he knew relatively little about the theater, amateur or otherwise.

How moved he was, by the young woman's warm response, which he'd elicited with his guileless, instinctive, American-male directness: the ritual of seduction programmed in Harry Steinhart that seemed, to him, always unpremeditated, thus innocent. And always for the first time.

He'd been married, and he'd been divorced, and all of it—the hurt, the befuddlement, the anger—belonged to the eighties, as to another man, and was behind him now. When he studied his face in the mirror he was grateful to see how, at the age of thirty-six, he bore so little of what he'd experienced. *Am I sliding through? I'm a statistic!* His new friends and colleagues knew nothing of his past.

Harry was amused, or was he in fact disgusted, by the notion of love in the old, sentimental sense: pledging fidelity, channeling one's very soul into the soul of another. The grasping needs, the anxieties. He thought: Apart from the sexual attraction of the female for the male, which is certainly powerful, there is the attraction of the mysterious. You fall in love with what is *not-known* in the other. And what is *not-known* becomes the identity of the other. Sexual intercourse is the miming of the desire to make the *not-known* into the known. The strongest desire in the species— and sometimes the most ephemeral.

*   *   *

When Harry Steinhart introduced himself to Andrea McClure that evening, he allowed her to believe she was encountering him for the first time. Yet in fact Harry had been aware of the young woman for months, since she'd come to work for the investment firm for which he was a market analyst. She was not a beautiful woman exactly, but rather odd-looking, with an asymmetrical face, pronounced cheekbones, large dark quick-darting eyes that nonetheless failed to take in much of their surroundings. Her hair was dark brown streaked with gray, she must have been in her early thirties and looked her age, with a perpetually crinkling forehead, a quizzical half-smile. Why Harry found her so interesting, he couldn't have said. Once he'd ridden alone with her in a swiftly rising elevator for twenty-two floors but she'd been distracted by a sheath of papers she was carrying and seemed quite genuinely unaware of him. Another time, sighting her by chance in a local park where she was running alone on a jogging trail, Harry followed her at a discreet distance and traversed a rocky strip where the trail doubled back upon itself and he knew she'd have to pass him, and so she did. He'd been excited, watching her. Watching her and not being seen. This small-boned woman with the prematurely graying hair, legs in loose-fitting white shorts slenderly muscular, small fists clenched. She wasn't a natural runner, her arms swung stiffly at her sides, not quite in rhythm. She was frowning and her mouth worked as if she were silently arguing with someone. How *interesting*, Harry thought her: Andrea whose last name, at that time, he hadn't known. How *mysterious*.

Harry Steinhart was not the kind of man to spy upon a lone woman in a deserted place. Not at all. In order not to be misunderstood, he climbed into full view on an outcropping of granite, in a blaze of warm sunshine—khaki shorts and dazzling white T-shirt, bronze-fuzzy arms and legs, affable smile. That is, Harry was prepared to smile. But the woman no more than lifted her eyes toward him than, running past, she glanced away. She seemed scarcely to have seen him, to have seen anyone, at all.

He'd stared after her, amazed. Not that he'd been rebuffed—he hadn't even been noticed. His *maleness* acknowledged, let alone absorbed. Yet he'd felt oddly amused. Not annoyed, nor even hurt, but rather amused. And protective.

He deliberately stayed away from that park, to put himself out of the temptation of seeking her out, watching her, again.

And then they formally met, and began to see each other in the evenings and on weekends, and through that spring and early summer Andrea's *mysteriousness* in Harry's eyes deepened—that vexation, almost at times like a physical chaffing, of the *not-known*: the sexually provocative. Though confident at first that he would quickly become her lover, Harry was surprised that he did not; which left him hurt, baffled, vaguely resentful—though not at Andrea, exactly. For she seemed to him so strangely oblivious, innocent. Even when she spoke with apparent artlessness, carelessness, as if baring her soul.

In his embrace she often stiffened, as if hearing a sound in the next room. She kissed him, and drew back from him, staring up at him searchingly. Making a joke of it—"You really should find someone normal, Harry!" so that Harry was provoked to say, smiling, "Hell, Andy, I'm crazy about *you*."

She'd told him the first evening they'd met, "My name is Andrea McClure and no one ever calls me 'Andy' "—which Harry interpreted not as a warning but a request.

When finally, in late summer, they made love, it was in silence, in the semidarkness of Andrea's bedroom into which one night, impulsively, she'd led Harry by the hand as if declaring to herself *Now! now or never!* Andrea's bedroom was on the ninth floor of a white-brick apartment building overlooking a narrow strip of green, her window open to a curious humming-vibrating sound of traffic from the Interstate a mile away. Penetrating this wash of sound through the night (Harry stayed the night) were distant sirens, mysterious cries, wails. Harry whispered, "You're so beautiful! I love you!"—the words torn from him, always for the first time.

It would be their custom, then, to make love in virtual silence, by night and not by day. By day, there was too much of the other to see and to respond to; by day, Harry felt himself too visible, and in lovemaking as opposed to mere sexual intercourse, it's preferable to be invisible. So Harry thought.

*   *   *

They were lovers, yet sporadically. They were not a couple.

So far as Harry knew, Andrea was not seeing other men; nor did she seem to have close women friends. Alone of the women he'd known intimately, including the woman who'd been, for six years, his wife, Andrea was the one who never inquired about his previous love affairs—how tactful she was, or how indifferent! *She doesn't want you to ask any questions of her,* Harry thought.

Harry told Andrea he'd been married and divorced and his ex-wife now lived in London and they were on "amicable" terms though they rarely communicated. He said, as if presenting her with a gift, the gift of himself, "It's over completely, emotionally, on both sides—luckily, we didn't have any children."

Andrea said, frowning, "That's too bad."

What was *not-known* in her. Which not even love-making could penetrate, after all.

Once lifting her deep-socketed eyes swiftly to his, startled as if he'd asked a question—"I'll need to trust you." This was not a statement but a question of her own. Harry said quickly, "Of course, darling. Trust me how?" And she looked at him searchingly, her smooth forehead suddenly creased, her mouth working. There was something ugly about the way, Harry thought, Andrea's mouth worked in an anguished sort of silence. He repeated, "Trust me how? What is it?"

Andrea stood and walked out of the room. (That evening, they were in Harry's apartment. He'd prepared an elaborate Italian meal for the evening, chosen special Italian wines—preparing meals for women had long been a crucial part of his ritual of seduction which perhaps he'd come to love for its own sake.) He followed Andrea, concerned she might leave, for the expression in her face was not one he recognized, a drawn, sallow, embittered look, as of a young girl biting her lips to keep from crying, but there she stood in a doorway weakly pressing her forehead against the doorframe, her eyes tightly shut and her thin shoulders trembling. "Andy, what is it?" Harry took her in his arms. He felt a sharp, simple happiness as if he were taking the *not-known* into his arms—and how easy it was, after all.

I will protect you: trust me!

Later, when she'd recovered, calmed and softened and sleepy by several glasses of wine, Andrea confessed to Harry she'd thought he'd asked her something. She knew he hadn't, but she thought she'd heard the words. When Harry asked, what were the words, Andrea said she didn't know. Her forehead, no longer creased with worry, kept the trace of thin horizontal lines.

Harry thought: We're drawn to the mystery of others' secrets, and not to those secrets. Do I really want to *know*?

In fact, Andrea would probably never have told him. For what would have been the occasion?—he could imagine none.

But: one day in March a telephone call came for Andrea which she took in her bedroom, where Harry overheard her raised voice, and her sudden crying—Andrea, whom he'd never heard cry before. He did not know what to do—to go comfort her, or to stay away. Hearing her cry tore at his heart. He felt he could not bear it. Thinking too, *Now I'll know!—now it will come out!* Yet he respected her privacy. In truth, he was a little frightened of her. (They were virtually living together now though hardly as a conventional couple. There was no sense of playing at marriage, domestic permanency as there usually is in such arrangements. Most of Harry's things remained in his apartment several miles away, and he retreated to his apartment frequently; sometimes, depending upon the needs of his work or Andrea's schedule or whether Harry might be booked for an early air flight in the morning, he spent the night in his own apartment, in his own bed.)

Harry entered Andrea's bedroom but stopped short seeing the look on her face which wasn't grief but fury, a knotted contorted fury, of a kind he's never seen in any woman's face before. And what are her incredulous, choked words into the receiver—"What do you mean? What are you saying? Who are you? I can't believe this! Parole hearing? He was sentenced to life! He was sentenced to life! That filthy *murderer was sentenced to life!*"

Later, Harry came to see how the dead sister had been an invisible third party in his relationship with Andrea. He recalled certain curiously insistent remarks she'd made about having been lonely growing up as an "only child"—her remoteness from her mother even as, with an edge of anxiety, she telephoned her mother every Sunday evening. She refused to read newspaper articles about violent crimes and asked Harry please to alert her so she could skip those pages. She refused to watch television except for cultural programs and there were few movies she consented to see with Harry—"I distrust the things a camera might pick up."

In a way, it was a relief of sorts, for Harry to learn that the *not-known* in Andrea's life had nothing to do with a previous lover, a disastrous marriage, a lost child or, what was most likely of all, an abortion. He had no male rival to contend with!

This much, Harry learned: In the early evening of April 13, 1973, Andrea's nineteen-year-old sister Frannie, visiting their widowed grandmother in Wakulla Beach, Florida, was assaulted while walking in a deserted area of the beach—beaten, raped, strangled with her shorts. Her body was dragged into a culvert where it was discovered by a couple walking their dog within an hour, before the grandmother would have had reason to report her missing. Naked from the waist down, her face so badly battered with a rock that her left eye dangled from its socket, the cartilage of her nose was smashed, and teeth broken—Frannie McClure was hardly recognizable. It would be discovered that her vagina and anus had been viciously lacerated and much of her pubic hair torn out. Rape may have occurred after her death.

The victim had died about approximately eight o'clock. By eleven, Wakulla Beach police had in custody a twenty-seven-year-old motorcyclist-drifter named Albert Jefferson Rooke, Caucasian, with a record of drug arrests, petty thefts, and misdemeanors in Tallahassee, Tampa, and his hometown Carbondale, Illinois, where he'd spent time in a facility for disturbed adolescent boys. When Rooke was arrested he was reported as drunk on malt liquor and high on amphetamines; he was disheveled, with long scraggly hair and filthy clothes, and violently resisted police officers. Several witnesses would report having seen a man who resembled him in the vicinity of the beach where the murdered girl's body was found and a drug-addicted teenage girl traveling with Rooke gave damaging testimony about his ravings of having "committed evil." In the Wakulla Beach police station, with no lawyer present, Rooke confessed to the crime, his confession was taped, and by two o'clock of the morning of April 14, 1973, police had their man. Rooke had relinquished his right to an attorney. He was booked for first-degree murder, among other charges, held in detention, and placed on suicide watch.

Months later, Rooke would retract this confession, claiming it was coerced. Police had beaten him and threatened to kill him, he said. He was drugged-out, spaced-out, didn't know what he'd said. But he hadn't confessed voluntarily. He knew nothing of the rape and murder of Frannie McClure—he'd never seen Frannie McClure. His lawyer, a public defender, entered a plea of not guilty to all charges but at his trial Rooke did so poorly on the witness stand that the lawyer requested a recess and conferred with Rooke and convinced him that he should plead guilty, so the case wouldn't go to the jurors who were sure to convict him and send him to the electric chair; Rooke could then appeal to the state court of appeals, on the grounds that his confession had been coerced, and he was innocent.

So Rooke waived his right to a jury trial, pleaded guilty, and was sentenced to life in prison. But the strategy misfired when, reversing his plea another time to not guilty and claiming that his confession was invalid, his case was summarily rejected by the court of appeals. That was in 1975. Now, in spring 1993, Rooke was eligible for parole, and the county attorney who contacted Andrea's mother under the auspices of the Florida Victim/Witness Program, and was directed by Andrea's mother to contact her, reported that Rooke seemed to have been a "model prisoner" for the past twelve years—there was a bulging file of supportive letters from prison guards, therapists, counsellors, literacy volunteers, a Catholic chaplain. The Victim/Witness Program allowed for the testimony to parole boards of victims and family members related to victims, and so Andrea McClure was invited to address Rooke's parole board when his hearing came up in April. If she wanted to be involved, if she had anything to say.

Her mother was too upset to be involved. She'd broken down, just discussing it on the phone with Andrea.

Except for a representative from the Wakulla County Attorney's Office, everyone who gave testimony at Albert Jefferson Rooke's parole hearing, if Andrea didn't attend, would be speaking on behalf of the prisoner.

Andrea said, wiping at her eyes, "If that man is freed, I swear I will kill him myself."

Andrea said, "I was fourteen years old at the time Frannie died. I was supposed to fly down with her to visit Grandma, at Easter, but I didn't want to go, and Frannie went alone, and if I'd gone with Frannie she'd be alive today, wouldn't she? I mean, it's a simple statement of fact. It isn't anything but a simple statement of fact."

Harry said, hesitantly, "Yes, but—" trying to think what to say in the face of knowing that Andrea had made this accusation against herself continuously over the past twenty years, "—a fact can distort. Facts need to be interpreted in context."

Andrea smiled impatiently. She was looking, not at Harry, but at something beyond Harry's shoulder. "You're either alive, or you're not alive. That's the only context."

Where in the past Andrea had kept the secret of her murdered sister wholly to herself, now, suddenly, she began to talk openly, in a rapid nervous voice, about what had happened. Frannie, and how Frannie's death had affected the family, and how, after the trial, they'd assumed it was over—"He *was* sentenced to life in prison. Instead of the electric chair. Doesn't that mean anything?"

Harry said, "There's always the possibility of parole, unless the judge sets the sentence otherwise. You must have known that."

Andrea seemed not to hear. Or, hearing, not to absorb.

Now she brought a scrapbook out of a closet. Showing Harry snapshots of the dead girl—pretty, thin-faced, with large expressive dark eyes like Andrea's own. Sifting through family snapshots, Andrea would have skipped over her own and seemed surprised that Harry would want to look at them. There were postcards and letters of Frannie's; there were clippings from a Roanoke paper—Frances McClure the recipient of a scholarship to Middlebury, Frances McClure embarked upon a six-week work-study program in Peru. (No clippings—none—pertaining to

the crime.) Andrea answered at length, with warmth and animation, Harry's questions; in the midst of other conversations, or silence, she'd begin suddenly to speak of Frannie as if, all along,
she and Harry had been discussing her.

Harry thought, It must be like a dream. An underground
stream. Never ceasing.

"For years," Andrea confessed, "I wouldn't think of Frannie.
After the trial, we were exhausted and we never talked about her.
I truly don't believe it's what psychiatry calls 'denial'—there was
nothing more to say. The dead don't change, do they? The dead
don't get any older, they don't get any less dead. It's funny how
Frannie was so old to me, so mature, now I see these pictures
and I see she was so young, only nineteen, and now I'm thirty-
four and I'd be so old to *her.* I almost wish I could say that Frannie and I didn't get along but we did—I loved her, I loved her so.
She was older than I was by just enough, five years, so we never
competed in anything, *she* was the one, everybody loved her, you
would have loved her, she had such a quick, warm way of laughing, she was so *alive.* Her roommate at Middlebury would say
how weird it was, that Frannie wasn't *alive* because Frannie was
the most *alive* person of anybody and that doesn't change. But
we stopped talking about her because it was too awful. I was
lonely for her but I stopped thinking about her. I went to a different high school, my parents moved to a different part of Roanoke,
it was possible to think different thoughts. I dream about Frannie
now and it's been twenty years but I really don't think I was
dreaming about her then. Except sometimes when I was alone,
especially if I was shopping, and this is true now, because Frannie used to take me shopping when I was young, I'd seem to be
with another person, I'd sort of be talking to, listening to, another
person—but not really. I mean, it wasn't Frannie. Sometimes I get
scared and think I've forgotten what she looks like exactly—my
memory is bleaching out. But I'll never forget. I'm all she has. The
memory of her—it's in my trust. She had a boyfriend, actually, but
he's long gone from my life—he's married, has kids. He's gone. If
he walked up to me on the street, if he turned up at work, if he
turned up as my supervisor some day—I wouldn't know him. I'd
look right through him. I look through my mother sometimes,

and I can see she looks through me. Because we're thinking of Frannie but we don't acknowledge it because we can't talk about it. But if she's thinking of Frannie, and at the moment I'm not, that's when she really *will* look through me. My father died of liver cancer and it was obviously from what Frannie's murderer did to us. We never said his name, and we never thought his name. We were at the trial and we saw him and I remember how relieved I was—I don't know about Mom and Dad, but I know *I* was—to see he truly was depraved. His face was all broken out in pimples. His eyes were bloodshot. He was always pretending to be trying to commit suicide, to get sympathy, or to make out he was crazy, so they had him drugged, and the drugs did something to his motor coordination. Also, he was pretending. *He* was an actor. But the act didn't work—he's in prison for life. I can't believe any parole board would take his case seriously. I know it's routine. The more I think about it, of course it's routine. They won't let him out. But I have to make sure of that because if I don't, and they let him out, I'll be to blame. It will all be on my head. I told you, didn't I?—I was supposed to go to Grandma's with Frannie, but I didn't. I was fourteen, I had my friends, I didn't want to go to Wakulla Beach exactly then. If I'd gone with Frannie, she'd be alive today. That's a simple, neutral fact. It isn't an accusation just a fact. My parents never blamed me, or anyway never spoke of it. They're good people, they're Christians I guess you could say. They must have wished I'd gone in Frannie's place but I can't say I blame them."

Harry wasn't sure he'd heard correctly. "Your parents must have—what? Wished you'd died in your sister's place? Are you serious?"

Andrea had been speaking breathlessly. Now she looked at Harry, the skin between her eyebrows puckered.

She said, "I didn't say that. You must have misunderstood."

Harry said, "I must have—all right."

"You must have heard wrong. What did I say?"

At such times Andrea would become agitated, running her hands through her hair so it stood in affrighted comical tufts; her mouth would tremble and twist. "It's all right, Andy," Harry would say, "—hey c'mon. It's fine." He would stop her hands and maybe kiss them, the moist palms. Or slide his arms around her playful and husbandly. How small Andrea was, how small an adult woman can be, bones you could fracture by squeezing, so be careful. Harry's heart seemed to hurt, in sympathy. "Don't think about it anymore today, Andy, okay? I love you."

And Andrea might say, vague, wondering, as if she were making this observation for the first time, which in fact she was not, "—The only other person who ever called me 'Andy' was Frannie. Did you know?"

He'd been trained as a lawyer. Not criminal law but corporate law. But he came to wonder if possibly Andrea had been attracted to him originally, that evening, because he had a law degree. When he'd mentioned law school, at Yale, her attention had quickened.

Unless he was imagining this? Human memory is notoriously unreliable, like film fading in amnesiac patches.

Memory: Frannie McClure now exists only in memory.

That's what's so terrible about being dead, Harry thought wryly. You depend for your existence as a historic fact upon the memories of others. Failing, finite, mortal themselves.

Though they'd never discussed it in such abstract terms, for Andrea seemed to shrink from speaking of her sister in anything but the most particular way, Harry understood that her anxiety was not simply that Albert Jefferson Rooke might be released on parole after having served only twenty years of a life sentence but that, if he was, Frannie McClure's claim to permanent, tragic significance would be challenged.

Also: for Frannie McClure to continue to exist as a historic fact, the memories that preserve her as a specific individual, not a mere name, sexual assault statistic, court case must continue to exist. These were still, after twenty years, fairly numerous, for as an American girl who'd gone to a large public high school and had just about completed two years of college, she'd known, and been known by, hundreds of people; but the number was naturally decreasing year by year. Andrea could count them on the fingers of both hands—relatives, neighbors who'd known Frannie from the time of her birth to the time of her death. The grandmother who'd lived in a splendid beachfront condominium overlooking Apalachee Bay of the Gulf of Mexico had been dead since 1979. She'd never recovered from the shock and grief, of course. And there was Andrea's father, dead since 1981. And Andrea's mother, whom Harry had yet to meet, and whom Andrea spoke of with purposeful vagueness as a "difficult" woman, living now in a retirement community in Roanoke, never spoke of her murdered daughter to anyone. So it was impossible to gauge to what extent the mother's memory did in fact preserve the dead girl.

Sometimes, when Andrea was out of the apartment, Harry contemplated the snapshots of Frannie McClure by himself. There was one of her dated Christmas 1969, she'd been fifteen at the time, hugging her ten-year-old sister Andy and clowning for the camera, a beautiful girl, in an oversized sweater and jeans, her brown eyes given an eerie red-maroon glisten by the camera's flash. Behind the girls, a seven-foot Christmas tree, resplendent with useless ornamentation.

Harry noted: When he and Andrea made love it was nearly always in complete silence except for Andrea's murmured incoherent words, her soft cries, muffled sobs. You could credit such sounds to love, passion. But essentially there was silence, a qualitatively different silence from what Harry recalled from their early nights together. Harry understood that Andrea was thinking of Frannie's struggling body as it, too, was penetrated by a man's penis; this excited Harry enormously but made him cautious about being gentle, not allowing his weight to rest too heavily upon Andrea. The challenge, too, for Harry as a lover was to shake Andrea free of her trance and force her into concentrating on *him*. If Harry could involve Andrea in physical sensation, in actual passion, he would have succeeded. At the same time Harry had to concentrate on Andrea, exclusively upon Andrea, and not allow his mind to swerve to the mysterious doomed girl of the snapshots.

The call from the Victim/Witness Program advocate came for Andrea in late March. Giving her only twenty-six days to prepare, emotionally and otherwise, for the hearing on April 20 in Tallahassee. Andrea mentioned casually to Harry it's only a coincidence of course—this first parole hearing for Rooke is scheduled for the Tuesday that's a week and two days following Easter, and it was 12:10 A.M. of the Tuesday following Easter 1973 that the call came from Wakulla Beach notifying the McClures of Frannie's death.

Andrea went on, wiping at her eyes, "It wasn't clear from that first call just how Frannie had died. What he'd done to her. She was dead, that was the fact. They said it was an 'assault' and they'd arrested the man but they didn't go into details over the telephone—of course. Not that kind of details. I suppose it's procedure. Notifying families when someone's been killed—that requires procedure. When they called Grandma, to make the identification, that night, *that* must have been difficult. She'd collapsed, she didn't remember much about it afterward. My mother and father had to make the identification, too. I suppose it was only Frannie's face?—but her face was so damaged. I didn't see, and the casket was closed, so I don't know. I shouldn't be talking about something I don't know, should I? I shouldn't be involving you in this, should I? So I'll stop."

"Of course I want to be involved, honey," Harry said. "I'm going with you. I'll help you all I can."

"No, really, you don't have to. Please don't feel that you have to."

"Of course I'm going with you to that goddamned hearing," Harry said. "I wouldn't let you go through something so terrible alone."

"But I could do it," Andrea said. "Don't you think I could? I'm not fourteen years old now. I'm all grown up."

Except: Harry heard Andrea crying when he woke in the night and discovered she was gone from bed, several nights in succession hearing her in the bathroom with the fan running to muffle her sobs. Or was it Andrea talking to herself in a low, rapid voice in the night. Rehearsing her testimony for the parole board. She'd been told it was best not to read a prepared statement, nor give the impression that she was repeating a prepared statement. So in the night locked in the bathroom with the fan running to muffle her words which are punctuated with sobs, or curses, Andrea rehearsed her role as Harry lay sleepless wondering, *Am I strong enough? What is required of me?*

This, without telling Andrea: A few days before they were scheduled to fly to Tallahassee, Harry drove to the Georgetown Law School library and looked up the transcript of the December 1975 appeal of the verdict of guilty in the *People of the State of Florida* v. *Albert Jefferson Rooke* of September 1973. He'd only begun reading Rooke's confession when he realized there was something wrong with it.

. . . That night I got a feeling I wanted to do it . . . hurt one of them real bad . . . so I went out to find her . . . a girl or a woman. . . I hate them . . . I really hate them . . . I get a kick out of hurting people . . . I get a kick out of putting something over on you guys . . . so I saw this girl on the beach . . . I'd never seen her before . . . I jumped her and she started to scream and that pissed me off and I got real mad . . . and so on through twenty-three pages of a rambling monologue Harry believed he'd read before, or something very like it; its Wakulla Beach, Florida, details specific but its essence, its tone familiar.

What was Albert Jefferson Rooke's "confession" but standard boilerplate of the kind that used to be used (in some parts of the country still is used?) by police who've arrested a vulnerable, highly suspicious person? In a particularly repulsive crime? Someone not a local resident so drunk or stoned or so marginal and despicable a human being witnesses take one look at him and say *He's the one!* cops take one look at him *He's the one!* and if the poor bastard hadn't committed this crime you can assume he's committed any number of other crimes he's never been caught for so let's help him remember, let's give him a little assistance. Harry could imagine it: this straggly-haired hippie-punk brought handcuffed to police headquarters raving and disoriented not knowing where the hell he is, waives his right to call an attorney or maybe they don't even read him the Miranda statement, he's eager to cooperate with these cops so they stop beating his head against the wall and won't "restrain" him with a choke-hold when he "resists" for it's self-evident to these professionals as eventually to a jury that this is exactly the kind of sick degenerate pervert who rapes, mutilates, murders. Sure we know "Albert Jefferson Rooke," he's our man.

Harry sat in the law library for a long time staring into space. He felt weak, sick. Can it be? *Is* it possible?

Andrea said, "Please don't feel you should care about this—obsession of mine. You have your own work, and you have your own life. It isn't—" and here she paused, her mouth working, "—as if we're married."

"What has that got to do with it?" Harry saw how the quickened light in Andrea's eyes for him, at his approach, had gone dead; she was shrinking from him. He'd come home from the law library and he'd told her just that he'd been reading about the Rooke trial and would she like to discuss it in strictly legal terms and she'd turned to him this waxy dead-white face, these pinched eyes, as if he'd confessed being unfaithful to her. "That isn't an issue."

"I shouldn't have told you about Frannie. It was selfish of me. You're the only person in my life now who knows and it was a mistake for me to tell you and I'm *sorry.*"

She walked blindly out of the room. This was the kind of apology that masks bitter resentment: Harry knew the tone, Harry had been there before.

Still, Harry followed Andrea, into another room, and to a window where she stood trembling refusing to look at him saying in a low rapid voice as if to herself how she shouldn't have involved him, he had never known her sister, what a burden to place upon him, a stranger to the family, how short-sighted she'd been, that night the call had come for her she should have asked him please to go home, this was a private matter—and Harry listened, Harry couldn't bring himself to interrupt, he loved this woman didn't he, in any case he can't hurt her, not now. She was saying, "I'm not a vengeful person, it's justice I want for Frannie. Her memory is in my trust—I'm all she has, now."

Harry said, carefully, "Andy, it's all right. We can discuss it some other time." On the plane to Tallahassee, maybe? They were leaving in the morning.

Andrea said, "We don't have to discuss it at all! I'm not a vengeful person."

"No one has said you're a vengeful person. Who's said that?"

"You didn't know Frannie and maybe you don't know me. I'm not always sure who I am. But I know what I have to *do*."

"That's the important thing, then. That's the—" Harry was searching for the absolutely right, the perfect word, which eluded him, unless, "—moral thing, then. Of course."

The moral thing, then. Of course. On the plane to Tallahassee, he'd tell her.

But that night Andrea slept poorly. And in the early morning, Harry believed he heard her being sick in the bathroom. And on their way to the airport and on the plane south Andrea's eyes were unnaturally bright, glistening and the pupils dilated and she was alternately silent and nervously loquacious gripping his hand much the time and how could he tell her, for what did he *know*, he *knew* nothing, only suspected, it was up to Rooke's defense attorney to raise such issues, how could he interfere, he could not.

Andrea said, her forehead creased like a chamois cloth that's been crumpled, "It's so strange: I keep seeing *his* face, *he's* my audience. I'm brought into this room that's darkened and at the front the parole board is sitting and the lights are on them and *he's* there—he hasn't changed in twenty years. As soon as he sees me, he knows. He sees, not me, of course not me, he wouldn't remember me, but Frannie. He sees Frannie. I've been reading these documents they've sent me, you know, and the most outrageous, the really obscene thing is, Rooke claims he doesn't remember Frannie's name, even! He claims he never saw her and he never raped her and he never tortured her and he never strangled her, he never knew her, and now, after twenty years, he's saying he wouldn't even remember her name if he isn't told it!" Andrea looked at Harry, to see if he was sharing her outrage. "But when he sees me, he'll see Frannie, and he'll remember everything. And he'll know. He'll know he's going back to prison for the rest of his life. Because Frannie wouldn't want revenge, she wasn't that kind of person, but she *would* want justice."

Harry considered: Is the truth worth it?—even if we can know the truth.

*   *   *

In the end, in the State Justice Building in Tallahassee, it wasn't clear whether Albert Jefferson Rooke was even on the premises when Andrea spoke with the parole board; and Andrea made no inquiries. In a blind blinking daze she was escorted into a room by a young woman attorney from the Victim/Witness Program and Harry Steinhart was allowed to accompany her as a friend of the McClure family, though not a witness. *At last,* Harry thought. *It will be over, something will be decided.*

The interview lasted one hour and forty minutes during which time Andrea held the undivided attention of the seven middle-aged Caucasian men who constituted the board—she'd brought along her cherished snapshots of her murdered sister, she read from letters written to her by Frannie, and by former teachers, friends, and acquaintances mourning Frannie's death in such a way as to make you realize (even Harry, as if for the first time, his eyes brimming with tears) that a young woman named Frances McClure did live, and that her loss to the world is a tragedy. The room in which Andrea spoke was windowless, on the eleventh floor of a sleekly modern building, not at all the room Andrea seemed to have envisioned but one brightly lit by recessed fluorescent lighting. No shadows here. The positioning of the chair in which Andrea sat, facing at an angle the long table at which the seven men sat, suggested a minimal, stylized stage. Andrea wore a dark blue linen suit and a creamy silk blouse and her slender legs were nearly hidden beneath the suit's fashionably long, flared skirt. Her face was pale, and her forehead finely crossed with the evidence of grief, her voice now and then trembling but over all she remained composed, speaking calmly, looking each of the parole board members in the eye, each in turn; answering their courteous questions unhesitatingly, with feeling, as if they were all companions involved in a single moral cause. *It's people like us against people like him.* By the end of the interview Andrea was beginning to crack, her voice not quite so composed and her eyes spilling tears but still she managed to speak calmly, softly, each word enunciated with care. "No one can ever undo what Albert Jefferson Rooke did to my sister—even if the State of Florida imprisons him for all his life, as he'd been sentenced. He escaped the electric chair by changing his plea and then he changed his plea again so we know how he values the truth and he's never expressed the slightest remorse for his crime so we know he's the same man who killed my sister, he can't have changed in twenty years. He hasn't come to terms with his crime, or his sickness. We know that violent sex offenders rarely change even with therapy, and this man has not had therapy relating to his sickness because he has always denied his sickness. So he'll rape and kill again. He'll take his revenge on the first young girl he can, the way he did with my sister—he can always pretend he doesn't remember any of it afterward. He's claiming now he doesn't even remember my sister's name but her name is Frances McClure and others remember. He claims he wants to be free on parole so he can 'begin again.' What is a man like that going to 'begin again'? I see he's collected a file of letters from well-intentioned fair-minded people he's deceived the way he hopes to deceive you gentlemen—you know what prison inmates call this strategy, it's a vulgar word I hesitate to say: 'bullshitting.' They learn to 'bullshit' the prison guards and the therapists and the social workers and the chaplains and, yes, the parole boards. Sometimes they claim they're sorry for their crimes and won't ever do such things again—they're 'remorseful.' But in this killer's case, there isn't even 'remorse.' He just wants to get out of prison to 'begin again.' I seem to know how he probably talked to you, tried to convince you it doesn't matter what he did twenty years ago this Easter because he's reformed *now*, no more drugs and no more crime *now*. He'll get a job, he's eager to work. I seem to know how you want to believe him, because we want to believe people when they speak like this. It's a Christian impulse. It's a humane impulse. It makes us feel good about ourselves—we can be 'charitable.' But a prisoner's word for this strategy is 'bullshitting' and that's what we need to keep in mind. This killer has appealed to you to release him on parole—to 'bullshit' you into believing him. But I've come to speak the truth. I'm here on my sister's behalf. She'd say, she'd plead—don't release this vicious, sick, murderous man back into society, to commit more crimes! Don't be the well-intentioned parties whose 'charity' will lead to another innocent girl being brutally raped and murdered. It's too late for me, Frannie would say, but potential victims—they can be spared."

Only a half-hour later, Andrea was informed that the parole board voted unanimously against releasing Albert Jefferson Rooke. She asked could she thank the board members and she was escorted back into the room and Harry waited for her smiling in relief as she thanked the men one by one, shook their hands. Now she did burst into tears but it was all right. Telling Harry afterward, in their hotel room, "Every one of those men thanked *me*. They thanked *me*. One of them said, 'If it wasn't for you, Miss McClure, we might've made a bad mistake.'"

Harry said, in a neutral voice, "It was a real triumph, then, wasn't it? You exerted your will, and you triumphed."

Andrea looked at him, puzzled. She was removing her linen jacket and hanging it carefully on a pink silk hanger. Her face was soft, that soft brimming of her eyes, soft curve of her mouth, the woman's most intimate look, the look Harry sees in her face after love. Yet there's a clarity to her voice, almost a sharpness. "Oh, no—it wasn't my will. It was Frannie's. I spoke for her and I told the truth for her and that was all. And now it's over."

That evening Andrea is too exhausted to eat anywhere except in their hotel room and midway through the dinner she's too exhausted to finish it and then too exhausted to undress herself, to take a bath, to climb into the enormous king-sized canopied bed without Harry's help. And he's exhausted, too. And he's been drinking, too. Since that afternoon foreseeing with calm, impersonal horror how, like clockwork, every several years Albert Jefferson Rooke will present himself to the parole board and Andrea will fly to Tallahassee to present herself in opposition to the man she believes to be her sister's murderer; and so it will go through the years, and Rooke might die one day in prison, and this would release them both, or Rooke might be freed on parole, finally—of that, Harry doesn't want to think. Not right now.

In the ridiculous elevated bed, the lights out; a murmurous indefinable sound that might be the air-conditioning, or someone in an adjacent room quietly and drunkenly arguing; the feverish damp warmth of Andrea's body, her mouth hungry against his, her slender arms around his neck. Naively, childishly, in a voice Harry has never heard before, as if this is, of all Andrea's voices, the one truly her own, she asks, "Do you love me, Harry? Will you always love me?" and he kisses her mouth, her breasts, bunching her nightgown in his fists, he whispers, "Yes."

Life After High School

~

"Sunny? Sun-ny?"

On that last night of March 1959, in soiled sheepskin parka, unbuckled overshoes, but bare-headed in the lightly falling snow, Zachary Graff, eighteen years old, six feet one and a half inches tall, weight 203 pounds, IQ 160, stood beneath Sunny Burhman's second-storey bedroom window, calling her name softly, urgently, as if his very life depended upon it. It was nearly midnight: Sunny had been in bed for a half hour, and woke from a thin dissolving sleep to hear her name rising mysteriously out of the dark, low, gravelly, repetitive as the surf. "*Sun*-ny—?" She had not spoken with Zachary Graff since the previous week, when she'd told him, quietly, tears shining in her eyes, that she did not love him; she could not accept his engagement ring, still less marry him. This was the first time in the twelve weeks of Zachary's pursuit of her that he'd dared to come to the rear of the Burhmans' house, by day or night; the first time, as Sunny would say afterward, he'd ever appealed to her in such a way.

They would ask, In what way?

Sunny would hesitate, and say, So—emotionally. In a way that scared me.

So you sent him away?

She did. She'd sent him away.

*   *   *

It was much talked-of, at South Lebanon High School, how, in this spring of their senior year, Zachary Graff, who had never to anyone's recollection asked a girl out before, let alone pursued her so publicly and with such clumsy devotion, seemed to have fallen in love with Sunny Burhman.

Of all people—Sunny Burhman.

Odd too that Zachary should seem to have discovered Sunny, when the two had been classmates in the South Lebanon, New York, public schools since first grade, back in 1947.

Zachary, whose father was Homer Graff, the town's preeminent physician, had, since ninth grade, cultivated a clipped, mock-gallant manner when speaking with female classmates; his Clifton Webb style. He was unfailingly courteous, but unfailingly cool; measured; formal. He seemed impervious to the giddy rise and ebb of adolescent emotion, moving, clumsy but determined, like a grizzly bear on its hind legs, through the school corridors, rarely glancing to left or right: *his* gaze, its myopia corrected by lenses encased in chunky black plastic frames, was firmly fixed on the horizon. Dr. Graff's son was not unpopular so much as feared, thus disliked.

If Zachary's excellent academic record continued uninterrupted through final papers, final exams, and there was no reason to suspect it would not, Zachary would be valedictorian of the Class of 1959. Barbara ("Sunny") Burhman, later to distinguish herself at Cornell, would graduate only ninth, in a class of eighty-two.

Zachary's attentiveness to Sunny had begun, with no warning, immediately after Christmas recess, when classes resumed in January. Suddenly, a half-dozen times a day, in Sunny's vicinity, looming large, eyeglasses glittering, there Zachary *was*. His Clifton Webb pose had dissolved, he was shy, stammering, yet forceful, even bold, waiting for the advantageous moment (for Sunny was always surrounded by friends) to push forward and say, "Hi, Sunny!" The greeting, utterly commonplace in content, sounded, in Zachary's mouth, like a Latin phrase tortuously translated.

Sunny, so-named for her really quite astonishing smile, that dazzling white Sunny-smile that transformed a girl of conventional freckled snub-nosed prettiness to true beauty, might have been surprised, initially, but gave no sign, saying, "Hi, Zach!"

In those years, the corridors of South Lebanon High School were lyric crossfires of *Hi!* and *H'lo!* and *Good to see ya!* uttered hundreds of times daily by the golden girls, the popular, confident, good-looking girls, club officers, prom queens, cheerleaders like Sunny Burhman and her friends, tossed out indiscriminately, for that was the style.

Most of the students were in fact practicing Christians, of Lutheran, Presbyterian, Methodist stock.

Like Sunny Burhman, who was, or seemed, even at the time of this story, too good to be true.

That's to say—*good.*

So, though Sunny soon wondered why on earth Zachary Graff was hanging around her, why, again, at her elbow, or lying in wait for her at the foot of a stairs, why, for the nth time that week, *him*, she was too *good* to indicate impatience, or exasperation; too *good* to tell him, as her friends advised, to get lost.

He telephoned her too. Poor Zachary. Stammering over the phone, his voice lowered as if he were in terror of being overheard, "Is S-Sunny there, Mrs. B-Burhman? May I speak with her, please?" And Mrs. Burhman, who knew Dr. Graff and his wife, of course, since everyone in South Lebanon, population 3,800, knew everyone else or knew of them, including frequently their family histories and facts about them of which their children were entirely unaware, hesitated, and said, "Yes, I'll put her on, but I hope you won't talk long—Sunny has homework tonight." Or, apologetically but firmly: "No, I'm afraid she isn't here. May I take a message?"

"N-no message," Zachary would murmur, and hurriedly hang up.

Sunny, standing close by, thumbnail between her just perceptibly gat-toothed front teeth, expression crinkled in dismay, would whisper, "Oh Mom. I feel so *bad.* I just feel so—*bad.*"

Mrs. Burhman said briskly, "You don't have time for all of them, honey."

Still, Zachary was not discouraged, and with the swift passage of time it began to be observed that Sunny engaged in conversations with him—the two of them sitting, alone, in a corner of the cafeteria, or walking together after a meeting of the Debate Club, of which Zachary was president, and Sunny a member. They were both on the staff of the South Lebanon High Beacon, and the South Lebanon High Yearbook 1959, and the South Lebanon Torch (the literary magazine). They were both members of the National Honor Society and the Quill & Scroll Society. Though Zachary Graff in his aloofness and impatience with most of his peers would be remembered as antisocial, a "loner," in fact, as his record of activities suggested, printed beneath his photograph in the yearbook, he had time, or made time, for things that mattered to him.

He shunned sports, however. High school sports, at least.

His life's game, he informed Sunny Burhman, unaware of the solemn pomposity with which he spoke, would be *golf.* His father had been instructing him, informally, since his twelfth birthday.

Said Zachary, "I have no natural talent for it, and I find it profoundly boring, but golf will be my game." And he pushed his chunky black glasses roughly against the bridge of his nose, as he did countless times a day, as if they were in danger of sliding off.

Zachary Graff had such a physical presence, few of his con-temporaries would have described him as unattractive, still less homely, ugly. His head appeared oversized, even for his massive body; his eyes were deep-set, with a look of watchfulness and se-crecy; his skin was tallow-colored, and blemished, in wavering patches like topographical maps. His big teeth glinted with fila-ments of silver, and his breath, oddly for one whose father was a doctor, was stale, musty, cobwebby—not that Sunny Burhman ever alluded to this fact, to others.

Her friends began to ask of her, a bit jealously, reproachfully, "What do you two talk about so much?—you and *him?*" and Sunny replied, taking care not to hint, with the slightest move-ment of her eyebrows, or rolling of her eyes, that, yes, she found the situation peculiar too, "Oh—Zachary and I talk about all kinds of things. *He* talks, mainly. He's brilliant. He's—" pausing, her forehead delicately crinkling in thought, her lovely brown eyes for a moment clouded, "—well, *brilliant.*"

In fact, at first, Zachary spoke, in his intense, obsessive way, of impersonal subjects: the meaning of life, the future of Earth, whether science or art best satisfies the human hunger for self-expression. He said, laughing nervously, fixing Sunny with his shyly bold stare, "Just to pose certain questions is, I guess, to show your hope they can be answered."

Early on, Zachary seemed to have understood that, if he expressed doubt, for instance about "whether God exists" and so forth, Sunny Burhman would listen seriously; and would talk with him earnestly, with the air of a nurse giving a transfusion to a patient in danger of expiring for loss of blood. She was not a religious fanatic, but she *was* a devout Christian—the Burhmans were members of the First Presbyterian Church of South Lebanon, and Sunny was president of her youth group, and, among other good deeds, did YWCA volunteer work on Saturday afternoons; she had not the slightest doubt that Jesus Christ, that's to say His spirit, dwelled in her heart, and that, simply by speaking the truth of what she believed, she could convince others.

Though one day, and soon, Sunny would examine her beliefs, and question the faith into which she'd been born; she had not done so by the age of seventeen and a half. She was a virgin, and virginal in all, or most, of her thoughts.

Sometimes, behind her back, even by friends, Sunny was laughed at, gently—never ridiculed, for no one would ridicule Sunny.

Once, when Sunny Burhman and her date and another couple were gazing up into the night sky, standing in the parking lot of the high school, following a prom, Sunny had said in a quavering voice, "It's so big it would be terrifying, wouldn't it?—except for Jesus, who makes us feel at home."

When popular Chuck Crueller, a quarterback for the South Lebanon varsity football team, was injured during a game, and carried off by ambulance to undergo emergency surgery, Sunny mobilized the other cheerleaders, tears fierce in her eyes, "We can do it for Chuck—we can *pray.*" And so the eight girls in their short-skirted crimson jumpers and starched white cotton blouses had gripped one another's hands tight, weeping, on the verge of hysteria, had prayed, prayed, *prayed*—hidden away in the depths of the girls' locker room for hours. Sunny had led the prayers, and Chuck Crueller recovered.

So you wouldn't ridicule Sunny Burhman, somehow it wouldn't have been appropriate.

As her classmate Tobias Shanks wrote of her, as one of his du-
ties as literary editor of the 1959 South Lebanon yearbook:
*"Sunny" Burhman!—an all-American girl too good to be true who
is nonetheless TRUE!*

If there was a slyly mocking tone to Tobias Shanks's praise, a
hint that such goodness was predictable, and superficial, and of
no genuine merit, the caption, mere print, beneath Sunny's dazzlingly beautiful photograph, conveyed nothing of this.

Surprisingly, for all his pose of skepticism and superiority,
Zachary Graff too was a Christian. He'd been baptized Lutheran,
and never failed to attend Sunday services with his parents at the
First Lutheran Church. Amid the congregation of somber,
somnambulant worshippers, Zachary Graff's frowning young face,
the very set of his beefy shoulders, drew the minister's uneasy
eye; it would be murmured of Dr. Graff's precocious son, in ret-
rospect, that he'd been perhaps too *serious.*

Before falling in love with Sunny Burhman, and discussing his
religious doubts with her, Zachary had often discussed them with
Tobias Shanks, who'd been his friend, you might say his only
friend, since seventh grade. (But only sporadically since seventh
grade, since the boys, each highly intelligent, inclined to impatience and sarcasm, got on each other's nerves.) Once, Zachary
confided in Tobias that he prayed every morning of his life—
immediately upon waking he scrambled out of bed, knelt, hid his
face in his hands, and prayed. For his sinful soul, for his sinful
thoughts, deeds, desires. He lacerated his soul the way he'd been
taught by his mother to tug a fine-toothed steel comb through his
coarse, oily hair, never less than once a day.

Tobias Shanks, a self-professed agnostic since the age of fourteen, laughed, and asked derisively, "Yes, but what do you pray *for,*
exactly?" and Zachary had thought a bit, and said, not ironically, but
altogether seriously, "To get through the day. Doesn't everyone?"

This melancholy reply, Tobias was never to reveal.

Zachary's parents were urging him to go to Muhlenberg College,
which was church-affiliated; Zachary hoped to go elsewhere. He
said, humbly, to Sunny Burhman, "If you go to Cornell, Sunny,
I—maybe I'll go there too?"

Sunny hesitated, then smiled. "Oh. That would be nice."

"You wouldn't mind, Sunny?"

"Why would I *mind*, Zachary?" Sunny laughed, to hide her impatience. They were headed for Zachary's car, parked just up the hill from the YM-YWCA building. It was a gusty Saturday afternoon in early March. Leaving the YWCA, Sunny had seen Zachary Graff standing at the curb, hands in the pockets of his sheepskin parka, head lowered, but eyes nervously alert. Standing there, as if accidentally.

It was impossible to avoid him, she had to allow him to drive her home. Though she was beginning to feel panic, like darting tongues of flame, at the prospect of Zachary Graff always *there*.

Tell the creep to get lost, her friends counseled. Even her nice friends were without sentiment regarding Zachary Graff.

Until sixth grade, Sunny had been plain little Barbara Burhman. Then, one day, her teacher had said, to all the class, in one of those moments of inspiration that can alter, by whim, the course of an entire life, "Tell you what, boys and girls—let's call Barbara 'Sunny' from now on—that's what she *is*."

Ever afterward, in South Lebanon, she was "Sunny" Burhman. Plain little Barbara had been left behind, seemingly forever.

So, of course, Sunny could not tell Zachary Graff to get lost. Such words were not part of her vocabulary.

Zachary owned a plum-colored 1956 Plymouth which other boys envied—it seemed to them distinctly unfair that Zachary, of all people, had his own car, when so few of them, who loved cars, did. But Zachary was oblivious of their envy, as, in a way, he seemed oblivious of his own good fortune. He drove the car as if it were an adult duty, with middle-aged fussiness and worry. He drove the car as if he were its own chauffeur. Yet, driving Sunny home, he talked—chattered—continuously. Speaking of college, and of religious "obligations," and of his parents' expectations of him; speaking of medical school; the future; the life— "beyond South Lebanon."

He asked again, in that gravelly, irksomely humble voice, if Sunny would mind if he went to Cornell. And Sunny said, trying to sound merely reasonable, "Zachary, it's a *free world*."

Zachary said, "Oh no it isn't, Sunny. For some of us, it isn't."

This enigmatic remark Sunny was determined not to follow up.

Braking to a careful stop in front of the Burhmans' house, Zachary said, with an almost boyish enthusiasm, "So—Cornell? In the fall? We'll both go to Cornell?"

Sunny was quickly out of the car before Zachary could put on the emergency brake and come around, ceremoniously, to open her door. Gaily, recklessly, infinitely relieved to be out of his company, she called back over her shoulder, "Why not?"

Sunny's secret vanity must have been what linked them.

For several times, gravely, Zachary had said to her, "When I'm with you, Sunny, it's possible for me to believe."

He meant, she thought, in God. In Jesus. In the life hereafter.

The next time Zachary maneuvered Sunny into his car, under the pretext of driving her home, it was to present the startled girl with an engagement ring.

He'd bought the ring at Stern's Jewelers, South Lebanon's single good jewelry store, with money secretly withdrawn from his savings account; that account to which, over a period of more than a decade, he'd deposited modest sums with a painstaking devotion. This was his "college fund," or had been—out of the $3,245 saved, only $1,090 remained. How astonished, upset, furious his parents would be when they learned—Zachary hadn't allowed himself to contemplate.

The Graffs knew nothing about Sunny Burhman. So far as they might have surmised, their son's frequent absences from home were nothing out of the ordinary—he'd always spent time at the public library, where his preferred reading was reference books. He'd begin with Volume One of an encyclopedia, and make his diligent way through each successive volume, like a horse grazing a field, rarely glancing up, uninterested in his surroundings.

"Please—will you accept it?"

Sunny was staring incredulously at the diamond ring, which was presented to her, not in Zachary's big clumsy fingers, with the dirt-edged nails, but in the plush-lined little box, as if it might be more attractive that way, more like a gift. The ring was 24-karat gold and the diamond was small but distinctive, and coldly glittering. A beautiful ring, but Sunny did not see it that way.

She whispered, "Oh. Zachary. Oh *no*—there must be some misunderstanding."

Zachary seemed prepared for her reaction, for he said, quickly, "Will you just try it on?—see if it fits?"

Sunny shook her head. No she couldn't.

"They'll take it back to adjust it, if it's too big," Zachary said. "They promised."

"Zachary, no," Sunny said gently. "I'm so sorry."

Tears flooded her eyes and spilled over onto her cheeks.

Zachary was saying, eagerly, his lips flecked with spittle, "I realize you don't l-love me, Sunny, at least not yet, but—you could wear the ring, couldn't you? Just—wear it?" He continued to hold the little box out to her, his hand visibly shaking. "On your right hand, if you don't want to wear it on your left? Please?"

"Zachary, no. That's impossible."

"Just, you know, as a, a gift—? Oh Sunny—"

They were sitting in the plum-colored Plymouth, parked, in an awkwardly public place, on Upchurch Avenue three blocks from Sunny's house. It was 4:25 P.M., March 26, a Thursday: Zachary had lingered after school in order to drive Sunny home after choir practice. Sunny would afterward recall, with an odd haltingness, as if her memory of the episode were blurred with tears, that, as usual, Zachary had done most of the talking. He had not argued with her, nor exactly begged, but spoke almost formally, as if setting out the basic points of his debating strategy: If Sunny did not love him, he could love enough for both; and, If Sunny did not want to be "officially" engaged, she could wear his ring anyway, couldn't she?

It would mean so much to him, Zachary said.

Life or death, Zachary said

Sunny closed the lid of the little box, and pushed it from her, gently. She was crying, and her smooth pageboy was now disheveled. "Oh Zachary, I'm *sorry*. I *can't*."

Sunny knelt by her bed, hid her face in her hands, prayed.

Please help Zachary not to be in love with me. Please help me not to be cruel. Have mercy on us both O God.

O God help him to realize he doesn't love me—doesn't know *me*.

Days passed, and Zachary did not call. If he was absent from school, Sunny did not seem to notice.

Sunny Burhman and Zachary Graff had two classes together, English and physics; but, in the busyness of Sunny's high school life, surrounded by friends, mesmerized by her own rapid motion as if she were lashed to the prow of a boat bearing swiftly through the water, she did not seem to notice.

She was not a girl of secrets. She was not a girl of stealth. Still, though she had confided in her mother all her life, she did not tell her mother about Zachary's desperate proposal; perhaps, so flattered, she did not acknowledge it as desperate. She reasoned that if she told either of her parents they would have telephoned Zachary's parents immediately. I can't betray him, she thought.

Nor did she tell her closest girlfriends, or the boy she was seeing most frequently at the time, knowing that the account would turn comical in the telling, that she and her listeners would collapse into laughter, and this too would be a betrayal of Zachary.

She happened to see Tobias Shanks, one day, looking oddly at *her*. That boy who might have been twelve years old, seen from a short distance. Sunny knew that he was, or had been, a friend of Zachary Graff's; she wondered if Zachary confided in him; yet made no effort to speak with him. He didn't like her, she sensed.

No, Sunny didn't tell anyone about Zachary and the engagement ring. Of all sins, she thought, betrayal is surely the worst.

"Sunny? Sun-ny?"

She did not believe she had been sleeping but the low, persistent, gravelly sound of Zachary's voice penetrated her consciousness like a dream-voice—felt, not heard.

Quickly, she got out of bed. Crouched at her window without turning on the light. Saw, to her horror, Zachary down below, standing in the shrubbery, his large head uplifted, face round like the moon, and shadowed like the moon's face. There was a light, damp snowfall; blossomlike clumps fell on the boy's broad shoulders, in his matted hair. Sighting her, he began to wave excitedly, like an impatient child.

"Oh. Zachary. My God."

In haste, fumbling, she put on a bulky-knit ski sweater over her flannel nightgown, kicked on bedroom slippers, hurried downstairs. The house was already darkened; the Burhmans were in the habit of going to bed early. Sunny's only concern was that she could send Zachary away without her parents knowing he was there. Even in her distress she was not thinking of the trouble Zachary might make for her: she was thinking of the trouble he might make for himself.

Yet, as soon as she saw him close up, she realized that something was gravely wrong. Here was Zachary Graff—yet not Zachary.

He told her he had to talk with her, and he had to talk with her now. His car was parked in the alley, he said.

He made a gesture as if to take her hand, but Sunny drew back. He loomed over her, his breath steaming. She could not see his eyes.

She said no she couldn't go with him. She said he must go home, at once, before her parents woke up.

He said he couldn't leave without her, he had to talk with her. There was a raw urgency, a forcefulness, in him, that Sunny had never seen before, and that frightened her.

She said no. He said yes.

He reached again for her hand, this time taking hold of her wrist.

His fingers were strong.

"I told you—I can love enough for both!"

Sunny stared up at him, for an instant mute, paralyzed, seeing not Zachary Graff's eyes but the lenses of his glasses which appeared, in the semidark, opaque. Large snowflakes were falling languidly, there was no wind. Sunny saw Zachary Graff's face which was pale and clenched as a muscle, and she heard his voice which was the voice of a stranger, and she felt him tug at her so roughly her arm was strained in its very socket, and she cried, "No! no! go away! no!"—and the spell was broken, the boy gaped at her another moment, then released her, turned, and ran.

No more than two or three minutes had passed since Sunny unlocked the rear door and stepped outside, and Zachary fled.

Yet, afterward, she would recall the encounter as if it had taken a very long time, like a scene in a protracted and repetitive nightmare.

It would be the last time Sunny Burhman saw Zachary Graff alive.

Next morning, all of South Lebanon talked of the death of Dr. Graff's son Zachary: he'd committed suicide by parking his car in a garage behind an unoccupied house on Upchurch Avenue, and letting the motor run until the gas tank was emptied. Death was diagnosed as the result of carbon monoxide poisoning, the time estimated at approximately 4:30 A.M. of April 1, 1959.

Was the date deliberate?—Zachary had left only a single note behind, printed in firm block letters and taped to the outside of the car windshield:

April Fool's Day 1959

To Whom It May (Or May Not) Concern:

I, Zachary A. Graff, being of sound mind & body, do hereby declare that I have taken my own life of my own free will & I hereby declare all others guiltless as they are ignorant of the death of the aforementioned & the life.

(signed)
ZACHARY A. GRAFF

Police officers, called to the scene at 7:45 A.M., reported finding Zachary, lifeless, stripped to his underwear, in the rear seat of the car; the sheepskin parka was oddly draped over the steering wheel, and the interior of the car was, again oddly, for a boy known for his fastidious habits, littered with numerous items: a Bible, several high school textbooks, a pizza carton and some uneaten crusts of pizza, several empty Pepsi bottles, an empty bag of M&M's candies, a pair of new, unlaced gym shoes (size eleven), a ten-foot length of clothesline (in the glove compartment), and the diamond ring in its plush-lined little box from Stern's Jewelers (in a pocket of the parka).

Sunny Burhman heard the news of Zachary's suicide before leaving for school that morning, when a friend telephoned. Within earshot of both her astonished parents, Sunny burst into tears, and sobbed, "Oh my God—it's my fault."

So the consensus in South Lebanon would be, following the police investigation, and much public speculation, not that it was Sunny Burhman's fault, exactly, not that the girl was to blame, exactly, but, yes, poor Zachary Graff, the doctor's son, had killed himself in despondency over her: her refusal of his engagement ring, her rejection of his love.

That was the final season of her life as "Sunny" Burhman.

She was out of school for a full week following Zachary's death, and, when she returned, conspicuously paler, more subdued, in all ways less sunnier, she did not speak, even with her closest friends, of the tragedy; nor did anyone bring up the subject with her. She withdrew her name from the balloting for the senior prom queen, she withdrew from her part in the senior play, she dropped out of the school choir, she did not participate in the annual statewide debating competition—in which, in previous years, Zachary Graff had excelled. Following her last class of the day she went home immediately, and rarely saw her friends on weekends. Was she in mourning?—or was she simply ashamed? Like the bearer of a deadly virus, herself unaffected, Sunny knew how, on all sides, her classmates and her teachers were regarding her: She was the girl for whose love a boy had thrown away his life, she was an unwitting agent of death.

Of course, her family told her that it wasn't her fault that Zachary Graff had been mentally unbalanced.

Even the Graffs did not blame her—or said they didn't.

Sunny said, "Yes. But it's my fault he's dead."

The Presbyterian minister, who counseled Sunny, and prayed with her, assured her that Jesus surely understood, and that there could be no sin in *her*—it wasn't her fault that Zachary Graff had been mentally unbalanced. And Sunny replied, not stubbornly, but matter-of-factly, sadly, as if stating a self-evident truth, "Yes. But it's my fault he's dead."

Her older sister, Helen, later that summer, meaning only well, said, in exasperation, "Sunny, when are you going to cheer *up?*" and Sunny turned on her with uncharacteristic fury, and said, "Don't call me that idiotic name ever again!—I want it *gone!*"

When in the fall she enrolled at Cornell University, she was "Barbara Burhman."

She would remain "Barbara Burhman" for the rest of her life.

Barbara Burhman excelled as an undergraduate, concentrating on academic work almost exclusively; she went on to graduate school at Harvard, in American studies; she taught at several prestigious universities, rising rapidly through administrative ranks before accepting a position, both highly paid and politically visible, with a well-known research foundation based in Manhattan. She was the author of numerous books and articles; she was married, and the mother of three children; she lectured widely, she was frequently interviewed in the popular press, she lent her name to good causes. She would not have wished to think of herself as extraordinary—in the world she now inhabited, she was surrounded by similarly active, energetic, professionally engaged men and women—except in recalling as she sometimes did, with a mild pang of nostalgia, her old, lost self, sweet "Sunny" Burhman of South Lebanon, New York.

She hadn't been queen of the senior prom. She hadn't even continued to be a Christian.

The irony had not escaped Barbara Burhman that, in casting away his young life so recklessly, Zachary Graff had freed her for hers.

With the passage of time, grief had lessened. Perhaps in fact it had disappeared. After twenty, and then twenty-five, and now thirty-one years, it was difficult for Barbara, known in her adult life as an exemplar of practical sense, to feel a kinship with the adolescent girl she'd been, or that claustrophobic high school world of the late 1950s. She'd never returned for a single reunion. If she thought of Zachary Graff—about whom, incidentally, she'd never told her husband of twenty-eight years—it was with the regret we think of remote acquaintances, lost to us by accidents of fate. Forever, Zachary Graff, the most brilliant member of the class of 1959 of South Lebanon High, would remain a high school boy, trapped, aged eighteen.

Of that class, the only other person to have acquired what might be called a national reputation was Tobias Shanks, now known as T. R. Shanks, a playwright and director of experimental drama; Barbara Burhman had followed Tobias's career with interest, and had sent him a telegram congratulating him on his most recent play, which went on to win a number of awards, dealing, as it did, with the vicissitudes of gay life in the 1980s. In the winter of 1990 Barbara and Tobias began to encounter each other socially, when Tobias was playwright-in-residence at Bard College, close by Hazelton-on-Hudson where Barbara lived. At first they were strangely shy of each other; even guarded; as if, in even this neutral setting, their South Lebanon ghost-selves exerted a powerful influence. The golden girl, the loner. The splendidly normal, the defiantly "odd." One night Tobias Shanks, shaking Barbara Burhman's hand, had smiled wryly, and said, "It *is* Sunny, isn't it?" and Barbara Burhman, laughing nervously, hoping no one had overheard, said, "No, in fact it isn't. It's Barbara."

They looked at each other, mildly dazed. For one saw a small-boned but solidly built man of youthful middle-age, sweet-faced, yet with ironic, pouched eyes, thinning gray hair, and a close-trimmed gray beard; the other saw a woman of youthful middle-age, striking in appearance, impeccably well-groomed, with fading hair of no distinctive color and faint, white, puckering lines at the edges of her eyes. Their ghost-selves *were* there—not aged, or not aged merely, but transformed, as the genes of a previous generation are transformed by the next.

Tobias stared at Barbara for a long moment, as if unable to speak. Finally he said, "I have something to tell you, Barbara. When can we meet?"

Tobias Shanks handed the much-folded letter across the table to Barbara Burhman, and watched as she opened it, and read it, with an expression of increasing astonishment and wonder.

"*He* wrote this? Zachary? To you?"

"He did."

"And you—? Did you—?"

Tobias shook his head.

His expression was carefully neutral, but his eyes swam suddenly with tears.

"We'd been friends, very close friends, for years. Each other's only friend, most of the time. The way kids that age can be, in certain restricted environments—kids who aren't what's called 'average' or 'normal.' We talked a good deal about religion— Zachary was afraid of hell. We both liked science fiction. We both had very strict parents. I suppose I might have been attracted to Zachary at times—I knew I was attracted to other guys—but of course I never acted upon it; I wouldn't have dared. Almost no one dared, in those days." He laughed, with a mild shudder. He passed a hand over his eyes. "I couldn't have *loved* Zachary Graff as he claimed he loved me, because—I couldn't. But I could have allowed him to know that he wasn't sick, crazy, 'perverted' as he called himself in that letter." He paused. For a long painful moment Barbara thought he wasn't going to continue. Then he said, with that same mirthless shuddering laugh, "I could have made him feel less lonely. But I didn't. I failed him. My only friend."

Barbara had taken out a tissue, and was dabbing at her eyes.

She felt as if she'd been dealt a blow so hard she could not gauge how she'd been hurt—if there was hurt at all.

She said, "Then it hadn't ever been 'Sunny'—she was an illusion."

Tobias said thoughtfully, "I don't know. I suppose so. There was the sense, at least as I saw it at the time, that, yes, he'd chosen you; decided upon you."

"As a symbol."

"Not just a symbol. We all adored you—we were all a little in love with you." Tobias laughed, embarrassed. "Even me."

"I wish you'd come to me and told me, back then. After—it happened."

"I was too cowardly. I was terrified of being exposed, and, maybe, doing to myself what he'd done to himself. Suicide is so very attractive to adolescents." Tobias paused, and reached over to touch Barbara's hand. His fingertips were cold. "I'm not proud of myself, Barbara, and I've tried to deal with it in my writing, but—that's how I was, back then." Again he paused. He pressed a little harder against Barbara's hand. "Another thing—after Zachary went to you, that night, he came to me."

"To you?"

"To me."

"And—?"

"And I refused to go with him too. I was furious with him for coming to the house like that, risking my parents discovering us. I guess I got a little hysterical. And he fled."

"He fled."

"Then, afterward, I just couldn't bring myself to come forward. Why I saved that letter, I don't know—I'd thrown away some others that were less incriminating. I suppose I figured—no one knew about me, everyone knew about you. 'Sunny' Burhman."

They were at lunch—they ordered two more drinks—they'd forgotten their surroundings—they talked.

After an hour or so Barbara Burhman leaned across the table, as at one of her professional meetings, to ask, in a tone of intellectual curiosity, "What do you think Zachary planned to do with the clothesline?"

The Goose-Girl

She wanted very much to know why, yet she dreaded knowing why, her son, newly home after four months away, was avoiding her. And then he reared up suddenly before her, as she was descending the stairs, tall, long-boned, his deep-set eyes shiny with misery, and said, "I'm—so ashamed of something." It was typical of Barry, Lydia's youngest child, twenty years old but as likely to appear, in strangers' eyes, older, as he was likely to behave, at home, as if he were younger, that, though he'd been replying to Lydia's remarks in laconic monosyllables, shrugging nervously, shifting his shoulders like a wild creature unaccountably trapped in clothing, as in this household now depopulated of all save his wanly attractive and resolutely cheery forty-six-year-old divorcée-mother, Barry would address Lydia as if, all along, they'd been having a conversation; as if this raw, mildly stammered, wholly unexpected statement was in response to a question of hers. And invited a question, which Lydia asked immediately, with warmth, her hand on his arm, "Oh Barry—what is it?"

He stood on the step below her, yet nearly of her height. Tense, perspiring, giving off a scent (though he'd showered, at length, that morning: Lydia had heard him, early) of anguish and excitement, that faintly briny smell she recalled, with a pang of nostalgia, from his high school days as an athlete. But now Lydia had asked the question, Barry was naturally on the defensive. He said, "I don't know if, if I can tell you, Mom. I mean," he said, shaking his head, turning away, "—right now."

Lydia, trying not to become alarmed, trying not to wonder what this intelligent and well-mannered and altogether admirable young man might mean by saying he was ashamed of something, followed Barry downstairs into the hall, it seemed he was headed for the kitchen, then he veered sharply in another direction and went into the garage, and Lydia was trying to stop herself from wondering, fearfully, had he been expelled from Amherst?—was the spring semester not really over, and Barry had come home early, banished, disgraced?—even as she reasoned this could not be so, she'd nearly memorized the salient dates of the school's academic calendar. She was calling, "Barry, honey—wait!" but of course he wasn't going to wait, like an arsonist who has dropped a lighted match on flammable material he wasn't about to wait, nor even to glance over his shoulder to see how the damage he'd caused was progressing. Barry opened the garage door, and wheeled his Yamaha out into the May sunshine, and Lydia, ever attentive, even in the exigency of worry, snatched up the grimy black helmet from the concrete floor, and followed after him. She said, calmly, "Barry, please. You can't run off. You've upset me by saying—"

Barry murmured, "Yeah, Mom, okay, I know, I'll tell you later, I just can't tell you now. I *can't.*"

"Is it about school?"

"No."

"Is it about—Chris?" Chris was Barry's girlfriend, from high school; now at Middlebury; or, rather, one of his girlfriends. He had not spoken of her lately but Lydia knew from her former husband, with whom she spoke frequently on the phone, that they still saw each other.

Quickly, irritably, his back to her, Barry said, "No, it isn't about Chris."

"Is it—"

"I'll tell you later, Mom. I *said.*" He paused, wiping the accumulation of cobwebs off the Yamaha, rubbing the chrome with spittle. "Don't bug me, okay?"

There was an old semijokey history in the family of Lydia's exaggerated dislike of the motorcycle, perceiving it, as Lydia thought quite reasonably, as the possible instrument of her son's death or disfigurement, but there was an old history of Barry's fanatic attachment to it: he'd worked at exhausting jobs, including emergency snow-removal for the State of New York, to pay for it. Lydia, with her anthropological-sociological bent, thought the shiny black vehicle with the flaring handlebars and high-backed seat, the near-deafening roar of which its motor was capable, a sign of Barry's rejection of his own natural introversion and good sense, a proclamation of his distinctly American, thus public, masculinity; Sam, her former husband, graced with a placidity regarding their children's welfare that Lydia sometimes thought maddening, at other times enviable, had merely shrugged, and said, "It's cheaper than a car."

Barry straddled the Yamaha, and labored to start it, and, after several abortive attempts, it started, roaring into demonic life, eager to be gone. Lydia handed Barry his helmet, for otherwise he might have forgotten it. A womanly figure in a medieval tapestry, handing over armor to a knight on a steed. A visor to obscure the youthful, and in this case embarrassed and sullen, face.

She asked where he was going, and he told her, naming names she'd heard from junior high school onward, and she asked when he thought he might be back, and he said, fumbling to fasten the helmet strap beneath his chin, lowering the smoked-plastic visor, "Maybe around lunch—I don't know," and he drove noisily off, like an upright insect on the black vehicle, down the sloping asphalt driveway, onto Somers Brook Road, within seconds curving out of sight. Lydia stood alone shading her eyes against the warm sunshine, feeling more than usually diminutive; diminished; a bit foolish, like a spurned woman. Except for the stink of the exhaust, and an agitation of the air, there was no evidence Barry had been there at all.

It was 9:35 A.M. He'd fled without eating breakfast. Lydia, who had set this day aside for Barry, canceling appointments, rearranging her schedule, saw that it would be a long day.

Of the three Manning children, Barry had taken his parents' protracted separation and speedy divorce the most seriously—with an almost romantic seriousness, Lydia and Sam thought. Believing that the erotic passion that had generated *him*, of all the world's population, was too extraordinary ever to be extinguished?

The week before, talking with Sam on the phone, Lydia had asked, "Does Barry talk to you?—confide in you?" steeling herself for information that might reawaken an old, demeaning jealousy, but Sam had laughed his explosive laugh, and said cheerfully, "Are you serious, Lydia? The kid hates my guts." Which wasn't true, for no one hated Sam, least of all his youngest and most tender-hearted child.

Lydia was thinking guiltily that she'd neglected Barry, this past year. She was working again, and she had her friends, and the days passed swiftly, and smoothly—as they had not passed smoothly during the years of her marriage. It was easy to comply with Barry's neglect of her, in the heady maelstrom of undergraduate life: a few late-night telephone calls, snatched from the waning day, postcards and not letters, no time, no time. Once, seated at the dining room table with his mother, his brother, and his sister, this would have been Christmas of his freshman year, Barry had solemnly denounced a friend, now at Berkeley, who'd sent out a computer-printed newsletter to Barry and many others, taking no time to make the individual letters individual, thus worthy of being read. Josh, Barry's brother, his elder by three years and so by family tradition his mentor, said, "Yes, but a newsletter is better than no letter, isn't it, assuming you care about your friend at all," and Barry said, incensed, his dark nostrils fairly flaring, "No! No, it isn't."

He was fierce and hawklike in profile, he wanted to be an "environmental science–writer," or maybe a lawyer, something in the line of environmental protection, yes but he was being drawn toward the classics too, what a mesmerizing professor he had, making Homer, the Greek lyric, the tragedies, come *alive*. Like many shy people, he could talk excitedly, and at length, as if words were pent up inside him, exerting a sweet painful pressure. Yet, listening to Barry, Lydia sometimes felt she didn't know him, at all. For the words he actually spoke did not somehow match the words she imagined pent up inside him; as his purchase of the Yamaha, and the fever of excitement surrounding it, had stunned her, his mother—yes, she wanted to protest, other boys do such things, but not *you.*

In families, courtships prevail. Someone is forever pursuing someone else; that person, another; and there are those who, so strangely, so perversely, prefer, yes unmistakably prefer to be alone.

For a long time, Lydia had believed herself to be in pursuit of her children, who, even as they clearly loved her, and behaved very decently to her, nonetheless eluded her. For a brief while, Lydia had believed herself in pursuit of her husband—talky, gregarious, clumsy Sam, who meant of course no harm, blundering amid the wreckage of their marriage, perennially meaning well. Then, by degrees, she'd realized, no, no, I am not like this at all, I am the person I always was, from the first, I don't need others to define me, it's in fact others who misdefine me. Armed with such knowledge, Lydia had surprised Sam—so conciliatory, so fairminded. When, another time, he'd asked if he could come back to her, try again, he loved her of course and she loved him, Lydia had laughed, and laid her hands on Sam's arms, in the manner of a coach springing the news to a dazed second-string player, "No, Sam. No. *No.*"

Now Sam was living with a woman friend, in Dobbs Ferry, a half-hour drive from his old house in Hazelton-on-Hudson. Lydia hoped they would marry soon, to restore tidiness, formality, to the situation.

Lydia herself had numerous male friends, amid the large, heterogeneous circle of her Hazelton friends, but no romantic prospects or interests—assuredly not. She was slim, impeccably groomed, beautiful in a fading, dusky-golden way, as if touched with pollen; like a day lily just past its prime; she supposed herself attractive to men, but gave no encouragement, made no overtures. Her women friends, those still married, made no secret of envying her what's called, in the simplest language, *peace-and-quiet.* Everyone loved Sam, but who would have wanted to live with him? And their own husbands? Who would want to live with *them?* So, lunching together at the tennis club, or in town, Lydia and her friends of many years would succumb to fits of girlish, exhilarating laughter, given a special buoyancy by glasses of white wine, cool, dry, tart, low in calories. The wittiest and most brazen among them (this would not be Lydia, however) might even be led to do imitations of certain husbands, and how the women laughed, laughed—for domestic life, seen from the perspective of youthful middle-age, is as amusing as a comic opera by Mozart. More hilarious still if the beautiful arias are sung by wavering, amateur voices, as in a summer-stock production.

Lydia wondered if, at such giddy times, she might not be betraying not only Sam, but her children?—Josh, Roslyn, Barry?—so defining herself as a *self* wholly independent of them?

Once, during the time of the divorce, Lydia confessed, of Sam, that while she still loved him she could not, often, *bear* him. "In a way the thing that upset me most," Lydia said, as her friends leaned forward attentively, like medical students at their first dissection, "—was his, I don't know, mendacity?—that's too strong a word. His ranking of people—of friends. For instance, when we'd give a dinner party," and here Lydia's friends did indeed listen attentively, for they and their husbands had many times been guests at the Mannings', as the Mannings had been guests at their homes, "—Sam would deliberate for days over the wine." Sam Manning's wine cellar was much talked-of in Hazelton; a good deal of the talk by Sam himself. "Everything he serves is precisely chosen—there are 'A' wines, red wines, from the 1960s, there are 'B' wines, God knows what the 'C' wines are, these days. And Sam would rank the wines to fit the guests, and I was always so worried the guests would *know*."

Lydia's friends erupted in laughter. "Of course we knew, we knew all along, everyone knew," they told her.

Lydia did something she'd promised herself she would never do, again. When Barry didn't return for lunch, she telephoned in pursuit of him—making three calls before she tracked him down, yes he'd been visiting his friend Trig, just home from Wesleyan, but he was gone now, off on his Yamaha.

"I see. Thanks!" Lydia said cheerfully.

She thought, The next thing will be going through his things.

She thought, I will *not*.

Lydia had been trained as an educational psychologist and had more recently taken graduate courses at SUNY-Purchase; she was working as a consultant for a film company that did educational films; she'd been contracted to prepare the script for such a film herself. And she had plans to invest, with a Hazelton friend, a divorcée like herself, in a documentary film series on children and the arts. Through the years of her marriage she had worked sporadically, but only part-time; she'd rarely had the luxury of periods of concentration that professional work requires; when the children and Sam had all been home, her consciousness was as easily broken and scattered as—what? A flock of sparrows pecking in the dirt, when a stone is tossed into their midst. Since Barry had come home she'd been reduced to *that* again—not just the edginess of confrontation, but the apprehension of it. She could not imagine how their conversation would go, only that there would be a conversation.

She recalled his words. The startling gravity of "ashamed." "—So ashamed."

She recalled his eyes, evasive, very dark, as if all pupil.

She recalled the awkwardness, and the hurt, of the previous evening, when Lydia had prepared a light supper for the two of them, and Barry had had little appetite, picking at his food, scarcely hearing what she said, answering her questions quickly and abstractly, as if with the most superficial part of his brain.

He'd been nervous, excited about something, yet, so strangely, he'd gone to bed early, at eleven. Lydia herself usually went to bed around midnight.

The thought had occurred to her, He's uncomfortable alone in the house with me. The two of us, now that the others are gone.

It was a thought she pushed from her.

It was a thought, yes, she'd had herself, without fully articulating. Quite deliberately, she pushed it from her.

The previous afternoon, Lydia had talked Barry into coming with her to a small, impromptu gathering at the home of neighbors on Somers Brook Road. Though he'd only been home a few hours, and might have pleaded tiredness, he'd agreed to accompany her, provided he didn't have to wear a coat or tie (Lydia assured him he didn't) and they wouldn't stay too long (Lydia promised no more than an hour). The Brewers were old family friends, they'd seen Barry grown up, Barry understood that they would be hurt if they knew he'd returned from school but hadn't cared to see them. He understood that, like other young men and women of his age, he represented something binding and reassuring to his parents' friends, particularly those of an older generation than his parents, and that this fact carried with it a curious obligation. *He meant something. He "stood for" something.* So he'd accompanied his mother, and they'd stayed for two hours, and Lydia was covertly proud of her tall, attractive, well-mannered son who now shook hands with adults as if he were one of them.

He'd even been drawn off, in a mysteriously intense conversation, by a local woman with whom the Mannings were slightly acquainted—the married daughter of friends of the Brewers, in her late twenties, back in Hazelton on a visit.

"How does Barry like Amherst?" Lydia was asked, and "Is he home for the summer?", and "What is he studying?" and "Is he still serious about—what was it, track? swimming? diving?" The Brewers, now well into their seventies, never tired of exclaiming, "How he's grown—!" out of Barry's earshot, to Lydia, as if his height were an accomplishment of Lydia's. She smiled, and blushed, as if, indeed, it were.

The day had been balmy, fragrant with the sweet catkins of pussy willows and Lombardy poplars. The party was held on the Brewers' terrace overlooking their lawn and cattail-choked pond, and Lydia watched absently as Barry and the young married woman strolled down to the pond, the woman leading the way, talking animatedly, gesturing, conspicuous in her tight-fitting glove of a dress and spike-heeled shoes, her hair, clay-colored, with a look of being glazed, springing in shoulder-length curls around her thin face. The woman's name was Phoebe Stone, and Lydia could not recall her husband's name, though she knew he was a prominent Manhattan financier, and much had been made, in Hazelton, when the wedding had taken place—surely no more than two years ago? Phoebe Stone was painfully and defiantly thin; she wore black silk, no doubt to emphasize her thinness; she was not beautiful, nor even pretty, with close-set wary eyes and a large dissatisfied mouth, yet she had an air of reckless glamor, inappropriate to the setting, comically out of place amid the Brewers and their guests, several of whom were white-haired. Of the gathering, only Barry was near Phoebe Stone's age, if twenty is near twenty-nine. Only Barry, lanky and self-conscious in jeans, pullover shirt, canvas shoes, with that maddening habit of continually brushing his hair out of his eyes, provided any interest for her.

Sam had had an apt name for the haughty Ms. Stone, whose parents were very wealthy. Now what was it?

It was after such Hazelton gatherings that Lydia most missed her husband. Her old pal, her confidant. Blunt, funny, unsparing and outrageous in his judgments, Sam had allowed Lydia, all those years, to remain *nice*; yet, with a delicious sense of abandon, to *laugh*.

So Barry had accompanied his mother to the Brewers' party, and had seemed to be enjoying himself. At least, saying goodbye, he'd shaken his host's hand vigorously, and leaned to accept a kiss and a cheek from his hostess, and thanked them both with his sweetly-shy dimpled smile. On the way home in the car, however, he lapsed quickly into one of his moods; staring out the window, fidgeting, replying in monosyllables to Lydia's remarks, as if he were, so suddenly, twelve years old again. Lydia was surprised, and Lydia was hurt. How like sunshine on a day of high scudding clouds these adolescent beings are—patchy, unpredictable, unreliable. She foresaw that the evening, the supper she'd so looked forward to, just Barry and her, would be an ordeal; and she was not mistaken.

He wasn't very hungry, Barry mumbled, picking at Lydia's food. He'd had a lot to eat, he guessed, at the Brewers'.

"I guess you know her. You and Dad. The woman at the Brewers'. Yesterday."

Barry was speaking haltingly, his face visibly warm, eyes lowered. There was a faintly sour smell of beer on his breath.

Lydia said, more perplexed than startled, "Phoebe Stone?"

"She— I— Oh Christ I'm so *ashamed*."

"What happened, Barry?"

Barry was sitting directly in front of Lydia; hunched a bit, flexing his big-knuckled hands. It was nearly six o'clock. He'd stayed away all day, and when Lydia had heard the motorcycle approaching the house, heard the damned thing sputter to a stop in front of the garage, she'd felt almost faint with anger and apprehension. She was in the sunporch at the rear of the house—the glassed-in room that was also her study—and she'd been working, though of course she'd been waiting, all day.

Lydia said, rather sharply, "What happened, Barry?"

Barry squirmed. Ran his fingers through his hair. Spoke in so soft a voice, Lydia could barely hear. Now plunging headfirst, with that air of calculated desperation he'd brought to high school swim meets . . . where, as a diver, he'd climbed the ladder to the high diving board as everyone watched, a skinny, scared-looking boy, near to naked, streaming water like rippling nerves. It had seemed to Lydia and Sam that their son ran the length of the board to fling himself into—what? Space, oblivion, destiny.

Barry told Lydia shamefaced that, at the party, Phoebe Stone had "come on pretty strong" to him; he'd been surprised, and, he guessed, flattered; he wasn't used to that sort of attention from older women—"Heck, from anyone." She was such a—beautiful woman. Such a glamorous woman. And married. And in her thirties.

Lydia, who was profoundly shocked, nonetheless corrected her son. "Oh, I don't think so. Phoebe Stone is no more than twenty-nine."

Barry shifted his shoulders miserably, and ran his fingers through his hair. His hair, though washed that morning, looked dirty—oily. It stood up in frantic tufts about his head like the damp-feathered tufts of a newly fledged bird.

Lydia had time too to register bemusement—of course, Phoebe Stone's exact age could hardly matter. She was *older*.

Gently, Lydia asked Barry again what had happened; and Barry hesitated, and said, still in a low, mumbly voice, "Mom, she wants me to come over to her place, tonight. She gave me the address, and all. She's staying with her parents but there's a separate house she's in—nobody would see, she said, if I came after dark. Her telephone number too." Barry removed from his jeans pocket a much-crumpled little piece of paper, and laid it on Lydia's desk, awkwardly smoothing it; this little task required several seconds. Lydia caught a glimpse of a harshly slanted handwriting, words and numerals in red felt-tip pen. "She said," Barry continued, suppressing a nervous belch, "she wanted me to—make love to her." Again he paused; swallowed; his face so darkly mottled with blood, it looked like a recrudescence of his old acne. "She, uh— didn't use that word, exactly. She used other words."

There was another pause; a pang of mutual misery; and now Lydia looked down at her own hands, whitely clenched in her lap. What were they talking about? How was this possible? Her Barry, her son? Recruited for a sexual adventure? Under her very eyes? At the Brewers' home on Somers Brook Road, of all unlikely places? Barry continued, rapidly, "—She said she didn't think she really knew *how*, the kind of man her husband is, something wrong with him I guess, or, maybe, with other men she'd been—involved with. She said I looked like I would know *how*. So I—" Barry broke off, giggling suddenly. "—I said yes."

"You said *yes*—?" Lydia's voice was faint.

"I was flattered, I guess. She's so beautiful and so—glamorous. So strange. Like nobody I know my own age, or any age. I didn't have time to think, it was like something in a movie—but the kind of movie that never would happen to *me*. She said she 'felt a rapport' with me—'felt desire' for me—as soon as she saw me arrive at the Brewers'. She didn't know who I was, or who you are, Mom— or anyway she pretended not to. Jesus, it was weird! I knew at the time it was weird, but I—couldn't say no. We were walking down by the pond and she looked at me, her eyes are so big, and her skin's so white, like she was getting over being sick, she's got a sort of feverish look, it just went through me. 'Promise me you'll come to me, and promise you'll never tell anyone,' she said, she squeezed my arm, dug in her nails so they hurt, '—promise, promise, promise.' I said yes, sure, I'd come, and I wouldn't ever tell anyone, I guess I'd have told her anything, she had me so—" Barry's face contorted as he searched for a word that eluded him, and Lydia, listening with a painfully beating heart, did not want to supply. "Anyway, I said those things. And now I'm telling you, Mom, so that makes me a liar, I guess, and I'm not going to her place tonight so I'm backing out on that too—oh God I'm so fucking *ashamed*."

He was too agitated apparently to notice the profanity that had slipped from him, which Lydia had never heard from his lips before. Not that she was surprised—much.

So he talked, confessed. Doubled back and repeated what he'd said, with amplification. It was clear that the situation greatly distressed him; that, apart from the sexual embarrassment, he simply did not know what to do. Where another young man would have torn up the note, or gone to the tryst and afterward boasted to his friends, Barry was too sensitive, and too inexperienced. In Lydia's place, Sam would have dropped a heavy hand on the boy's shoulder and told him the incident was funny, why not just laugh? For Sam, that would about sum it up—*funny*. And maybe that was so.

Lydia said, suddenly, " 'The Goose-Girl'!"

Barry squinted at her, perplexed.

Lydia explained, "That was what your father used to call Phoebe Stone—not to her face, of course. It was one of his comical names. She reminded him—and me too—of the drawing of the poor Goose-Girl, in our copy of Grimms' *Fairy Tales*: that sort of gangly frazzled look, the enormous staring eyes, stork legs—do you remember the Goose-Girl? No?" Barry's eyes had gone opaque. Any attempt on Lydia's part to remind her children of their common childhood, especially their remote babyhood, was usually met with such blank resistance. "Phoebe used always to dress conspicuously, as she did yesterday. For a while it was tie-dyed things, like rags. Once she wore what looked like a P.L.O. uniform, khaki fatigues, leather boots to the knee. Now it's black. And always skin-tight. She's so terribly thin—anorexic, I suppose. And the extreme high heels, with her height—she must be five feet ten. And the bizarre makeup." Lydia paused, breathless. She was unable to recall whether in fact Phoebe had been excessively made up the day before, or whether she'd worn no makeup at all. The young woman's pale, pinched face floated before her, indistinct as a ghost's. "We'd heard that she was having 'emotional problems,' a breakdown in college. Then she got involved in demonstrating against—I think it was nuclear power plants. She was always what you'd call eye-catching. Always seeming to cry, 'Look! look at *me*!' "

Barry was too caught up in his own emotion to notice his mother's. He said, face contorted as a small boy's, "If only she hadn't made me promise. If only I hadn't been such an asshole. I had a quick glass of wine, and it's sort of, you know, disorienting, to be back home, and—everything went to my head. And now—"

Lydia smiled, encouragingly. "And now—"

"—I'm not going."

The words were a vow, vehemently uttered.

Lydia said, "Well, I wouldn't think, under the circumstances, you would."

Still he stared at her, imploring her. To what? Saying, tears glistening in his eyes, "I'm not going and I—I can't call her." There was a pause. Lydia, now knowing what was coming, began to shake her head. Barry pleaded, "Mom please, would *you*? Just call her, and tell her—some excuse? Anything? Like, I'm gone out of town, had to go back to school, I'm not—*here?*"

Lydia said sharply, "Barry. *No.*"

"You could make up any excuse, you could simply—"

"—lie? For you? And you're twenty years old, and you got yourself into this predicament?" Lydia laughed, though without much mirth. She could scarcely force herself to look at Barry: such adolescent misery quivered in his face, he seemed about to cry.

She got abruptly to her feet, anger coursing quicksilver along her veins. Why she was so radiantly angry she didn't know, and didn't want to know. She seized Barry's forearms, each in a tight grip, and said, firmly, "No. No. *No.*"

Lydia hid herself away upstairs, she was so upset.

Was she furious with the Goose-Girl for daring to proposition her son, her young, beautiful, innocent son, or was she furious with her son for being so propositioned—and so flattered? So, it was clear, sexually mesmerized? Wryly Lydia thought, I'm angry because it's the one thing, for her son, a mother can't do.

And then, of course, she relented.

For Barry *was* miserable, as only the young can be miserable, perceiving their betrayal of another person as self-betrayal; too humiliating, at the core, to be remedied. "And please don't tell

Sam," Barry pleaded. (Lydia's former husband was one of those fathers who request that their children call them by their given names, as if, apprehended as equals, they might then be expected to bear less parental responsibility.) Lydia sighed, and Lydia laughed, and Lydia said, in disgust, "Oh all right. *But never again.*"

Barry stared at her as if she'd uttered an obscenity.

So Lydia relented, and, at 10:15 P.M., with Barry out for the evening, she poured herself a glass of dry white wine, and smoothed out the wrinkled scrap of paper bearing Phoebe Stone's telephone number, and, her hands slightly trembling, dialed the number. By Barry's account, Phoebe had asked him to come to her house, a former carriage house on the Stones' property, "anytime after 9:30." So she would have been waiting for him, expecting him, for forty-five minutes.

As the phone rang, and rang, Lydia's face burned. She felt— what? Vindictive, elated?—gloating? Why should *she* have him, even for a night, Lydia's son?—the gawky-gangly Goose-Girl, who deserved only rejection, repudiation?

The phone was answered at the other end, a faint, guarded voice ventured, "Hello?" and Lydia, swallowing, suddenly very nervous, said, "Hello? Is this Phoebe Stone?"

There was a pause. Then, Phoebe Stone said, yes, yes this is she, and Lydia cleared her throat, and said, in a voice of warmth and apology, as evenly as if she'd practiced this little speech for hours, "Phoebe, this is Lydia Manning—Sam Manning's wife—we were both at the Brewers' yesterday, but I don't believe we had a chance to speak?" There was no reply to this cast-out remark, casual and imprecise as it was, not even the usual murmured assent or encouragement for Lydia to continue, so Lydia plunged forward, a bit clumsily, her face now burning, "I—I'm calling for my son Barry. He said you'd invited him and some of his friends over tonight," a lie, but an inspired lie, one which, Lydia reasoned, would allow the Goose-Girl to save face, "—and he's asked me to call you and apologize, something came up, a friend from college—" Lydia's voice trailed off in just the right tone of exasperation and indulgence.

A pause. No reply.

Lydia added, with a weak laugh, "You know how they are—at that age."

Then came Phoebe Stone's voice, clear and distinct and small, like crystal being struck, "I'm afraid I don't, Mrs. Manning." In that instant Lydia could see the young woman's thin, pinched-pale face, the eyes brimming with tears. That Goose-Girl tumble of curly, crinkly hair with its synthetic lustre. "But thank you for calling, you're very kind."

Exhausted, Lydia went to bed early. But, though the house was empty, and silent as a tomb, and the painful ordeal was over, she couldn't sleep. (No, she wasn't waiting for Barry to come home: she'd given up such wasted effort, years ago.) Toward 2:00 A.M. she got out of bed, and wandered downstairs, switching on lights as she passed. She was drawn as if by instinct to a sway-backed old Workbench bookshelf in one of the spare bedrooms, located the aged copy of Grimms' *Fairy Tales*, leafed through it . . . the book was a children's edition, hardcover, oversized, with illustrations for most of the tales . . . in very bad condition (in fact, hadn't it slipped from her, or Sam's hands, once, and fallen into the tub where one of the children was being bathed?) . . . untouched for years. Lydia located the Goose-Girl, and was startled to see that the drawing bore very little resemblance to Phoebe Stone after all.

The Goose-Girl in the book was pretty in a conventional way, plump-cheeked, curly-haired, sweet-faced, vacuous. Lydia scanned the tale and saw, too, that it wasn't the fairy tale she might have surmised, from the title, but a rather cruel, primitive tale—yet another variation on the "mistaken princess." The Goose-Girl *was* a princess, mistaken as a commoner.

So Sam had been wrong, after all. But then, Sam had been wrong about so many things.

Lydia closed up the book, her eyes stinging with tears. Poor Goose-Girl! She'd deserved better treatment, at the hands of such good people.

American, Abroad

In the unmarked government sedan with the olive-tinted windows, en route to the Consul-General's residence in a leafier, less traffic- and bicycle-clogged part of the city, the cultural attaché's wife leaned forward to tell Caroline Carmichael, in a lowered voice, "You won't mention this to anyone tonight, of course, Miss Carmichael— but Mr. Price has been under a good deal of pressure lately. Our office was warned by Intelligence that he has been definitely targeted by an Iranian terrorist team. His daughter—" Mr. Price, Norman Price, was the Consul-General at whose home Caroline Carmichael would be dining that evening; the occasion of the dinner was, in fact, to honor her, as an American visitor, a "feminist" art historian traveling through Europe under the auspices of a culturally-minded United States agency. After thirty-five days of hotels chosen to accommodate the agency's modest per diem and the alarmingly diminished American dollar, and brief, often rackety air flights, and lecture halls mysteriously packed with people or as mysteriously empty, and the usual insomniac and dyspeptic miseries, Caroline Carmichael had begun to think of herself as a seasoned or in any case resigned traveler; a zealous, uncomplaining cultural emissary, as her sponsoring agency surely believed her. But—a terrorist team? Iranian? "Targeted"? The casual remark shocked her; but she managed merely to nod, to nod gravely and with sympathy, as if such a disclosure, such a revelation of the heightened drama of the diplomat's life, were not at all foreign to her, or terrifying.

The cultural attaché, seated up front with the driver, glanced back at his wife, possibly to give warning, but she ignored him, and continued breathlessly, "—His daughter Inge—you'll be meeting her tonight—she's visiting them from the States—was followed yesterday for several hours, and there have been other incidents reported. But the Prices didn't want to cancel tonight—so many people, so many *cultural* people, invited by the Consulate, are coming. It's an important event, actually. Of course the residence is heavily guarded. Security isn't perfect in this post because there hasn't been trouble since the early seventies but—" The cultural attaché turned sharply to say, as if this were an old point, and a sore one, "I've put in a request I don't know how many times for a bullet-proof sedan. The Consulate has other cars of course, limos, and most of them are equipped, but *this*, the one assigned to our division . . ." His voice trailed off into a bemused silence.

As if in response to this remark the driver, who did not speak but seemed to comprehend English, began to drive faster; they were rattling over a bridge over one of the wide, placid, usually rain-pocked canals. Caroline Carmichael's heart too accelerated; she stared out at a grim urban landscape of dull brick, rowhouses, tenements, shabby municipal buildings, with here and there signs of "modernization"—cheap high-rise office and apartment buildings, parking garages. Most distracting, and demoralizing—Caroline had arrived in this city only the day before—were the miles of walls, sidewalks, public benches, even trees—enormous dignified elms, oaks, plane trees—defaced by graffiti in wild fluorescent Day-Glo colors. How strange! How ugly! The angry yet idle iconography of youth, seemingly transported from the New York City subway to *this* legendary city—Caroline Carmichael had asked her hosts about it, who does it, and why, why is it tolerated, why isn't it cleaned up, but the answers were rather vague. Youth. The drug culture. "Revolutionaries" without a revolution.

Now she wondered if, out of nowhere, at the next intersection perhaps, or as the driver turned off onto a quieter boulevard, death might come flying at them. Machine-gun fire, a bomb? Caroline Carmichael was of that generation of thoroughly modern, indeed post-modern men and women who expect their deaths to spring from no logical or predictable sequence of events, let alone any ethically coherent algorithm of the soul; why not, then, in the company of such seeming ordinary, good-hearted Americans (the cultural attaché and his wife were both, like Caroline Carmichael, Midwesterners: two decades of living abroad had not neutralized their accents), in an automobile of such ordinary dimensions, sudden death by assassination? Misguided political assassination? She laughed uneasily and said, "But you don't think there is any danger, do you?—really?"

Having aroused their guest's alarm the Bonners were quick now to extinguish it; the wife even patted Caroline's arm. No, they assured her, of course not, there was no real danger—if there were, Security would have insisted that the Prices cancel the evening.

"Why do the Iranians want to kill Mr. Price?" Caroline asked.

"Not 'the' Iranians, 'some' Iranians," the cultural attaché said. "In fact, Intelligence hasn't been able to learn the name of the terrorist team yet—it must be a small splinter group, only a few men. They can be the most deadly. —They want to kill Mr. Price because he was in Tehran up until the end; he has many Iranian friends in and outside the country."

"They loved him there, him and Georgine both," Mrs. Bonner said passionately.

"I see," said Caroline Carmichael, though she didn't, quite.

The Consul-General's residence was an immense foursquare stone and stucco mansion, painted an improbable, though quite attractive, pale pink; set like a fortress behind fifteen-foot stone walls, with a medieval-looking iron gate and a security booth manned by Marine guards. Caroline Carmichael disliked these young Americans with their blunt shaved heads and purposefully expressionless eyes: in an American embassy in West Germany she had chanced to overhear two of them talking about her, carelessly, rather loudly, having mistaken her for a German woman presumably, for at that moment she'd been alone, and not engaged in conversation with any of her embassy hosts. The brief experience had angered her; yet had made a deeper, more profound impression on her; for she'd felt not only the raw helplessness of being female in a world of men but the helplessness of being non-American in a world organized along military lines of power and influence. But tonight the Marine guards were courteous, if mechanical; for Caroline Carmichael had her passport, her identification, her Consulate escorts.

Elsewhere in Europe, brought into one or another palatial residence, Caroline Carmichael had several times been informed that the property now belonging to the United States government had once been commandeered by Nazi authorities during World War II; that, indeed, Adolf Hitler himself *had* very likely slept beneath its roof. She waited now for the Bonners to make this remark—it was usually accompanied by an embarrassed laugh—but they did not. Caroline said, looking up at the elegant facade, the graceful portico, "How lovely!" The cultural attaché's wife said, "But Georgine Price would rather live anywhere else."

Fanning the side entrance of the house was a double row of yellow, golden, and pale orange roses, blossoming like an exposed vein of gold in the fading daylight.

A hysterically barking dog, a small terrier with a pink ribbon bouncing from its collar, rushed forward to greet the little party, and had to be restrained by one of the young Marines, as the door swung outward, and Mrs. Price—tall, regal, bony-faced, in a long brocaded gown—welcomed them and ushered them in, all the while chattering at the terrier, which leapt against Caroline Carmichael's legs and licked her hands with a tongue like a wet chamois cloth. "Suzie, be good!" Mrs. Price cried, "—we're all skittish enough tonight without *you*." This was so clear an allusion to the terrorist warning, Caroline supposed it an open secret; though of course she said nothing. She was tonight's guest of honor and meant to acquit herself well.

Mrs. Price, given to lavish gestures, seized Caroline Carmichael's hand and drew it up to her bosom, asking how she was, how she was adjusting to so much travel, not exhausted they all hoped— "After that perfectly marvelous lecture of yours this afternoon. I learned *so much*."

She linked her arm through Caroline's, and led her sweepingly into the enormous living room, there to endure several vertiginous minutes of introductions, handshakes, studied Old World gallantry, reiterated and perhaps even genuine praise for the afternoon's lecture ("The Iconography of Female Martyrdom in European Art"), and the repeated offering of glasses of white wine and elaborate appetizers borne on silver trays by uniformed servants. As always in such situations Caroline Carmichael felt sheerly diamagnetic impulses: the wish to be elsewhere, *any*where; the conviction that, yes, she was in the right place, and deserved her good fortune.

For what after all was the alternative?

Mrs. Price clapped her hands, raised her voice shrilly, "Norman hopes you will all excuse him for being late," then repeated, as if for the benefit of those who had not quite understood, "—The Consul-General begs your forgiveness, he will be a few minutes late." Mrs. Price was in her mid-sixties but her manner was youthful, even frenetic; with her widened eyes, her mobile mouth, her graying hair frizzed out electrically about her face, she reminded Caroline Carmichael of John Tenniel's drawing of the Red Queen in Alice's adventures in the looking-glass world. She was gazing at Caroline now with an expression of extreme if muddled solicitude. "Did you say you *were* exhausted, Miss Carmichael? Would you like to lie down for a few minutes upstairs, and rest?" she asked suddenly.

Everyone looked at Caroline Carmichael, awaiting her reply, and Caroline, embarrassed, wondering if she looked so very awful, assured her hostess she wasn't at all exhausted—"I'm really very happy to be here." But Mrs. Price's jittery attention was diverted by new arrivals and a furious spasm of yipping out in the foyer.

Caroline accepted a glass of white wine with a hand that shook just slightly, and found herself in a conversational group that included the insufferable "Parisian cultural critic" who had introduced her that afternoon—the only person they could find, Mr. Bonner rather tactlessly explained, who could do a "creditable job" of introducing Caroline Carmichael to an audience that knew nothing of her work. François was the slender, sinewy, sloe-eyed youngish man's name; he had very white teeth, and a courtly condescending manner. As if to soothe Caroline Carmichael's flurried nerves he murmured confidentially in her ear, "Please do not worry, Miss Carmichael—your C.I.A. people have everything under control, I am certain." "I'm not worried," Caroline said, startled; she did not want to be drawn into an exchange of confidences.

For what seemed like a very long period of time but was probably no more than half an hour the guests in the Prices' living room—there were about fifteen, including a Dutch journalist, a Dutch documentary filmmaker, a German professor and translator, the curator of the city's museum of contemporary art, several members of the United States Consulate and their wives, and a visiting American economist named Zaller who fumbled an unlit pipe in his left hand—talked together animatedly; a neutral observer might have sensed a palpable strain in the atmosphere, a nerved-up giddiness to the air, but might have attributed it to the usual cocktail party excitement. It was nearly time for dinner but the Consul-General had not appeared; Mrs. Price herself was continually disappearing from the gathering, and reappearing, her beringed hands clasped against her bosom, her eyes darting about, mildly glazed over, seeing nothing. A hostess's nightmare, Caroline Carmichael thought. Why don't we all go home? She thought of her own mother, whom she had loved very much, dead now for nearly ten years. She thought of her aging, ailing father, from whom she was estranged; and wondered what sort of telegram the United States government would send him in the event of her sudden death. A stroke victim, Mr. Carmichael decoded the world's myriad hieroglyphics in terms specific to him; his cosmology allowed for nothing so innocently crude as mere accident.

She had a vision, quick, silent, cinematic, of an explosion of fire through the satin-draped windows of the living room; a rolling uncoiling ball of flame that ignited them all in a cataclysmic death. The vision frightened her, yet comforted: for if one had to die it was surely preferable to die suddenly, and in a sense anonymously, among strangers? Her mother's protracted dying had torn all their hearts and it was likely that her father had never quite recovered from that death though within a stunning eighteen months he'd remarried—a woman young enough, as the inevitable expression would have it, to be his daughter; but in no way sisterly to his daughter. Mr. Carmichael was professor of philology, emeritus, Oberlin College, formerly a gentleman of authority and cantankerous charm, now a thoroughly routed old man in whom a mild stroke two years before and a subsequent intermittent aphasia had encouraged a true paranoia—a lifelong penchant for imagining others' assessments of him and "plots" in regard to him had now blossomed into a feverish, tireless cycle of fears, recriminations, doubts, pleas for forgiveness, farewell scenes of Shakespearean intensity. For most of my father's life he believed himself Hamlet, Caroline Carmichael told her friends, now he believes himself Lear. Mr. Carmichael had never fully approved of his daughter's choice of a career in its specifics—for was there not something reductive and vulgar about the phenomenon of feminism itself—but he had seemingly wished her well; since his stroke the mere sight of her, the sound of her voice raised in appeal, stirred him to angry tears. His charge seemed to be that she did not love him, or did not love him *enough*—"But what would be 'enough'?" Caroline Carmichael asked the second Mrs. Carmichael, whose pinched smile and ungenerous eyes filled her with foreboding, and was told, in all artless sincerity, "I don't think anything would be enough, Caroline. Maybe you'd better just leave your father alone."

In another part of the world, as through a looking-glass, Caroline Carmichael's twin-self was going through the motions of her routine, domestic life, even as, here, in this splendidly if somewhat overly decorated living room, Caroline Carmichael was being ostensibly honored; at home, in her little rented house in a suburb of a large, sprawling, rather featureless Midwestern American city, an hour's commute from the state university at which she taught, she was possibly having dinner with friends, or with a male companion (there were two or three extant, rather more friends than admirers, colleagues of hers at the university), though more likely she would be eating alone, in her vague distracted way, as she glanced through her mail, or the next-day's lecture notes, or made an effort to read one or another of the professional books she invariably agreed to review, and was invariably behind in reviewing. The great danger in living alone is that you will read or work while you eat, Caroline Carmichael knew, but, again, the alternate did not appeal; food had not much taste, eaten without company. At home, too, geographical proximity (four hundred sixty-odd miles separated them: a mere day's drive) urged her to think of her father more than she wished to think of him, since such thoughts were to no purpose, and devolved fairly quickly into self-pity.

It was not specifically to flee her father that Caroline Carmichael had agreed to her government's invitation to do an ambitious tour of Western Europe that spring and early summer but it had to be confessed that the benefits of being "at home"— in any sense of the term—were not apparent. She read Pavase, and with satisfaction more than dread underscored the words, *Traveling is a brutality. It forces you to trust strangers and to lose sight of all that familiar comfort of home and friends. You are constantly off balance. Nothing is yours except the essential things—air, sleep, dreams, the sun, the sky—all things tending toward the eternal, or what we imagine of it.* But that ecstatic flight had not been Caroline Carmichael's experience for her days were crowded and cacophonous with people: very nice people for the most part, but people nonetheless, all of them strangers, with smiles, handshakes, special requests, questions phrased in careful but sometimes perplexing English. In giddy loops and zigzags Caroline was making her way north, giving variations of her lecture, meeting with students, teachers, translators, fellow art historians and feminists, Americans living abroad; she had begun the tour in Athens and would end it in Oslo in another twelve days barring disaster—a sudden physical collapse, a "political" assassination. She was thirty-seven years old; an attractive woman with level, rather brooding eyes, limp fine blond-streaked hair, a habit of smiling too quickly, and insincerely; tall, straight-backed, a bit tense; holding herself, as a former lover had meanly observed, like a bow about to spring an arrow. Though she was a professionally successful woman—to the degree that "success" can be measured, without cynicism, in public, official terms—she harbored nonetheless an adolescent, romantic hope of meeting, when she traveled, her "fate": recognizing at first sight the individual, or individuals, or scene, or vision, that might give to her journey its unique validity. Otherwise, why leave home?

So she felt disproportionately upset, as if personally insulted, by *this* fabled city: Amsterdam: a jewel of canals, sixteenth- and seventeenth-century houses, numberless museums. Its dereliction had begun at the airport; Caroline had seen, on the drive in, defaced walls and buildings and sidewalks, faded and fresh graffiti side by side, a witless public littering that seemed to proffer a statement, a cultural critique, but what was the statement? Even the parks, oases of civic pride in other western European cities, were here derelict, and sad to see; young people slept sprawled on the grass in midday, or sat on benches, drugged, dazed, utterly vacuous, and seemingly utterly content. It was a nightmare of the welfare state, Caroline Carmichael supposed: a reminder that after all the fundamental integrity and dignity of the individual could not be assumed. The city was staggering under the financial burden of enormous welfare rolls; there was an army, ever-increasing, of the professionally unemployed; there were squatters' unions, there were even drug users' unions . . . ! Yet Caroline's "The Iconography of Female Martyrdom in European Art" had gone well; it had been surprisingly well attended. No one is so completely alone as the lecturer addressing her audience, Caroline thought, yet this sort of aloneness suited her; excited her; invested her with an eloquent, fiery passion, very much in keeping with the controversial nature of the ideas she presented.

The Parisian critic's introduction, however, had been affable, uninformed, and charmingly condescending; "François" had clearly read nothing of her work, and knew nothing of her, except for a recitation of facts provided him by the Consulate. He dwelled upon the fact, which he seemed to find amusing, that Caroline Carmichael was the first woman to receive tenure at her university; the first woman officer of her professional-academic society; the first woman art historian to have been invited to the American Consulate in Amsterdam to speak. In the guise of praising Caroline Carmichael, and flattering her American organizers for bringing her here ("for the first time in Professor Carmichael's distinguished career!"), the smiling, dapper little man with his exotically accented English was actually insulting her. But Caroline Carmichael stoically maintained an expression of equanimity, even cheerfulness. She would never betray her feelings, in public.

Not even murderous rage could force itself to the surface of her being, in public.

She'd taken the podium from François with a gracious smile, and set about winning over the audience, as she knew she could not fail to do. How perfect Caroline Carmichael would be, she thought, how thoroughly good, kind, courageous, if only she could live out her life in public.

"Your talk was brilliant, Miss Carmichael. *You* were brilliant."

The Prices' twenty-year-old daughter Inge, introduced to Caroline Carmichael by Mrs. Price, grasped her hand fiercely in hers, as if taking possession; leaned so close, and so urgently, it seemed for a disconcerting moment she meant to kiss Caroline on the lips. What an extraordinarily forceful young woman! How completely different from the college-age women Caroline Carmichael taught! An angry light flared up in Inge Price's eyes, as if in Caroline's defense; her big-boned face—full, fleshy, freckled, warmly pink as if just slapped—loomed large as a moon; her soft young body was suffused with energy, intent, impudence. At first glance it looked as if she were wearing, simply, rags, but there was a logic of sorts, even a slapdash tatterdemalion style, to the two or three layers of skirts, the gauzy open-throated peasant blouse, the shapeless black sweater, or was it a handwoven shawl, unraveling down her back. Her hair was long, frizzed and knotted, a magnificent copper color, swinging in her face and in her eyes; her full, soft breasts were loose inside her clothing; her hips were wide, stolid, fleshy; she reminded Caroline Carmichael of a young Flemish girl in a painting, ruddy with health, unthinking in beauty. Clearly, her mother was both proud of and intimidated by Inge, who had swept into the living room with the intention of helping the servants (with whom, perhaps, she claimed a spiritual kinship?), but displayed no self-consciousness whatsoever about talking animatedly with the guest of honor, and plying her with questions. Inge was particularly interested in the iconography of female martyrdom, she told Caroline Carmichael, as it applied to life today and not just to the past; she wanted to know more about "Inquisitional politics" (of which Caroline has spoken briefly at the end of her talk) as it applied to reality and not just to some old art that nobody looks at, or almost nobody. "How long will you be in Amsterdam? Maybe we could meet sometime? Maybe tomorrow? As soon as possible—like, for breakfast?" Inge asked Caroline, breathless, leaning close, staring at Caroline with her damp, slightly protuberant green eyes. She exuded a rich mesmerizing scent of something powdery, heated, not frequently washed; a mustiness of well-worn clothes, like slept-in bed-clothes. Mrs. Price in her brocaded hostess's gown and scimitar-like jewelry professed a mother's horror, or was it simply embarrassment—"Why Inge, for heaven's sake, Miss Carmichael is *busy,* I'm sure she has a dozen appointments for tomorrow, in-terviews—" Caroline Carmichael had taken an unconscious step back from the impertinent young Inge, and now caught her breath, and laughed, rather amazed, startled, smiling—"Why, I'm sure we can meet—breakfast would be fine."

So distinct a victory of daughter over mother was this, Inge nudged Mrs. Price and muttered, "Okay, Mother, go *on,* Miss Carmichael and I need to talk," and Mrs. Price shrank away, im-mediately routed, and Caroline Carmichael continued smiling, continued a bit dazed, for Inge was so striking a young woman, so spectacularly forceful a presence, a ball of flame might have swept into the decorous gathering, contrasting painfully with the older men and women, the majority of them middle-aged, so carefully, even elegantly dressed and groomed. Caroline recalled now having seen this flamboyant young American girl at her lec-ture that afternoon, she'd been struck by the vehemence with which the girl had nodded, and during the question and answer period Inge had ventured a not entirely coherent question about a point Caroline had made on the "enantiomorphic" relationship between asceticism and sadism in religious art of the late me-dieval, early Renaissance period, a question that was both arro-gant and perceptive—for were not "asceticism" and "sadism" both simply patriarchal expressions?—and her loud, self-assertive voice, so distinctly American, caused people in the audience to look at her. Caroline had not known of course that the outspoken young woman was the daughter of the Consul-General and Mrs. Price: she'd disappeared after the lecture without coming forward to be introduced.

Now she was talking to Caroline Carmichael in a great rush of words, smiling, smiling a dazzling smile, gripping Caroline's wrist as if they were old, intimate friends, repeating her praise of the lecture, how she'd been blasted by it, it'd blown her mind, some of the slides Caroline had shown, the gouged-out eyes, the martyrs' breasts on trays, the madonna with the greenish sickish skin nursing the spiteful-looking little Jesus, was that German? medieval? or Flemish? or were they all the same, mostly? Inge had dropped out of Bennington in the middle of her sophomore year, she said, and she didn't intend to return, or maybe she would, but not right now; she wasn't going to succumb to parental pressure—"You can't imagine what it's like! I'm a foreign service brat, my daddy is the *biggest* deal anywhere he's posted, and the hell of it is, Caroline," she said, drawing near to murmur in Caroline Carmichael's ear, "he's a dear sweet noble man and I love him, he's a saint practically, like everybody says. And Mommy too in case she has misled you. She's *too weird*. But they're both good people, they're ready to die, just about, doing their duty, representing the United States fucking foreign policy, my daddy was almost killed already two times I know about and other times I'm not supposed to know about. They're *good* people, that's all. I love them, they're crazy, it's weird! They're not *evil*. You quoted the feminist, I forget her name, she was one of the suffragist pioneers I guess, she said 'women don't have enough evil in them—'?"

Caroline Carmichael laughed with pleasure since this remark was one that had made a strong impression on her when, years before, she'd first come upon it. "Rebecca West said that. But she was speaking of the women of Great Britain, a certain caste of women, in 1912—"

Inge nodded vehemently, but must not have been listening for she said, leaning close to Caroline Carmichael again, her eyes humid and dilated, a marvelous pellucid green like a child's marble, "—Have you been introduced to that guy with the pipe over there, standing over there by the door, 'Peter Zaller'?—he's C.I.A. but 'analysis' as they call it, not 'covert.' " She snorted with indignation and turned her lower lip inside out in a razzing derisory gesture. "Like he doesn't know what a dirty war is, or a friendly assassination!" Caroline glanced over at the fairly ordinary-appearing gentleman in question; asked what "analysis" was; but Inge's interest in Mr. Zaller had already consumed itself. She returned to her earlier, more passionate topic of Caroline Carmichael's lecture—images of severed hands, severed heads, madonnas as martyrs, the ecstasy of death—maybe Caroline could provide her with a list of books to read, paintings to look up, the names of the most important radical feminists back in the States? And when could they meet? *Could* they meet tomorrow? Sometime in the mid-morning, at Caroline's hotel? Which hotel was it? "—All the hours between your lecture and now," the breathless young woman said, fixing her eyes on Caroline's in a way that was both annoying and flattering, "—I was just walking mainly, by the canals, though they don't like me to because of— some problem they're having with security—and all that while can you guess what I was thinking?"

She stared at Caroline Carmichael so intently, Caroline felt a stab of simple fear. "Yes—?"

"I want to be you."

The remark hung in the air as if uttered but not received: for Caroline Carmichael was quite nonplussed by it.

Then Mrs. Price returned, the Consul-General in tow, for at last Mr. Price had come home—a tall white-haired gentleman with sad eyes, a rather ashen skin, a handsome courtly mouth. "Miss Carmichael! How good to meet you! And how terribly sorry I am for being late!" he exclaimed, quite as if he meant it; as if he'd been hurrying, these hours, simply to meet *her*. It was the diplomatic style par excellence and Caroline Carmichael, not at all deceived, was nonetheless charmed. She shook hands with him— his hand was warm, dry, reassuring, strong. As they talked she noticed, to her mild regret—or was it sheerly relief—that Inge Price was slipping away. At last it was time for dinner.

During this stately meal Caroline Carmichael was distracted by the appearance, at regular, almost predictable intervals, of Inge, who was helping the two uniformed servants serve the food; emerging like a sunburst through the swinging door that led to the kitchen pantry, tray in her hands, lower lip caught in her teeth. Her waist-long coppery hair gleamed with static electricity; she'd tied a crimson sash tight around her waist, ethnic-style, as if to empha-size her full, shapely, exuberant young body. Approaching Caro-line Carmichael—Inge had made certain, it seemed, that she, and not the others, served Caroline's and Mr. Price's end of the table—she smiled like a clever child. Clearly the girl was enjoying her handmaiden role, and had played it before: "helping out" with her parents' social obligations. She appeared too to be on companionable terms with the household staff. How striking she is, Caroline thought, trying not to stare. And how perverse, her imagining she would want to be *me*.

Nonetheless it was flattering. In her mind Caroline Carmichael rapidly catalogued the titles and names she would provide Inge with in the morning. Yes and she must remember to get Inge's address so that she could mail her paperback copies of her own two books.

The Consul-General, seated at the head of the table, with Caro-line Carmichael to his right, showed none of the distractedness one might be excused for showing if one were purportedly on a terror-ist "target list" but engaged his guest of honor in polite, even quite animated conversation, inquiring after Caroline's background, her work, her impressions of Europe and of her foreign service hosts thus far,—and what did she think of Amsterdam? "It's a beautiful city," Caroline said, then, faltering a bit, "—except for the neglect." "Ah yes indeed," Mr. Price murmured, smiling, "—the 'neglect.'" At the far end of the sumptuously set table, barely visible beyond the many-branched candelabrum, Mrs. Price kept up an exclamatory hostess's dialogue with guests, punctuated by peals of girlish laughter. The food was Middle Eastern, Iranian in fact, rich and de-licious and altogether new to Caroline Carmichael; the wines too were delicious, and seemed to be going rapidly to her head. Inge appeared through the swinging door, this time to collect the first-course dishes; there was an innocence in her head-on plunging manner. She smiled in Caroline Carmichael's direction.

Caroline's heart lifted in simple happiness. She said to Mr. Price, "How lovely this is!—all of this! The room, the table! What fascinating lives you all must lead!"

Norman Price looked at Caroline Carmichael and smiled, po-litely at first, then with more animation. "Yes, do you know," he said, considering, "—all in all, that's so. I have had nearly forty years of it—Georgine and I, both—and, yes, that's so: fascinating."

The Prices had been posted in the U.S.S.R., in Western Africa, in Iran, in Japan, in Germany, and again in Iran, and Norway; their foreign posts had alternated with posts in Washington, but they had always preferred to live abroad, even with the difficulties of bringing up children. Mr. Price had learned the languages of each of the countries in which he had lived, he'd learned as much as possible about their histories and cultures, and, yes, he said, in reply to a question of Caroline's, Iran remained their favorite country, by far—"We miss it terribly, still, to this day, Georgine and I both." Before the Revolution, when Mr. Price had been deputy chief of mission in Tehran, the Iranians they had known—"Not the Shah and his associates, but the others"—were wonderfully sensitive, well-educated people, superior people, educators, intellectuals, doctors, scientists, artists. What a tragedy had befallen them! A tragedy, really, for the world! Caroline said awkwardly, "You must have been very upset, when—" Mr. Price said, smiling, " 'Upset' isn't a word allowed in a diplomat's vocabulary, Miss Carmichael." He was breathing not quickly but deeply; in that instant he looked his age, and rather hunted. Caroline saw that he had drained his wineglass and was staring at the dregs.

Later, midway in the meal, Mr. Price seemed to regain his interest in Caroline Carmichael, and asked her about her parents—were they still living? She told him about her father; but only minimally; stressing his accomplishments, his long and productive and seemingly happy professional life. For that is how she meant to remember him after all. For that is how she *would* remember him. Mr. Price's father, he told her, smiling fondly, nostalgically, had been a jack-of-all-trades, even, as a young man, a semiprofessional boxer, boxing in clubs, possibly not quite legal clubs, in the metropolitan New York area. "Sometimes he just boxed for wristwatches," Mr. Price said. "I have an old snapshot of him with a half-dozen wristwatches on each arm. "Really!" Caroline Carmichael exclaimed. Her eyes filled with tears of sentiment as if the snapshot—sepia-tinted, much-wrinkled—were before her. Glancing up she saw Inge Price just emerging through the swinging door, bearing an enormous cut-glass salad bowl in her arms.

After the salad course was served Mr. Price said, "—I see you've made my daughter's acquaintance, Miss Carmichael," and Caroline murmured a vague assent. In a neutral voice Mr. Price said, "Our youngest daughter is a fiercely independent young woman. Perhaps because she has always been the baby of the family—there are eighteen years separating her and our eldest, Robert. She left Bennington, for instance, without informing us— or the college—and went 'backpacking' in Canada. For a while." He paused, shaking his head; sighing. Caroline could not determine whether his tone was wry or troubled. Careful to show no inordinate curiosity she asked a few questions about Inge Price, what was Inge interested in studying, how had she responded to being brought up in a series of foreign countries, how long was she visiting him and Mrs. Price here in Amsterdam? "Ah, not long, I hope!" Mr. Price said. "—Amsterdam is dangerous." Seeing Caroline's look of inquiry he amended, "I mean for young people. Young people without work and resources who have a special penchant for"—he paused to select the perfect word—"drift."

Drift! Caroline Carmichael, whose life was so much a matter of schedules, time-tables, deadlines, and obligations, thought the idea uniquely appealing.

Elsewhere at the long table were conversations of a more abstract, less personal nature, and to one or another of these the Consul-General and Caroline Carmichael now sought to attach themselves, for it was uncommon for two people to talk together so exclusively at so formal a gathering—talk of air, water, and soil pollution ("East Germany is the most criminal but France is not far behind"), and of AIDS in Europe ("*We* will not make the mistake the United States is making—refusing to distribute free needles to narcotics addicts"), and of World War II memories, still distressingly fresh ("The Dutch were starving and living like animals well into 1945 when most of the rest of Europe was liberated"). There was talk, even, though it was brief and rather vague, of the C.I.A. and its recent actions, that very day headlined in the *International Herald Tribune*, in Central America, and Peter Zaller gained the attention of the table by saying in an aggrieved voice, "What no one seems to realize, even otherwise well-informed people, is that Central Intelligence is primarily concerned with analysis—only three percent of the staff is engaged in covert operations." "And there is no direct link between the two?" the German professor asked skeptically. "There is very little communication," Mr. Zaller said. "Then perhaps there should be more communication," the German professor said. It was time for coffee to be served; Mr. Zaller, unlit pipe still in hand, like a talisman, slipped away from the table—to make a telephone call, Caroline wondered, or simply to use the guest bathroom?—and Mrs. Price said gaily, "It's so enormously thoughtful of Peter, I *adore* that man, he refrains from smoking that ghastly pipe of his in company." Thus conversation shifted to smoking, and those at the table who had once smoked and no longer did declared themselves, and those who continued to smoke but wished they could break the habit declared themselves, and those who smoked and were adamant in their intentions to continue to smoke declared themselves, and Mrs. Price, scarcely listening, with the euphoria of a hostess who has feared the worst for her dinner party and has seemingly been spared, called out shrilly, "Everything in moderation, my father always said! Vices not excepted!" And now the German professor, whose name was Fredrich, a plump stolid bespectacled man of late middle age who taught American literature at the University of Mainz and who was an old friend of the Prices, entertained the table by telling of how he had participated in World War II for "approximately fifteen minutes": aged eighteen, he had been parachuted into Allied-occupied territory in France, in 1943, was taken prisoner at once, and spent the remainder of the war in a POW camp in Galesburg, Illinois. "Galesburg!" Caroline Carmichael exclaimed unthinkingly. "I was born in Galesburg!" Fredrich smiled at her, showing broad discolored teeth. "—But long after my time there, Miss Carmichael, surely!" he said gallantly.

And then the alarm went off.

A piercingly loud, shrill noise, more substantial than a whistle, not quite a siren—and Caroline Carmichael thought, almost calmly, Now it is going to happen.

Suddenly the Prices and the Consulate people were all efficiency: quick and brisk and methodical, as if this very scene had been rehearsed countless times. Georgine Price, from whom one might have expected hysteria, was immediately mobilized, rising from her chair to push open the French doors at her rear and helping to usher out onto the terrace, and from there down a short flight of stone steps to the grass, her frightened guests. Like the others Caroline Carmichael turned docile at once, for there was no time for panic, and, like a grammar school student in a fire drill, acquiesced to the Consul-General's lowered, wonderfully authoritative voice, "This way, please. Out these doors. Inge?—come along. Here. Out here. Yes. Step right along." Caroline Carmichael stood shivering in the grass, breathing in the fresh chill damp night air that smelled of roses, or so she imagined, hugging herself as if to forestall an attack of convulsive shuddering. She felt it in her bowels more powerfully than elsewhere, the shock of it, the irony, that the very possibility with which she had been toying for hours—of suffering chaos—of being attacked and murdered by faceless strangers—had been no idle anecdotal fantasy after all.

The residence had been activated into a state of emergency within seconds. Every window blazed with light; spotlights in the shrubbery had switched on, exposing the pink stone and stucco mansion like a garish movie set; there were men's voices, the sounds of heavy footsteps. The high-pitched wailing continued. Caroline Carmichael wondered: Was the residence under siege? Had shots already been fired? Was a bomb about to detonate? She backed off in the grass, choked with emotion. She did not want to die. She was terrified of dying. Overhead the night sky was very black, numberless winking stars scrambled her vision, she thought of her father who was a lonely frightened dying old man trapped inside the frail encasement of his skull. If she survived, she thought, she would fly home at once, and beg his forgiveness. For he was quite right: she hadn't ever loved him enough.

A hand closed about hers, with a hard little squeeze. Inge whispered in her ear, "Don't worry! Daddy won't let anything happen to us!"

The alarm stopped abruptly. Mr. Price, who had evidently reentered the house, appeared now in the doorway, cupping his hands to his mouth to call out, with a joviality that sounded unforced, "Sorry! False alarm! It was only the smoke detector!"

*   *   *

"I'm so terribly sorry, and so terribly embarrassed," Peter Zaller said, red-faced, sweating with shame, but they told him not to be sorry and not to be embarrassed in the slightest—they much preferred him and his pipe, after all, to the real thing. "But I feel like such a damned fool," he said. Mrs. Price laughed wildly and, seizing one of her guest's hands simply because the woman was seated close by, said, "No, no, *no*. *We* are the fools. The damned detectors are too *sensitive!*"

The brief remainder of the evening passed in this way, convivial, a bit giddy, and Caroline Carmichael thought how comical, life, how fundamentally silly and farcical, yes, and anecdotal, finally—it would make a perfect little story after all, that a formal dinner party in her honor at the Consul-General's residence in Amsterdam had been routed, the guests thrown into terror for their lives, because a man had crept off to smoke his outlawed pipe in a bathroom. *And who was this individual but an officer of the C.I.A.*

As if on cue the dinner party dissolved promptly at 11 P.M. Before Caroline left, driven back by the Bonners to her little hotel near the Stedelijk Museum, she made a date with Inge Price for 9 A.M. the next morning in the coffee shop of her hotel. ("I'll be there!—and I can take you to some museums afterward!" Inge said.) Mr. Price shook Caroline's hand in farewell and seemed genuinely sorry she was leaving Amsterdam in two days—"I so much enjoyed our conversation, Miss Carmichael." As if they had indeed come through a siege together, Mrs. Price warmly embraced Caroline, and complained hoarsely in her ear, "How I wish my daughter could take a tutorial course with someone like you, Miss Carmichael!—by mail, if no other way! It would do her a world of good to use her brains for once. All Inge seems to do is waste time, court disaster—she's forever taking up strays—lame ducks—" The Consul-General laid a hand on his wife's arm and said, gently, "Georgine, dear, Miss Carmichael's car is waiting." The frenzied terrier Suzie, thrown into a seemingly permanent state of excitation by the alarm and the evacuation of the house, was yipping wildly, her toenails clicking on the marble foyer floor and her damp cold busy little nose poking about against Caroline Carmichael's knees.

Outside, a Marine guard stood by the opened rear door of the sedan, stony-faced with fury, or contempt, or simple boredom.

And in the morning, though Caroline Carmichael waited patiently in the coffee shop of her hotel, well past 10 A.M., sipping coffee, adding to the list of names and titles she'd devised for Inge Price, the young woman failed to appear. Caroline's little table overlooked the street where movements—traffic, pedestrians, bicyclists—continually drew her attention. But Inge failed to appear, nor did she telephone.

Caroline had a small breakfast, hard rolls and jam, a glass of rather synthetic orange juice, left a note for Inge with the proprietress ("I'll be upstairs in my room until 11—please come right up: 302"), went back to her room telling herself that in the event Inge had not arrived by 11:00 she would go out, to the Stedelijk Museum in fact. And possibly, since it was so close, the Van Gogh Museum as well.

So she sat in her cramped, dour little room, telling herself now that she wasn't waiting exactly, she was simply reading, for she had always intended to read *The Diary of Anne Frank* and with the Frank house only a few miles away what more fitting opportunity. And so engrossing was the book, so beautifully and tragically modulated the young girl's voice, it was nearly 11:30 when she checked the time. Out of nervousness—the aftermath, no doubt, of the previous evening's bad scare—and the intervening night's insomnia—she had not been able to read the Frank diary in chronological sequence, fearing the accumulation of suspense and tension, she'd been skipping about, and in a sort of numbed horror she read, near the end, *I am saying goodbye to you before our death. Dear Father: I am saying goodbye to you. We are so anxious to live, but all is lost—we are not allowed! I am so afraid of this death, because little children are thrown into graves alive. Goodbye forever.*

I kiss you.

Caroline Carmichael snatched up her trench coat and umbrella, and hurried out. Walking in the rain, beneath the slanted umbrella, dodging bicyclists who came hurtling at her, she told herself it was nothing, her hurt and disappointment were nothing,

think of true disappointment, true hurt, true terrorism and terror, think of Anne Frank and the millions of others, children
tossed living into graves, think of anyone and anything other
than Caroline Carmichael, thirty-seven years old, alone, walking
blindly in the rain in a city the color of pewter, telling herself
strays, lame ducks, what else did you expect!

I want to be you.

She spent an absorbed ninety minutes in the Stedelijk Museum, might have had lunch in the stylish little café but returned
to her hotel just in case, for what if Inge Price, breathless, apologetic, hair in her eyes, had arrived in her absence. . . . Though she
could see that her mail box was empty save for her oversized key
Caroline Carmichael nonetheless asked the desk clerk if there
were any messages for her. No messages, she was told.

So she wrote out a message herself for Inge, for the desk clerk
to give her should she arrive, and went out again in the rain, and
had lunch alone in a crowded neighborhood restaurant, not an
expensive and certainly not an elegant place by the look of it,
but, the American dollar being so low, expensive enough. As if to
spite her own mean-spirited inclination, she left a generous tip.
Then she went to the Van Gogh Museum though this was, in a
sense, out of spite, for of all museums the Van Gogh was surely
the one Inge Price would have liked to take her to—what more
appropriate, for two Americans visiting Amsterdam? At 3:00 P.M.
she was scheduled for an interview in the coffee shop of her hotel so she returned, and quite enjoyed, or appeared to enjoy, the
well-informed and provocative questions put to her by the young
Dutch woman journalist, and if she was hurt, indeed dismayed
and bewildered, by Inge Price's failure to contact her, she gave
no sign.

She left the hotel again, desperate to be in the open air. No
matter the perpetual rain, the graffiti-scrawls that assaulted the
eye. The Dutch flew by on their grim high-seated and -handled
old bicycles, unpainted bicycles, and the Dutch faces pale and
grim too, pale hard plain-pewter faces, sexless, with strong
bones. She would telephone the Consulate in the morning, before
she left for the airport, she would leave a message for Inge Price,
some sort of brisk matter-of-fact message, she'd mail the list of

names and titles to the girl too for why not be generous in the face of another's rudeness. She had made up her mind to continue with her tour—on to Hamburg, to Copenhagen, to Stockholm, to Oslo. She would not return home to her father only to be rebuffed another time, the very thought was absurd and sentimental, serving no purpose. Caroline Carmichael was of all things purposeful.

"I am an American," she thought, "—at least." She was walking by an open-air flower market, the rain had turned to mere drizzle, she folded up her umbrella and carried it under her arm. The thought, conceived in meanness, blossomed in her heart; and so transformed her face that, for several blocks, passersby glanced at her, some of them fellow Americans perhaps, with faint quizzical stares, half-smiles, almost of recognition.

The Track

Their yearling pacer, Navajo, the first racehorse they had ever owned, was scheduled to leave shortly for winter training quarters in Florida, so, one day in mid-October, McCullen and his wife Lydia drove to the Belle Acres Horse Farm to see the colt a final time before he was shipped off. They lived in East Orange, New Jersey, a two-hour drive from the farm north of Netcong.

"Do you think we'll recognize him?" Lydia asked. "He might have changed some since the auction."

"He's maybe grown a little," McCullen said, "but he won't have changed." In the McCullens' kitchen, affixed to their refrigerator by tiny magnetized decals, were numerous Polaroid snapshots of the bay colt taken immediately after the sale in August: Navajo with McCullen holding his bridle, Navajo with Lydia, Navajo with McCullen and Lydia beaming like startled parents, Navajo with McCullen and Lydia and Indian-dark Jake Crotty, the trainer. One hundred seventy-three standardbred yearlings had been sold at the auction, the highest for prices in the range of $300,000; Navajo, though of promising stock, had gone for only $39,000—an extraordinary bargain, as McCullen was assured. (Navajo's sire, though descended from million-dollar stallions, had acquired, over the course of his foreshortened career in harness racing, a problematic reputation: he had balked at starting at the gate several times and was notoriously headstrong. Navajo's dam, however, was the first-born of the filly Stormy Weather, the second fastest pacer in history.) Before McCullen had signed on for the auction he'd been informed, as of course he already knew, that not all yearling standardbreds, despite their bloodlines, and the prestige of their breeders and trainers, were guaranteed to actually race; to qualify for professional racing; even to train successfully. It was a risk, McCullen thought, you had to take.

At the time of the auction the farm had resembled a fair or a carnival: hundreds of cars parked in a roped-off pasture, an enormous candy-cane-striped tent with rows of red canvas chairs to which names—*Mr.* and *Mrs. T. J. McCullen* among them—had been taped, a raised dais for the three tuxedo-clad auctioneers, and raised platforms for the spotters, and free champagne, and much excitement and apprehension as, one by one, the horses were led into the ring for bidding, by young women grooms in riding costumes; now, in the cooler, more sober air of October, with a high wind in the trees and leaves underfoot and no more than three or four cars and a pickup truck parked in the graveled lot in front of the horse barns, the farm looked very different. A beautiful place, but quiet; seemingly deserted. "You wouldn't think it was the same place, would you?" Lydia said, shivering. There were a half-dozen barns painted mint-green, with smart white trim; there was a large, old, clearly refurbished white farm-house, in which the farm manager lived; a mile away (the McCullens had had a glimpse of it, in August) was the fieldstone manor house in which the owner of Belle Acres Farm lived when he was in residence in New Jersey. (The McCullens had never met the owner, a Mr. Marks: their dealings had been with intermediaries.) On all sides were pastures bounded by dazzling white fences in which horses grazed, and beyond the farm buildings were a quarter-mile dirt track and a shorter exercise track on which, at this time, horses were being exercised—trotting, pacing, frequently breaking into gallops, behind motorized carts manned by young grooms. McCullen shaded his eyes, looking around. Where was Crotty? They were to meet him here at two o'clock and it was nearly ten after and no one seemed to be taking note of them. He wondered if he and Lydia should try to locate Navajo on their own . . . unless he was out to pasture, and, if so, even if he were within sight, how could they be certain they knew him?

McCullen stared hard at a small group of horses grazing close by, most of them dark, browns or bays, young, supple, sleekly groomed, oblivious to everything but their eating.

As if following McCullen's thought Lydia said with her soft, uneasy laugh, "They all look alike, don't they?—I remember that from the auction. Unless a horse has white markings it's impossible to tell them apart. You can't even tell the colts from the fillies—at least I can't."

"You can tell the stallions," McCullen said. "The stallions are bigger."

A black groom was leading a spirited horse to a van a short distance away and it looked as if the man might call over greetings to the McCullens, but he did not. McCullen, trembling slightly, with anticipation and perhaps annoyance, said, "It's frustrating to be here and not to know where he is—Navajo, I mean. You don't think Crotty has forgotten our appointment?"

"I'm sure he hasn't," Lydia said. But she sounded uncertain.

For today's excursion Lydia had dressed with care in a purplish-brown cable-knit sweater with carved wooden buttons, and a black cashmere turtleneck, and Ann Taylor jeans, and good shoes, Italian snakeskin pumps with a small heel. Her ashy blond hair was caught up in a purple turbanlike scarf and she wore her darkest sunglasses to protect her eyes, which were sensitive to light, from the whitish autumn glare. The sunglasses gave her an assured, even arrogant look, which pleased McCullen, who knew it was misleading. It was a look he cultivated, not always successfully, in himself.

McCullen wore light flannel trousers, a sports shirt open at the throat, and his heather-brown tweed coat, which fitted his broad shoulders snugly and gave him the air—controlled, affable, rather rumpled—of an English country squire in an illustrated advertisement. He was hatless, his graying hair blowing freely in the wind, and he wore steel-rimmed glasses with prescription lenses tinted dark green. Of his two current cars, a metallic-blue Mercedes 450SL sedan and a Chevy station wagon, McCullen had driven the Mercedes today though it was in fact the less reliable of the two—a client of his had been hard pressed for cash and had had to sell the car quickly and cheaply, and McCullen, who loved special things, classy things, things that defined their owners as differing slightly, but significantly, from the quotidian, had been unable to resist. He was a tax accountant, a partner in his firm, in East Orange, but a dropout, as he described himself, from the academic world—he'd once taught in the School of Business Administration at Rutgers—where salaries were too low and advancement too uncertain. Not that he was a man who was defined by his employment. He was forty-nine years old and did not think of himself as defined at all.

After several more minutes they went to look for Crotty in a barn marked PACING COLTS, where a young woman groom directed them out to the track at the rear. The wind was brisker here, and overhead a small private plane was soaring, banking, cutting its engine, and Lydia said, her hands over her ears, "Those little planes make me so nervous—I always think they're about to crash." Crotty and an assistant were just bringing in a horse from the track, dismantling the hobble, the gear, the practice sulky. He apologized for being late, if he was late, and McCullen said quickly, "No, no, you weren't late," and Lydia said apologetically, "We were early."

Crotty shook hands with them formally. He was a head shorter than McCullen, in his mid-fifties, darkly tanned, with a much-weathered gnomish face, small shrewd watchful eyes, a cautious smile. For a moment he stared rather openly at Lydia, as McCullen remembered him staring at her the other time they'd met. Then Crotty asked if they were looking for Molly-O, and McCullen said no, Navajo was their horse's name, a young colt they'd bought in August, and Crotty said yes, that was the horse he meant, in fact; around the barns they were in the habit of referring to young horses by their dams' names. "So many foals get born," Crotty said, grinning, "it's hard to keep them straight."

Lydia asked, "How many in a season?"

"One hundred ninety-two, this year."

"One hundred ninety-two foals!"

Lydia smiled wide-eyed at Crotty, and at McCullen, who felt a stab of impatience: she seemed to have forgotten, but she'd asked the identical question of another Belle Acres employee, at the time of the auction, and had responded the same way.

Crotty said, tactfully, "Of course Navajo isn't just any foal. I know Navajo very well."

He led them out of the sunshine and back into the barn marked PACING COLTS, along the row of barred stalls, and there, number eleven, was Navajo, the McCullens' horse, lifting his head alertly as they approached. The young horse was beautifully groomed, sleek, glossy, with large pricked-up ears and very large very intense liquidy-brown eyes that seemed to McCullen, though of course he knew better, to flash with recognition. Lydia exclaimed at his beauty and McCullen swallowed hard, staring. Beautiful, yes. But beauty was the least of it.

Ceremoniously, Crotty led Navajo out of his stall and stood him, ears nervously pricking, hindquarters quivering, in the aisle. All the while he murmured to the horse with what seemed like genuine affection, stroking him and encouraging the McCullens to come closer. "He won't panic," Crotty said, "—he won't bite, will ya, fella? He's a little skittish sometimes, mainly outdoors, horses are wary of being led into strange places, asked to do strange things—like all of us, eh?" Crotty smiled at the McCullens, who were feeling shy and self-conscious, like overage parents. "C'mon, friends, stroke the good boy's nose, horses love to have their noses stroked, right, Navajo?" So the McCullens came forward, and petted Navajo, cautiously at first and then with more confidence. "Oh, how soft!—how beautiful his coat is!" Lydia cried. It was not the first time she had so exclaimed but the russet-brown coat always surprised McCullen, too—it was soft as fur. Even the mane, with its look of coarseness, seemed to McCullen wonderfully fine to the touch. But most surprising was the horse's nose—its softness, its velvety coolish damp. And the enormous eyes with their look of watchful intelligence. *I own this,* McCullen thought, his heart quickening with love and wonder. *This is my horse I own.* Stroking the young horse's superb muscled shoulders, his back, his flanks, his sides, and again his head, his nose, his wide solid standardbred's chest . . . even as McCullen knew that the fact of his ownership, stated in legal documents, and confirmed in monthly $1,600 bills payable to Belle Acres Horse Farm, was a fact of absolutely no significance to Navajo. This was a horse who would never know his owners.

Yet it seemed to McCullen that October day as if his very life stood outside him, in the figure of the young horse. Unconscious of him, and indifferent to him. And therein lay the mystery—that it did not, could not, know *him.*

Over the horse's burnished, just perceptibly rippling back, McCullen and Lydia smiled happily at each other, as if, for the instant, surprised to see each other there, in this strange, unlikely, in a way improbable and even absurd place, their eyes shining as if with tears.

Lydia exclaimed over Navajo in her rich melodic tones, flattering the trainer with questions about him, about his training schedule, how in Crotty's opinion was he "shaping up," how did he take to the sulky and the track, was he healthy as he seemed, and, well, *happy* as he seemed, and McCullen listened, or half listened, for these were things he already knew, had been told over the telephone, and things Lydia too more or less knew and may not even have forgotten but simply wanted to hear again, perhaps so that she could hear Navajo's name spoken, and speak it, querying, herself. Crotty said that Navajo had "banged" his left rear leg a few days ago but it was "nothing serious, nothing to worry about," and Lydia began speaking, too quickly for McCullen's comfort, of how surprisingly delicate horses are, these special racing breeds in particular, susceptible to respiratory ailments, and infections, spraining and breaking their legs so easily, sometimes for no other reason than, racing, they come down too hard at the wrong angle, and how puzzling it was, how ironic, at least, Lydia said, laughing nervously, in her eyes it seemed so, that the horse is also an animal that contains such power: a symbol, you might say, of that kind of power. Crotty listened politely to all this, and said again that the banged leg was nothing serious, staring frankly at Lydia, this almost-beautiful woman in her stylish costume, carefully made up, in fact elegantly made up, her pink-toned skin seemingly flawless, her ashy blond hair seemingly untouched by gray, the soft puckering flesh around her eyes hidden by dark sunglasses. A diamond cluster ring flashed on her left hand, a bulky topaz on her right, hand-fashioned silver earrings, geometrically shaped, outsized, swung from her earlobes, and though she was in her late thirties it was probable Crotty thought her younger. (McCullen, her elder by nearly a decade, would certainly have thought her younger.) There are American women who conscientiously remain girls through their lives, and McCullen had fallen in love with and married one of them, had in fact quite deliberately married one of them, out of fear and repugnance of the other kind. And he did not regret it.

McCullen interrupted Lydia to ask Crotty a few questions of his own, shrewder questions perhaps, which of the stakes engagements he thought—"I'm asking of course just for your off-hand estimation"—Navajo might compete in next year. The Meadowlands? the Kentucky Pacing Derby? the New Jersey Memorial? These questions Crotty answered simply, they'd have to wait and see, he said, it all depends, he said, training horses like living your own life is mostly a matter of waiting and seeing how things come out. "Hoping for the best, you know," Crotty said, rubbing vigorously at his nose, "but not, maybe, if you're smart, setting yourself up for disappointment." McCullen nodded quickly. He was a novice racehorse owner but he was smart. And if, deep inside him, unexamined as a heartbeat, was the conviction that his horse *would* do well, *would* triumph over the others, McCullen knew enough—he had gambled a bit at the racetrack over the years, and at Atlantic City, and with friends, in monthly poker games at which he was rather good if not consistently good—not to allow that conviction to be uttered. He saw that there was a wicked six-inch scar along Crotty's jaw, and that two of the fingers of his left hand were misshapen.

"You know what I almost forgot, Jerry?" Lydia said suddenly. "*We* almost forgot? To take some more pictures of Navajo. I left the camera in the car."

They took several snapshots, McCullen holding Navajo's bridle, Lydia holding Navajo's bridle, the McCullens together, and each of them in turn with Crotty, smiling, beside Navajo. And then Crotty led Navajo back into his stall, and the visit was ended, and there seemed, abruptly, a kind of sadness about it: the animal led back so tractably into what amounted to his cage, and the barred door bolted. At once Navajo appeared to lose interest in his visitors, or forgot them, turning negligently away.

A single fly buzzed near McCullen's head. He brushed it away, thinking how clean the horse barn was kept: this was the first fly he'd noticed.

Crotty seemed pleased to be given one of the Polaroids, Crotty holding the bridle and Lydia with an arm around Navajo's mane, both smiling as if with enormous happiness. In the snapshot Crotty looked dark as an Indian and Lydia oddly pale except for her red, red mouth and the delicately penciled arch of her eyebrows. "Would you like to show us the most beautiful horse of all?" McCullen asked suddenly, with a heartiness he didn't quite feel. "—I mean, of course," he said, winking, "after ours."

So Crotty led the McCullens into an adjoining stable, and from there into the next, to the stall of Belle Acres's most famous stallion, Rondeley. He was a trotter who had earned over $2 million for his owner Mr. Marks during his three-year racing career (he'd been a Hambletonian winner and the second fastest standardbred in racing history) and many millions since, having sired one hundred sixty-six trotters, among whom, as Crotty proudly said, were twenty-two world champions. "In all, the old boy has made fifty-one million dollars change hands," he said.

McCullen whistled in astonishment, and Lydia said, laughing, "That *is* a lot of money."

"Not all of it is Mr. Marks's, of course," Crotty said. "There are other owners involved, and lots of other mares. But he's been a golden boy here."

The stallion appeared, to McCullen's eye, conspicuously larger than Navajo; he was a dark, very nearly black horse, nervously alert to his visitors, softly snorting and nuzzling his nose against the bars of the door, even biting, or mock-biting, the metal. The three interior walls of his stall were padded in dark red and a narrow mirror ran horizontally across the rear wall. Rondeley was seven years old and long past his prime for trotting, Crotty said, but in the pasture he was in the habit of "going crazy" and trying to race cars up the driveway. He'd torn up certain stretches of various pastures with his running and in his stall he sometimes threw himself against the walls, for no reason anyone could figure, just his craziness, or too much energy, so they had to pad the walls; also, sometimes he got so lonely he'd whinny and stamp and carry on like a baby, so they installed a mirror for him, so he could look at himself and be less lonely. "Less lonely—!" McCullen echoed softly. He felt deeply moved.

Rondeley certainly was a beautiful horse, an impressive horse, and you couldn't tell, at least McCullen would have had to admit he couldn't have told, that he was past his prime: he looked damn good. Lydia was addressing him in admiring cooing tones but when she put out her hand to stroke his nose Crotty said sharply, "Watch it, lady!" and she quickly withdrew her hand. There was a moment's embarrassment. Then Crotty said apologetically, "This old boy *bites*. He doesn't even need to be mad at you, sometimes, he just *bites*. The other day he was being shod, and he's used to that, you'd think, and he just turned his head sort of casually, they said, and sank his teeth into his groom's hand, this is a real sweet girl who's been grooming him for two years and almost never had any trouble, for no reason the s.o.b. reached over and sank his teeth in her hand down through the knuckles and it was nasty, I mean it was *real* nasty."

Lydia said stiffly, "I'm sorry, I didn't realize," her face lightly flushed, "—didn't realize horses bite." McCullen felt sorry for her and tried to catch her eye but she looked away.

"Oh yes they bite," Crotty said, laughing, "—they do lots of things you wouldn't say were in anybody's best interests, theirs or ours."

"How long have you been training horses?" McCullen asked.

"I've been around horses, one way or another, all my life," Crotty said. "But working here, for Mr. Marks, maybe ten years."

"And Mr. Marks—" McCullen said, not knowing what he meant to ask, "—has he been around horses all his life?"

"His father, and his father's father, owned this farm first," Crotty said. He paused, then said, rather vaguely, "Mr. Marks travels a lot. He's in Sweden right now. We have this November auction coming up, you know, not here I mean but at another farm he has, in New York State, bigger than the August one, and, you know, or maybe you don't know, Swedes are crazy about horses: some of them have a lot of money, to spend on horses."

They were strolling out of the barn, toward the sunshine which looked, from inside, blindingly bright; that autumnal cast, or clarity, that seems to reflect from all surfaces, the consequence,

McCullen supposed, of an absence of moisture in the air. He did not want to leave, much: he drew in a deep shuddering breath, inhaling the rich, sweet odors of hay, feed, horse manure, urine . . . the indefinable but unmistakable smell of a barn, of horses. And the almost vertiginous phenomenon of being inside and gazing out on a brightly sunny day. . . . What did it remind him of? A vagrant childhood memory of his grandfather's farm in northern Minnesota which he'd visited, summers, but where he had never lived and would not have wanted, at that time, to have lived? *Less lonely,* he thought. The expression had hooked into him as expressions sometimes did, often the remarks of strangers, or scraps of dialogue from films or television, hooking into him for years, very likely the remainder of his life. He'd once asked Lydia if she was the same way, susceptible to the same thing, and she frowned, and thought, and seemed to say yes she was, then she shook her head and said no, she guessed she didn't really know what he was talking about.

A thought came to McCullen suddenly: the notion of asking Crotty if they could come back again soon, very soon, maybe even tomorrow, before Navajo and the other yearlings went south, and get here early enough (that meant 7 A.M.) to watch them work out on the track. He'd loved to have seen a little of that and not just his poor colt closed up in a stall. . . . But he hesitated to ask. He felt shy of asking. He didn't want to be, Christ he sure didn't want to be, the kind of racehorse owner who worries too much about his horse like an anxious parent or a paranoid of some kind convinced the world is out to cheat him. Before signing over his $39,000 to Belle Acres he had done a good deal of homework on the farm and came away satisfied that Marks and his associates were absolutely honest; they were famous, in fact, for their integrity and the high quality of their horses in general. So he had nothing to worry about. He should have had nothing to worry about.

Lydia and Crotty were getting along well again, Crotty was making her laugh telling her about one or another racing mishap or irony such as the time when a million-dollar filly named Sheba, leading the pack at the New Jersey Classic, decided for some reason to return to her stable . . . nothing her driver could do, the damned horse simply kept veering out toward the edge of the track, out and away while everyone in the stands including the owner (who was Mr. Marks's father) stared in astonishment and horror. And the time only a few years ago when a competitor's pacer, a hot-blooded young colt, turned into the path of one of theirs, the odds-on favorite to win the race, this was the Kentucky Futurity and there was a lot, repeat: a lot, of money riding on it, and there was a tangle of bikes, and a spill, and damned lucky nobody's neck was broken. And the time a while back when Rondeley's sire Macheath refused to go to the gate at Meadowlands . . . "refused" not once but twice and not twice but three times and that was it for the day and no explanation was ever put forward except that horses get crazy sometimes and you can't make them do what they don't want to do any more than you can make a woman do what she doesn't want to do, and Crotty and Lydia laughed together, and Lydia said isn't it the male horses, the stallions, who are the most temperamental and dangerous, and Crotty said yes, sure: but only after they stop racing and begin breeding. Then they get hard, real hard, to handle.

And Lydia laughed again, sharply.

As if he'd just now thought of it, turning back to include McCullen in his question, Crotty said, "Would you folks like to go around the track a few times? In one of our practice sulkies? Just to see what it's like?"

Like surprised children Lydia and McCullen exclaimed together, "Yes of *course!*"

Crotty and one of his assistants were preparing to exercise, with a timing watch, a two-year-old chestnut filly who'd had a problem with a knee the previous season but was, in Crotty's opinion, in excellent shape now; a beautiful horse, Crotty said, his eyes lighting with pleasure, a first foal from Irish Princess by Rondeley, and Mr. Marks hoped for good things from her. They all did.

Shivering in the wind, which had picked up considerably, McCullen and Lydia watched as the rather skittish horse was harnessed to a black-lacquered sulky—not the practice sulky, McCullen gathered, but one for visitors, for VIPs perhaps—and fitted with a pacing hobble, and even a headbandlike cloth coil above her nostrils, and their excitement verged upon something else, apprehension perhaps, for though the sky was still that hard, bright, ceramic October blue the tops of trees writhed in gusts, and dried leaves were blowing, swirling, on all sides. Lydia hugged herself in her bulky sweater, McCullen braced himself, wishing he'd worn a sweater beneath his coat, and a hat. He asked Crotty what the red band was around the filly's snout and Crotty said, "That's a shadow-roll—so she won't get spooked seeing her own shadow on the ground." "Her own *shadow*—?" McCullen asked, but Crotty did not pick up his tone, saying, "Mrs. McCullen first, ladies first, while we warm 'er up," grinning happily at Lydia and helping her into the sulky, "—maybe you'd like to borrow your husband's gloves, Mrs. McCullen, so your fingers won't get cold." So Lydia took McCullen's suede gloves, and Crotty took up his little whip, and off they moved onto the track, and McCullen framed them in the camera's viewfinder and snapped a picture as the horse pulled them away, prancing a little, shaking her head, not quite in stride but it didn't look at all dangerous so McCullen began to relax a little, reasoning that nothing much could go wrong, at that modest speed. And that Crotty must know what he was doing.

As the sulky approached the starting point McCullen snapped another photograph though Lydia, staring fixedly at the horse's flying tail, was oblivious of him, and Crotty, smiling, affable, flicking the reins and talking to the horse, did not notice him either. Poor Lydia was hunched stiffly forward in her seat, gripping the bar in front of her with her right hand and the bar at her side with her left, holding on, it seemed, for dear life. She had been to the racetrack with McCullen only a few times—the world of professional harness-racing was entirely alien to her—though as she told their friends repeatedly, and assured McCullen, buying Navajo was "exciting," "a new adventure"—and at one of the races McCullen took her to, at Meadowlands, there had been a freak accident involving several horses and drivers, one driver bullying another and that driver refusing to be bullied and suddenly horses, drivers, bikes had spilled in a terrifying tangle, and one man had been seriously injured, and one horse's leg shattered, and Lydia had been appalled, she'd said naively that she had never dreamt that that kind of racing, not sports cars but horses, and harness-racing horses at that, could be so dangerous. McCullen had laughed and said, Every kind of racing is dangerous, otherwise why do it?

They had been married nearly fifteen years and this was the first marriage, the only marriage, for each, though McCullen had had several love affairs before meeting Lydia, entanglements you could call them, and he knew that Lydia had been involved with at least one man, seriously . . . of whom McCullen did not allow himself to think. He was not a jealous man and he was certain he wasn't any sort of possessive or proprietary man but there were things of which it was simply better for him, for him and for Lydia, not to think. Through their years together—first in New Brunswick, then in Philadelphia, then in a Newark suburb, and the past seven years in East Orange—moving each time to a larger and costlier residence—they had wanted, had hoped for, a baby; Lydia perhaps more passionately and certainly more consistently than McCullen; though McCullen had looked forward to fatherhood, had speculated dreamily of fatherhood, as a way of . . . but how to express it . . . a way of anchoring himself, knowing himself truly *here*. But there were so many other factors to consider: the market unpredictable as it was, or almost always was; whether they were really settled at any particular point, or just, as McCullen thought of it, biding time, awaiting the opportunity for another move, another upward leap. And then Lydia was thirty-seven, and then she was thirty-eight, and McCullen felt a panicked sense that time was running out but yet, almost simultaneously, a narcotized sense that time *was* running out, and perhaps it was better so. Easier, at any rate. With the passage of time Lydia had gradually stopped talking about having a baby, starting a family, though McCullen supposed she still wanted to be a mother, as he in his way still wanted to be a father, but they rarely spoke of it now and McCullen thought that best too since after all such wants and hopes, such passions, hurts, puzzles, ironies, do exhaust themselves in time, like natural forces: tidal waves, hurricanes: working their terrible devastation for a while, but only for a while.

At the last turn Crotty gave Lydia the reins and the horse immediately slowed her pace, broke stride—it was really remarkable, how quickly!—turned outward clumsily, sensing another driver, a weak-willed driver, and this too, this embarrassing moment for Lydia, McCullen could not resist photographing. So skittish and easily panicked in some ways, horses were so damned smart in other ways, McCullen thought, approvingly. You had to show them who was master at once. There could be no hesitation.

Then it was McCullen's turn, and Lydia gave him back his gloves, and took the camera, her face flushed, her eyes shining behind the dark lenses; and McCullen climbed into the sulky; and Crotty flicked the reins; and off they went, at a companionable pace, a little faster than Lydia had gone, but not really fast; though McCullen found himself sitting as Lydia had, in a stiff forward-leaning posture, one hand gripping the front bar, the other the side bar, and his head lowered. "Now girl, now girl, be a good girl, mind your manners girl," Crotty was saying, as the filly began, unaccountably McCullen thought, to shake and twist her head, yanking the sulky about, "—it's her friends over there, in that barn, hear 'em?" Crotty said, and McCullen, listening hard, could hear, faintly, horses neighing somewhere close by, and he said, "She isn't going to bolt, is she?" and Crotty said, "Naw she's got more sense, don't you girl? Hey girl? Hey *girl*? Mind your manners girl come *on*!" Then they were all right, or so it seemed, the filly back in stride, and an accelerated stride it was, the wind rushing against McCullen's face, chilling his ears, "We're going to go a little faster, going to time 'er," Crotty said, and now he was all business, and the sulky was being pulled swiftly behind the filly though even now she seemed distracted, headstrong, on the verge of bolting, "—it's the wind, those fucking leaves," Crotty said, "—damn you, *behave*!—you hear?—*behave!*" As they approached the starting point McCullen was conscious of Lydia and the other trainer watching them but he could not tear his eyes away from the horse's streaming tail and muscular haunches less than twelve inches in front of him, he had the impression that Lydia had the camera raised and the thought entered his mind, swift as a ray of light penetrating an eye, that his wife would not only witness, but would record, on perishable Polaroid stock, his very death.

Another time around the track. And another. And always the horse seemed about to bolt, or rear, or turn sharply to capsize the sulky, for not only the wind and the flying leaves but *the very tire tracks in the dirt, the very shadow of her mane and tail* evidently upset her. McCullen gripped the sulky bars so tight his knuckles ached. Shut his eyes against pellets of dirt and mud flying against him, peppering the front of his coat, his face, his stylish glasses, like buckshot. Trying to control his panic, thinking *I am not going to die, not like this. Not now, not today* recalling how in a luxurious hotel suite in Mexico City twelve years before during an earthquake that had lasted a terrifying twenty-eight seconds he had instructed himself, through the taste of bile in his mouth *I am not going to die, I am not ready to die* yet it had seemed to him that his death had been drawn from him to stand before him as in a mirror mocking and taunting the mere mortal body, and now too he knew, he seemed to know *Yes I will die: like this* his heart pounding violently, the first sharp tinges of angina in his chest, and this frightened him even more, the prospect of pain, real pain, of suffocation, of terror, of death. Yet at his side Crotty took no heed, continued to urge the damned horse on, chuckling and scolding C'mon girl faster, let's see it, mind your manners, miss *c'mon*, and McCullen could not speak, fear encasing him like ice, a fear not only of dying, and dying in a paroxysm of pain, but that he would, in Crotty's presence, and in the presence of his wife, simply break down: disintegrate as a man.

Then, to Crotty's horror, the little airplane reappeared overhead, flying low, as if for a prank, and of course the skittish horse reacted at once: almost veered from the track. McCullen's eyes, shut tight, flew open, sightless. But still Crotty took no notice of his passenger's anguish, urging the horse on with sharp clicks of his tongue, scolding, cajoling like a lover, and apologizing to McCullen—how absurdly!—for the horse's "bad manners." It seemed to McCullen that the horse was, if not crazy, crazed: listing from side to side: tossing her head: as if struggling to free herself of the burdensome sulky—of harness, blinders, hobble, shadow-roll—the weight of the men behind her. McCullen's angina attack was a sequence of pains, stabbing pains, more severe than any he'd ever had, and not only had he not brought his pills with him, his glycerine, he hadn't remembered to store some in the car in case of emergency, and now this was an emergency, and the pills were one hundred miles away in his home in East Orange. And the pain was increasing. And he was breathing desperately, sucking in air, oxygen, no matter the dirt-pellets thrown up against his face, no matter the humiliation, the shame. And still the fancy black-lacquered sulky flew forward. And still the track flew beneath them. And still Crotty, oblivious of McCullen, urged the filly on, *using his whip.*

Why didn't he tell Crotty what was happening to him, why didn't he ask Crotty to stop, yes but he couldn't, he could not, simply could not. Paralyzed as sky—track—horse's pounding hooves—windblown tail jolting about him, mixed with the ferocity of the wind, that drew tears from his eyes; seeing there at the side of the track, again, his wife Lydia and the assistant trainer waving, smiling as if this was great sport, a festive occasion, beautiful self-assured Lydia in her purple scarf and dark glasses, Lydia in designer jeans, a woman McCullen scarcely knew whose body he had imagined he'd possessed now raising a camera with ring-glittering fingers to record her husband's collapse. Yet in the next instant the sulky had flown past, they were circling the track another time, Crotty using his stick-like little whip, dear God it would never end. McCullen sat hunched, head lowered, as if to ease the pain in his chest, telling himself he was not going to die, don't be absurd, not like this, not like this, trying to see the humor of the situation, a cartoon-humor you might say, the filly's head not only veering drunkenly from side to side but now her tongue was protruding from her mouth!—lathered, flecked with foam, a look of madness, frenzy. By this time both McCullen and Crotty were covered with dirt, and the sensation in McCullen's chest was no longer a single pain but a dense network of pains like electrical charges, a spider's web, a sheet of ice fracturing along unknown fault lines. He understood: he was helpless in the face of death, all men are helpless in the face of death, for the wild ride would not end except in death, *there is nothing to be done but endure it.*

And he would never see Navajo again. Never see his own horse race.

*   *   *

"Is it—?" Lydia saw his deathly-pale face, his expression of pain as he climbed from the sulky, hurrying to him to slide her arm around him, and McCullen murmured, "No, no I'm fine," quickly, to forestall her alarm, and the unwanted solicitude of Crotty and his young assistant. How old he must seem to them, how *other* than they, so at ease in their bodies, and masters of these untamable, unknowable animals! He shrank from their eyes, he was curt, abrupt, giving the excuse of a stomach cramp, nothing serious. By now, now that he was on solid ground, out of the sulky and off the hellish track and his own man again, the pain had lightened, and he could breathe much better. Crotty asked did he want to come inside to lie down, did he want a glass of water, McCullen waved him away thanking him but no, no: they had to leave. Sorry, so abruptly they had to leave. They'd be back another time.

Knowing that Crotty and his assistant were watching them walk to the parking lot. Watching, as McCullen moved his legs with such caution, leaning, not quite conspicuously, on Lydia's arm. But at the Mercedes he knew Lydia must drive, not he; he wasn't in a condition to drive. "Just sit back, calm yourself and be very still," Lydia whispered, her face taut, eyes bright and alert, and she helped him buckle the seat belt and she drove them to Netcong, located a drugstore and hurried inside and, after twenty maddening minutes, the pharmacist managed to get through to McCullen's doctor in East Orange so that he could fill a prescription for McCullen for a four-ounce vial of glycerine pills.

And then McCullen was sitting, eyes shut, in the Mercedes, in the passenger's seat, a seat to which he was not accustomed. And Lydia was tense beside him, Lydia who loved him holding his icy hand hard as they waited for the pill to dissolve under his tongue, and to melt into his bloodstream, into his body, to be carried to those tricky arteries circling his heart, feeding his heart, though, as McCullen assured Lydia, assured her repeatedly, in a hoarse voice, he really was all right now—really, he was *all right.* He had not died on the track and he would not die in the Mercedes and in another few minutes he might be capable of driving the car and in fact he would insist upon it, as soon as his breathing was completely under control, and the eerie chill gone from his hands and feet.

Smiling suddenly, opening his eyes, McCullen said, "He was beautiful, wasn't he," and Lydia said, squeezing his hand, saying, half-angrily, "Yes. He was. Beautiful."

The Handclasp

He saw something in her face she had not known was there.

He gripped her shoulders, gently, not hard, as if to comfort, or to constrain, and asked, "Is it beginning again, Edith?" He was a kindly man, they had been married for twenty-two years. Edith said quickly, guiltily, "Is what beginning again?" and Mark said, "You know," and Edith, beginning to be frightened, though she spoke calmly enough, lips vacant as a ventriloquist's, said, "But I don't know," and, not seeming to realize how she contradicted herself, "—I would tell you, wouldn't I, if it was? Beginning again?" and Mark, staring at her, said, "Would you?" The moment passed like a bubble in the heart.

The Gotschalks, Edith and Mark, had friends who owned a seventeen-year-old West African gray parrot.

What an exquisite bird!—standing about twenty inches tall with pearly-gray sculpted feathers, and tail feathers a bright arterial red, but the parrot had plucked a ring cruelly bare around its neck, picking out feathers one by one with its chunky hooked beak and dropping them on the floor of its cage, and Edith asked, "Oh but why?—it's so beautiful, why would it want to disfigure itself?" and her friend said, "Out of boredom, I guess, or loneliness—we're away so often," and Edith asked, "But how can it—she?—manage, reaching around so far with its beak?" and her friend reached his arm boldly into the large brass cage so that, after a moment's hesitation, the parrot chose not to stab at him but to leap familiarly onto his arm and walk up the arm, using its beak to haul itself along, as if wounded, until, splendidly, the parrot was out of the cage and on Edith's friend's shoulder, and he said, "She has an amazingly elastic neck, don't you Gigi?—she can turn her head almost three hundred sixty degrees. Show us, Gigi?" he said fondly. Edith stared half in fascination, half in dread, as the parrot twitched, jerked its head, opened and closed its beak as if compulsively, showing its tongue, an arched squirming tongue twisting inside the beak as if with its own life, but the parrot did not stretch its neck to demonstrate the neck's elasticity nor did the parrot flap its wings, which seemed odd, so Edith asked, "Doesn't it—she—fly?" and her friend said, stroking the parrot's crested head, "Oh—caged parrots' wings are always clipped," and, not seeming to realize how he contradicted himself, "Gigi forgot how to fly years ago, haven't you Gigi?" And Edith Gotschalk stared and had no more questions to ask.

Edith Gotschalk was in the habit, sometimes, of getting in her car and driving. In no particular direction, and with no particular destination.

One morning in early autumn she found herself driving in the Poconos, high above the Delaware River. Thinking, I'm happy, and she was happy, in her car, drawn by something she could not have named but knew, the beat of happiness in the brain like an artery swelling to burst.

Clear simple facts, and pleasure in these facts: that the mountainous area through which she drove had a name, and the wide froth-splashed river had a name, men had named all things, and mapped them, or so they believed. And this season too with its hard blue sky, tarnished gold of leaves like coins carelessly scattered on the slopes: "autumn."

Edith parked her car on one of the convenient scenic overlooks, and walked, for hours. Until she felt sweat run in chill rivulets down her sides and back, beneath her cotton shirt. How happiness frightens us. She had no idea where it came from, or why; or to what it might lead. Or had led.

How, in such places, the margin of what's human dissolves.

No name and no face. No maps really. You can forget not only who you are but who you are supposed, elsewhere, to be.

Still, Edith Gotschalk came back, that day, and others. She always did. Happiness swelling in her brain to the point of bursting but not, quite.

So the danger passed. Unless it was the season that passed.

She was a writer and an adjunct university instructor: she had her work. Even when not working (as she was not working now) she had her work. And she had her friends; and the comforting routine of her life; and most of all, for only from this source could redemption come, she had her husband of twenty-two years who loved her and did not judge her harshly and built, blowy winter evenings, crackling birchwood fires in their fireplace so they could sit together on the sofa reading, or watching the flames, fingers clasped dreamily together. It's just that I can't bear it, Edith thought. The effort.

Kronberg the lawyer from Detroit represented a party named Koenig and the similarity of the names, their harsh Teutonic sound, was irrelevant but, for a moment or two, distracting.

Kronberg shook Edith Gotschalk's hand and pretended to have knowledge of her books, admiration for her talent and all that, perhaps he'd heard of her name before this, perhaps not, she was that kind of writer: known, but not known. She cared not in the slightest for strangers' acknowledgment of her work or that wisp of smoke, her reputation, no more than she cared for it herself, these fading winter days. The effort of following one breath with another, walking into a room with a backbone erect and personality reasonably in place was quite enough for her to concentrate upon, take pride in. "An honor!" said Kronberg, who had fattish lips and a frank friendly disingenuous smile, fading red hair, gravelly baritone voice, and Edith Gotschalk smiled at him in return, and laughed.

Kronberg had telephoned from Detroit, a mysterious mission, yes he might come to see her in her office at the university (the university was a distinguished one, the office large, sparely furnished, drafty), and as soon as the flattery was out of the way, business at hand, he asked if Edith remembered a young man named Roger Koenig who had been a student of hers in Detroit in the mid-1970s. And Edith said she thought, yes, the name was familiar.

Kronberg frowned, as if disappointed. "No more than the name, Miss Gotschalk?"

Edith said, "In fact I'm Mrs. Gotschalk."

"Ah! Sorry!"

Edith tried to think: sat at her desk pressing her fingertips against her eyelids in an effort to summon, out of the depths of years, a face. The name "Roger Koenig" was hauntingly familiar but had ambiguous associations. She seemed to recall an earnest, persistent young man, something melancholy about him, that air of febrile hope tinged with despair characteristic of many young people, particularly young men, who imagine themselves to be artists of some kind. But Edith could not recall his face.

She said, "The mid-1970s were a long time ago."

She did not care to think how much of her life she was forgetting, had already forgotten. Great chunks of irretrievable time washed away like a seacoast riddled with erosion.

"In a sense, yes," said Kronberg. "In another, it might have been yesterday."

He provided Edith with a photograph of Roger Koenig, a formally posed yearbook photograph, and Edith recognized the face at once, boyish, very young, a look to the mouth as if the teeth didn't quite fit the narrow jaws, but those intelligent eyes, yes. Edith said, "I remember him now. He was a good student."

Kronberg said emphatically, "He *was*, indeed. His records bear that out." Now Edith was given transcripts to examine, which she rapidly skimmed, with no idea why she was doing so, noting, in fact, that Roger Koenig had grades of C scattered amid the columns of A's and B's: he'd been a good student perhaps but nothing more, at even the modest university in Detroit in which she'd taught for several years.

Kronberg was saying, ". . . He took three courses with you, Mrs. Gotschalk, as you see, received A's in all three. In his journal for that period he speaks of you often, with enormous respect. Of all his professors you were the one who most touched him . . . changed his life."

Edith glanced up at the mention of a journal. She said, uneasily, "You speak of him as if it's all past tense."

Kronberg sighed, said with a sober shake of his head, "I'm afraid—yes. Young Roger Koenig is dead." After a pause, "That's why I'm here, Mrs. Gotschalk."

"Dead?"

And he'd only just now been made to come alive for her.

"Why that's . . . terrible," Edith said. Strange how tears of immediate sympathy flooded her eyes. "How did it happen?"

Suicide, she thought.

"Yes," said Kronberg, "it *was* terrible. And needless. He was undergoing surgery in Detroit Memorial Hospital a few weeks ago, minor surgery to repair an abdominal hernia, and he died on the operating table as a consequence of an anesthetist's error. A tragic death . . . a clear case of malpractice." Edith continued to stare, eyes brimming with tears like pain. Childless herself, she responded to news of others' children with an almost visceral sympathy. "His parents are devastated with grief, as you might imagine. They've retained me in their suit against the guilty parties: the anesthetist, the surgeon, and Detroit Memorial Hospital."

"I see," Edith said slowly, though in fact she did not.

For some minutes Kronberg talked. He was impassioned, articulate. As if arguing before a jury he denounced the hospital, the hospital's attorneys, the current state of medical ethics. Edith nodded, murmured in agreement, it might almost have been that Kronberg with his morose eyes and flashy necktie and gravelly voice was Roger Koenig's father, the proper object of commiseration. When Edith interrupted finally to ask, "I'm sorry—but what has this to do with me?" it seemed, in the context, a rude question.

Kronberg said, "Roger's parents strongly believe that their son was a writer of unusual promise, and that his literary career was ended before he had a chance to prove himself. You recognized his talent while he was still an undergraduate, Mrs. Gotschalk. He'd published a few short pieces in little, local magazines but it seems to have been a long, ambitious novel he was working on for years, it might have made his reputation when it was published, catapulted him into—" Kronberg was taking portions of a heavy manuscript out of his briefcase, an alarming quantity of paper at which

Edith Gotschalk stared as it was set down on her desk. ". . . Your encouragement was the single most influential factor in this young man's career decision," Kronberg was saying, his breath now audible, "—the Koenigs told me how he used to talk of you, 'incessantly,' they said; and there's the evidence of the journal, as you'll see. Because of your kindness in giving him criticism and advice Roger Koenig decided not to go on to graduate school as he'd planned but to stay home and help in the family business—the Koenigs own a small hardware store on Grand Boulevard—and devote himself to his writing. It was a brave decision and who knows what success this gifted young man might have had except for this terrible, absolutely terrible medical blunder!"

Edith, staring at the piles of manuscript, felt a wave of sickness rise in her. It would fall to her, fittingly, to read this material—maybe to help get it published?

Kronberg said, "And Roger was an only son."

"How old was he when he died?"

"Thirty-four."

"Thirty-four!" Edith remembered a very young man, scarcely more than a boy.

Now that the lawyer's briefcase was empty he sat back, crossed his legs, clasped his hands over his knee, spoke as if conspiratorially. "The court will require some estimate of this unfortunate young man's probable earning power over the course of his career had he lived, as everyone expected him to, a full and productive life. As an expert witness, Mrs. Gotschalk, you could be extremely helpful. If you might, after you've read some of Roger's work, give us a sense of his probable reputation had he lived to complete the novel and publish it . . . ranking him, if you can, in terms of contemporary writers . . . novelists whose names the court would recognize. Not their incomes, of course; I can take care of that."

"Wait," Edith said. "Let me get this clear: you want me to help you . . . in the trial?"

"The Koenigs are depending on you. They are absolutely stunned with grief and—they're depending on you."

"You want me to 'rank' an unknown, unpublished writer in terms of . . . ?"

Seeing the expression of incredulity in Edith's face, Kronberg said hurriedly, "In terms of commercially successful contemporary American writers, Mrs. Gotschalk. Updike, Vonnegut, Styron—" his voice trailed off vaguely, "—writers of your own 'literary' quality who are nonetheless popular. Who make good livings by their writing."

Edith protested, "But Roger didn't publish anything while he was alive—he doesn't even seem to have finished this novel. How can anyone possibly expect—"

"The grieving family is depending upon you, Mrs. Gotschalk, for the literary side of the case," Kronberg said, an air of subtle reproach in his voice. "Of course, we have abundant medical evidence that the death was an error—*that* won't be difficult to prove. In malpractice suits of this sort it's common procedure to make an estimate of the deceased's probable earning power over the course of a normal lifetime. In terms of—"

Edith interrupted, "Mr. Kronberg, I can't be a party to this."

"What do you mean, Mrs. Gotschalk? 'Can't'—?"

"Roger was only an undergraduate student of mine. I'm sure I didn't do anything more than encourage him as I've encouraged countless students over the years. It's a teacher's duty to encourage—"

"But not falsely, I hope?"

"Of course not falsely! But—I've been teaching since 1971, I've had literally hundreds of students. I wasn't even in contact with—"

"Roger wrote to you, four times. You never replied."

"I . . . don't remember that."

"*He* did. He kept a record."

Edith sat very still and pressed her fingertips against her eyes. Now the danger of tears was passed, she dreaded bursting into laughter.

Kronberg said carefully, "I should have made it clear, Mrs. Gotschalk, that any expenses you incur while helping us will be paid promptly. Should, for instance, the court require your testimony in person."

He paused. He asked warily, "Is something wrong, Mrs. Gotschalk?"

Edith said quietly, "Much is wrong, Mr. Kronberg."

Kronberg did not seem to hear. He was already on his feet, energized, prepared to leave. "I'll leave Roger's manuscript with you: you can't make any decision until you've looked at it. Fair enough? I'll telephone you in a few days and we can talk. After all, Mrs. Gotschalk, it was your encouragement that inspired this young man to devote his life to his art . . . you were his model, his guiding star, so to speak. You were," Kronberg added ominously, "responsible."

Edith shivered.

But she was a polite woman, politeness in the very set of her bones, she walked Kronberg the lawyer from Detroit to her office door and kept her ironic smile to herself, a little pulse of fury in her throat. She even shook hands with the man, as if a deal of some sort had been struck.

Backing off, Kronberg said with a smile, "You'll enjoy it: it's fascinating material!"

Edith asked, "You've read it?"

Kronberg hesitated for the merest fraction of a second.

"Let's say I've looked into it," he said.

Hundreds of manuscript pages, many of them poorly typed (and poorly photocopied); outlines, scribbled notes, paragraphs broken off in mid-sentence; here and there X's drawn through passages of text with such violence the original paper seemed to have torn. The novel, titled only "Work-in-Progress," was in fact not a single work but a discontinuous, episodic narrative in which insubstantial characters disappeared, reappeared, changed their names, clearly written at disparate times, with no effort to unify sections or provide transitions. There were lengthy, sometimes beautiful lyric descriptions (of skies, landscapes, city scenes, the Detroit River); there were sequences of dialogue running for as long as thirty pages at a stretch spoken by unidentified characters. Bursts of inspiration flanked by pages of inert prose like isolated flares of light in the dark. Even the journal entries were haphazardly organized as if the writer were unable to bring himself to read what he'd written, only pushed on. A terrible manic energy propelled him forward but there was no retroflexive energy urging him back. Edith thought, sickened, Did he give up his life for this? Am I responsible?

Her head rang with pain and self-recrimination but she continued to read, the door of her office locked so she couldn't be interrupted in her task, her duty, her obligation . . . then it was night and the telephone rang and Mark asked what was wrong, why hadn't she come home and she told him the situation, I'll be home when I'm home, please don't wait up for me. She turned from the incoherent narrative to the journal, noting with embarrassment the numerous checked passages (checked by Kronberg?) in which a woman professor named "E.G." appeared, in lengthy unpunctuated entries for 1974 and 1975. Her face heated; her heart beat painfully against her ribs; for here was a vision of herself, a younger, lost self, an elusive presence filtered through the eyes of a dead youth who had not only taken courses with Edith Gotschalk but audited other courses of hers, read her novels and short stories with intense, uncritical admiration, followed her about. Even her clothes were described . . . an old camel's hair coat, a crimson scarf . . . white angora gloves. The portrait of Edith Gotschalk was a preposterous one: "brilliant woman," "genius," "mind like darting flames," "the most decent & kind-hearted & perceptive & <u>beautiful</u> human being I have ever encountered." There were asterisks and rows of exclamation marks in the text. Edith thought, through a haze of pain, or was it happiness beating in her brain like pain, He loved me, he loved his idea of me, now we're both dead.

She glanced up to see him, the doomed boy, a shy but persistent figure lurking about her office door. He'd waited for her after her lecture class, he'd walked with her on the stairs, across campus. Talking excitedly of Camus . . . of Genet . . . of Peter Weiss's *The Persecution and Assassination of Marat as Performed by the Inmates of the Asylum of Charenton Under the Direction of the Marquis de Sade* . . . modish works everyone had imagined would endure forever. Outside of class, Roger Koenig was eager, talkative, stammering in excitement; inside class he'd tended to sit silent and brooding, frowning as if in disagreement with his professor. Or had it been so profound a sympathy he could not bring himself to speak.

Roger Koenig. Soft damp hopeful eyes. A defensive, ironic smile. The lower part of his face narrow, receding, with a look of defiant weakness. Yet he wasn't an unattractive boy . . . young man. Yet she'd liked him. (When she thought of him: for of course at this time in her life, in her late twenties, she'd had many other things to absorb her. A husband, an ambitious career. A love affair approaching its zenith.) She'd been kind to Roger Koenig, tirelessly annotating his long, rambling course papers; commenting tactfully, always constructively, on his creative work; offering as much criticism as she gauged his sensitive nerves could bear; giving him grades just slightly higher than his work probably merited. She had not the heart to disappoint or discourage for Roger Koenig had been one of those students who tries so hard, so piteously hard . . . a shadowy image, as in a distorting mirror, of Edith Gotschalk herself for whom the effort of writing, like the effort of resisting madness, was so exhausting that no degree of public acknowledgment, or acclaim, or honor, or, indeed, the commercial success Kronberg understood she'd never won, could ever compensate.

Am I to blame? I, the "genius"!

One windy November day Roger Koenig was lying in wait for Edith Gotschalk, yes, it came back to her now, a memory of that encounter, one of their final encounters out of class, he'd seen quite clearly that, caught up in a mood, or simply tired, in a hurry, Edith didn't want to talk but there he was alongside her, chattering away, plying her with questions, a shy stubborn suitor. Yes and Roger Koenig had a habit . . . it came back to her forcibly now . . . of shaking hands when saying goodbye, and that day, in the university parking lot, a dark gritty wind howling about them, he'd thrust out his hand, bare, small-boned, peremptory, and Edith had hesitated just a fraction of a second before shaking it, she'd been impatient with his talk that afternoon and his persistent trailing of her and she'd hesitated just long enough for him to notice then shook his hand firmly and vigorously as if nothing were wrong.

And in parting she'd told him, quite seriously, a gentle sort of warning, "Don't expect too much from a 'literary career,' Roger," and Roger Koenig had responded with nervous boyish laughter, "Oh, I always expect too much!" Doomed boy, hair blowing in his eyes.

*   *   *

"But why should you feel upset?—least of all *guilty?*" Mark asked, staring at her. "If you haven't given this what's-his-name a thought in fifteen years?"

Edith composed a tactful, formal statement to read to Kronberg over the telephone, but, when they spoke, she became suddenly emotional, angry. "I'm sorry: it's just impossible. I can't in all conscience testify that Roger Koenig would have completed this novel, got it published, made money,"—hearing her voice begin to falter, "I can't in all conscience testify to the quality of his talent."

Kronberg said reproachfully, "But you did encourage this impressionable young man, Mrs. Gotschalk, we have ample evidence of that."

Edith said, "I admit I was mistaken—I'm hardly infallible."

Kronberg said, "You could be served a subpoena under these circumstances," but Edith knew he was bluffing, how absurd to threaten her, and she said, "You wouldn't want my testimony, Mr. Kronberg," and there was a moment's silence, Edith could see the man's thick lips shaping a silent obscenity, could hear his harsh breath, then he said, "Well. So be it. Sorry to have wasted your precious time, Miss Gotschalk," and Edith said, "How much are you suing the hospital for?—I'm just curious," and Kronberg said, "Thirty million."

Christmas came, too swiftly; and New Year's. Occasions where public gaiety is required. The Gotschalks did their part, entertained relatives, gave a party for their many friends amid a frenetic cycle of similar parties. "Circles of winter warmth," Mark observed, with a smile. His tone was not ironic.

Childless, the Gotschalks needed their friends, at least in theory.

Childless, the Gotschalks never aged. At least in each other's eyes.

On New Year's Day Edith said to Mark, as if conversationally, "It's strange isn't it . . . how some of us are dead, and some of us aren't."

Mark winced, and said, "An odd way of putting it."

"It's an odd situation."

When the incident involving Roger Koenig was fresh and raw and thrummed along her nerves Edith had discussed it with Mark, for of course Mark wanted to talk about it with her, the Gotschalks were a couple who shared all things save those things unspeakable and unsharable. He'd told her it was absurd to feel guilt; yes the medical blunder was unconscionable—a man of thirty-four going to sleep on an operating table and never waking up; but such things happen all the time, the world is a capricious place. Yes, said Edith. And if, before that, he'd wasted his life working on something he couldn't complete, in a field for which he seems not to have had enough talent, whose fault was that? Surely not hers?

Yes, said Edith. You're right.

Feeling the fissure begin to open in her brain.

In childhood these spells or fugues were her secret place about which she never spoke, but they were mild enough, then, to have been diagnosed as moods by others; Edith was a "high-strung" child. In adolescence she'd cultivated them to a dangerous degree as a sign of her specialness, in young adulthood she'd resisted them as a sign of her normality. Now in her mid-forties she began to feel that her normal consciousness was stunted and diminished, and only the other, the bouts of happiness, of happiness sharp as pain, were real. Regarding her husband who was the kindest most reasonable most practical-minded of men, sane as a white-walled room blazing with lights, she thought, Please let me go, stay away from me, I don't want to involve you in this.

But he was involved of course, and years ago, when Edith had gone for nights without sleeping, would not speak with anyone except him and, with him, only vaguely, in a flat, indifferent voice, clearly suicidal, clearly in need (Mark had believed: Mark believed in such things) of professional care, he'd insisted upon taking her to a doctor, a psychiatrist, in Detroit; and the doctor had prescribed pills for Edith, barbiturates as it turned out, a single dose powerful enough to fell a horse and yes certainly they were habit-forming, within two weeks an addiction, so one day

Edith in desperation emptied the container into the toilet and flushed it quickly before she could retrieve the pills with her convulsively shaking fingers.

Never again would Edith go to a psychiatrist for help, never she vowed, and Mark, humbled in guilt, could not protest.

It was happiness that was not happiness, as an eye-piercing beam of light is not light but blindness.

Still, Edith had no other name for it: the fissure opening in her skull pouring radiance through her, a paralysis, an obliteration. . . . All directions are equally futile. All human action to no purpose.

In January there were many days of bright fierce sunshine: hard-crusted snow underfoot, razor-sharp blue skies and nowhere safe to look. Edith thought of the parrot's twisty coiled tongue inside its beak that opened and closed . . . opened and closed. She thought of Roger Koenig hidden away in a room of his parents' house transcribing his life into a work-in-progress with no coherence, no end. She thought of "Edith Gotschalk" and "Roger Koenig" as a drowned couple locked in each other's arms, it was a dream image perhaps, retrieved from a night of unhappy dreams.

Without having discussed it beforehand with Mark, Edith decided not to teach the spring semester at the university, as she'd planned. "I want to concentrate on my own work," she said. Adding, "My work that's going so badly."

Though she knew, or should have known, that long hours of winter solitude would not help her concentration but merely free her to sit for unclocked minutes staring mesmerized at the trees outside her study window . . . and, as darkness came on, her own ghostly reflection in the window pane. She felt how her soul might slip out of her body to fly *there*.

In the evening Mark asked, concerned, "I tried to call you five or six times today, Edith—weren't you here?"

Edith said, "I must have been outside."

"All day? Did you drive somewhere? Where were you?"

She hadn't heard the telephone ring, or, hearing, had immediately forgotten. She said, "I'm sorry. I must have been outside."

Mark regarded her doubtfully. He was a tall big-boned man, creases deepening around his mouth and eyes, his love and dread of her evident in his face. "I don't believe you, Edith, I'm sure you were here, you simply didn't want to talk to me and I'd like to know why."

Then let me go, Edith thought.

She said, "Maybe you shouldn't telephone home, then. I don't like to be spied on."

On a counter in her study, in several piles, was Roger Koenig's "Work-in-Progress" (Kronberg had not wanted the photocopied material returned, perhaps he hoped Edith would have a change of heart), and sometimes, thwarted in her own writing, Edith reread sections of it. She no longer judged the quality of the writing but read to lose herself in the act of reading; hearing the dead man's voice, the idiosyncratic cadences of his speech, in his language. But the face was fading.

Edith wished bitterly that she'd asked Kronberg if she could keep the photograph, but she hadn't.

Belatedly, in February, she wrote to the Koenigs, a simple condolence letter. Of course, she made no mention of the lawsuit or of her inability to help them; nor did she, after all, though she'd wanted to, request a photograph of the deceased young man. Her letter was handwritten, only three brief sentences but it took her a full afternoon to compose.

The Koenigs never replied. Edith thought, Of course, they blame me for their only son's death. Why should they reply!

"Edith, please. Get rid of it. I insist."

"But it's irreplaceable."

"For your own good, darling, will you?—*I'll* do it, if you can't."

So Mark threw out the unwieldy manuscript. Edith gave in knowing she could retrieve it from the trash, which, that night, quietly, stealthily, as her husband slept, she did.

And this time she was shrewd enough to hide it where Mark would never find it. Even if he suspected her, which he didn't. She scattered the pages through her files containing her own work, from 1964 to the present.

*   *   *

Through that interminable winter Edith often lay awake in the
night listening to deer grazing outside the bedroom windows. At
first, the sound was alarming, as if a trespasser were approaching
the house, then it became routine, strangely comforting. How
shy-sounding, how tentative the deer's hooves in the hard-crusted
snow . . . white-tailed Virginia deer exquisitely beautiful in even
their dun-colored winter coats. (By now the fawns, born in June,
were old enough to have lost their delicate patterned stripes.
Though distinctly smaller than their elders, they were no longer
immediately recognizable as fawns.) In the Gotschalks' neighborhood there were small herds of famished deer, a plague to home-
owners, capable of destroying shrubs and ivy with the voracity
almost of locusts; Edith did not want to think of them as preda-
tors, nor even as suburban nuisances, for they were so beautiful
after all. Above all she did not want to think of them as starving—
starving because overbreeding. Somehow the idea of Roger
Koenig was bound up in her mind with the grazing deer: Edith
heard the deer outside her bedroom windows and found herself a
moment later thinking of the dead boy. In a state between wakefulness and sleep Edith thought of Roger Koenig as if he were,
not a person, nor even a dead body, but a living force; a palpably
living force snug-fitting in her as an eye in its socket, a fetus in
her womb.

Oh Christ save me. If I could believe. Help me, help him.

It was a windblown night in March that, listening to the deer
in the snow outside the windows, Edith understood suddenly that
she could bear it no longer—the happiness that was no happiness, the terrible pulsing in her brain that never reached climax.
She slipped out of bed careful not to wake her sleeping husband,
seeing how his face in repose was younger than the face by
which she knew him, by day.

She went into the bathroom. She opened the medicine cabi-
net, avoiding her bright damp eyes in the mirror. She took out a
razor blade, one of those thin aluminum blades that seem harmless, being so thin and so light.

I'm not this kind of person, Edith reasoned. *I must act quickly.*

Her bladder ached, with anxiety. So she had to use the toilet first, and listening to her urine splash in the bowl she thought, At least that works; and flushing the toilet she thought, At least *that* works. And she laughed, knowing how inconsequential it was whether she continued living, or died; whether she died, or continued living. But now that she had begun, now that she had the razor blade in her hand, she was obliged to go through with the gesture. Once the momentum was initiated, it could not be stopped. She held the small thin blade with surprisingly steady fingers and drew it lightly, a feather's touch, lengthwise against the inside of her left forearm, as if she were sketching. And poised there she heard Mark's footsteps, and his voice, "Edith? Honey? Are you in there?" turning the doorknob which was locked, and in sudden shame Edith dropped the razor blade into a wastebasket. She hadn't any choice goddamn it except to unlock the door since he would break it down if she didn't.

She unlocked the door, and opened it. And there stood her husband blinking and suspicious, frightened, knowing by her eyes the condition of her soul. For he knew her, he knew her deeply, with an intimacy she could not bear. Saying, "Why are you *here*, Edith? Come back to bed, will you?" and Edith said angrily, "Why don't you let me go, Mark, for Christ's sake you know it's hopeless, there are people like me who are hopeless, what is there is you that won't let us *go*," and he led her out of the bathroom and sat her in a chair, so strange to Edith to be sitting in this chair in the middle of the night, in her nightgown. She was sobbing, she was mortified, she was furious with this man for bringing her back again, another time. As if he too had no choice. Saying to her, gently, "You'll be all right, darling. Trust me, you'll be all right."

How tired she was: the long nights, weeks, months of being tired, yearning for sleep.

Mark was close beside her murmuring to her, comforting her, stroking her hair, her bare shoulders inside the nightgown, and Edith felt herself give way to him, leaning suddenly forward onto a table, her head on her arms in abject weariness. She slipped off the edge of a pale-glittering surface like ice, she was in dark rushing water being borne away. Always, they'd promised it would be sleep. As when Toby had had to be "put to sleep" his stomach bunched with tumors and his beautiful eyes fever-glazed and

Edith was instructed not to cry, not to cry it's only sleep as the needle was injected into her vein so she'd thought with relief she could always sleep, a profound relief to know yes she could always slip away and sleep, and now in this house she could scarcely remember except to know it belonged to a late part of her life and that she'd been happy here she seemed to have fallen asleep leaning her head in her cradled arms but she slept only a few minutes in this awkward position waking dry-mouthed and disoriented, frightened as a child, and her hand was firmly clasped, someone gripped the fingers tight in his and would not let her slip away.

So that was how it was, that night.

The Girl Who Was to Die

The girl who was to die wasn't a girl any longer but a young woman of twenty-four, with a small, shapely, perky body and a china-doll face that, to Beverly Crystal's eye, was almost too small, the perfect features too squeezed together, like a midget's. She was a nurse at Yewville General Hospital and in her trim, white nylon uniform, gauzy white stockings and spotless white lace-up shoes, her honey-brown curly hair shaken loose from her nurse's cap, she looked striking, out of place in the Crystals' gloomy living room, sitting on the old Italian Provincial sofa, toes just touching the carpet, speaking in an earnest, breathless, little-girl voice. Her name was Audrey McDermitt and she was a friend of Beverly Crystal's stepdaughter Ednella from high school, though Beverly hadn't known the girls were so close.

It was late afternoon of November 6, two nights before her death, that Audrey McDermitt dropped by the Crystals' to visit with Ednella. Beverly, who observed the girls in the living room, uncertain at first whether to come out and say hello, hadn't known whether Ednella had invited Audrey to stop by after her hospital shift or whether Audrey had invited herself. Beverly's relations with her deceased husband's twenty-five-year-old daughter were amicable and warm, for the most part, but not intimate; Beverly could chat companionably with Ednella about many things, then offend her with the most inadvertent innocent question, if it touched upon something private. So Beverly wouldn't have asked about Audrey McDermitt for fear of drawing some quick, quiet, coldly hurtful rebuff from Ednella. She was never to ask.

That day, a Wednesday, it was dark by 5:45 P.M. Beverly, upstairs, had heard someone come in the front door, had been hearing voices, muffled laughter, assumed it was Ednella and a visitor; and so came downstairs by the back way. (The Crystals' house, in which Beverly and her stepdaughter now lived by themselves, without Wally Crystal, Beverly's husband and Ednella's father, to connect them, was one of the old, spacious, well-kept Victorian houses on Church Street. It had a broad staircase off the front foyer and a narrow, steep, almost ladderlike staircase at the rear, off the kitchen.) Beverly in flannel slacks and a strawberry-pink hand-knitted cardigan appeared at the doorway of the dining room, smiling hesitantly in the direction of Ednella and her friend in the nurse's uniform that looked so dazzlingly white. Beverly wondered, Would the girls like some coffee? tea? something sweet? It was like Ednella not to have thought to offer her visitor anything. But neither took the slightest notice of Beverly, they were so intent upon their conversation. Audrey McDermitt was saying in her hushed, little-girl voice, "—so I said to him, I was crying, but I was damned mad, too! I said, 'Mister, if you think so low of me, maybe I just better give you this back right now,'" making a weak tugging gesture at the ring on her left hand, and Ednella asked something in a soft, wondering voice that Beverly couldn't hear, and Audrey said, with a nervous giggle, "Well, then, *he* started crying! Said he'd kill himself, blast his head off with a shotgun, if—"

What on earth were the girls talking about, Beverly wondered. There was the McDermitt girl fluttering her hands, her small face heated and self-important, like a face on afternoon television prettily made-up for some dramatic purpose, and there was Ednella Crystal who usually scorned her former high-school classmates, as she scorned most Yewville residents, dismissing them as provincial, narrow-minded, dull—Ednella in a chair facing Audrey, leaning far forward, elbows on knees, chin resting on clasped hands, staring at her friend. Ednella was a lean knife-blade of a girl with dark ironic eyes and dry, sallow skin. She was between jobs at the moment, and had not been out of the house all day; she wore the shapeless beige corduroy slacks she'd been wearing for weeks and a much-laundered, shrunken sweatshirt that emphasized her gaunt, flat torso. Beverly winced, seeing that damned sweatshirt on Ednella: it was steel-gray with an insipid, faded image of Mickey Mouse on its front and the letters VASSAR COLLEGE fanning beneath. A memento, and a ridiculous one, of Ednella's undergraduate college where, for all the girl's intelligence and talent, she'd come close to not graduating with her class. (Poor Wally, still alive at the time, had to make several urgent telephone calls to the college president, to get things straight. Beverly never learned just what the problem was.) Ednella was, in Beverly's eyes, a beautiful young woman, far more striking in appearance than the little McDermitt girl who resembled a kewpie doll; but she wore no makeup, neglected her limp, fine black hair, seemed more naturally inclined to frown than to smile, and was unpredictable in her moods. For instance, Beverly could never have predicted that she would come downstairs to find Ednella in an intense conversation with Audrey McDermitt, of all people.

Audrey was saying, breathlessly, wiping at her eyes, "Damn it, he *knows* there isn't the least reason to be jealous. Of Ron Carpenter, of all people! What girl would look twice at Ron, if Harvey Mercer was in the room! My goodness, Ron and I have known each other since fifth grade, and now that Ron's mother has chemotherapy at the hospital, and Ron brings her, we just naturally see each other, and if I have time we talk. Ron's worried sick about his mother, and—"

Ednella leaned farther forward. She had taken acting lessons at Vassar and had had a year of law school at Albany; there was often something histrionic and coiled about her. "That's all?" she interrupted. "Just 'talk'?"

"Well—we've had coffee in the cafeteria together, once or twice," Audrey said. She crinkled her little-girl's face in appeal. "And, I guess, he drove me out to Piketown"—Piketown, named for a local road, was the area's largest mall—"once, after my shift. But—"

"Did someone tell Harvey?"

"I guess so! Goddamn it! You know Yewville—such a damned small town." Audrey paused, wiping at her eyes with a tissue. Her pretty face shimmered with tears as if about to dissolve. "The thing is, he scares me. Harv, I mean. I love him and I can't live without him and that's never going to change no matter what my parents say, but—"

Ednella said, nodding, "Harv doesn't mean it really, he's just a hot-headed guy. I could talk to him, maybe. I could explain."

"Oh, Ednella, I don't know!" Audrey said. "He respects you, I know that, but if he even guessed I was talking about him behind his back, saying I was scared of him, he'd—well, maybe take it as betrayal. That's a word he says all the time now—'betrayal.' "

Ednella continued in a low, intense voice, as if she hadn't heard. "He just needs someone to *explain*. Someone he can *trust*." Ednella had run her fingers through her hair so that it looked spiky and electrified, as if with the urgency of her thought. "Harvey isn't superficial like most people, he's *deep*. Passionate, and *deep*."

At this moment, just when Beverly had decided she had better not intrude, and might just retreat quietly back into the kitchen, Audrey McDermitt glanced up and saw her. Immediately she cried, "Oh, Mrs. Crystal! Hello!" like the sweet, good, uncomplicated Yewville girl she was; her smile seemed genuine, though her eyes glittered with tears. Beverly, who had been feeling so critical about the girl, now felt a rush of affection for her—my goodness, she *was* pretty, and quite winning in her nurse's uniform. Ednella, turning to squint at Beverly, did not smile, at first, at all—blinked and stared at her stepmother, the handsome, soft-spoken, easily wounded fifty-three-year-old woman with whom she shared the house, as if, for a long pained moment, she failed to recognize her.

Then, with coolly forced animation, "Hello, Beverly! Come in! You know Audrey, of course?"

So Beverly, blushing, had no choice but to come forward and join the girls. She smiled warmly, graciously, hopefully. (If she'd been stung by Ednella's greeting, the dissonant sound of "Beverly" where, at another time, Ednella might have murmured, "Mother," she gave not the slightest sign.) She switched on a second lamp. "You girls, sitting in the dark!" She asked them, putting the question to Audrey in particular, would they like some coffee? tea? something sweet? "It wouldn't take me but a minute to get things ready."

There was such appeal in Beverly's voice, her eyes behind her new mother-of-pearl glasses so hopeful, Audrey McDermitt hesitated a moment before saying apologetically, "Oh, thank you, Mrs. Crystal—but I'm just on my way. In fact—" a quick glance at the wristwatch on her child-sized wrist, "—I'm *late*."

And she jumped up, with a high-school cheerleader's energy, and was on her way.

After the girl had gone Beverly asked Ednella what was wrong, for of course it was only natural for her to ask under the circumstances; even as she dreaded her stepdaughter's probable response. But Ednella surprised Beverly by saying, thoughtfully, "You can see why she's a nurse, can't you—just as, in high school, she was a cheerleader. That bounce. That optimism." Ednella shook her head, as if mildly disapproving, yet in wonder. "Even with her life at risk—Audrey is what she *is*."

Beverly was astonished. " 'Life at risk'? What on earth do you mean, Ednella?"

Ednella shrugged, headed for the stairs. "I can't say, Beverly. I can't violate Audrey's confidence. Anyway, probably I'm exaggerating—you know me."

"But, Ednella—"

Beverly stared after Ednella as, lithe and springy on her feet as a wild creature, she bounded up the stairs, taking them two at a time. She called back over her shoulder, almost gaily, "You know *me*."

In fact, Beverely didn't.

She knew that she admired her stepdaughter, yes, and she felt a strong if inchoate emotion for her, with which Beverly's hope of being accepted at last in Yewville was naively bound up—but she would not have said she knew Ednella Crystal, really. Nine years ago, brought to the house on Church Street, Yewville, as Wally Crystal's new wife (his second wife, the first, Ednella's mother, had died when Ednella was four years old), Beverly had told Wally, "Your daughter is a special person—I can see it in her eyes!" But Wally, gruff, good-natured, vaguely embarrassed, had turned the compliment back upon Beverly. "Ednella? Hell, she's just spoiled."

Which was true, Beverly supposed. But only a fraction of the truth.

When Beverly was first introduced to Ednella, by Wally, it was only a week before the wedding. The girl was sixteen, but looking much younger. Her skin was fair, but mildly blemished; her eyes were clear, dark, beautiful, but marred by an expression of subtle derision. Her hand in Beverly's was cool, limp, unresisting; her cheek, kissed, was cool too, impassive as marble. In bleached jeans and a black turtleneck sweater, Ednella had stood straight and tall, as tall as Beverly, gazing at her imperturbably, as Beverly nervously chattered. Then she'd interrupted, as if gently. "You know, all this isn't necessary—really."

"What isn't necessary?" Beverly asked.

"All this *trying* so hard."

Beverly stared at the girl, speechless. She had never been so hurt. So cut to the quick. So found out. So helpless. Forty-four years old, a woman of some independence; never married; shortly to be the bride of a well-to-do small-city banker whose name she had not known twelve weeks before. But how to reply to his daughter? How to define herself to this eerily composed child who seemed to be looking not at, but through her? Beverly stammered, "I—don't know what you mean, Ednella. *'Trying'?*"

Still imperturbed, the girl said, as calmly as if she'd memorized the words, "You're here to be my father's wife, Beverly. Not my mother. My mother has been dead a long time and everyone has adjusted."

But I love you, Beverly wanted to plead. *I want to love you.*

It seemed the most improbable, in a way the most mysterious culmination of her life as a woman—to discover herself, in middle age, anxiously courting the moody daughter of a woman she had never known.

How clumsy it was, how supremely mawkish! Like an oversized package Beverly had to carry everywhere with her, fearful of setting it down and misplacing it.

She was to be Wallace Crystal's wife for only five years, but those five years would alter the course of her life irrevocably. Now, years after his death, she was known in Yewville as Wally Crystal's *widow*; as, while he'd lived, one of the town's most prominent citizens, she'd been Wally Crystal's *second wife*.

Not that Beverly minded, of course. She was very happy in Yewville, if lonely. Her life before marrying and coming here had not been a happy one, nor even clearly defined.

Yewville was curious about Wally Crystal's *second wife*, but not really interested in her. Even the women Beverly wished to count as friends. "Where's your family?" "Where're you from?" "*How* did you and Wally meet?" Their questions were prying, but never deep. Beverly answered them simply and honestly, knowing herself on trial. (But for what?) Virtually every answer she gave misrepresented her, for her marriage to Wally Crystal had been anything but calculated; in fact, it had come about sheerly by chance.

They had met on a Caribbean cruise, of all unlikely places: the first Wally had ever taken, and so very reluctantly, in his life. (As he would confide in Beverly, he'd had a heart attack the year before, not a serious one but a heart attack nonetheless, and it had "scared the bejesus" out of him. He'd wanted to do something romantic, extravagant, before it was too late.) Beverly herself was on the cruise in the role of "social director"—her first voyage too, and in a position she'd accepted in desperation for a job. (On this issue, Beverly blurred the precise facts in speaking about herself. She'd been trained as a teacher of high-school French but, somehow, through the course of humbling, exhausting years, had never found a teaching position that was suitable; or, if suitable, permanent. Where a school board was eager to hire a teacher of her qualifications, she was reluctant to be hired; where she would have wished to be hired, budgets suddenly evaporated, and French-teaching jobs. But how to explain this, without sounding defensive? self-pitying? a failure?) On the tackily expensive cruise ship amid the over-bright days and the balmy, calypso nights, enjoying a distinct advantage because of her age (Beverly, at forty-four, was perhaps the youngest woman on the cruise), she'd somehow cultivated a bubbly outgoing personality, at odds with her real personality; she was the ship's "social director," after all. With stylish frost-tipped hair, chic new glasses, an ascending laugh of sheer uncomplicated gaiety, Beverly had won over, within a few hours, the lonely, homesick, brooding, slightly dyspeptic Wally Crystal, who hadn't understood, he confided in Beverly afterward, how badly he wanted to be married again, until he'd seen her.

Which was flattering, wasn't it? Of course it was.

Wally Crystal was a man of evident means, if little formal education, in his early fifties: near-bald, heavy, though not fat; with a weatherworn, lined, ugly-attractive face, a froggish sort of face, slack-jowled, but shrewd about the eyes, intelligent. (That intelligence, an unmistakable ironic sharpness of the eye, Beverly would note in Ednella. But little else of Wally.) He had the gruffly shy manner of a man accustomed to ordering employees about, but uneasy in social situations involving women. His most common expletive was a nervous expulsion of breath, "Well!—*well!*" and a wide, strained helpless smile.

Beverly had known at once, seeing him: *widower.*

Beverly was an attractive woman whose youth had passed rapidly by, like scenery glimpsed from a speeding car. Where it had gone, she did not want to think. Yes, she'd had romances in her life ("romances" being a kinder word than "affairs"), but she had never married; she had never had a child. It was too late for the child but not too late to marry and, mildly drunk, Beverly accepted Wally Crystal's proposal not with an air of startled gratitude, which might have alarmed him, but with that newly acquired ascending laugh that sounded like crushed ice being dropped into a glass. It bespoke marital good times, uncomplicated bliss. It bespoke a future.

True, Beverly was not in love with Wally Crystal. The man was not—had he ever been?—the kind of man with whom a woman might be in love. But she grew to like him, very much. In time, she grew to love him. And then, after a second heart attack, in their sixth year together, Wally died.

So Wally Crystal's *second wife* became Wally Crystal's *widow.*

At that time, after having dropped out of law school, Ednella was living in New York and working as an assistant stage manager at a small theater in SoHo. She was twenty-two years old and had stayed away from Yewville since her father's remarriage, except for brief visits at holidays and during the summers. (At which times she was unfailingly polite, if rather cool, with her father's new wife. The three syllables of "Bev-er-ly" sounded in her mouth like a droll foreign word, each syllable equally stressed.) When Beverly telephoned Ednella with the news of her father's death, Ednella screamed at her and slammed down the receiver. Later, when Beverly managed to speak with her, Ednella did not cry but was raving, incoherent; as it happened, Ednella herself was ill, had been seriously ill for days, with what would be diagnosed as mononucleosis. In the midst of funeral preparations, Beverly flew to New York to bring Ednella home. She nearly fainted, seeing her beautiful stepdaughter skeleton-thin, with enormous scared eyes in a ravaged face. (Beverly's first panicked thought was that the girl had AIDS.) On the plane coming home, Ednella leaned weakly into Beverly's arms, calling her "Mother."

The shock and the pleasure of the word passed through Beverly like an electric current.

Afterward, yes, and fairly frequently, the two quarreled; or, rather, Ednella quarreled with Beverly. But that was all right. That was to be expected. Beverly consoled herself, *I can wait.*

SEVERAL TIMES DURING THE DAY following Audrey McDermitt's visit to the house, Beverly was aware of Ednella on the telephone; not that she eavesdropped on the extension, of course. (Beverly was too respectful of Ednella's privacy to do such a thing. Besides, quick-witted Ednella would have detected her at once.) In the early afternoon, lifting the receiver to make a call of her own, Beverly happened to overhear a man's voice, a snatch of some slurred, sarcastic words: "—expect me to believe that shit? I—" Beverly replaced the receiver at once, as if it burnt her fingers.

So far as Beverly knew, her stepdaughter was seeing no man, or men, at the present time. There had been no one in Yewville in recent memory. Ednella had remarked to Beverly that she'd long ago outgrown her contemporaries in Yewville; in New York, she'd "overdosed." Her wan, ironic, rather wistful smile suggested that the situation was not ideal, but Beverly had not felt welcome to inquire.

In high school, Ednella had had no boyfriends, but she had cultivated passionate friendships with two or three boys. To Beverly's surprise, the boys hadn't been the kind one might have expected Ednella Crystal to associate with—boys who, like Ednella, were taking college-entrance courses—they were rough, coarse, problematic types, prototypical dropouts, losers. Aggressive, masculine. From backgrounds very different from her own. One of them, Beverly suddenly remembered, was named Harvey Mercer—whom Audrey McDermitt had mentioned the previous day. A tall, blond, hulking boy with unkempt hair and Presley-style sideburns and a stubbled chin, good-looking in that way of swaggering adolescence that so quickly loses its edge. Ednella had spent weeks, or had it been months, helping Harvey Mercer rebuild a car after school and on weekends: she'd chattered excitedly of two cars to "wreck" and one to "build" and "V-8 engines" and "hot-wiring" and "stripping" and "sanding" and "painting with primer" and the "pick-up" the car would have when finished. Wally had been annoyed that Ednella seemed so willing to devote her energies to an effort of the kind, but he'd supposed it was harmless as long as the garage was well ventilated (Ednella assured him it was: she knew better than to breathe in stripper fumes); Beverly worried about Ednella, so naive for all her surface sophistication and intelligence, being gang-raped one terrible day by Harvey Mercer and his buddies. But to confront a girl of seventeen with one's wishes for her well-being, still less her future, was, Beverly knew, ill-advised. Of Harvey Mercer, Ednella would say, with a defiant, mysterious smile, "We get along. There's no bullshit with *him*."

Nothing came of such friendships, in the end. Not so far as Beverly knew. There must have been a day, an hour, when Ednella Crystal realized that she wasn't—finally, ultimately—wanted; when a car having been test driven, and brought to its highest level of performance, it was used to impress other girls, a vehicle for romance, passion, sex. The swaggering boys with sideburns went out with girls very different from Ednella Crystal: if they were lucky, girls like Audrey McDermitt.

At six o'clock on November 7, a drizzly dusk smelling of winter, Beverly heard a car pull up in front of the house, and saw Ednella, bareheaded, run out and get inside. The car's headlights were on, its windshield wipers in operation. Wasn't that Audrey McDermitt's little VW? Perplexed, Beverly watched out the vestibule window for some minutes; then, unable to resist, she clumsily draped a raincoat over her head, hurried out to the car, rapped on a window, smiling, admonitory, hopeful—"Girls! Please come inside! It's so nasty out here." The young women stared blinking at her as if she were a fantastical apparition. Ednella's expression was severe, and Audrey seemed to be crying, a lighted cigarette in her fingers. The interior of the little car was hazy with smoke.

Ednella rolled down her window a grudging inch or two. "Beverly," she said, her voice trembling, "Audrey and I are having a private conversation. *Please*."

"Oh, I know, I'm sorry, but I thought—"

"Please."

So, her cheeks burning, Beverly retreated to the house.

Thinking, *Why don't they need me? I'm a woman, too.*

Thinking, *Nurses of all people shouldn't smoke.*

It was to be the last time Beverly Crystal would see Audrey McDermitt alive.

That evening, though Beverly prepared dinner as usual, Ednella refused to sit down at the table with her. She was much too excited, distracted. When, at 10:20 P.M., the telephone rang, she hurried to get it (downstairs: Beverly sitting in the television room, staring without interest at a BBC-made rebroadcast of one or another English-style soap opera of the monied classes, heard her rapid, surprisingly heavy footsteps overhead); minutes later, to Beverly's astonishment, she hurried down the rear stairs, and would surely have rushed out of the house without a word of explanation, or even a shouted "Goodbye!" if Beverly, breathless, had not hurried after her. "Ednella, what on earth? Where are you going?" she cried.

Ednella turned to her as if, indeed, she'd forgotten that she shared the house with another person. Beverly saw that Ednella was flush-faced, and breathless; she'd shampooed and brushed her hair so that it shone, and she was wearing trim black wool trousers and a scarlet Shetland pullover. How severe, yet how attractive, she looked! Carelessly she said, "I'm going to talk with him—Audrey's fiancé. The one who's so jealous. They need me, it's urgent, I won't be long. Don't wait up for me, Beverly? Please?" She was already at the back door, car keys rattling in her hand. Beverly called after her, "Ednella, dear, *who*? *Who* are you going to talk to?"

Ednella called back over her shoulder, annoyed, but elated too, "Just don't wait up. *Please.*"

Beverly did not dare wait up for Ednella; but, of course, she was unable to sleep. Where had the girl gone, what danger might she be in! The ghostly luminous dials of Beverly's bedside clock, the slow hands circling the face, exerted a morbid fascination upon her. Midnight, 1:05 A.M., 2:40 A.M. . . . at last, car headlights swung across the bedroom ceiling, Ednella's car turned into the drive. Beverly had been in such a state of apprehension that, released, she nearly wept.

"Ednella. Thank God."

She heard Ednella enter the house by the rear, quietly. Heard footsteps in the kitchen. Quiet. As if in stealth.

It would occur to her later that Ednella must have refrained from slamming her car door shut. To spare waking her. To spare disturbing her any further.

Beverly rose from bed, slipped on her bathrobe, went soundlessly to the rear stairs. Then, seeing that Ednella had not switched on the stairway light, and that the only light was at the foot of the stairs where the kitchen door had been left ajar, Beverly realized that she must not intrude; must not let Ednella know that she was awake at this hour, and so clearly waiting for her. Yet she could not resist descending the stairs, as quietly as she could. Her heart was beating painfully hard. She would tell herself afterward that she had not been spying on her stepdaughter: she had only wanted to see, with her own eyes, that Ednella was all right.

I loved her . . . love her. Where was the harm.

As Beverly cautiously neared the foot of the stairs, she was puzzled to hear Ednella murmuring to herself; she heard the girl's quickened breath, the opening and closing of the refrigerator door. A rattling as of ice cubes? Then, abruptly, Ednella was speaking over the phone, in a low, urgent voice, "Audrey? It's me. Yes. Yes, it *is*. Listen!—*he* is." A pause. Beverly listened, fascinated. She drew closer, peering through the doorway at a slant. Where was Ednella? The kitchen telephone was a wall phone, and Ednella was leaning against the sink, the cord stretched almost horizontal. "I've been there all this time. Sobered him up—made him drink black coffee—talked him out of—you know." Another pause. A deep, exhilarated breath. Then, more animated, as if she were trying to talk reason into a stubborn child, "Give him a call, say you're coming over. He's waiting. He keeps saying he isn't 'worthy.' We won't ever know how serious he was, I guess—'Blowing his head off.' My God! He was crying off and on. Said he was so ashamed! Didn't know what in hell came over him, hurting you like he did, but he knew—" here there was another pause, a quick intake of breath as if Ednella were suppressing a sob, or laughter, "—knew he loves *you*. Wants to marry you. If—"

Part in fascination, part in dread, Beverly drew closer to the doorway, seeing, then, an extraordinary sight: even as Ednella was speaking so passionately to Audrey McDermitt over the telephone, the receiver gripped tight between her shoulder and her chin, she was leaning back against the sink, spine arched, head dropped back and eyes shut in a pained sort of euphoria; she'd drawn her bright-colored sweater up, baring her breasts, small, hard, faintly bluish breasts with childlike nipples, and she was rubbing several ice cubes against them, in slow languorous circular motions. As the ice melted in contact with her heated skin it ran in glistening rivulets down her midriff.

Beverly stared, shocked and uncomprehending.

The thought came to her, unbidden, *Has Ednella had sex with that girl's young man!*—even as she knew this was not likely. No, it was not likely.

Beverly shrank back from the doorway, anxious now not to

be seen. Quickly turned, retreated up the stairs as silently as she'd come down. Returning to her bed, exhausted, dazed, ready for sleep. Seeing the time on her bedside clock: a few minutes before three.

She's safe! She's in the house! That's all that matters.

Next day, by noon, word had spread through Yewville: Audrey McDermitt had been killed by Harvey Mercer, who had then apparently (so eyewitnesses claimed) killed himself by deliberately smashing his car against a concrete abutment a few miles north of Yewville.

Even as local television and radio stations were issuing news bulletins of the "tragedy"—variously known as the "double tragedy" and the "lovers' tragedy"—Yewville residents, acquainted with the young people, were telephoning one another, stopping one another on the street, in stores. The sheriff's office was beginning its investigation. It had not been until Harvey Mercer's death at 9:20 A.M. that a search was made for Audrey McDermitt, who had failed to arrive at the hospital for her shift that morning, and who had not been home the previous night. Audrey often stayed with her fiancé Harvey Mercer in his rented house on the south side of Yewville, according to her family, and it was there, amid the wreckage of Mercer's bedroom, that her badly bruised naked body was found.

The coroner's report would list strangulation as the official cause of death. The young woman had died sometime between 4:00 A.M. and 5:30 A.M.

Audrey McDermitt, nurse, twenty-four years old, 1985 graduate of Yewville High School.

Harvey Mercer, employed by Valley Lumber, twenty-seven years old, attended Yewville High School without graduating.

Both had been born in Yewville. Both were survived by numerous relatives.

Both had been drinking for some time before their deaths.

The young couple had become engaged the previous April. The engagement, despite "disagreements," had not been broken.

Audrey McDermitt was wearing her engagement ring, a one-carat diamond, at the time of her death.

Police were investigating reports that Mercer, jealous of his fi-
ancée's alleged friendships with other men, had acted violently in
the past and had made threats against her life, before witnesses.

Anyone who could help with the police investigation was
urged to come forward.

Beverly, hearing the first news on her kitchen radio, at noon, was
overcome with shock and disbelief. Aloud she whispered, "My
God. No. That little girl. It can't be." She turned the radio volume
up higher, listened. She was paralyzed, she could not think.
Then, beginning to tremble, she shut off the radio. Thinking, *Ednella must not know, just yet.*

Thinking, *Does Ednella know?*

Of course, Ednella had not known. When Beverly told her the
news, Ednella stared at her uncomprehendingly; even, so very
queerly, smiling slightly, as if she suspected a joke. "Beverly,
what? What are you saying?" Beverly, her own eyes filling with
tears, repeated what she'd said, supplying what details she knew
from the news bulletin, and Ednella interrupted, panicked. "What?
What? What? You're crazy!" she cried. In an instant the blood was
draining rapidly out of her face. Her lips, already pale, were turning a ghastly sickish blue.

Beverly made a gesture as if to hold Ednella, to help her to a
chair (they were in the kitchen: Ednella had just come downstairs,
sallow-faced and groggy), but Ednella pushed away as if in terror.
She turned, ran out of the room. Up the stairs, her footsteps
heavy, pounding. Her voice lifted like a child's wail—aggrieved,
incredulous.

No. Ednella had not known.

That afternoon, Yewville police, two detectives, came to the Crystal home at 8 Church Street, to question Ednella Crystal about the
murder-suicide. Ednella had telephoned in, to volunteer the information that she'd seen Harvey Mercer the previous night; it was
possible that she was the last person (except, of course, for Audrey McDermitt) to have seen the young man alive.

Yes, and she'd seen the young murdered woman, too. Earlier

in the evening. Audrey had been desperate to talk with her, to enlist her help with Harvey; she'd driven over, and Ednella had sat out in her car with her, talking. For about an hour.

The detectives asked, gently, had Ednella been a friend of both?

"I was. I was a friend of—both."

Ednella's voice was soft, faint, toneless. Her face was mottled, her eyes threaded with blood. She wore black—a long black wool skirt, a black silk blouse with an elaborate lace collar. (A beautiful blouse, which Beverly had not seen before: bought, perhaps, at an antique clothing store in New York?) Her hair, shining still, had been brushed back severely from her face, emphasizing her sharp cheekbones and the angular thinness of her face. As she answered the detectives' questions her eyes moved restlessly over them, to Beverly; and back. (Beverly, of course, had insisted upon being present. She had a strong impulse to grip her stepdaughter's hand, tight.) The detectives were middle-aged, solid men, the elder resembling Wally Crystal—bald, with a lined, jowly, kindly face and a habit of sighing audibly. In fact, both police officers had known, or had known of, Wally Crystal. They spoke of him, respectfully, as "Mr. Crystal."

Ednella was telling the detectives, with an air of choosing her words precisely, that she had been asked by Audrey—by both Audrey and Harvey, but Audrey first—to help smooth over their difficulties. She'd known Harvey in high school, just as a friend— "We got along, understood each other"—but had been closer to Audrey since coming back to Yewville: it was strange, how friendships evolved. You couldn't predict.

The detectives asked if Ednella had gone to Harvey Mercer's house at Audrey McDermitt's request?

Ednella nodded. Her eyes were bright with tears. "Yes, I did. Audrey was so upset, crying, almost hysterical—I couldn't say no."

Had she intervened between the two in the past?

"No! Oh, no," Ednella said quickly. "I didn't feel comfortable in such a position. I—have my own life. I only did it because Audrey begged me, and I wanted her to be happy. Her, and Harvey."

Audrey McDermitt had been upset? Worried for her life?

"No, I think—I think she was worried that, because Harvey

was so jealous, and tended to exaggerate when he drank, he would stop loving her and break off their engagement. She was always saying, 'I can't live without him.' "

But hadn't Audrey McDermitt been frightened, too, that Mercer might seriously injure her? kill her? According to her family—

Ednella interrupted, shaking her head. As if this were an old issue, she said, "Audrey had to know Harvey loved her, was crazy for her. He'd gone out with other girls—there was even some married woman in town he'd see—but he was in love with Audrey, and that was that. He wouldn't have hurt her—I mean, under ordinary circumstances."

These hadn't been ordinary circumstances, last night? Why?

"I—really don't know. I—" Ednella paused, wiping at her eyes. She spoke slowly, falteringly, "—don't *know*. They'd always had a stormy relationship. Harvey is—was—well, passionate. Hot-headed. And he'd gotten a drinking problem, I guess you'd have to say. And Audrey was so pretty, flighty—she didn't always know the effect she was having on him, how jealous she could make him." Ednella paused. Then said, almost bitterly, "She knew, but didn't *know*. Didn't let on."

Had Audrey McDermitt been going out with other men? Had there been any basis for Mercer's jealousy?

"No! Not really. And I told him so. I tried to kid him, I said, 'Don't be stupid, Audrey loves *you*. These other guys don't mean anything—to a girl like her, friends are a dime a dozen.' " Ednella laughed sharply. Then, more soberly, "At any rate, he seemed to believe me. By the time I left—"

But hadn't Ednella been worried, meeting Mercer like that? At his house? Alone? When he'd been drinking? When he'd already knocked Audrey McDermitt around, and threatened her life?

Ednella shook her head, annoyed. "Of course I wasn't worried. Not *me*."

But why not?

Ednella said impatiently, "Because he was my friend! My buddy. We got along." A pause. Ednella's lips twitched. She glanced over at Beverly, with a look of confusion and grief. "My God. I can't believe I'll never see him again! Either of them! *I can't believe it*."

Yet the detectives persisted: Ednella hadn't been afraid of Mercer, last night, only a few hours before he was to murder Audrey McDermitt, and take his own life?

"I said, *no*! Not *me*. Harvey would never have killed *me*—he didn't love me." Ednella smiled ironically. As if baiting the detectives, she said, "A man has to love you to kill you—right?"

But the detectives merely snorted with quick laughter, an obligatory and fleeting mirth.

They persisted: when Ednella had left Mercer's house, he was showing no signs, so far as Ednella could detect, of potential violence? He'd calmed down?

"Yes! Definitely. I'd swear."

So Ednella's intervention had helped, she'd thought?

Ednella gnawed at a thumbnail. Her eyes were clouded with doubt, fear. "That's what is so—horrible! So—unbelievable. I'd told Harvey just to get some sleep, he looked terrible, really strung-out, he should get some sleep and see Audrey the next day—call her in the morning. I'm wondering now if somebody else got to him—some of his friends, maybe. Poisoning him against her. You know how guys can be. When I left him, he shook my hand and thanked me. He really did. There were tears in his eyes. My God! Poor Harvey! And I was feeling pretty good about it! My God!"

And when had Ednella left Mercer?

At this, Ednella blinked. She was sitting very straight and poised in her black wool skirt, her black silk blouse with the exquisite lace collar. The faint bruised crescents beneath her eyes gave her an air of ravaged dignity. Ednella met the detectives' gazes levelly, and said, "Let's see: Harvey telephoned around 10:30, sounding desperate, and I drove out to his place right away afterward; I was talking to him for, maybe, an hour; maybe a little more." Ednella paused. She was breathing quickly, almost eagerly. She said, "I—was back here by about midnight, I guess. I—went to bed. I'd gotten Harvey to promise he'd call Audrey in the morning, *I* didn't want to call her, I didn't want to be involved any further in such a private, intimate matter, so—I went home, and I went to bed. I guess—around midnight. I was so exhausted—" Ednella's voice trailed off, childlike and forlorn.

There was a moment's silence. Then, as the detectives were about to continue, Beverly said, quickly, "Yes—it was around midnight." She had been sitting unobtrusively to one side, hands clasped in her lap, head racked with pain, and now she spoke, helpfully, yet with an air of apology for interrupting. "I'd been asleep, but Ednella's car turning in the driveway woke me. Five minutes after twelve, I think."

The detectives nodded, and smiled, and believed her, for why should they not?

She was Wally Crystal's second wife, Wally Crystal's widow: a handsome middle-aged woman in a good magenta jersey dress, mother-of-pearl eyeglasses, black patent leather shoes. She was immaculately if fussily well-groomed. Her silver-blond hair was permed; her just perceptibly softening face was lightly powdered; she wore a pale coral lipstick. The detectives, smiling at her, saw this woman. Ednella, staring, might have seen someone else.

When the detectives rose to leave, Beverly was the one to see them to the door; Ednella remained in the living room, sobbing bitterly. The detectives thanked Beverly and apologized for disturbing her and Ednella: it was simply routine, part of their investigation, which would probably be completed in another day or two. The case, after all, was open and shut—cases of murder-suicide usually were.

Beverly winced, and managed a weak smile. "Oh, yes! I can see how they would be."

Just don't wait up for me, Beverly. Please!

This time Ednella had run out of the house in silence. Beverly, hearing her pounding feet on the stairs, had not called out after her, had not so much as glanced out a window at Ednella's car as it was backed, swiftly, recklessly, out of the driveway.

Prowling the house, the empty house. Not waiting, nor even thinking of the fact that she was not waiting. There was a glass of tart red wine in her unsteady hand and perhaps, after the two massive headache pills she'd swallowed down, that was unwise?

How swiftly dusk had come, and then night. November was

gusty and damp. Leaves were blown against her windows with a sound suggesting giddiness, hilarity. Already, the girl had been dead more than twelve hours.

"It doesn't seem possible."

Where had Ednella gone, well, she did not know, nor care, where Ednella had gone, that was none of her business. Shortly after the detectives left, Ednella had fled (possibly to visit with the McDermitts? to share their grief? Offer commiseration? Or was she, more likely, simply driving into the country, into the night?) and it was none of Beverly Crystal's business. They were not related by blood, nor by sentiment. That was a fact, an implacable fact, Beverly had not wanted to know.

A life consists of many facts, implacable facts, you do not want to know.

Beverly Crystal, a widow, prowling a strange house in the dark. As if she feared putting on lights. Feared what she might see.

Just don't wait up for me. Please!

She had not had so blinding a headache since Wally Crystal's heart attack. Finding him groaning in the upstairs bathroom, telephoning for an ambulance, trying to keep the hysteria out of her voice. They'd come for him within five minutes, taken him away. Brief, brave, doomed hours in the intensive care ward of Yewville General Hospital.

Beverly, who are you? I'm just curious.

Who am—?

Who are you, beside my father's widow?

Why, what a thing to—ask!

And in the hired limousine, bringing them back to Church Street from the cemetery.

Beverly, stunned, had blinked at her fierce, cruel, beautiful stepdaughter not knowing whether the girl's question was sincere or meant, simply, to hurt. She'd managed a smile, she'd drawn a deep breath. *Do I have to be anyone? Anyone special?*

Her head was throbbing, the capillaries heated, swollen! Yes, surely it was a mistake to be drinking (was this Beverly's third glass?) after taking such powerful medication—but who would know?

"No witnesses."

She was going to go to bed, but, somehow, she did not go to bed. Somehow, another time, to her disgust, there she was, in the television room, watching, again, local television coverage of the deaths. It was 11:00 P.M. So late. Mesmerized, watching. The empty creaking house and a woman in nightgown, bathrobe, watching. What?—images of the dead. Familiar images at which one stared in the hope of—what?—that they might come alive, refute the fact of their deaths? These were mainly reruns of tapes shown earlier, yet they exerted an irresistible spell. Blurred with tears. "Oh, damn!"—the wineglass tilting, spilling. Beverly was too dizzy to pick it up, staring another time at pretty Audrey McDermitt in her blue-and-gold cheerleader's costume, in her gravely black high school graduation costume, now, so proudly, in her crisp, white nurse's costume, a cap smartly set on her honey-brown curly hair. Smiling her dazzling smile for the camera, for a television audience she could not see. Not hearing, either, the newscaster's solemn voice-over speaking of funeral arrangements.

And here were images of the "murderer-suicide" Harvey Mercer. None so formal or posed as those of the victim, none in any kind of uniform. In one snapshot, the husky young man, dirty-blond hair worn long, stood leaning against the hood of a car with over-sized tires (was this the car Ednella Crystal had helped Mercer re-build? Sanding, stripping, painting, polishing? As if her young life had depended upon it?), grinning at the camera. In another snap-shot, a close-up, Mercer smiled almost shyly, his arms tightly folded across his muscular chest. A handsome young man, but with something too intense about him. Furrowed forehead, heavy eyebrows, blond-glinting stubble on his jaws. *A man has to love you to kill you—right?*

In fact, Beverly did remember Harvey Mercer. Not by name, but by appearance. She'd seen him occasionally in Yewville, on the street, in a store; she seemed to recall he'd worked for a while at one of the local service stations where she went for gas. Of course, he had not known her as Ednella Crystal's stepmother. He hadn't even seen her, probably.

Beyond the excited buzz of the television set, there was the sound of a door quietly opening, shutting. Footsteps?

"No. Never again."

Beverly shut her eyes. It was a way of keeping the tears from running down her cheeks. She wasn't drunk, she was just very sad. She *was* crying, but no one would see. Having grabbed from somewhere (the hall closet? but much larger than she recalled the closet being) that heavy, soiled, quilted L.L. Bean coat of Ednella's the girl hadn't worn for years, and she was walking swiftly, half running, along the alley behind the house, the darkened alley where Church Street residents or their servants set out garbage and trash cans for the twice-weekly pickup, snowflakes melting against her heated skin and *Where am I? why am I here?* panting staring frightened at the shadows surrounding her, she was a girl of eleven or twelve again, in a distant city, returning home from school at dusk, wintry dusk, in lightly falling snow peering into the lighted houses of strangers, catching glimpses of unknown, inaccessible lives, warm-lit kitchens, parlors with their shades not yet drawn (sometimes, even as Beverly stood on the sidewalk staring, a man or a woman would come to pull the blind: so casually excluding her!), she was not crying but she was staring in resentful longing, yes, in envy, yes, in a kind of bitter love, for her own home was not a happy home—*Don't! don't think of that!*—so she would not think of it, for she was also a mature woman, an adult, staring astonished into the rear of a kitchen where a young girl, breasts bared, was leaning back ecstatically, eyes closed, rubbing something glistening against her heated skin, and Beverly knew she should look away; but could not.

What did you tell him? Did you let that girl die? Did you let that girl die?

"Beverly?"

The voice was so faint and hoarse, Beverly would not have recognized it.

She opened her eyes, disoriented. Her headache was blinding. For a moment she did not know where she was. In the doorway stood Ednella, staring at her. The girl's hair was disheveled, her face pale, ravaged, ugly, eyes bloodshot with crying. Simulated laughter sounded raucous and demented from the television set.

This, then, confusedly, was what happened.

By a gesture of grief and repugnance, Beverly indicated that she did not wish to speak with, no nor even look at, her distraught stepdaughter. Ednella, stung, turned away at once, and retreated back along the darkened corridor, to the kitchen. For some minutes Beverly remained where she was, seated on the sofa, trying to get the better of the throbbing pain in her head. Aloud she murmured, "No. I won't. I don't have to." Elsewhere in the house there was silence. Had Ednella run out again? Beverly saw that there was nothing else to be done, she found herself already in motion, though moving unsteadily, back to the kitchen where, looking as if she'd been slapped hard in the face, Ednella was sitting at the table. Seeing Beverly, however, Ednella rose, came eagerly forward, whispering, "I—didn't mean—I never meant— Oh, Mother!" She burst into tears. She was shivering convulsively. Beverly found herself embracing Ednella, comforting her, even as the girl gripped her tight, tight, to the point of pain. She was murmuring, "It's all right, dear, it will be all right, I love you." For that was the one thing she knew, amid all that she didn't.

June Birthing

She was one of those who had always believed that mere chance is unworthy of changing a life. But this is how it happened.

Driving home from work that sun-splotched June afternoon thinking how orderly, how newly happy her life, quiet, private, protected from hurt; smooth as the asphalt country highway over which she drove her car so frequently she had almost ceased to see her surroundings—hilly farmland bordered by deciduous trees, fields luminous at this time of year with white-blooming wild rose, the deep ditch beside the road dense with cattails. She was thirty-seven years old and believed she had earned this privacy, this protection. And turning onto the narrower gravel road that led, in a sequence of uphill curves, another two miles to her house, she saw something moving by the side of the road, and at once braked the car to a stop. Something moving, something living. Her first panicked thought was *A baby? Abandoned?*

There, in damp flattened grass at the shoulder of the road, was a new-born fawn.

Kathe approached the creature in amazement. Incredibly, it was no larger than an adult cat. The smallest deer she had ever seen. It was motionless now, though alive; regarding her with large, unperturbed moist brown eyes; its smooth furry coat was freckled and streaked with white. It seemed to be lying on its knees, its head lifted. "Poor thing!" Kathe murmured. "Where is your mother?" She crouched beside the fawn, uncertain what to do. It did not appear to be injured but it was obviously too young to be separated from its mother. Had it been abandoned? Had the mother deer been injured, frightened away by dogs, struck by a car? Hunting was forbidden in this part of north central New Jersey but deer were frequently struck by cars on rural and even suburban roads, the deer population had so increased in recent years.

Kathe was crouched trembling with excitement on the shoulder of the road, staring at the baby fawn which in turn stared back at her. So small! So vulnerable! It could not have been more than a few hours old. Kathe saw no sign of any other deer, no movement in a field of tall grasses and wild rose that lifted to a woods some distance away. She was thinking, *I must do something, I must do something,* but the immediacy of the tiny creature, its extraordinary physical beauty and terrible frailty distracted her, scattered her thoughts like a flock of birds frightened by a gunshot. Strange how she was trembling, as if for a moment she'd actually thought the fawn might be a human baby, abandoned here by the side of the road; delivered, by the madness of chance, to *her.*

Another vehicle approached, taking the curve fast; seeing Kathe's car, the driver hit his brakes, his van skidded a few yards and stopped. A door swung open, a man called out angrily, "Goddamn, what's going on here? This curve is blind—I almost hit you."

The stranger appeared behind Kathe, breathing quickly. A big man in work clothes, torso like the trunk of a thick tree, brawny bare forearms and a broad, heavy-jawed face, dark-tinted glasses flashing light. There was something familiar about him and his mud-splattered Toyota van but Kathe did not know him and his ferocity, his male disgust, made her wince. When he drew nearer, however, and saw the baby fawn in the grass, his expression softened. "Is that a *deer*? Is it alive? My God."

Kathe said quickly, "It's alive, it hasn't been injured. It's just *small.*"

The man whistled, squatting nearby. "It sure *is.*"

Kathe was greatly relieved that the man was sympathetic. He was even willing to confer with her about what should be done.

Clearly, the fawn couldn't be left here by itself—it would shortly die, or be killed. The man suggested an animal shelter in Schuylersville, a country town seven miles away—"They'd know what to do with it." Kathe was surprised and grateful that this stranger should be taking an interest in the tiny creature as intense, or nearly, as her own.

It seemed they would go to the animal shelter together. Neither had exactly agreed yet here was Kathe removing the keys from her car ignition and locking the doors.

When she tried to lift the fawn in her arms, however, it began to tremble violently and made a frantic bleating sound. Kathe was in a sudden terror it would die at her touch, its tiny heart might stop.

The man squatted beside her making cajoling clucking sounds to comfort the fawn. After a moment he carefully slid his hands, which were big work-callused hands, beneath the fawn, and gently lifted it. The fawn was small enough to fit in the palms of his cupped hands.

He has been a father, Kathe thought. He's had experience with babies.

Kathe climbed eagerly into the Toyota van, whose motor was still running. The van was mud-splattered along its passenger's side and it was not a recent model but it appeared otherwise in good condition. Kathe pushed aside a jacket, and sat on the high front seat, positioning her knees so that the man, his breath still audible, as if he were mildly asthmatic, set the fawn tenderly into her lap. She was not thinking of the strangeness of this adventure, its dreamlike abruptness and shifts of action. She was not thinking there might be some danger to herself in so trustingly climbing into a stranger's van. Instead she stared as if hypnotized by the tiny creature entrusted to her, trembling in her lap. It had ceased to struggle and was gazing at her with fine-lashed liquid-brown eyes. So beautiful!—the miniature eyes, nose, muzzle, pert upright ears—the smooth fine honey-colored fur—the slender folded legs, no more than six inches long, and the perfect miniature hooves—the animal's blood-warmth and the pulse of its rapidly beating heart: Kathe had never seen, had never held, in her arms, anything so extraordinary.

The man, the burly stranger, climbed up beside her into the van with a grunt and backed the van around so that he could continue on the country highway north and east to Schuylersville. It was past six o'clock but the summer sky was flooded with light as if it were midday. A warm fragrant breeze smelling of wild rose blew through the van's open windows, cooling Kathe's warm skin. She felt feverish. Her heart was beating uncomfortably hard and her mouth had gone dry. As if to relieve the tension the man was speaking casually, commenting on how developed the area was getting; he'd lived out here for the past twelve years, and he'd seen dozens of new houses go up, old farmhouses converted. In fact he'd been involved in some of this—he was a self-employed carpenter and a cabinetmaker. He bred horses for the pleasure of it. His name was—

Kathe was only half listening, staring at the fawn. She sat hunched carefully forward, securing the creature with both hands, pressing it against her belly and thighs; if the van struck a pothole, the fawn could not slip from her grasp.

She said, "I guess I'm a little upset right now, I don't know why. If you don't mind I'd rather not talk."

They rode in silence to the animal shelter in Schuylersville.

Where, as soon as the young woman receptionist sighted them entering with the fawn in Kathe's arms, they were rebuffed.

Sorry, no deer, it was state policy. Absolutely no deer.

Kathe confronted the young woman, leaning against the counter, the fawn in her arms blinking in the harsh fluorescent light. She pleaded, she was angry, she was persistent—the fawn was newly born, it was lost from its mother, lying by the side of a road, we can't just let it die, can we? The man too spoke aggressively, arguing that it was the shelter's duty to take in lost and injured animals—wasn't it tax-supported? Her face flushed, the young woman repeated it was policy and there was nothing she could do about it: the deer population in the state was five times denser than it had been in the 1700s—think of that. Anxiously, beginning to be frightened, Kathe held the fawn up for the young woman to see. "But—look how beautiful it is, how tiny and helpless! Look at these eyes! See how it's trembling, it doesn't want to die." The young woman said sullenly, "Sure, I know, all baby animals are darling, but I can't help it, the vet's on duty in the back and he'll tell you the same thing: it's state policy." Kathe asked desperately, "What can I do with it, then? Can I feed it milk, cow's milk, would it drink milk from a baby's bottle?"

The young woman avoided looking at the fawn. The flush in her face, rising from her throat, was deeper. She said, "Frankly, I'd take it back where I found it if I were you. If nothing has happened to the mother deer she'll return to her fawn." The man objected, "But now we've handled the fawn, the doe will smell our scent," and the young woman said, "That won't matter. It really won't. If the doe is all right she won't have forgotten where she left the fawn and she'll come back to get it, probably after dark," and Kathe said, "But it was by the side of a road we found it, in a dangerous place," and the young woman said, patiently, as if speaking to a frightened child or a hysterical person, "Then leave it a few yards away, in a safer place. The doe will find it, I'm sure." Kathe was trembling, hugging the fawn to her breasts. A sudden sense of hopelessness in the face of the world's cold logic struck her; she felt weak, desolate. Absurdly, she was almost in tears. "Please, you wouldn't be lying to us, would you?" she asked. The young woman said curtly, "You shouldn't have taken the fawn away in the first place. Next time, you'll know better."

So the man, now Kathe's infuriated companion, drove them back to the exact spot where Kathe had found the fawn. And there was her car, startling to her eye, as if unexpected, parked at a crooked angle on the shoulder. "Poor thing," Kathe murmured, stepping down from the cab with the fawn in her arms, "I hope your mother hasn't forgotten you." She crossed the ditch, making her way cautiously, and lowered the fawn into a patch of chicory and wild grass. Her heart was beating so hard now that she could scarcely catch her breath. *No, I can't, I can't do this* but wisely, practicably, she turned back to the man, who was out of the van, at the side of the road, watching her, and said, "Should we wait a while? And see what happens? In case there's some danger?" She was trying to speak normally and she believed she was speaking normally though her voice quavered and her eyes stung with tears. "In case there are dogs?—or—" The man said quickly, "We can wait a while, sure," surprising her with his reasonableness.

Kathe thought, He has had experience with women, or girls, or children, in just such a state. He knows, but he doesn't judge.

So they waited in the van a short distance away. Cars passed from time to time but the fawn, on the far side of the ditch, was safe. Dusk came slowly, by degrees lifting from the earth; out of the woods, out of the undersides of hills, out of the ditch choked with cattails and wild rose. It was nearly eight o'clock and the sky in the west was a brilliant dreamlike wash of pale orange and blue. The man had introduced himself as Lyle Carter, and this time Kathe retained the name, and offered her own, Kathe Connor, which was her maiden name, her unmarried name, startling her ear with its freshness. But she was staring at the fawn, and distracted from Lyle Carter's conversation, she could not concentrate, jamming her knuckles against her mouth and waiting, praying *Let the doe come! God, please! Just this once and I will never ask again.* Several times she had to restrain herself from getting out of the van and going to check to see if the fawn was all right—that small, almost indiscernible shape in the gathering shadows.

It was as if she were hypnotized. She was aware of Lyle Carter's presence, and she could hear his low-pitched, casual voice, and she understood that her behavior was not fully within her control, yet she could not remove her eyes from the fawn, or from the hilly field lifting behind it. An eighth of a mile away there was a woods, and near this woods, at dusk, or very early in the morning, she'd sometimes noticed a small herd of deer when she'd driven by. She narrowed her eyes and tried to see deer there now, or a single deer, a doe; but there was nothing.

Lyle Carter said, "Why don't we go somewhere and wait? Then, when we come back, after dark, the doe will probably have taken away the fawn."

Kathe did not answer at first. Then she said, for she knew she must be reasonable, "If you think the fawn will be safe. If we're not abandoning it . . ."

Lyle Carter said, turning the key in the ignition, "Sure the fawn will be safe. We're not abandoning it."

So they drove now in Lyle Carter's van to the Horseshoe Tavern on the highway which Kathe had passed numerous times but had never entered, nor thought of entering. Inside, the bartender and several men at the bar called out hello to Lyle Carter and he greeted them cheerfully in turn. Kathe noticed that he had a slight limp, favoring his right leg. He led Kathe to a booth by a front window where they had a view of the slow-dissolving sky at dusk and where Kathe ordered a club soda for her first drink and then switched to beer since beer was what Lyle Carter was drinking. She was anxious, but she smiled and responded to Lyle Carter's conversation; by degrees she became more relaxed, and dared to look fully at him. He'd removed his dark glasses and was looking at her. It was not clear if he was smiling or frowning. His eyes were shadowed deep in their sockets, intelligent, watchful, curious. His face was weathered with the sun-creases of early middle age; Kathe guessed him to be in his mid-forties, one of those fair-skinned men who look older than their age. Yet he had an air of good humor, generosity. He was telling her that he knew what it was to feel strongly about an animal—one of his daughters had been distraught for weeks after a young horse of hers died. Kathe did not know how to reply, and so sat silent; she wondered why this information was being offered to her. After a moment Lyle Carter asked Kathe did she have a family?—which was his way, she surmised, of asking if she was married. She told him yes, a family, but no, not a marriage, no longer; and no children. And what about him? Lyle Carter shrugged, and sucked at his beer, as if the effort of self-assessment was physically taxing. He said finally that he'd become accustomed to being alone in this phase of his life and he didn't know if it was good for him, or not so good; or if he had much choice. He laughed, he seemed genuinely amused. "Some things happen, and then other things happen," he said. He seemed about to say more, but did not.

He ordered two more beers for them. Suddenly it was dark. Kathe said, "Should we go back and check? The fawn . . ." and Lyle Carter said, "Let's give the doe another half-hour. Our headlights might scare her off." Kathe looked at the man, raising her eyes to his face, which seemed to her familiar, yes probably she'd been seeing Lyle Carter, and his battered Toyota van, for months, even for years, in and around the country towns in the vicinity, and she smiled at him, for he had such good sense; she guessed him one of those men who pride themselves on their manual dexterity, their physical strength, their moral stubbornness, their rock-bottom common good sense.

She said, "You wouldn't think a single fawn would matter so much, would you?"

The Undesirable Table

With mumbled apologies, the maître d' seated us at an undesirable table in our favorite restaurant Le Coq d'Or. The men in our party protested. But there was nothing to be done. It was a Saturday night in the holiday season, the more desirable tables had been booked weeks in advance. Our reservation had been made practically at the last minute, what could we expect? Even though we were—are—frequent patrons of Le Coq d'Or, and had imagined ourselves on special terms with the management.

As we took our seats, reluctantly, at the undesirable table, in a front bay window of the dining room, one of our party remarked, bemused, yet serious, that perhaps the maître d' had expected a twenty-dollar bill to be slipped surreptitiously to him. Was *that* it?

Seated at the undesirable table, in a front bay window of the dining room of Le Coq d'Or, we discussed this possibility in lowered, incensed voices. We are highly verbal people and much of dispute in our lives is resolved, if not satisfied, by speech. The more cynical among our party believed that yes, this might be so; though, in the past, and we'd dined in this restaurant innumerable times, the maître d' had not behaved like an extortionist. The more optimistic among our party believed that, no, that wasn't it, at all; surely not; our reservation had been made late, just the day before, the holiday season was frenzied this year, it *was* a Saturday night. And so why not enjoy ourselves? As we'd come out to do?

Even if it was something of a disappointment, and a rude surprise in a way, to be seated at an undesirable table in Le Coq d'Or.

And so, seated at the undesirable table, in a front bay window of the dining room of Le Coq d'Or, with an unwanted view of the street outside, we gave our drink orders to the waiter; we smiled gamely, and took up our hefty Le Coq d'Or menus (parchment-bound, gilt-printed, gold-tasseled, with elegantly scripted French, and English translations below) and perused the familiar categories of appetizers, first courses, entrees, desserts, wines. We chattered to one another discussing the dishes we might order, recalling previous meals at Le Coq d'Or, previous evenings in one another's company that had been both intellectually stimulating and emotionally rewarding, evenings that had had *meaning* of a kind, precious to consider. For food consumed in the presence of dear friends is not mere food but sustenance; a sustenance of the soul. A formal meal, with excellent wines, in a restaurant of the quality of Le Coq d'Or, in the right company, is a celebration. Yes?

So it was, we smiled gamely. We chattered happily. We were not to be cheated of our evening's pleasure—for most of us, a well-deserved reward for the rigors of the previous week—by the accident of being seated at an undesirable table. We gave our orders to the waiter, who was all courtesy and attentiveness. We handed back our hefty menus. When our drinks arrived, we lifted them to drink with pleasure and relief. We were almost successfully ignoring two facts: that the undesirable table in the bay window of the dining room was even more undesirable than the most pessimistic of us had anticipated; and that those of us unfortunate enough to be seated facing the bay window were particularly afflicted. Yet such was our courtesy with one another, even after years of friendship, and so awkward was the situation, that no one, not even those facing the bay window and the street, chose to speak of it. For to *name* a problem is *to invest it with too much significance.*

We, who are so highly verbal, whose lives, it might be said, are ingeniously amassed cities of words, understand the danger as few others do. Ah, yes!

There followed then, with much animation, a discussion of

wines—in which several of our company, male, participated with great gusto and expertise, while others listened with varying degrees of attentiveness and indulgence. Which wines, of the many wines of Le Coq d'Or's excellent list, were to be ordered?—considering that the party was to dine variously on seafood, fish, poultry, and meat. Our conversations about wine are always lengthy and passionate, and touched with a heartfelt urgency; even pedantry; yet there is an undercurrent of bemused self-consciousness, too—for the wine connoisseurs are well aware of the absurdity of their almost mystical fanaticism even as they unapologetically indulge in it. After all, if there is a simple, direct, unalloyed ecstasy to be taken by the mouth, savored by the tongue like a liquid communion wafer, how can it be denied to those with the means to purchase it?—and by whom?

So, the usual spirited talk of wine among our party. And some argument. Where there is passion there *is* argument. Not that the wine connoisseurs dominated completely, despite their loud voices. Conversation became more general, there were parenthetical asides, the usual warm queries of health? recent trips? family? work? gossip of mutual acquaintances, colleagues? If there was a distracting scene outside the window, on the street (which was in fact an avenue, broad, windy, littered, eerily lit by streetlamps whose light seemed to withhold, not give, illumination) or even on the sidewalk a few yards away from those of our company with our backs stolidly to the window *we knew nothing of it: saw nothing.*

At last, our appetizers were brought to us. And the first of the wines. The ceremonial uncorking, the tasting—exquisite!

Red caviar, and arugula salads. Giant shrimp delicately marinated. Pâté maison. Escargots. Coquilles St. Jacques. Consommé à la Barigoule. Steak tartare. And of course the thick crusty brown bread that is a specialty of Le Coq d'Or. As we talked now of politics. Foreign, national, state, local. We talked of religion—is there any *demonstrable difference* between the actions of "believers" and "nonbelievers"? We asked after our friends' children in the hope and expectation that they would ask after ours.

(One of our party, her gaze drawn repeatedly to something outside the window, which, facing it as she was, at this undesirable table in the dining room of Le Coq d'Or, seemed to possess a morbid attraction for her, suddenly laid her fork down. Shut her eyes. As conversation swirled around her. But she said nothing, and nothing was said to her, and after a pause of some seconds she opened her eyes and, gazing now resolutely at her plate, picked up her fork and resumed eating.)

(Another of our party weakened. Laid his fork down too, pressed the back of his hand against his forehead. Again, conversation continued. Our eyes were firmly fixed on one another. And after a minute or so he, too, revived, with steely resolution lifting his wineglass to his mouth and draining it in a single swallow.)

Boeuf Stroganoff. Pompano à la Meunière. Bouillabaisse. Sweetbreads à la York. Chateaubriand. Blanquette of veal, coq au vin, sole Lyonnaise, and an elegantly grilled terrapin with black mushrooms. And julienne vegetables, lightly sauteed in olive oil. And another generous basket of crusty brown bread. And another bottle of wine, this time a Bordeaux.

One of our party, a woman with widened moist eyes, said, Oh!—what are they doing—? staring out the window in an attitude of disbelieving horror. But adding quickly, a hot blush mottling her face, No really—*don't look.*

No one of us having looked, nor even heard. In any case.

(Yes, certainly it crossed the minds of those gentlemen of our party with their backs to the offending scene to offer to exchange seats with the women facing it. Yet we hesitated. And finally, as if by mutual consent, said nothing. For to *name* a problem, in particular an upsetting and demoralizing problem over which none of us has any control, is *to invest it with too much significance.*)

How popular Le Coq d'Or is!—a region, an atmosphere, an exquisite state of the soul rather than merely a *restaurant.* In such surroundings, amid the glitter of flashing cutlery, expensive glassware, and crystal chandeliers, animal gluttony is so tamed as to appear a kind of asceticism.

At Le Coq d'Or, a perfectly orchestrated meal—which, we were determined, ours would be, even at an undesirable table—is rarely a matter of less than two hours.

Casting our eyes resolutely *not* in the direction of the window, the avenue, the luckless creatures outside. But, rather, with some envy at parties seated at desirable tables. Impossible not to feel resentment, bitterness, rancor. Even as we smiled, smiled. Even as the maître d' hovered guiltily near, inquiring after the quality of our food and drink and service, which we assured him, with impeccable politeness, and a measure of coolness, was excellent as always. Yet: *Why are these other patrons favored with desirable tables, while we, equally deserving, possibly more deserving, are not?*

Perennial questions of philosophy. The mystery of good, evil. God, devil. More wine?—a final bottle uncorked. Through the plate glass bay window an occasional unwelcome, unheard stridency of sound. Keening wails, or sirens? No, mere vibrations. All sound *is* vibrations, devoid of meaning. Coffee, liqueurs. Desserts so delicious they must be shared: Sorbet à la Bruxelles, profiteroles au chocolate, meringue glacé, zabaglione frappé, strawberries flambé. And those luscious Swiss mints. It was observed that the rose-tinted wax candles in the center of the table had burned low, their flames had begun to flicker. A romance of candlelight. The circular table, draped in a fine oyster-white linen cloth—the rose-patterned cushioned chairs—were floating in a pool of darkness. Staring intensely at one another, friends, dear friends, the fever of our love for one another, our desperate faith in one another, transfixed by one another's faces. For there lies *meaning.* Yes?

You expected me to weaken. To surrender to an instinctive narrative momentum. In which the *not-named* is suddenly, and therefore irrevocably, *named.* Following the conventions of narration, I might have proceeded then to Events B, C, D, the horror of disclosure increasing in rhythm with the courses of our elaborate meal. By the climax—the emptying of the very last bottle of wine, the paying of the check, our rising to leave—a revelation would have occurred. *We would never be the same again after our experience at the undesirable table.* You expected that.

But that was not my way, because it did not happen that way. There was no *naming,* thus no *narrative.*

The check was paid, we rose to leave. One of us, fumbling for her hand bag, dropped it and it fell onto a chair and from the chair to the floor spilling some of its contents with a startled little cry.

We walked through the dining room of Le Coq d'Or without a backward glance at the undesirable table.

(Let the maître d', who wished us happy holidays with a forced smile, worry that we'll never return to his damned restaurant. Let him worry he's insulted us, and we'll spread the word to others. Our revenge!)

Fortunately, there is a high-rise parking structure directly accessible from Le Coq d'Or so that patrons are spared walking along the windswept, littered avenue, and the possible danger of this walk. We'd parked our cars there, on Level A, and in the cooler air felt a sudden giddy sense of release, like children freed from confinement. We were talking loudly, we were laughing. We shook hands warmly saying goodnight, we hugged one another, we kissed. Old friends, dear friends. Now the ordeal of the undesirable table was behind us it was possible to forget it. In fact, we were rapidly forgetting it. We would retain instead the far more meaningful memory of another superb shared meal at Le Coq d'Or, another memorable evening in one another's company. Of course we'll be back—many times.

For Le Coq d'Or is, quite simply, the finest restaurant available to us. It might be said we have no choice.

Is Laughter Contagious?

Is laughter contagious?—driving on North Pearl Street, Franklin Village, Mrs. D. began suddenly to hear laughter on all sides, a wash of laughter gold-spangled like coins, just perceptibly louder issuing from the rear of her car, and she found herself smiling, her brooding thoughtful expression erased as if by force, on the verge of spontaneous laughter herself for isn't there a natural buoyancy to the heart when we hear laughter? even, or particularly, the laughter of strangers? even an unexpected, inexplicable, mysterious laughter?—though Mrs. D. understood that the laughter surrounding her was in no way mysterious, at least its source was in no way mysterious, for, evidently, she had forgotten to switch off the car radio the last time she had driven the car, and the laughter was issuing from the radio's speakers, the most powerful of which was in the rear of the Mercedes.

What were they laughing about, these phantom radio-people?

Men's laughter—and, here and there, the isolated sound of a woman's higher-pitched laughter?—delicious, cascading, like a sound of icicles touching?

Though laughing by this time herself, Mrs. D., who was a serious person, with a good deal on her mind—and most of it private, secret, not to be shared even with Mr. D.—switched the radio off, preferring silence.

There.

* * *

Christine Delahunt. Thirty-nine years old. Wife, mother. Recently returned to work—a "career." A woman of moral scruples, but not prim, puritanical, dogmatic. Isn't that how Mrs. D. has defined herself to herself? Isn't Mrs. D., in so defining herself, one of us?—determined, for no reason we can understand, to define ourselves to—ourselves?

As if we doubt that anyone else is concerned?

Mrs. D. was to tell us, certain of her friendly acquaintances. Last Thursday it seemed to begin. Did others in Franklin Village notice?—that afternoon, sometime before six o'clock? The time of suburban car-errands, family-tasks, last-minute shopping and dry cleaners pickup and the drugstore, quickening pace of the waning day, yes and Thursday is the day-preceding-Friday when the week itself notoriously quickens, a panic-sensation to it, as a river seemingly placid and navigable begins to accelerate, visibly, as it approaches a cataract?—though there is, yet, no clear sign of danger? no reason for alarm?

Outbursts of laughter. Gay infectious laughter. In the Franklin Food Mart, our "quality" grocery store, at one of the checkout counters when the deaf-and-dumb packer wearing the badge FRITZ (pasty-skinned, in his fifties: the Franklin Food Mart is one of several area businesses that have "made it a policy" to employ the handicapped) spilled a bag of fresh produce onto the floor, and Washington State winesaps, bright-dyed Florida navel oranges, hairy-pungent little kiwi fruit, several pygmy-heads of Boston lettuce, a dozen Idaho red potatoes, a single California melon—all went tumbling, rolling, startling yet comical as the deaf-and-dumb packer gaped and blinked standing frozen in a kind of terror that for all its public expression seemed to us, witnessing, to be private: thus somehow funnier: and the very customer who had paid extravagant prices for these items laughed, if a bit angrily; and other customers, seeing, burst into laughter too; and the checkout cashier, and other cashiers, and employees of the store, peering over, craning their necks to see what the commotion is, their laughter tentative at first since the look in poor Fritz's eyes *was* terror wasn't it?—then exploding forth, an honest, candid, gut-laughter, not malicious surely, but, yes, *loud*?

Mrs. D. was at an adjacent checkout counter, methodically

making out a check to the Franklin Food Mart, a weekly custom this is, perhaps it might better be called a blood-sacrifice, this week's check for—how can it be? $328.98 for an unexceptional week's shopping? for a family of four? no supplies for a dinner party? no beer, wine, liquor? not even any seafood? making out the check with resigned fingers when she heard the strange laughter rising around her, rising, erupting, childlike raucous laughter, and turning, smiling, wanting to join in, Mrs. D. saw the cause—a bag of groceries had overturned, things were rolling on the floor, and that look on that poor man's face, it *was* amusing, but Mrs. D. suppressed laughter for, oh dear, really it *wasn't* amusing, not at all, that poor man backing off and staring at the produce on the floor paralyzed as everyone laughed so cruelly, what are people thinking of? how can it be? in the Franklin Food Mart of all places?

Are the Delahunts neighbors of ours?—not exactly.

We don't have "neighbors," in the old sense of that word, in Franklin Village. Our houses are constructed on three- and four-acre lots, which means considerable distance between houses, and with our elaborate landscaping (trees of all varieties, shrubs, twelve-foot redwood fences, electrically charged wire-mesh "deer-deterrent" fences) it's possible for the residents of one house to be unable to glimpse even the facade of the house next door, certainly it's possible to go for years without glimpsing the faces of the people who live next door, unless, of course, and this is frequently the case, we encounter one another socially—on neutral territory, you might say. Nor have we sidewalks in residential Franklin Village. Nor have we streets, in the old sense of that word—we have "lanes," we have "drives," we have "passes," "circles," "courts," even "ways," but we do not have "streets."

Are Mr. and Mrs. Delahunt friends of ours?—not exactly.

We don't have "friends," in the old sense of that word, in Franklin Village. Most of us are relatively new here, and a number of us are scheduled to move soon. Spring is the busiest time for moving. (Of course there are residents in this area who are known as "oldtime." Who can recall, for instance, when the Franklin Hills Shopping Mall was nothing but an immense tract of open, wild, useless land, and when Main Street in the Village was residential from Pearl Street onward, and when Route 26 was a mere country highway!) Thus the majority of us make no claims to have (or to be) "friends"—but we *are* "friendly acquaintances" of one another and we *are* social. Very!

The Delahunts, Mr. and Mrs., became friendly acquaintances of ours within days of their arrival, they are highly respected, warmly regarded, attractive, energetic, invited almost immediately to join the Franklin Hills Golf Club and the yet more prestigious Franklin Hills Tennis Club. Mr. D. moved his family here three years ago from Rye, Connecticut, or was it Grosse Pointe, Michigan, when he became sales director at W.W.C. & M., and Mrs. D. has recently begun public relations work part-time, for our Republican congressman Gordon Frayne—Gordon's the man whom the papers so frequently chide, urging him to "upscale" his image. The Delahunts live in a six-bedroom French Normandy house on Fairway Circle, their fourteen-year-old daughter Tracey and their eleven-year-old son Jamey both attend Franklin Hills Day School. Mrs. D. like many of us tries to participate in parent-teacher activities at the school, but—when on earth is there *time*?

"Upscaling" Gordon Frayne's image is a challenge, Mrs. D. laughingly, if somewhat worriedly, confesses. But Gordy Frayne— some folks even call him Gordo—wins elections. He's a big-hearted ruddy-faced shooting-from-the-hip character, often in the headlines and on television, one or another controversy, last year he was interviewed on network television and made a statement warning that "ethnic minorities" had better man their own oars "or the venerable Ship of State's gonna capsize and sink"— which naturally led to protests from certain quarters but a good deal of support from other quarters. Mrs. D. like other associates and friendly acquaintances of Gordon Frayne has learned to frown as she smiles at his witticisms, just slightly reprovingly, as Franklin Village women often do, she has unconsciously mastered this response, this facial expression, as adroitly as any professional actress—"Oh Gordy! Oh *really*!" It was at a party on Saturday night (the Saturday following the Thursday) that Gordy launched into one of his comical diatribes, the guy could have been a stand-up comedian for sure, cruel but ingenious mimicry of Jesse Jackson, another in his series of jokes about gays, faggots, AIDS "victims," and he and some others fell to discussing a feature in the *Detroit News* about elderly inner-city residents living on food stamps and forced to buy dog food as the price of food rises and Gordy screwed up his face in that dead-serious way of his like he's Dan Rather the voice of reason and fair play: "Hell, maybe they *like* dog food? It's a free country isn't it?" And most, though not all, of the company laughed, Mrs. D. among them, not wanting to be a prude, but smiling and shaking her head, avoiding the others' eyes, wondering why, why, why, and what will come of this?

Five girls from the Franklin Hills Day School jogging on Park Ridge Road, Monday after school, pumping legs and arms, high-held heads, shorts and loose-fitting school T-shirts and identical expensive jogging shoes, and according to the girls' testimonies after the "vehicular assault" they were running single file, they were keeping to the left side of the road, facing oncoming traffic, careful to keep off the road itself and to run on the asphalt-paved shoulder. As usual one of the girls was falling behind, there were three girls running close together, then, a few yards behind them, the fourth, and approximately twenty feet behind her the fifth, poor Bonnie, Bonnie S., fourteen years old, second-year in the upper form at the Day School, Bonnie S. is a few pounds overweight, not fat, the most accurate word would be plump but who wants to be plump? who can bear to be plump? fourteen years old and plump in Franklin Village, New York?—poor Bonnie S. whom the other girls like well enough, feel sort of sorry for, she's sweet she tries so hard she's so generous but it's pathetic, Bonnie trying to keep up with the tall thin girls the girls she envies letting it be known at school that her problem isn't overeating it's glandular it's "genetic—like fate" and maybe that's true since none of Bonnie's classmates ever sees her eating anything other than apples, carrot sticks, narrow slices of honeydew melon she'll devour fleshy-fruit and rind both—poor Bonnie S.! (But *is* her weight problem "glandular"? Maybe she binges?—in secret?—tries to stick her finger down her throat and vomit it up?—but can't quite *succeed*?—enough to make a difference?) In any case there was Bonnie S. running fifth in the line of girls, breathless, clumsy, a sweaty sheen to her round flushed face, a glazed look to her damp brown eyes, and the carload of boys swerved around the curve, that curve just beyond Grouse Hill Lane, six older students from the Day School jammed together in a newly purchased white Acura, the girls could hear the car radio blasting heavy metal rock even before the car came into sight, they could hear the boys yelling and laughing as the car bore down upon them, they saw the faces of the boys in the front seat clearly, wide grins, gleeful-malicious eyes, a raised beer can or two, then the girls were screaming, scattering, it was Bonnie S. who was the target, poor Bonnie arousing male derision pumping away there twenty feet behind the others, poor plump sweaty Bonnie S. with her expression of incredulous shock and terror as the white car aimed for her, boyish-prankish braying laughter, she threw herself desperately to the left, the car skidded by missing the screaming girl by perhaps a single inch then righted itself, regained the road, on shrieking tires it sped away and there was Bonnie S. lying insensible in the shallow concrete drainage ditch like something tossed down, bleeding so profusely from a gash in her forehead that the first of her friends to reach her nearly fainted.

Tracey Delahunt tells her mother afterward, she'll confess to her mother solely, knowing her mother will understand, or, failing to understand, for who after all *can* understand?—will sympathize with the hungry wish to understand, "—It happened so fast—oh God!—we looked back and there was Bonnie sort of *flying* off the road like something in a kid's cartoon—and it was horrible—it was just, just horrible, but—" lowering her teary eyes, thick-lashed tawny-green eyes Mrs. D. thinks are far more beautiful than her own though closely resembling her own, "—sort of, in a way—oh God!—*comical* too."

Pressing her fingertips hard against her lips but unable to keep from bursting into a peal of hysterical laughter.

Three days later, the most upsetting incident of all.

Not that Mrs. D. allowed herself to think of it very much afterward. Certainly not obsessively. She isn't that type of mother—the obsessive-neurotic mother. Fantasizing about her children, worrying, suspicious.

She'd entered the house from the rear, as usual. About to step into the kitchen when she'd overheard, coming up from the basement, the family room in the basement, the sound of juvenile laughter, boys' laughter, and ordinarily she would not have paused for a moment since Jamey and his friends often took over that room after school to watch videos, yes some of the videos the boys watched were questionable, yes Mrs. D. knew and, yes, she'd tried to exercise some restraint while at the same time she'd tried not to be, nor even to appear to be, censorious and interfering, but that day there was something chilling about the tone of the boys' laughter, and wasn't there, beneath it, another sound?—as of a creature *bleating?*—a queer high-pitched sound that worried Mrs. D. so she went to the door of the family room (which was shut) and pressed her ear against it, hearing the laughter, the giggling, more distinctly, and the other sound too, and carefully, almost timidly—she, Christine Delahunt, nearly forty years old, wife, mother, self-respecting surely?—self-determined, surely?—opening a door timidly in her own house?—and saw there a sight that froze her in her tracks even as, in that instant, she was already shoving it from her, banishing it from her consciousness, denying its power to qualify her love for her son: for there were Jamey and several of his boy friends, eighth graders at the Day School whose faces Mrs. D. knew well, Evan, Allen, Terry, red-haired impish Terry, and who was there with them? a girl? a stranger? and *strange?*—slightly older than the boys, with dull coarse features, eyes puckered at the corners, wet-dribbly mouth, no one Mrs. D. knew or had ever glimpsed before and this girl was sprawled on her back on the braided colonial-style carpet in front of the fireplace, in the Delahunts' family room, her plump knees raised, and spread, naked from the waist down, and what was red-haired Terry doing?—poking something (too large to be a pencil, an object plastic and chunky, was it a child's play baseball bat?), or trying to poke something, into the girl's vagina?—while the other boys, as if transfixed, crouched in a circle, staring, blinking, grinning, giggling.

Mrs. D. cried, without thinking, "Oh what are you doing! Boys! Jamey! And you—you filthy, disgusting *girl!*"

Her voice was unlike any voice she'd ever heard springing from her. Breathless, disbelieving, angry, wounded.

She slammed the door upon the children's startled-guilty-grinning faces, and fled. Upstairs.

That evening, at dinner, not a word! not a word! not a word! to Jamey, who, frightened, subdued, ate his food almost shyly, and cast looks of appeal to Mrs. D. who behaved as—as usual?—knowing that the child *knew*.

"I'm so afraid."

Mrs. D. was sitting, yes in the family room, which Mr. D. preferred to call the recreation room, with a drink in her hand. Her voice was quiet, apologetic.

Mr. D. sipped his drink. Peered at the newspaper. Said, vague, but polite, "Yes?"

"Harry. I'm so afraid."

"Well, all right."

Mr. D. was scanning the paper with increasing impatience. "Christ, it's always the same! AIDS, crack, crime! 'Ghetto!' " He squinted at a photograph of several black youths being herded into a police van, he laughed harshly. "*I'm* a subscriber, for Christ's sake, d'you think these punks subscribe? Why the hell am I always reading about *them?*"

Upstairs a telephone rang. Tracey's private number.

Mrs. D. raised her glass to her lips but did not sip from it. She feared the taste of it—that first slip-sliding taste. She pressed her fingertips to her eyes and sat very still.

After a few minutes Mr. D. inquired, glancing in her direction even as his attention remained on the newspaper, "Chris—are you all right?"

"I'm so afraid."

"Cramps, eh? Migraine?"

"I'm *afraid.*"

Mr. D. was scanning the editorial page. A sudden smile illuminated his face. He nodded, then, suddenly bored, let the newspaper fall. "Everyone has an *opinion*. 'Put your money where your mouth is' my father used to say."

Mr. D. rose—majestically. A solid figure, ham-thighed, with a faintly flushed face, quick eyes. At its edges Mr. D.'s face appeared to have eroded but his mouth was still that "sculpted" mouth which Mrs. D., a very long time ago, so long ago now as to seem laughable, like a scene in a low-budget science-fiction film, had once avidly, ravenously, *insatiably* kissed.

Mr. D. said, walking away, "Two Bufferin. That'll do it."

After dinner, rinsing dishes and setting them carefully into the dishwasher, Mrs. D. smiled tentatively at her reflection in the window above the sink. Why was she afraid? Wasn't she being a bit silly? Where, so often recently, she was thinking of what she was *not* thinking of, now, abruptly, she was *not* thinking of what she was *not* thinking of.

Elsewhere in the house, issuing from the family room, and from Tracey's room upstairs, laughter rippled, peaked—television laughter by the sound of it.

Simple boredom with the subject, maybe.

Which subject?

Mr. H., father of one of the girls who had been jogging on Park Ridge Road on the day of the infamous "vehicular assault," telephoned Mr. D. another time, and, another time, Mr. D. took the call in private, the door to his study firmly shut; and, as they were undressing for bed that night, when Mrs. D. asked cautiously what had been decided, Mr. D. replied affably, "We don't get involved."

Mrs. D. had understood from the very first, even as Tracey was sobbing in her arms, that, given the litigious character of Franklin Hills, this would be the wisest, as it was the most practical, course of action; she gathered too, as things developed, despite Tracey's protestations and bouts of tears, temper, and hysteria, that Tracey concurred, as her girlfriends, apart from Bonnie, concurred, perhaps even before their worried parents advised them. Yet she heard herself saying weakly, "Oh Harry—if Tracey *saw* those boys' faces, Tracey wants to *say*," and Mr. D., yawning, stretching, on his way into his bathroom, nodded vaguely in her direction and said, "Set the alarm for 6:15, hon, will you?—the limo's picking me up at 6:45."

*　　*　　*

Tracey no longer discusses the incident with Mr. and Mrs. D. *Ugly!—horrible!—nightmare!—never never forget!*—but she restricts all discussions of it to her girlfriends, as they restrict their discussions of it too.

That is, the girls who were witnesses to the incident, not Bonnie S. to whom it happened. Not pathetic Bonnie S. to whom they no longer speak, much, at all.

For weeks, red-haired Terry was banished from the Delahunts' house. Not that Mrs. D. spoke of such a banishment, nor even suggested it to Jamey, who watched her cautiously, one might say shrewdly, his gaze shifting from her if she chanced to look at him.

No need to chastise and embarrass the poor child, Mrs. D. has begun to think. He's a good decent sensitive civilized child, he *knows* how he has upset me.

Poor Mrs. K.!—poor "Vivvie"!

Since the start of her problem eighteen months ago, the first mastectomy, and the second mastectomy, and then the chemotherapy treatments, her circle of friendly acquaintances has shrunken; and those who visit her, primarily women, have had difficulties.

Yes it's so sad it's *so* sad.

Vivvie Kern of all women.

A few of us visited her at the hospital, some of us waited to visit her at home, it's awkward not knowing what to do or to say it sometimes seems there isn't anything *to* do or to say and there's the extra burden of having to exchange greetings with Mr. K. who appears almost resentful, reproachful, that's how men are sometimes in such cases, husbands of ex-prom-queen-type women, and Mrs. K. was, a bit boastfully, one of these. Of course it's wisest to avoid *the subject* but how can you avoid *the subject* with that poor man staring at you unsmiling?—just *staring?*

But it's lovely in their new solarium, at least. So much to look at, outside and in, and you aren't forced to look at *her*, I mean exclusively at *her*, poor thing! chattering away so bravely!—and that gorgeous red-blond hair she'd been so vain about mostly fallen out now, the wig just sort of *perches* there on her head, and her eyebrows are drawn on so crudely, and with her eyelashes gone it's *naked eyes* you have to look at if you can't avoid it but in such close quarters and with the woman leaning toward you sometimes even gripping your arm as if for dear life how can you avoid it?—except by not visiting poor Mrs. K. at all?

(Of course, some in our circle have stopped seeing her, and it's embarrassing, how painful, Mrs. K. joking to disguise her bitterness. Saying, "My God, it isn't as if I have AIDS after all, this isn't *contagious*, you know!")

Visiting Mrs. K. in late June, having procrastinated for weeks, Mrs. D. was nervously admiring the numerous hanging plants in the solarium, the startlingly beautiful pastel hues of the cactus flowers, she was listening to Mrs. K. speaking animatedly of mutual acquaintances, complaining good-naturedly of the Hispanic cleaning woman she and Mrs. D. shared, perhaps half-listening was more accurate, not thinking of what she was not thinking but she *was* thinking of the ceremonies of grief, death, mourning, how brave of human beings yet how futile, how futile yet how brave, for here was a terminally ill woman now speaking aggressively of regaining her lost weight—"muscle tone" she called it—and returning to the Tennis Club, and Mrs. D. smiled at the woman's wide smiling mouth, a thin mouth now and the lips garishly crimson, yes but you must keep up the pretense, yes but you must be brave, and smile, and nod, and agree, for isn't it too terrible otherwise?

Sharp-eyed, Mrs. K. has noticed that Mrs. D. has another time glanced surreptitiously at her wristwatch, as a starving animal can sense the presence of food, however inaccessible, or even abstract, so does Mrs. K. sense her visitor's yearning to escape, thus she leans abruptly forward across the glass-topped table, nearly upsetting both their glasses of white wine, she seems about to bare her heart, *oh why does Vivvie do such things! with each of us, as if for the first and only time!* seizing Mrs. D.'s hand in her skeletal but strong fingers and speaking rapidly, intensely, naked bright-druggy eyes fixed upon Mrs. D.'s, thus holding her captive.

"... *can't* bear to think of leaving them ... abandoning them

. . . poor Gene! poor Robbie! . . . devastated . . . unmoored . . . already Robbie's been having . . . only thirteen . . . the counselor he's been seeing . . . specializes in adolescent boys . . . says it's a particularly sensitive age . . . traumatic . . . for a boy to lose . . . a mother."

Mrs. D., though giving the impression of having been listening closely, and being deeply moved, has, in fact, not been listening to Mrs. K.'s passionate outburst very closely. She has been thinking of, no she has *not* been thinking of. What?

With a startled, gentle little laugh, Mrs. D. says, "Oh—do you really think so? *Really?*"

Frightened, Mrs. K. says, "Do I really think—what?"

Calmly and unflinching, Mrs. D. looks the doomed woman in the face for the first time.

"That your husband and son will be 'devastated' when you die? That they will even miss you, much? I mean, after the initial shock—the upset to their routines?"

A long moment.

A *very* long moment.

Mrs. K. is staring incredulously at Mrs. D. Slowly, her fingers relax their death-grip on Mrs. D.'s fingers. Her bright lips move, tremble—but no sound emerges.

It's as if, in this instant, the oxygen in the solarium is being sucked out. There's a sense of something, an invisible flame, a radiance, about to go *out.*

"Oh! my goodness!" Mrs. D. exclaims, rising. "—I must leave, I still have shopping to do, it's after *six.*"

She would tell us, confide in us, yes we'd had similar experiences lately, unsettling experiences, sudden laughter like sneezes, giggles like carbonated bubbles breaking the surface of something you'd believed was firm, solid, permanent, unbreakable, the way in her car that day fleeing Mrs. K. Mrs. D. found herself driving like a drunken woman, dizzy-drunk, scary-drunk, but also *happy*-drunk as she never is in real life, she was hearing laughter in the Mercedes, washing tickling over her, *so* funny! so wild! you should have seen that woman's face! that bully! that bore! how dare she! intimidating us! touching us! like that! how dare! *as if I wasn't, for once, telling the truth!*

Hardly a five-minute drive from the Kerns' house on Juniper Way to the Delahunts' house on Fairway Circle but Mrs. D. switched on the radio to keep her company.

There.

The Brothers

They came for him one windy October dusk when he was walking alone after his final class of the day. It might have been a Friday—his final class of the week. He looked up, and he was descending the steep hill behind the old Hubbard Street neighborhood. His eyes were watering in the wind lifting from the river beyond the Erie Central Railroad yard a few blocks from the brick rowhouse where his family had lived. The neighborhood had been razed, bulldozed into oblivion and recast as expressway ramps, cloverleafs and soaring lanes in the years since he'd left, gone away to college and begun his adult life; his family too had moved, like all the families and all the merchants of Hubbard Street. Yet here he was on the hill he'd sledded on as a child, a smell of snow in the air and his heart beating in anticipation as if it knew what he did not *They are coming for me!* glancing up to see them where a moment before there'd been no one: an empty stretch of field grasses and scrub trees, of that bleak, sere, wind-tormented color of autumn after the first frost.

They greeted him with boyish excitement.

"John Michael!—you're just in time."

"John Michael!—we've been waiting for you."

At first, they seemed to have corduroy faces, sand-colored. Shiny black button eyes. Sleek shiny black hair like painted-on hair. And it was impossible to gauge how old they were, even how tall they were; he hesitated to stare, not wanting to seem rude. Their voices rang warmly in his ears without actual sound. He was allowed to know *This is the truest way of communication.* What surprised him most, as if it were a revelation of a part of himself hidden until now, was his own childlike excitement, even happiness, in greeting them.

Though his words were strange, and oddly formal: "I tried not to be late. I had to come a long distance."

And this was true, for he lived far away now from the city of his boyhood. Far away, and nearly twenty years, from Hubbard Street.

"John Michael!—we must hurry."

"John Michael!—there isn't much time."

They reached out boldly for him. Their faces were brightened by smiles and were almost blinding. This intense light obscured their features; or their features were fluid, not yet coalesced. *Which is so superior to the average.* He seemed to know there was a plan, everything had been agreed upon beforehand, but he could not remember the plan. At the same time, it had already happened. A buoyant sensation began in his chest as if his heart was swelling.

"My name is—"

"*My* name is—"

He understood that they were brothers though he hadn't been able to hear their names. The vibrations reached his ears as if through an element dense as water but scattered in teasing ripples.

One of them seized his left hand, and the other seized his right hand, and both tugged at him. He was standing on a dirt path slightly above the brothers and the effect of their tugging was to pull him off balance so that he had no choice but to join them; at the same time, he was overjoyed to be with them.

The three of them ran down the hill slipping and sliding and shouting with excitement. The hill was the scrubby field above Hubbard Street, where in John Michael Wells's memory wind-blown litter had marred the striated surface of the tall grasses, like lint in the nap of a carpet, yet it was suddenly an unknown place, steep and treacherous and coated in ice. Or something sly-slippery underfoot as ice. Shiny, blinding. Intense pleasure and the knowledge *This is the truest way of happiness* rose in him from the ground, through his feet and into his legs and so up into his groin, his belly, his chest *There is no other way of happiness* as the brothers yanked him forward, down the hill. Their breaths were steaming. "It's cold! It's so cold!" he cried, laughing. Knowing that they, his brothers, would warm him.

The next night, he learned their names.

"He's Damm—"

"*He's* Vann—"

Each pointed to the other in an identical mirror gesture, as if practiced. Yet they were not twins, exactly—one appeared to be distinctly older, stockier, than the other; one's hair was that curious sleek-shiny black, and the other had thick deep-textured hair, black also, but separated into sections, with measured parts. They were on Hubbard Street though nothing looked familiar, the background passed in a blur as if the brothers had not yet worked out where they were taking him exactly, in fact they seemed to be quarreling about this even as they spoke nonstop to him, their warm-rippling soundless words washing over him like caresses. The brothers were on either side of him—Damm to his left, Vann to his right—and they were gripping his hands tight so that he understood he was a little boy, a child, despite his height which he was trying awkwardly to conceal. They were not on Hubbard Street but in the playground of his elementary school which was not as he remembered it but close enough for him to know what it was meant to be and that there was danger here as so frequently there'd been danger for him in that playground when he was a child attending this school and so suddenly he tried to wrench himself away, his muscles went into a kind of spasm and Damm and Vann murmured words of comfort and gripped his hands tight to calm, to steady. He wanted to cry *Seeing how your brothers care for you, that is the only truth* but this too he managed to conceal.

"John Michael!—you want to."

"John Michael!—that's *good.*"

They were pulling him forward forcing him to go where he didn't but at the same time did want to go—to another child, or children, in a corner of the playground where the school's brick walls formed an L. Here, certain acts occurred. There were no names given to these acts and so there was no memory accruing to these acts except the memory of revulsion and shame.

Yes but you know nothing ever happened there. You know there was nothing.

Damm was tugging at him, and Vann was tugging at him, and the danger was close by but *Your brothers will protect you* and so he felt a radiant buoyancy that shifted into quicksilver anger, strange laughing anger. He saw the face, blurred as if glimpsed through water, of one whom he hated, and of whom he had not thought in thirty years; and other jeering child faces; but he was laughing, and Damm and Vann were laughing, so it was all right. He passed through these figures as if in fact they were water.

Anger grew in him like a flame rising from his groin into his chest, and into his throat. An actual heat, a flamey tingling in his throat. He was trying to speak to that child face blankly jeering as a mask but there was something wrong with his tongue, his mouth, the sounds that came from him were guttural and staccato, a rattling in his throat. He was choking, he was dying! Was this dying? Help me! help me! he begged the brothers. Swallowing compulsively to quench the fire at the back of his mouth but he could not and as Damm and Vann cried *John Michael! John Michael!* he slipped from the grip of their hands helpless as a child falling on the playground's cracked asphalt pavement. *Don't let me go, where are you?—not so soon.* His head jerked on the damp pillow bunched beneath his neck, his eyes flew open for a long moment sightless, his throat was raw as if abraded— he'd been deeply asleep with his head back, mouth agape. Breathing through his mouth so that his throat had become dehydrated and the uncomfortable sensation had waked him.

Snoring, too—he must have been snoring, like a hog. He'd been hearing it, dry-rasping saw-notched sounds coming, it seemed, from a distance.

Awake, he felt such loss. A sensation as of falling. Paralysis. The lineaments of the dream were rapidly fading like a cinematic image on a screen when the lights are switched on but he felt such loss!—the grip of the brothers' hands on his, his fingers in theirs, only a dream, a phantasm. Nothing.

Awake, and through the day—a day of many hours populated by many individuals, some of them professional colleagues at the university, some of them social acquaintances, friends, and in the evening his lover Crista and her six-year-old son, with whom he did not live but whom he saw almost daily—Jack retained the vivid, disturbing memory of the brothers like the afterglow of erotic consummation, suffused through his entire body. *Where I really am, and who I really am.*

Did anyone notice his uncharacteristic distraction? The vagueness of his replies, his smiles? Jack Wells who was so skeptical by nature, a specialist in differential geometry and an amateur musician-composer, known among his circle of acquaintances for his dry, acerbic humor, his strong political opinions, how was it possible he felt such yearning—such heartsick yearning? To return as quickly as possible to his dreams, these strange unbidden mysterious dreams that had nothing to do with his life; no connection with the present, nor, really, with the past. *To get back to them, my brothers.*

He'd had the first dream only a few nights before. Yet it seemed to him he'd been having such dreams for years. Or, rather, he'd been experiencing this strange, almost unbearable yearning for years.

How was it possible?—it wasn't. "It's absurd."

Who the brothers were, and why Jack should care so much for them, he had no idea. He could not even remember them clearly. They were young, and there was something not quite normal about them—he seemed to know that. But he could not summon back their faces. *To ourselves, we're invisible. The brain has no face.* And what had happened in the dream of Hubbard Street, the playground of Benjamin Franklin Elementary School? *What you must not remember, you won't be able to.*

He'd never had faith that dreams meant much. Considering them in the stark light of day was largely a waste of time. He was not a man who liked to waste time. He was the kind of man who, at the periphery of a meeting or social gathering that is about to break up, jingles his car keys in his pocket.

He was the kind of man who, if someone begins speaking of his dreams, pointedly conceals a yawn.

Yet the brothers had shown him *the truest way of happiness* which he could not comprehend and which frightened him in its intensity.

For knowing how passionately he felt in these dreams he was forced to realize with what little passion he lived his life—even his sexual, erotic life.

And there were mysteries about the dreams that intrigued him: Why, for instance, did the brothers call him "John Michael"?—he'd been "Jack" or "Jacky" most of his life. His baptismal name "John Michael Wells" was as remote to him as the long-deceased grandfather for whom he'd been named and whom he had scarcely known. And why a dream of *brothers* at all? Jack had one brother, Steven, five years his senior, an engineering consultant who lived with his wife and children in an upscale Chicago suburb; even as an adolescent Steve had shared few of Jack's interests in math, science, music—they'd gotten along amicably enough, for the most part, but had not been close. Now, they exchanged Christmas cards and ignored each other's birthdays and went sometimes for as long as a year without speaking on the phone. A good, dull, decent man, Steve Wells. About whom Jack would have had to rack his brains to say anything interesting.

But what is there to say about most men and women, after all? Jack was in the habit of observing that human beings are no more *mysteries* than a banana is a *mystery*. You could never deduce what's inside a banana by examining the peel and the inside is entirely different from the peel, but so what? Why is it important?

"Jack, you're so cynical!" Crista sometimes exclaimed, as if his random remarks truly shocked her. Jack supposed she meant to flatter him. Sexual flirtation, sexual banter. But he did not consider himself cynical, only matter-of-fact; a man not given to exaggeration.

Which was why he'd been drawn to math, geometry—figures, pure structures—uninhabited by personalities—unaffected by personalities.

At the university Jack was Mr. Wells, or Professor Wells to his students. Since years ago there had ceased to be surprises in his work as in the very textbook adopted for his undergraduate course—to which Jack himself had contributed—he had no need to be deeply engaged. He was thirty-seven years old. With his steel-gray metal-rimmed glasses and his graying brown hair combed in two severe wings behind his ears and his playful habit of anticipating his students' questions even as they raised their hands he seemed virtually of no age: not young, as his students were young; yet hardly old, smiling and youthful in his affect, with an unlined face, large dark intelligent sympathetic-seeming eyes, the body of a moderately active man—he swam, dutifully if without enthusiasm. At tennis, he was not competitive enough to be a good player. Why is it important?

One day after the dream of the playground while teaching an honors seminar in Riemannian geometry Jack heard his voice echoing from the room's corners and he realized *If these individuals see and hear me I must be here!* The profundity of this insight overwhelmed him.

And so it was, through the hours of wakefulness: Meeting with colleagues and friends, deftly scanning student work with that part of his mind that operated like a computer independent of Jack Wells's moods or "self"—even with Crista and the child whom he loved and to whom he'd become "family" of a kind. *They see me and hear me, am I deceiving them?*

Even making love with Crista, pushing her and himself to the release of orgasm, he felt the tug of that other yearning and wondered if all human beings harbored such secret, inexpressible desires—for the solace of dreams. If solace was what the brothers offered him.

"John Michael!—you're just in time."

"John Michael!—we've been waiting for you."

And eagerly Jack saw his brothers were not angry.

Yanked the covers off him where he was naked.

Except, bicycling, pedaling frantically to keep up with the brothers, he was wearing oversized flannel pajamas. The elastic waistband was too loose and the pants cuffs got in the way of his pedaling and the brothers were laughing at him. He was laughing too, breathing through his mouth and gasping for air. His bicycle was too big for him and seemed to be made of lengths of pipe with large spoked wheels. Damm's and Vann's bicycles were similar but their legs were longer, they were older boys. Hurtling through the street, which was Hubbard Street except not really. And the corner by the tire shop, the intersection with Mohegan where he lived in the brick rowhouse in a block of such rowhouses distinguishable from one another by painted front doors and shutters, crimped little lawns, flowerbeds. But there was much that was blurred. Open spaces like the edge of the world, blank like a television screen with no picture. "John Michael!—John Michael!" The brothers' voices were liquidy and caressing, vibrating in his head, "John Michael!—come *on*." Laughing and teasing and just slightly impatient because he was so slow. Jack's house was fourth from the corner and a hot wave of shame washed over him seeing it so shabby, walls of rust-brown brick and the shutters painted creamy yellow for a cheery look as Jack's mother insisted but something had happened to the house which was like a deformed face, a face born to a baby genetically doomed to horror, he was ashamed that the brothers saw but of course the brothers knew for they lived in that house themselves. *If it's too soon if I haven't been born yet where can I go?* He dreaded seeing his parents before they were his parents. There was a shame to this prospect he could taste as something tarry at the back of his mouth.

Sobbing gasping for breath pedaling frantically to keep up with Damm, and with Vann, who were shouting instructions to him he could not hear—such a roaring in his ears! He saw a human shape hurtle toward him and there was a sickening *crack!* as the big front wheel of his bicycle which might have been (the details were fluid, shifting) the front wheel of a car too passed over this figure, a child, or an elderly man, and he could not stop pedaling and did not want to stop pedaling following after the brothers who were drawing farther and farther away now scolding, playfully mocking "John Mi-chael!—*what have you done!*"

In terror then Jack woke, heart pounding and naked body which felt large, clumsy *something not myself* covered in sticky sweat. His mouth was aflame with dryness. His eyes oscillated sideways in his head. Crista who was a light sleeper, a woman given to quick maternal solicitude, was smoothing his damp hair back from his forehead asking was something wrong? had he had a bad dream? and in his confusion Jack pushed at her with his elbow, not hard enough to hurt but unmistakably. Then he saw where he was, and with whom. In his woman friend's bed. *I'm safe, it hasn't happened yet.* He assured Crista it had only been a dream, a confused dream of playing tennis—"Sorry! Try to go back to sleep."

He stumbled sleep-dazed into the hall, to use the bathroom hearing Crista's low anxious voice behind him. As if, poor woman, she half feared Jack might slip away in one of his moods in the night without a farewell kiss.

Of course, Jack would never do such a thing. Even if he could have grabbed his clothes and dressed in the bathroom without Crista's knowing.

He was shaken, for something terrible had happened. It helped to rinse his guilty heated face in cold water. Avoiding his eyes in the mirror. *But nobody saw. Nobody except my brothers.*

But he was fully awake, and he was all right. Never can you deduce: The banana is *not* the peel.

He used the toilet and flushed it reluctantly and self-consciously hoping he wouldn't wake Lonnie whose room was across the hall. Small quarters here in Crista's rented house. She was a legal secretary and the firm for which she worked had suffered financial losses through the recession, she'd had no raise for two years but was embarrassed taking money from Jack though sometimes she had no choice, if not taking money from him then allowing him to pay Lonnie's dentist bills, or for a new winter jacket, as if, if he married her, if he brought her and Lonnie to his own more spacious living quarters in a high-rise condominium tower on the hilly, leafy side of the enormous university campus, that would make a significant moral difference.

Fantasizing a note he'd leave for her affixed to the refrigerator door by one of those little dinosaur magnets he'd bought in a packet for the boy *Yes I love you I love you both but I have no heart for marrying you, the walls closing in on us. When I'm away from you I'm lonely for you but when I'm with you—I'm lonely for that part of myself that's somewhere else.* But he'd never do such a thing, he wasn't a cruel man except by accident.

The dream of the hurtling bicycle, the mysterious collision came in early November. The following day Jack canceled a dinner engagement with Crista and another couple, despite Crista's extreme disappointment—she'd been planning this evening for weeks. Jack stayed home to work on a musical composition he'd begun, set aside in frustration and forgotten a decade ago. It was a strange little piece scored for piano and strings, highly experimental, dissonant and lyric and meditative; neoclassic, but with startling juxtapositions and leaps inspired by Stravinsky and Varèse; an undercurrent of passionate yearning beneath. No one in this phase of his life even knew he'd once had a hope of writing music—"inventing music," he'd called it. It was his secret, or one of them.

Why Jack decided to work on this old, failed composition, he could not have said. So suddenly inspired, excited. *Yearning—for what?* It was almost a physical sensation, a hunger so extreme as to pass over into rapture. Working at the piano, emending his old composition and pushing ahead, he was so absorbed in the strange musical notes springing from his fingertips he glanced up to see with astonishment that it was nearly two A.M.—he'd been working for six hours virtually nonstop.

Outside, a wet-gusty November night. Leaves blown against the windows of his study like a fluttering of fingers.

How happy I am, and am meant to be.

There came back to Jack Wells now, by degrees, as, at night, not every night nor with any reliable regularity but with consoling frequency, he dreamed of the brothers, a memory of how, as a boy, he'd felt a flamelike excitement when working on mathematical problems; playing piano, and for a while the cello, for which he'd had more feeling than aptitude; trying, in secret, to "invent" original music. He'd been embarrassed by his secret vanity, his conviction at certain incandescent moments *You are a born composer, your destiny is music* and somehow this was bound up with his talent for math, geometry. That remarkable ease with which, as a schoolboy, he'd been able to "solve" problems in his head which his teachers had had to work out on paper.

He'd known, and had not wanted to know. He'd known, and had repudiated the knowledge, as one might hide away in a drawer a gift of disturbing mystery.

As a small child Jack had been brightly inquisitive and persistent in his questions put to adults. *How much are all the numbers in the universe added up? Where does the sun go at night? Where are my dreams during the day? If God is in the sky, why can't we see Him with a telescope?* And as a high school student, with his air of intense skeptical wonderment, *Why is Benedict Arnold a "traitor," and George Washington a "hero"? Why does the liver work the way it does, and not some other way? Why didn't parthenogenesis evolve as the most efficient means of reproduction?* He was far more intellectually curious than his brother Steven, though Steven always got high grades in school, too; he was nothing like his parents, who were sometimes proud of him but more often puzzled and annoyed by him. Mr. Wells was a low-level public schools administrator, Mrs. Wells a substitute junior high school teacher—they'd met at State Teachers' College in Albany and seemed to have married as a way of putting youth behind them. Jack resembled neither of them, he was sure. His most vivid memory was his father's counsel on the eve of Jack's high school graduation, at which he was to deliver the valedictory speech—"Just don't make a fool of yourself, son!"

Jack had started piano lessons in junior high school, though the Wellses owned no piano; in senior high, inspired by a televised concert of Pablo Casals, he'd started cello lessons, so avid to learn the instrument, or to try, the school music teacher allowed him to use hers. Later, an adult, Jack had acquired a cello of his own, an exquisite instrument he remembered with feeling, like an old, long-lost lover, but at the time he'd never been serious about taking lessons and eventually he'd sold it. Nor had he been serious about "inventing" music. It became a weekend preoccupation, in time a hobby more contemplated than pursued. Jack's academic work intervened, his dutiful if uninspired citizenship in the university community. He was a vain man and did not want to become one of those mathematicians of whom there are altogether too many characterized as *eccentric*.

His music was a candle flame flickering in his cupped hands and one day he happened to notice that the flame had gone out.

So with his mathematics. Highly promising in graduate school, winner of a prestigious fellowship, one of the more energetic younger professors at the first university at which he'd taught; then, by degrees, after a move to a less demanding university that brought with it promotion to associate professor and tenure, he'd let his research projects atrophy. Too much stress. Too much isolation. And always the risk of failure—*Just don't make a fool of yourself!* Jack found the routines of teaching, the superficial camaraderie of the academic life, the clockwork security of weeks, semesters, years sufficiently rewarding. Differential geometry, curves, surfaces, ghost structures in three-dimensional space, the mind's very play in pursuit of "higher" knowledge—what was it but a hobby, intriguing and respectable as hobbies go; reasonably well-paying; reasonably secure; to be taken up, put down, taken up again like any hobby. Professor Wells was capable of performing in class, or in the company of his colleagues, like an "animated," "passionate" mathematician, which role he played purposefully from time to time. He was an actor playing his own, old self, and he wondered, amused, if he wasn't more publicly effective as an actor than he'd been as that old self.

And there were women, a slow succession of women. Romances that shifted to friendships, with the passage of time. The compass direction of sexual feeling—could it be plotted? Jack supposed, in his case, it could. You move through points a, b, c . . . by the time you get to z, you aren't there any longer.

Fantasizing leaving on Crista's refrigerator door a note that had come to him in one of those waking dreams in which consciousness emerges and recedes and emerges again, where the daylight self touches fingertips with the nighttime self *A family is a four-dimensional structure one plane of which is Time. A vector originating at a finite point but, since it curves into infinity, unchartable. Unknowable. Terrifying.*

December, the week of the first heavy snowfall, he'd been working several nights in succession on his "Trio in C# minor" and dreaming intermittently of the brothers and his relations with

Crista were courteous if strained and guarded *She knows there is someone else, something else: she's jealous* and he felt guilty, sorry for her and at the same time resentful and there came to him a dream of Damm suddenly at his left hand! and Vann suddenly at his right hand! as if springing out of the earth, wholly unexpected. "You are always new to me, no one can invent you," Jack said. The brothers laughed loudly, their eyes squinting up in merriment.

"John Michael!—a surprise for you."

"John Michael!—come with us."

Pulling roughly at him, hands gripping his, tight. He felt a moment's panic. As if he'd pushed his hands into a narrow space and now they were stuck.

"John Michael!—we love you so much—"

"—we have made a place to put you inside of us—"

Though he was dreaming and should not have been capable of such lucidity Jack felt such warmth, such joy thinking *It doesn't matter that they aren't real, nothing in the real world is like this.*

They brought Jack to a clearing in the snow in which there was a tunnel like a rabbit hole and on his hands and knees Jack crawled into it and now Damm and Vann were somehow beside him, or in him, or he was in them, the three of them pushing through the snow tunnel butting with their heads. *If they abandon me I won't be able to find my way back.* But he felt only mild anxiety knowing *This is the truest way of happiness* and his trust in them was not misplaced for now they were in an open space, it seemed to be a room, overheated and airless and strangely lit as in the reflective, oscillating light of fireworks. There'd been a small boy crawling ahead squealing with excitement or alarm and now it was revealed that this boy was a brother, too—his face a vague sweet blur, his hair the color and texture of butterscotch. His name sounded like "Hänne"—"Hänn-*eh*"—a high vibrating syllable that rang in Jack's head.

"John Michael!—see who this is?"

"John Michael!—we've brought him here for a reason."

Jack asked, "What is the reason?" eager to know but his question came out garbled, like snorting, hiccuping. Damm and Vann laughed even louder than before.

"We thought he was the baby, but *you* are."

"John Michael!—why are you so—"

Cold, or *scared,* or *slow,* or—*old?* Jack was listening intensely yet could not hear. Even as, staring at Damm and Vann and now the boy Hänne who was about the size of an eight-year-old he could not seem to see their faces. *That is because they are inside your head, on the wrong side of your eyes.*

There was a fraction of a moment when Jack seemed to know he'd been in this place before. And Hänne was no surprise to him but someone he knew. And what was going to happen though he could not remember it.

It was expected that Jack stoop to kiss the little brother Hänne with whom he was now alone in this warm, airless cavity but he could not do it, his legs were twisted and his backbone stiff to the point of breaking. And his mouth so damned dry, that snorting-rattling in his throat. Damm and Vann were gone yet were watching and grinning lewdly through a kind of half window, an old-fashioned Dutch door. The strobelike lights pulsed weirdly in their eyes. They were—Jack was about to "see" them because he wasn't looking directly at them and they didn't think to disguise themselves—animated wooden figures, with astonishingly de-tailed, realistic features, liquidy eyes, thick dark eyelashes, glisten-ing mouths—even their clothing was carved of wood, slick and shiny. At the same time they were thick-muscled high school boys with blunt, handsome faces, about sixteen years old, the kind of boys who, in Jack Wells's high school, might have re-spected his intelligence but stared coolly through him as if, in his place, *no one at all had stood.* Except in gym class maybe where they'd expressed mild contempt for his tall skinny-puny body, his pigeon-sized muscles and weak eyes and the sullen-superior frown that was his defense.

But now it was, so delicious, "John Michael!—*we love you.*"

The littlest brother too loved Jack and now came giggling and rushing at him flailing his chubby baby arms in imitation of a bird—a hummingbird—aiming a wet kiss at Jack's mouth. But Jack panicked ducking and shielding his head with his arms and in a spasm of coughing woke dazed to find his legs twisted in damp bedclothes, his mouth agape in an enormous O and his penis too enormous pulsing stiff with an erection that throbbed to the point of pain.

It was 6:20 A.M. A high whining wind outside. Pitch black, but the night's dreaming was over. In horror of touching himself Jack staggered from his bed.

The week before Christmas, Jack's father had an accident driving his car, suffered minor injuries and had to be hospitalized and Jack went to visit him and saw by the look in his father's face, in and about the cringing eyes, that this was no longer the man Jack had known. Here was an aging man, a badly frightened man, forcing a jaunty smile to ashy lips; trading wisecracks with the nurses to whom he introduced his "professor" son; insisting, "One minute the damned steering wheel was in my hand, the next—it wasn't." He blamed the icy pavement but Jack knew from his mother that he'd had a blackout, he'd simply lost consciousness and woke up in the hospital.

Fortunately, Jack's father's car had been moving at only about twenty miles an hour. It had swerved across several lanes of traffic, sideswiping another car and striking the rear of a motorcycle driven by a young man and coming to a jolting stop against a guardrail.

Jack asked, "Was the cyclist injured?"

"Well—" His mother's eyes were veiled. "—not badly."

"He wasn't killed, for God's sake, was he?"

"Why are you so excited?" Jack's mother asked, staring at him. She'd always been a nervous woman, quick to take offense; you risked insulting her by simply asking questions of the kind that must be asked. "No, certainly he was *not*. He was treated in the emergency room same as your father and *he* was released that same night."

Jack shut his eyes, feeling the *crack!* of the front wheel striking an invisible victim. But that was only a dream, and not at all like his father's experience, really.

"Why am I so excited?" he asked his mother quietly. "In matters of life and death, shouldn't we all be excited?"

And there was another incident at about that time, a spilling over of his dreams of the brothers into real life, or a spilling over of real life into his dreams of the brothers: In the university swimming pool where he hadn't swum for months, he was doing laps one frigid January morning when he sighted, padding across his line of vision, a stocky-muscled young man covered in darkish ape-fuzz, pink hose of a penis bobbing at his groin—an undergraduate football player who was the model, unmistakably, for Damm and Vann. Jack stared, appalled: *him?* It was a males-only hour at the pool and in this atmosphere of naked men the young football player, shouting to a friend and diving noisily into the pool, was the most truly *naked.*

Jack Wells swam on in his lane, fumbling, so stricken he swallowed a mouthful of water.

John Michael!—now you know.

And he noted too, one evening at Crista's, when Lonnie in his pajamas was running in and out of the living room, squealing breathlessly hoping to avoid being put to bed by his mother—for Jack had been coming less frequently lately, there was tension in his presence—that the child's curly hair was the color of butterscotch. *Hänne—Lonnie?* Jack passed a hand over his eyes, laughing weakly. He must have looked as if he was about to get up and walk out, for Crista said sharply, "Lonnie, *stop.*" And to Jack, apologetically, "Jack, I'm sorry. It's past his bedtime and he knows better but—I guess—he's been missing you, and—"

"Well, I've been missing him," Jack said. This was true, or true enough. Lonnie approached him and Crista where they were sitting together, wineglasses in hand, and the boy's brown-amber eyes were wide in that way of a shy child's impetuosity and Jack felt his heart contract with an emotion sharp as pain. *Why don't you love me!* Lonnie demanded with those eyes *Why aren't you my daddy!*

Afterward, when they were alone, Crista asked, "Is there someone else?" quickly amending, in that way of hers that touched Jack deeply, it spoke of such instinctive solicitude for the other's position, "—unless you'd rather not talk about it with me." And Jack said, slowly, "No. No one." They were at the dining room table reluctant to shift into the next phase of the evening inevitable as a locomotive bearing down upon them—would they make love as they had not done in some time, would Jack stay through the night—or would he, very shortly now, glance at his watch, make a comment about the time and his work waiting for him at home. And there was silence.

A long awkward moment of silence. Crista rested her hand on Jack's in sympathy. *Where I really am, and who I really am.* Almost, she seemed to know. To forgive, and to release. Outside, a light snowfall fine and gritty as sand was being blown against the windows; there was a humming or vibrating in the air, a teasing, nearly inaudible strain of music.

Crista said, "Jack, good night."

He was hunched at the piano. His eyes ached, and his hands. He'd lost track of the time *Which is how you know you are where you are meant to be and that no other could be in your place.* Outside his twelfth-floor window the nighttime city was an attenuated cobweb of lights. It was late, and very cold—the temperature hovering near zero. Jack thought, Good, nobody will interrupt. Even the wind had died down.

The "Trio in C♯ minor" emerged from his fingertips feverishly, but had to be continuously revised. For every movement forward there was a movement back. Some nights, the labor of the previous night, hours of finger-stretching chords, annotations and revisions, was totally unraveled. *If I could just press forward, race to the end* but even in this heightened state of consciousness Jack was cautious, conservative. It filled him with a chill, subdued terror to think that he might never complete the composition. He would work, like this, night after night, week following week into infinity.

Already it was February. He'd arranged to take an unpaid leave of absence from the university, to the surprise of his colleagues and friends. Why? they asked. What are you working on that's so demanding? Or are you going to travel?—where? He told them nothing, he was alone much of the time.

He'd called Crista not long ago simply to be friendly, for he did miss her and the child, and Crista had been cool and curt saying she was fine and busy and, no, she couldn't put Lonnie on the phone—"He's too angry with you."

Jack wanted to say, "I'm angry with myself—" but the remark would have sounded facetious, insincere.

Damm laid a heavy, meaty hand on Jack's right shoulder, and Vann laid a heavy, meaty hand on Jack's left shoulder. The child Hänne was crouched nearby in his red pajamas, making a design in the snow with his hands. The butterscotch hair lifted in thick, hardened-syrupy tufts. There was something wrong with Hänne's left eye which Jack had never noticed before.

"John Michael!—you're an angry man."

"John Michael!—don't be a coward."

It was the first time the brothers had spoken quite so harshly to him and he recoiled with the hurt even as he wriggled his shoulders in such a way as to make himself smaller.

In recent dreams of the brothers Jack seemed to be his full size—an adult man. He stood taller than his father had ever stood before his father had begun his downward shrinking the farthest point of which was infinity. Yet, strangely, for all their shrewdness the brothers had no apparent knowledge that Jack Wells was a university professor, a mathematician. Nor did they know anything about his musical life *and so I have protected myself— haven't I?* He seemed to know that the brothers would have been bitterly jealous if they'd known of his other life.

"John Michael!—you don't lie to *us.*"

"John Michael!—you can't get away with that *here.*"

The threat they wielded was the threat of taking away their love for him. Even when the love was a warm golden liquid making his heart float he was fearful of its loss.

Hänne was running squealing and giggling in the snow and it was not clear if he was leading his brothers or whether his brothers, panting and lolling their tongues like wolves, were in pursuit. Suddenly there was excitement! danger! skidding descending the snowy-icy hill above Hubbard Street. A freight train was rattling close by, boxcar after boxcar ERIE CENTRAL RAILROAD ERIE CENTRAL RAILROAD and the noise was deafening vibrating inside Jack's head so hard his teeth chattered. They were in a forbidden place PRIVATE PROPERTY DANGER KEEP OUT having scaled the ten-foot chain-link fence and Jack was very frightened. And he understood he could not turn back.

Here has nothing to do with there. Once you climb the fence and jump down it doesn't matter where you come from.

The locomotive's whistle was a high-pitched shriek. Frantic as a hunted rabbit Hänne ran slipping in the snow in danger of falling beneath the train's wheels but when Jack reached out to grab him the older brothers jerked him back. "John Michael!—you have to choose."

"Choose what?" Jack asked. "Choose who?"

They were in the Erie Central Railroad yard but they were also in the L-shaped corner of Benjamin Franklin Elementary School. The noise of the train was also the noise of the wind blowing leaves and dirt into Jack's eyes. Jack saw Hänne's blunder but could not warn him *It's a corner! a trap!* for Damm and Vann gripped his shoulders too hard as running panicked from his enemies Hänne rushed into the corner and could not escape. His enemies who were the size of rabbits too, but large, vicious rabbits, knocked him down deftly and undid his corduroy trousers pulling them to his ankles and pulling down his underwear as well and rubbing dirt and dead leaves on his tender penis which shrank up inside him like a tiny turtle retracting its head. *Why do they hate me* Hänne was sobbing but the answer was *Oh no it's just play, it just happens to be you in the corner.* Damm and Vann knew better, however. They were laughing angrily in shame of their little brother who could not defend himself. Jack wanted to protest that when it had happened to him he'd learned to stay inside at recess and noon with other quiet children doing their homework in the cafeteria and amassing "extra credit" so at Parents' Day in June there was a row of shiny stars ***************************** beside John Michael Wells's name on the bulletin board far ahead of the next-nearest name.

Jack wanted to explain to Hänne who was sobbing *You won't remember the origin of those stars—I promise.*

Damm was shaking Jack's shoulder in disgust, "John Michael!—you'd better choose." And Vann shook Jack's shoulder even harder, as if hoping to dislocate it, "John Michael!—make up your mind."

The terrible locomotive was close behind them. Jack understood that he was to sacrifice one of the brothers, push him beneath the wheels, but he could not. "No, no please," he was pleading, "—don't make me, please—" He was paralyzed and his words too were stopped in his throat like great clots of phlegm. Damm and Vann were panting their harsh steamy breaths in his face saying, "Coward!—*choose*. Coward!—*choose*." But Jack was whimpering, his bladder threatened to spill, and in the manner of adolescent boys thrusting another from them in physical repugnance the older brothers shoved him so roughly he woke not at the piano (where with part of his delirious dreaming mind he'd believed himself to be) but fallen like a dead man across his bed. He was fully clothed, even his shoes on. Eyes burning in their sockets as if he'd been staring into a fierce light though his bedroom was darkened, and absolutely still. *Choose! choose!* the voices were fading *Coward, choose!* already the brothers' voices were fading into the wind against the windows, or into a locomotive's whistle miles away across the river, or into a child's nighttime fretting in the apartment above and though Jack sat up quickly, fully awake now and his senses alert as if he had narrowly escaped great danger he heard nothing, no one.

How rapidly, how helplessly they were fading, the voices. And the luminous human figures. And the names of these figures. Receding to the size of a spark, a pinprick. Infinity. *What you must not remember, you won't be able to.* The brothers were gone and would not return but what that would mean, what Jack's life would be from now on, he had no idea. It had happened already, but he could not remember.

The Lost Child

Our lives of secrecy, as children.

The secrets never to be uttered, to adults. Even after so long a passage of time we've become adults ourselves.

"Here's something!" one of us said, and snatched it up.

Beneath the rotting pier, at the end of the spit of land called Fox Point, amid muddy sand and beach debris, the torn snapshot, a color Polaroid, lay partly buried.

It was Jean, twelve years old, the oldest among us, who'd found the snapshot and ran out from beneath the pier with it, into daylight, to see it better. There was no sun, the sky was mottled with pearly incandescent cloud. Across Lake Ontario waves were wild, choppy, angry-looking, capped with froth and there was that smell that came with wind from the north—sharp and briny, like wet sand, decaying fish.

"What is it? Let's see—" Seeing the expression on Jean's face we crowded around her, but Jean backed off, staring at what she held in her hand, "What is it, what *is* it?"

Jean was a tall, stocky girl whose parents were divorced and whose mother worked in a plastics factory. Her face reddened easily, showing every emotion. Whatever the Polaroid was, it surprised and intrigued her, she stared at it with a look of incredulity, and alarm, and extreme embarrassment. "Something nasty," Jean mumbled, holding the snapshot out of reach, "—never *mind*." Her cheeks were ruddy as if they'd been slapped. Her eyes were damp and narrowed. These were signals to be wary with Jean, she was a big, strong girl, with a quick temper; the kind to lash out with an elbow or a fist if you got too close when she didn't want you close.

Another girl, Bobbie, insisted upon looking, and reluctantly Jean showed it to her, and Bobbie snorted with disbelief, "Je*sus*," and stood stock-still. "What're they doing?—d'you know who it *is*?" Bobbie and Jean began to giggle, wildly. There was nothing mirthful in their giggling which had a sharp, hurtful sound, like pebbles flung at the underside of the abandoned pier.

The rest of us, three or four of us, including Jean's nine-year-old brother Mickey, clamored to see, too, but were rebuffed, as Bobbie and Jean passed the Polaroid between them, now shrieking with laughter, not wanting to be in possession of the snapshot but not wanting to surrender it to us, either, and this went on for a while, the wind was up and a smell of rain in the air, late August just before Labor Day when there was a quickened sense of urgency among us as if we knew, but how could we have known, that this was the last summer we would be children together quite like this, and farther up the beach, where the boardwalk began, there were young mothers with babies in strollers, there were older kids, familiar faces, there was the risk—but of course this was part, now, of the game—that someone would take note of us, of Jean and Bobbie making such a commotion, and come down, and demand to see, too.

Finally, another girl, Brenda, was allowed to see, for Brenda was Jean's best friend, a red-haired freckled girl with a reliable capacity for surprise, and Brenda too stared, and stared, "—who is it?—oh God," and as I pushed forward impatiently, thinking to snatch the Polaroid from them, Brenda cried, not in meanness but in caution, as one stricken with alarm, "—Don't let Junie see!" and so they rebuffed me another time, and my eyes flooded with tears of resentment.

I saw that the three of them would share a secret forever, and I would be one of those, like nine-year-old Mickey, like Sharon Scott who was a little slow, relegated to *not knowing*. Banished to *not included*.

A flame passed over my brain, a terrible feverish need. Yet I could not beg, "Hey c'mon please,—please Jean c'mon," as I'd so often done in the past, for as long as I could remember. I sensed that this was different, for my protection somehow, as Mickey might be protected, and Sharon Scott, who was a little slow, but quick to tears, might be protected; and this startling perception of myself, as in an unexpected mirror or reflecting surface, was disturbing, too, for wasn't Junie the quickest and cleverest of her friends? didn't she get, seemingly without effort, the highest grades in school?

As if here, on the beach, this windy late summer day, the secret Polaroid snapshot hidden from me, school mattered in the slightest.

Sometimes on the boardwalk, down behind the grimy stucco changing rooms for men and women, older boys might call our attention to words and drawings scrawled on walls, we'd be urged to see what had been done overnight to posters, for instance the mutilated breasts of a grinning girl in a cowboy hat, or had the curving plume of smoke issuing from her mouth been turned into something tubular and solid, both comic and threatening, and, to me, mysterious—though always, as in Jean's mumbled words, *something nasty.*

In the older boys' presence, I did not want to know. When the boys laughed in that excited, sniggering way, I did not want to know why.

Something nasty.

Which was how the boys asserted their power over us—the threat of embarrassment, shame.

With my girlfriends Jean, Bobbie, Brenda, it was different. My need to know wasn't just curiosity but something stronger I could not have named. *I hate you, and I can't bear not to be one of you.* I rushed at Jean, who had the Polaroid again, and I snatched it out of her fingers, and ran off along the beach with it as they shouted after me, and when I saw they weren't following me I stopped to examine it—peering at it as at one of those puzzles in the children's magazine *Jack and Jill,* where, slyly hidden amid line-drawings of foliage and clouds, were faces, human figures, even animals. *What was this!*

The snapshot has been torn, folded, left out in the wet, dried

and baked by the sun. Its Polaroid colors had faded and its images were blurred as in a dream. But it showed, so strangely, to
my eyes astoundingly, a frightened little girl of perhaps four in
the grip of a man, a naked man, pressed against his belly and
groin, and what was she being forced to do, her jaws forced
open, her cheeks wet with tears, I could not see, I saw but could
not comprehend, staring as my eyes too filled with moisture,
shocked, yet puzzled, more puzzled at first than shocked, because incredulous, "—What *is* it?" called out for my friends to
hear. Only the naked torso, belly, and groin of the man showed,
and his forearms, his head was cut off so he might have been
anyone, was that the special horror of it, he might have been anyone, any man here at Fox Point, a man with a fatty slack belly
covered in dark rippling hairs like fur, muscular forearms like
our fathers' covered too in thick dark hairs. The little girl who
was a stranger wore a tiny, torn undershirt and no panties; her
skin was drained of all color by the Polaroid's flash, and hairless.
Her face was partly hidden by the man's belly and hands—
big-knuckled hands, a signet ring on one of the fingers—gripping
her jaws and the back of her head. Her pale hair was matted and
disheveled and her eyes narrowed in such pain and terror I
crumpled the snapshot in my hand, and looked away blinking,
blind, out at the lake. Choppy white-capped waves, circling gulls.
What was it!

My heart was beating strangely. I felt the shock in my body
I felt when I jumped from a risky height, always as a child I
jumped to impress my friends who watched but dared not emu-
late me, jumping from a lakefront retaining wall down to the
beach, jumping from the roof of our garage, landing hard on my
heels, the shock waves shooting up my body leaving me stunned,
giddy.

Jean ran up, flush-faced, scared and angry, "Junie, damn you, I
told you!" and snatched the Polaroid back, and tore it into tiny
bits, and let the wind take them, and I turned and ran, ran and
ran until I was off the beach and far away, frantic to get home to
the bungalow my parents rented for August, on a sandy lane
lined with similar bungalows, hard to distinguish one from the
other except by the towels and bathing suits tossed over railings

to dry, or a car parked out front. I didn't know what Jean meant
by "I told you!" but I wished I had not seen what I'd seen.
Something nasty.

I avoided my friends for what seemed like a long time but was
probably a single day, drawn out and seemingly endless as such
summer days are for children, and down at the beach with my
mother and little brother I was quiet, sullen, my mother asked
was something wrong and I said no but don't touch me, and it
was so: my skin smarted as with sunburn or fever. Not wanting to
look at people around me, at men in their bathing suits, my eyes
filling with moisture: no, don't look: I *told* you! Later I wandered
off to the pier, not on top (where you weren't supposed to walk,
it was blocked with a sign DANGER PIER NOT MAINTAINED BY COUNTY)
but beneath, where waves sopped up into the muddy sand, and
there was debris of all kinds, beer cans and bottles and the remains of fires (though for miles along the beach were signs FIRES
FORBIDDEN ON BEACH BY ORDER OF COUNTY SHERIFF'S DEPT.) and I
poked around with a stick unearthing bottle caps, broken combs,
pearly shells, what looked like the charred remains of snapshots,
maybe.

But I found nothing. So I could begin to forget.

Next day, I was back with Jean, Bobbie, Brenda, Sharon, as if
nothing had happened. We never spoke of the Polaroid. We told
no one about it. There were many secrets we never told our parents, or any adult, or even an older sister, secrets too certain of us
shared with one girl but did not share with the others, for that
was what we did, that was the happiness of our lives, such secrets, and the Polaroid Jean had ripped into bits and let the wind
take was only one of these secrets, more perishable in fact than
the others because it was something nasty of which, even among
ourselves, we could not speak; and where a thing is not named, it
is soon surrendered to oblivion.

But I remember: looking at the men on the beach for those remaining days of summer, their bodies which were naked except
for swim trunks, sometimes the trunks were tight-fitting, you
could see the bulge of what was inside, you could sense the
weight of it, that secret too, and the fatty-muscular arms, shoul-

ders, torsos, the hard lean muscles of the younger men, the slacker flesh of the older men, some of them deeply tanned, some pale as curdled milk, the arms of some ropy, the legs of some surprisingly thin, and some were near-hairless but most were covered in hairs, kinky-curly, matted or silky or frizzy, there were enormous paunches straining against elastic waistbands to the point of pain, there were chests with muscles hard as armor, chests flabby as melting chicken fat, and I saw with relief that my father was one of the younger men, arriving at the bungalow late Friday afternoon and changing right away into his trunks, just slightly soft at the waist but flat-chested and -bellied, with a thick frizzy swirl of reddish hairs on his torso, belly, legs, and his arms hard and muscular, yes and I saw that he wore no ring on either hand, I saw that right away.

Christmas Night 1962

Come on then! he said. Goddamn you I'll take you.

My mother was in the back bedroom crying. Christmas night, you wouldn't think it could still be the same day. She'd been crying seeing the raggedy doll thrown across the room. She'd been drinking too except with her, unlike the men, it made the freckles come out in her face, and the skin beneath like skim milk. It made her walk strange like the floor was tilted and laugh when nothing was funny and rub her knuckles into her eyes like she was trying to wake up and not succeeding. Her hair red-frizzed like mine except it was coarser than mine which was so fine I'd squirm and whimper when she ran the hairbrush through, then the steel comb. Frantic to get every last one of the snarls out she said, damn you hush! don't be a baby.

It started after we got home from Grandpa's. He was on the sofa watching the same TV football they'd had on at the other house then he said something making her laugh that sharp laugh like scraping your finger on a blackboard and that was the mistake. For always there was a mistake you could point to. First he slapped her with his open hand and she screamed and turned over the table where some of the presents were from that morning, and his beer, and somehow it happened the raggedy doll that was Grandma's present for me went flying across the room hitting the doorframe banging its head *crack!*

She'd tried to stop him but she'd run into his fist—more than his fist. When it happens it happens fast. Like the boxing he took us to in Port Oriskany, the men up in the ring in the lights coming at each other slow and wary so you think nothing's going to happen you could shut your eyes seeing something far away but suddenly people are yelling and it's happening faster than you can see so you have to invent what it was to account for one of the boxers down on the canvas, blood leaking from his mouth. Just like that, that fast, in the living room with the TV on high and the Christmas tree in the corner knocked now on its side and some of the glass bulbs shattered.

I cried, I wasn't to blame. I knew I would be blamed.

The red-swirled glass bulbs shaped like pears, that Grandma gave us, the ones that were so beautiful. And the frosted white ones with the glitter dust. Home by myself I'd drag the cardboard box of ornaments out of the closet just to look through them, touch them. The tinsel for looping over the tree branches, the colored lights in the shape of candles, the angel for the top of the tree with her pretty painted-on face and gold halo like the statue of the Blessed Virgin Mary in church. Where the tree was fallen over, the angel hung upside down like something in a cartoon.

Come on Honey, he said, wiping his mouth, squatting over where the raggedy doll was broken on the floor. You know you're okay.

If you'd stop that goddamn fucking crying, he said. His face going white like the blood was being squeezed out of it.

My mother came out of the back bedroom running with towels and a blanket and she screamed at him to get away, she was going to take me to Yewville to the hospital and he shoved at her saying she was too pissed to drive and she screamed *he* was too pissed, *he* was the crazy one, if he took me out of the house she'd call the police. He said, You call the police and I'll rip you apart, go for that phone to call anybody you'll wish you were never born, nor her either. She was trying to wrap the towel around my head where I was bleeding and they both pulled at me, *he* was going to take me he said, he guessed my leg might be broken, and my mother ran back into the bedroom then returned with the gun waving it at him, holding it in both hands waving it at him, You think I won't? You bastard, you think I won't?

This pistol he'd brought home last summer, he'd won playing poker. My mother was scared to have it in the house but later on, back in the woods, he'd target practice shooting bottles and got my mother to try too, giggling and nervous and I'd crouch behind them pressing my hands against my ears as he held her with his right arm around her to steady her, helping her aim, pull the trigger, absorb the kick. And her hiding her face in his neck afterward, breathless from what she'd done.

Now my mother in a velour shirt the color of crushed strawberries ripped off the shoulder from where he'd grabbed her and her black slacks glistening with blood holding that pistol trembling in her hands. Screaming and waving it her eyes wild so he backed off on his haunches, Okay Anna, okay just don't pull that trigger, you're crazy enough to do it, and she said, That's right! I am! Just try me, mister, I *am*!

So she lifted me and wrapped me in the blanket holding him off with the gun. The blood soaked into the gray wool making it wet. I was crying, I couldn't stop, like hiccups when you can't stop. She was sobbing too saying, Don't fight me, Honey, you're going to be all right but it hurt so when she lifted me I had to scream.

That Christmas night. Snow blowing gritty as sand. She had to carry me, I couldn't walk where the bone was cracked. My left leg below the knee where I'd hit against the doorframe, and my forehead bleeding and swollen already to the size of a hen's egg. And my mouth, there was something wrong with my mouth Mommy was trying to hold the towel against slipping and sliding out to the car, Oh! oh! oh! our breaths were steaming, she'd grabbed her coat but hadn't time to put on boots. Saying, Honey don't cry Mommy has you safe now okay? trying to fit me in the front seat but I screamed with the pain so she had to put me in back laying me out flat wrapped in the blanket. I screamed and held onto her not wanting to let go.

Christmas night, and the morning so long ago. Snowdrifts up to the windows, taller than a man by the garage, giant icicles glittering like knife blades hanging down from the roof's edge frozen solid in the minus-ten-degree-fahrenheit cold. That morning the windows were blinding with snow-light and now it was dark, snowflakes swirling in the car headlights like something you could stare and stare into and lose your way not remembering who you are.

I can't tell this. I don't have the words. I remember everything but I don't have the words. Even when I say them, the words are not the right words.

The raggedy doll sewed by my grandmother, it was big enough for me to need both arms to carry it. A floppy head with shiny black button eyes and a button nose and a smile and orange-red pigtails braided out of yarn. Her top was cotton printed in tiny flowers and her bottom was cotton printed in bright yellow checks and her legs which had no bones were white wool stockings and she was stuffed with something soft like cotton batting. Every year for all the years I could remember Grandma sewed me a Christmas doll, and things to wear.

I loved Grandma so much. She was his mother so she had to take his side. My other grandmother wasn't here they said and when I asked where was she they said with God in Heaven. But I knew what that was—buried in the cemetery that's just a hilly field behind the church.

That morning my mother dressed me for Christmas before she dressed herself. Only a few times a year we'd go to church and Christmas morning was one but *he* didn't go. Mommy brushed my hair wetting and shaping the curls into corkscrew-curls around her fingers then tickling blowing in my ear, Pretty girl! who's my pretty girl! Mommy loves you so. She pulled on over my head the new jumper Grandma had sewed for me for Christmas, soft velour to match Mommy's shirt she'd sewed too with a big patch pocket green like a strawberry leaf. White woolly socks, black patent-leather shoes but the same old scuffed boots to fit over them.

A little velour bow too in my hair. A row of bobby pins, barrettes. Corkscrew curls to my shoulders so I'd turn my head and feel them moving, tickling. Before Mommy and I went to church he squatted down in front of me staring at me. Cupped my face in his hands looking at me for a long time his eyes like that kind of marble with a glaze to them so the colors inside look cracked. That way I knew he wasn't seeing me though he said, Merry Christmas, sweetheart! The big day's here, eh?

Mommy said in her careful voice, Don't scare her. You scare her looking at her like that.

Like what? he said. Now straightening up, and taking Mommy's chin in his hand, holding her so she had to look at him. Like this?

He used to be Daddy but says not to call him that any more but sometimes I forget. But after Christmas night I won't forget.

It was at my grandparents' place the drinking started. The big old farmhouse, the long table for Christmas dinner. So much food at two in the afternoon, your stomach isn't ready for it. The men were playing poker and they were loud and laughing and my father was loud winning a hand but louder losing, red-faced and squinting up his eyes laughing like it was a joke only he got. Uncle Dwight who's married to Aunt Helen, Uncle Marcus who's married to Auntie Irene, Uncle Bud who used to be married but isn't now and you're not to ask why, you never ask *why* of adults. Grandpa and Uncle Dwight worked in the gypsum plant on the Jamestown Road where my father did except they were laid off through January. How long after that nobody knew. They'd been laid off, the factory gates chained shut, since before the first snow.

Who can you believe, they said. What any one of them tells you, or you read in the paper, if it's somebody in a suit and tie for sure he's lying to you because he makes his money off you. And if it's a politician he's already lied to get where he is. So fuck it.

Once when I was real little I said that word. My cousins whispered it in my ear and afterward when I said it some people laughed except not Grandma, and not Mommy. Mommy scolded saying that's not a nice word, nice little girls don't say that word. I giggled saying Yes they do! yes they do! and said the word again running around the table where she couldn't catch me. Except this time the way she looked at me I was sorry so I didn't say it ever again, that Mommy could hear.

My mother was driving our old 1957 Chevy along the Canal Road trying to keep the car's tires in the ruts in the snow made by other cars. The snow plow had come by in the morning and all day it had been snowing and now in the night the narrow road was drifting over and she was praying Holy Mary Mother of God! Holy Mary Mother of God! and in the back seat the limp sobbing raggedy doll. Leg cracked below the knee, bleeding from a swelling cut above her eye. And vomit, and the stink of vomit, on the gray blanket. No other cars were on the road. The headlights swung and lurched, snowflakes rushed at the windshield, the car's stops and starts and skids and jolts were stabs of pain Oh! oh! oh! At the steep ramp to the Yewville bridge the drifts are so high the car's front wheels get stuck. Back up, go forward, back up, go forward rocking the car until momentum carries it onto the ramp.

Honey, are you all right?—Honey?—your Mommy's going to take care of you. Don't cry! Don't cry!

Then, scared and angry-sounding as the car moves slowly so slowly not five miles an hour across the high windblown shaky plank-floored bridge, Holy Mary Mother of God have mercy on us!

The water tower at the top of Church Street. The steep drop to Memorial Avenue, the ice-slick pavement where the car skids, begins to slide. The front tire jolting against the curb Oh! oh! Seneca Street, Ontario, Locust. The redbrick Episcopal Church with the high tower, the big stained-glass window. Bell Telephone Co. where my mother worked as an operator before she fell in love and married the man who would be my father. Before she came to live in the country nine miles north of Yewville where I was born, where she became a woman who was a mother and where her life changed and could never return to what it was. And now at Locust near Main there are cars moving with painstaking slowness in the blizzard and my mother has no choice but to follow behind them sobbing Holy Mary help us! help us! God help us! like it was a curse.

At Providence Hospital on Locust and Van Buren there's a Christmas tree blinking red lights over the front entrance and the parking lot is two-thirds empty, drifted over in snow but my mother parks the car and carries me through the snow stinging gritty as sand in our faces and into the brightly lit reception area where there's only a single nurse behind the counter whose eyes swing onto us startled and disapproving. My mother begins to speak and the nurse cuts her off saying there's no emergency room in this hospital you'll have to go to Yewville General don't you know this isn't that kind of hospital, and my mother says, My little girl's hurt, she fell and hurt herself and I think her leg is broken, I think she's hurt her head bad, please can we see a doctor? please is there a doctor? I'll pay—and another nurse comes out and says in a loud voice like my mother might be hard of hearing, Ma'am? would you like us to call ahead to Yewville General? would you like us to call an ambulance to take you there? the two nurses staring at us, keeping their distance. My young mother with her windblown red-frizzed hair, her white skin splotched with freckles like tiny rust-stains, a purplish bruise swelling the right side of her face. Shivering, swaying with the weight of the child in her arms, a girl of about four years of age, wrapped in a blanket stained with blood and vomit. And my mother asks again for a doctor raising her voice and again the nurses raising their voices say you'll have to go to Yewville General, there's no doctor on duty here tonight and there are no emergency room facilities in this hospital and my mother says begging will you look at her, then? please help us will you please help us? coming forward so the nurses speak more sharply saying Sorry ma'am, sorry you'll have to go to Yewville General, we have no emergency room facilities in this hospital ma'am, and my mother begins to shout, Aren't you nurses? what the hell are you if you aren't nurses? my little girl's hurt, my little girl's in pain Goddamn you! and the older nurse says angrily, Ma'am, we'll have to ask you to leave these premises, picks up a telephone receiver threatening to call the police. So my mother backs off, sobbing and cursing carrying me back outside to the car where the headlights are on, the back door's wide open, the back seat already filling up with snow.

Driving then along Van Buren skidding through a red light then stuck behind a sanding truck moving at five miles an hour all the way to East Avenue where the big hospital Yewville General is. Where Auntie Irene was for her surgery and I was brought to visit one Sunday but we don't go to the front entrance, my mother drives around to the rear where the parking lot is filled with snow and almost empty of cars too and she parks at the curb and carries me half-staggering into another bright-lit reception area larger than the other but there's no one in the waiting room and just one woman at the desk saying Yes? What is it? How can we help you? and Mommy says, quick and scared like she knows she's going to be turned away, It's my little girl, she's hurt, I need to see a doctor!—coming forward past the desk toward the double swinging doors NO ADMITTANCE EMERGENCY and the woman calls out, Ma'am! Stop! and a young man in a white uniform appears to block her way and Mommy is saying, We need a doctor, please help us, my little girl is hurt bad, her head! her leg! I think her leg is broken please help us! her voice shrill and her eyes wild like she's been drinking. There's a nurse too saying, You'll have to check in at reception first, ma'am, ma'am?—you have to check in at reception first. My mother is pleading with the young man, Doctor? help us please, will you examine my little girl? she hit her head running, she fell down and I think her leg is broken, please Doctor? her voice rising as if to prevent the young man from interrupting saying he isn't a doctor, he isn't in charge.

Mommy is a thin woman, you wouldn't think she'd be strong enough to carry me, to hold me like this in her arms. The tight hard muscle tensing in her upper arms and shoulders like it's lifting from the bone.

And everybody in this bright lit place staring at the limp raggedy doll, bleeding from a cut about the left eye. Wrapped in a filthy blanket. Frizzy red corkscrew curls messy as a rat's nest.

The strong smell pierces my nostrils like the dentist's office to make me gag. Mommy hugs me, whispering Honey it's all right, Honey you're safe now, but there's a woman's voice running on and on repeating no patients can be treated at Yewville General Hospital without first filling out the proper forms at reception, yes and you need insurance identification, this is hospital policy, this is New York State law. There's an artificial silver-tinsel Christmas tree, three feet high, on a table, glittery sequin-snow sprinkled onto the green cloth beneath. And brightly wrapped Christmas presents, the kind of presents that if you lift them are just empty boxes. At the reception desk there's a radio playing "Rudolph the Red-Nosed Reindeer." My mother is saying, pleading, I don't know about our insurance, I don't know the name of the insurance, I came out without my wallet and I.D. speaking fast so they can't interrupt, then angry, saying, You're going to take this child! this is a hurt child, an injured child, Goddamn you! And a nurse, an older woman with peach-colored hair and a little fringe of bangs says making her voice steely calm, Ma'am, this is a private hospital and we are not obliged to accept any patient not adequately covered by hospital and medical insurance so if you will please cooperate—, and my mother says screaming, I told you! I don't have my wallet! There isn't time! This is an emergency! Her arms are weakening and give way and she almost drops me on the floor carrying me to a couch in the waiting room, now the voices are louder, there are more of them and more disapproving and Mommy is saying, furious, You think we're trash, is that it, we're white trash is that it! We're poor, we're from the country, we don't count, we're shit on your shoes is that it! Now there's another, older man wearing a white coat, a doctor this time asking what's going on here, and the nurse tells him, and my mother interrupts, You're not going to let my daughter die, Goddamn you, you sons of bitches you're not going to let my daughter die, taking the pistol out of her coat pocket and waving it in their faces her hand trembling and her eyes wild and frightened as everybody goes Oh! oh! shrinking back in astonishment and the quick terror of animals you see in their eyes in a car's headlights at night but my mother lets the pistol fall, she's sobbing Goddamn you, Goddamn you, letting it fall clattering onto the floor and for a long long moment there's no sound except over the radio the tinkly jingly "Rudolph the Red-Nosed Reindeer" coming to an end.

Then the older man, the doctor, stoops quickly to pick up the pistol. He hands it to the young man saying call the police, please.

And Mommy is standing there panting like she's been running, turning her head from side to side like she's trying to clear it, to wake up. And the doctor says, Yes I will examine your little girl but you'll remain out here until the police arrive. Do you understand, ma'am?—you will remain out here. And Mommy says her lips moving slow, Yes Doctor.

There's a stretcher brought out to where I'm lying and they lift me onto it and Mommy wants to help but they make her stand back. Staring at me seeing the ugly bruised cut on my forehead, the slack wet mouth and the bloody root of a missing front tooth, the blanket falls open showing the surprise of the strawberry-red velour jumper sewed by Grandma who loves me. White woolly socks and shiny patent-leather shoes and the skinny leg hanging limp, swelling below the knee like a giant bee had stung it.

On the radio, a woman's happy voice singing "Walking in the Winter Wonder-Land."

This woman who's my mother stands watching as I'm carried into the emergency room of Yewville General Hospital, Yewville, New York, 9:25 P.M. of Christmas night 1962. Standing clenching her fingers into fists her head slightly lowered as if to hide her own injuries and her lips moving and she begins to cry giving herself up to hoarse racking angry sobs, helpless sobs as if, now she's got what she has wanted, now she sees her child taken from her by strangers, now these strangers have yielded as if by magic to her desperate will, bearing me through the doors below NO ADMITTANCE EMERGENCY, she's surrendered me forever. It's over.

The Passion
of Rydcie Mather

Rydcie Mather, fifty-one years old, is making her final run. Fifteen years driving a glaring-yellow school bus with the words HARTSHILL JUNIOR HIGH SCHOOL in black on its sides, the lone female driver for any of the township schools. The vehicle rattles, wheezes. The brakes, when Rydcie hits them, sound like a goose whose neck is being wrung. It has been raining all day but now in the afternoon the sky is glowering-white, like a metallic surface, slightly corrugated.

Along Shepherd Road, Rydcie stops to let off Bobby Stitt, the Harkness sisters, Dewey Laird. Then a sharp turn onto Trumper, and Joan Caen gets off. At Ferry Street, where the old arsenal has been rebuilt, overlooking the Yewville River, the kids who live in the old millworkers' rowhouses get off, including Byron and Marinda Cass, the only black children who ride Rydcie's bus this year. When Rydcie stops her bus and the red lights flash, front and rear, no other motorists dare pass her—it's a state law, and there's Rydcie behind the wheel alert to see that no one disobeys, nor even creeps slyly forward. She isn't afraid to use her horn, and to use it long and hard. Even today, which is to be her final day, she's sharp-eyed, alert. She's maybe gripping the steering wheel a little more tightly than usual.

When Rydcie guns the motor, shifts to first, presses the gas pedal down hard, the bus shudders and heaves itself into motion; its tires protest with faint, satisfying squeals. The rowdier boys—

Bobo Lundt, Pete Erlicht—mimic the motor's sound deep in their throats, or cheer, in an undertone, "Go, Miz Mat'er!" Never once has Rydcie acknowledged this, nor does she acknowledge it this afternoon. She drives with her head high, shoulders ramrod straight, eyes ahead. She's a tall, flaring-shouldered woman with a fierce-eyed face like something carved on a totem pole, skin dark and grainy as stained wood. This past year, Rydcie's smoky-dark hair has become streaked in white, like a skunk's, which gives her a savage, rakish look. The kids riding her bus never see her so she has become, over the years, invisible to herself. There's a satisfaction in that.

On upper Post Road, Rydcie begins talking with Graeme Stearns, an eighth grader who lives on Shanker Road, off Post, three stops up from the bridge. Graeme is a plump-faced boy of thirteen with horn-rimmed glasses that give him the alert, affable air of a television newscaster; he sits near the front of the bus, like several others, to avoid the bullying and roughhousing elsewhere on the bus, which, in recent weeks, Rydcie has been negligent about controlling. Bobo, Pete, Budd Schier—their silly girlfriends Betsey Ann Waller, Irene McGhee—their snappy wisecracks and squealing laughter and the frantic beat of a forbidden transistor radio turned low, but still tauntingly audible: in avoidance, the good, quiet, meek kids like Graeme sit near the front, and hope for the best. In the driver's vicinity, there's safety.

How many times Graeme Stearns will repeat what he can remember of the last conversation Rydcie Mather is known to have had with anyone, before the accident!—Graeme will recount it, with varying embellishments, through his life.

Driving just perceptibly faster than usual, and rather jerkily, Rydcie lifts one hand from the wheel to gesture out the windshield at a stretch of vacant, partly wooded land, and says to Graeme, with no preamble, wholly unexpectedly, "Out there it was all a glacier once, millions of years ago, and then it melted and was all water, a *sea*. It's always changing. It never stops. God has nothing to do with it." Rydcie's deep voice, gritty as steel wool, sounds as if it hasn't been used in some time. At first, startled, Graeme isn't certain that Rydcie is addressing him—she'd never spoken to him in the past, nor to anyone, much, except to scold, in the nearly two years Graeme has been riding her bus. But Rydcie squints around at him, so he can't not know she means him, saying, "It's called *perpetual motion.*"

For some reason Graeme, a straight-A student, blurts out, "There can't ever be a perpetual motion machine."

Rydcie squints harder at him. She says, sharply, "Yes? Why?"

Graeme thinks a bit. "Our science teacher told us. There just can't be."

Rydcie makes a scoffing sound but says nothing more.

At Shanker Road, Rydcie brakes the bus to a shuddering halt, to let Graeme and two other children out. The time is 3:35 P.M., of Thursday, April 18. The rain is lightening but the Yewville River, a quarter-mile away at the foot of the Post Road hill, is swollen and fast-moving from days of rain.

The name was pronounced "Rid-see"—though she was also called in a burry rush of syllables, for people were shy of her, "Miz Mat'er." Only after her death would Hartshill residents who'd known her learn, from the newspaper, that her baptismal name was Eurydice.

Some of them would recall that she'd had a younger sister, long since vanished from the area. The sister's name was something peculiar too—"Gonne." Short for Antigone.

These were names that must have been inflicted upon the two girls by the late Orren Mather, their father. He was a locally prominent lawyer who'd invested his money unwisely, and who had died in a riding accident, falling drunk from his horse. Mr. Mather had been a convivial drinker whose only cranky trait was his habit of lapsing into high-sounding quotations from—was it Greek, or Latin?—the Bible? (But if Orren Mather quoted the Bible, you could be sure it wasn't any familiar verse.)

After her father's scandalous death, when she'd been still respectfully employed as a librarian at the Hartshill Public Library (in the old sandstone building behind the courthouse, not the new glass-fronted building on Trumper Road), poor Rydcie had tried to get a manuscript of his published, a thousand pages of translations of some ancient Greek tragedies Orren had been working on, it was rumored, for a quarter of a century. Rydcie

had had no luck, and the massive manuscript would be discovered in the Mathers' family vault at the First Chautauqua Savings &
Loan, by the executor of Rydcie's estate.

What became of it after that, isn't generally known.

Except for the three and a half years Rydcie Mather was away at
the State University learning to be a librarian, she lived with her
parents—after her father's death, alone with her mother—in the
pebble-colored colonial on Church Street. Since adolescence Rydcie had been tall, sinewy-thin, with heavy dark brows and staring
hyperthyroid eyes, a cleft chin like the late Orren Mather's, and
an air of bristling impatience. Even as a high school student, Rydcie had described herself as a "nonpracticing non-Christian"—a
"pure rationalist." Yet, each Sunday, when Mrs. Mather was feeling well enough, Rydcie brought her to the eleven o'clock service
at Faith Lutheran Church.

Mrs. Mather attended Faith Lutheran her entire life. She'd out-
lived several ministers, whom she recalled fondly, as if, like her
husband, they'd fallen by the wayside in a marathon race the dimensions of which they'd never quite grasped, while she, Violet
Mather, with all her maladies, had just kept on—"I thank the living God every hour of every day, for all my blessings!"

If Rydcie was within earshot, she would sigh, and roll her
eyes, and murmur, "Oh, Momma, *really*!"

In their pew at Faith Lutheran, directly in front of the pulpit,
the Mather women were a familiar sight. Mrs. Mather was placid
and sweet-faced; fattish; appearing, with her soft layered chin, her
plump arms and swollen legs, as if she were floating amid a rustle
of fabric, skirts and undergarments and thick flesh-colored support hosiery. Rydcie was fierce, straight, unyielding. For perhaps
the first half of Reverend Cogdon's sermon, Mrs. Mather would be
frowning and attentive; then, by abrupt degrees, her pale-powdered
face would go slack, and she would slip into a light doze, while
Rydcie, beside her, would listen, staring—simply staring, as if the
minister's gently-phrased pieties and invocations of Jesus Christ
were beyond scorn. In the face of Miss Mather's stony gaze, Reverend Cogdon, an oldish-young man in his thirties, began to perspire and stammer. It pained him to acknowledge that, though

Rydcie Mather was the single nonbeliever in his congregation, she was also the only person who listened unwaveringly to him.

Mrs. Mather, a Christian lady, was content with her life, even when short of breath, or when arthritis made her small, shapely hands swell. As she said, "Look at the poor souls so much worse off!—they're *everywhere*." She was an avid television watcher, and was rarely disappointed in her search for men and women worse off than herself.

Rydcie, who loved her mother, considered how, for her mother, life was routine, almost entirely. The solace of routine. The infantile happiness of routine. Mrs. Mather's Lutheranism was in fact a form of routine—like her eagerly anticipated meals and snacks, her long afternoon naps, her visits with a gradually shrinking circle of friends, her television programs, and the company of her canary Zasu. Each night, sinking, with Rydcie's aid, into bed, surfeited with a sugary snack (raspberry ripple ice cream, Dutch chocolate cake were her favorites), Mrs. Mather would sigh, "The Lord has me in His bosom, I shall not fear!" shivering with the anticipation of sleep, which she loved even beyond eating. Rydcie grunted, helping raise her mother's legs, and settle her back against her goose-feather pillows; she might grimace, or murmur, "Oh, Momma!" But she would never speak harshly or cruelly.

Nor say aloud, in her mother's hearing, "Yes, Momma—but what about *me?*"

As one of two librarians in the Hartshill Public Library, Rydcie Mather had seemed dedicated to her job. Yet, abruptly, after an incident that brought her local attention, and much admiration, she quit the job, with no explanation.

This is what happened: One Sunday afternoon in June, Rydcie hiked out to the War Memorial Park, where she frequently hiked by herself on weekends; she'd just emerged from a wooded area and was walking by the lake, when a canoe carrying a young couple overturned (no doubt, the young couple had been playfully tussling), and both fell screaming and thrashing into the water. Without hesitating, Rydcie tore off her shoes and waded into the lake, yelling, "Hold on! I'm coming!" Fully clothed, Rydcie pushed off into the deep water and swam to the canoe, where the young man was clinging squealing like a pig to the canoe and the girl, a few yards away, was swallowing water, choking, flailing about helplessly. "I'm coming! I'm here!" Rydcie cried.

Rydcie seemed not to have considered, for an instant, that, in such a desperate situation, there might be danger to herself—the lake was deep where the canoe was overturned, and Rydcie was not a practiced swimmer.

Rydcie seemed not to have considered any other course of action at all, except doing what she did, and saving the drowning girl.

So she swam to Amanda Curle, grabbed her roughly by her long yellow hair, looped an arm around her shoulders, and, after a brief sputtering struggle, succeeded in overpowering her, and hauling her to shore.

By the time Rydcie dragged her onto the bank, Amanda was unconscious. So, straddling her body, Rydcie began to apply mouth-to-mouth resuscitation, counting under her breath *twelve times per sixty seconds! twelve times per sixty seconds!* until the girl began breathing again—groaning, and retching, and weakly vomiting up lake water. By now, others had come running over to help. The young man was still clinging to the canoe, crying for help: Rydcie had ignored him entirely.

Rydcie rose, swaying, to her feet. Did she know Amanda Curle?—the girl, twenty-two years old, lying on the grassy bank amid the droppings of ducks and geese, hair now the shade of wet sand, skin sickly-white and doughy, floral-print halter-top dress clinging to her young body—was she recognizable? Rydcie might well have seen her in the library, a few years before, when the girl had used it for high school assignments; probably she'd noticed Amanda, and her gaggle of friends, annoyed as they whispered, giggled, passed notes to one another disturbing the decorum of the library—the decorum Rydcie Mather was determined to maintain. But Rydcie didn't remember Amanda Curle and had no interest in remembering.

Now, so many people were gathered around, Rydcie wanted only to slip away.

She snatched up her shoes, walked off. People tried to stop her, but she walked off. She was deeply embarrassed by the attention she'd drawn; in a growing fury of irritation, as, hurrying out of the park, hurrying two miles back to Church Street, she found she was drawing any number of quizzical stares and a few smiles. What a sight she must have been, hair and clothes soaked! What a figure of mirth for fools to gape at!

Not until hours later would the fact strike her, like a virtual blow—she had saved a human life.

She'd saved a human life without knowing what she did, and without any conscious choice.

And there was the matter too of the mouth-to-mouth resuscitation.

Witnesses swore that Rydcie Mather obviously knew what she was doing, but in fact, though Rydcie had taken a course in first-aid, it had been sixteen years before, in college, and she had not thought of the procedure since then. She was certain she had not thought of the procedure since then.

Yet, she'd remembered. Evidently.

Swimming, too. Rescuing a drowning, struggling girl. Rydcie had loved to swim as a child but had not been near the water for—how long? Ten years?

Not that she feared or disliked water. Exposing her body in a bathing suit, soaking wet, bedraggled—that was what filled her with revulsion.

Exposing herself, to others' eyes. Their rude assessments, their nudging smiles.

Recalling Amanda Curle's cold, slack, dead mouth, Rydcie shuddered. A violent paroxysm that weakened her, left her short of breath. The lips rolling back from the teeth, the tongue with a swamp-water taste. No breath, until Rydcie Mather forced it out of her.

At night, in sleep, Rydcie would taste Amanda Curle's mouth. Her eyes swooning back in her skull, as if she herself had drowned.

Of course, in a small town like Hartshill, where nothing ever happens, it was not possible for Rydcie Mather to avoid the fuss that followed her "heroic" "courageous" rescue of Amanda Curle from drowning.

Why, wasn't Rydcie the very incarnation of "The Good Samaritan," sitting right there, stony-faced with embarrassment, in the pew directly before Reverend Cogdon's pulpit as the reverend, rosy-cheeked, sparkling-eyed, delivered his most impassioned sermon in months?

Rydcie had to comply, to a degree. Though grumbling, and scowling, she had to sit for her photograph for the Hartshill *Gazette*—Mrs. Mather, who was in a delirium of maternal pride, would have had a fainting spell otherwise. She had to accept profuse, tearful thanks from Amanda Curle and her family, which was a large family, including even a ninety-six-year-old ancestor of indeterminate sex in a wheelchair. (How different Amanda looked, upright, hair dry and dazzlingly curly, color in her cheeks and wide-set baby-blue eyes shining with gratitude? A beautiful girl, whom Rydcie did in fact now remember, with a stir of displeasure, from the library.)

Even in the library, where Rydcie was accustomed to being in control, capable of silencing obstreperous patrons with fierce looks of disapprobation, she was suddenly vulnerable—people came boldly up to her to shake her hand, marveling at her "heroism"—her "courage." When, blushing brick-red, Rydcie muttered, "Oh for God's sake, I didn't do anything anyone else wouldn't have done, in my place," she was refuted ecstatically, as if everyone knew her better than she knew herself, "Oh, but you *did*, Rydcie Mather! Oh yes you *did*!"

And so it went. Weeks, months. The fact of Hartshill watching her, without her consent. Smiling. Whispering. Pointing as she passed. *Yes—that's the one. The Mather woman—you know. Saved a girl from drowning.*

It made Rydcie furious—sick. For how could she endure it, knowing that she'd torn off her shoes, flung herself blindly into the water to save Amanda Curle only because a force had compelled her—no thought, no *choice*, at all. As if Rydcie had inadvertently touched a wire, and a powerful current had rushed through her, to the drowning figure, to complete its circuit.

One evening when Mrs. Mather was admiring the cheap brass plaque given by the Township of Hartshill, at a Fourth of July ceremony, to *Eurydice Mather*, Rydcie said scornfully, "Oh, Momma, damn: it was just some force that went through me, that saved her. It was just something I *did.*" But Mrs. Mather merely smiled, and said, with maddening complacency, "Why, dear, that's what people mean by God. *God acted through you.*"

For a moment Rydcie was too shocked to protest. Then she said, weakly, "But—I don't believe. I'm beyond all that."

Mrs. Mather continued to smile, serenely. "Oh no, 'Eurydice Mather,' you're not."

Shortly afterward, to the astonishment of Hartshill, and to the dismay of poor Violet Mather, Rydcie resigned her position at the library, where she'd worked, with such evident devotion, for eleven years.

She then applied for a license allowing her to drive a school bus in the State of New York. She took the required training, and passed both the written and the road tests with exemplary scores. She was thirty-six years old.

In this way, with a vengeful ardor, Rydcie Mather took up a new life. Driving a bus during the school year, working intermittently at Cale's Nursery and Country Produce in the summer. She never offered any explanation for her behavior and few dared to ask.

Mrs. Mather sighed to her friends, "Oh, the ways of the Lord are mysterious, sometimes!" But, wisely, Mrs. Mather did not complain. She knew what a temper her daughter had, however taciturn and poker-faced she was in public.

Rydcie was observed dumping, with a look of zestful satisfaction, a carton of her old suits, dresses, blouses, skirts, "good" shoes onto the grimy counter of the Second-Time-Around Shop, and demanding a generous price in return. She then stocked up on bargain male gear from K Mart—khakis, wools, serges, gabardines, plaid flannel shirts, gloves. And boots! Leather look-alikes. Slick plastic-shiny boots, to the knee. The township required its safety officers, as they were called, to wear badges identifying themselves, and this Rydcie wore, carelessly affixed to her chest. In cold weather she wore an enormous sheepskin windbreaker; at other times, jackets with the look of uniforms.

Clearly, Rydcie liked to drive the bus assigned her by the

Hartshill township. Maneuvering its clumsy bulk around tight corners, bullying her way through intersections, sounding her horn, hitting the brakes and setting her red lights flashing front and rear, to halt traffic in both directions—this was power, this was authority, and Rydcie exulted in it. Her downturned lips and staring eyes exuded a look of unbending irony.

She was to drive solely for the Hartshill Junior High School, and her route would be unvarying for nearly fifteen years. Each school day of the year from 7:45 A.M. to 8:25 A.M. and then again from 3:20 P.M. to 4:00 P.M. The buses she drove were manufactured by International Harvester and seated thirty-six passengers in eighteen rows.

The boys and girls who rode Rydcie's bus were between the ages of twelve and fourteen, generally. Partly because they were so ephemeral in her eyes, never riding the bus for more than three years, and partly because she disliked children, Rydcie rarely troubled to learn their names, nor even their faces. Except when they appealed to her for one or another mysterious reason, or, more likely, when they came to her attention as "hooligans." In her consciousness, they were simply *there*, in some cases the children of her old high school classmates, or of her neighbors, yet undifferentiated by her, simply *there*, like any sort of cargo.

In the beginning, Mrs. Mather often asked Rydcie how her drive had been that day, and Rydcie, laughing, would reply, "Momma, please! The 'drive' is always the same drive, and the day is always the same day, so why ask?" Mrs. Mather never knew if she were being rudely rebuffed by this strange daughter of hers, or invited to share a melancholy joke.

Eventually, Mrs. Mather ceased asking her question.

In time, the twittering canary Zasu died, and was replaced by Tootsie; when Tootsie died, he was replaced by Pippa. All were yellow American males and inspired, happy singers, except during moulting season when their miniature feathers littered the floor of their cage and the kitchen floor beneath.

Each evening, at dusk, Rydcie drew an opaque dark cloth over the bird cage, since it was Mrs. Mather's belief that her canary could not sleep well otherwise. Often, the canary had already retired for the night, standing, on one leg, on the topmost perch, small head neatly tucked beneath small wing.

"What a damned nuisance you are!" Rydcie muttered. "Every one of you."

When her television programs were over for the night, Mrs. Mather too was put to bed; a procedure that, with the passage of years, had grown ever more complicated and arduous for both mother and daughter. Now Mrs. Mather suffered from degenerative arthritis, afflicting her hands, ankles, and spine, sleep did not come so readily as it once had. On bad nights she had to sleep, or doze, in an upright position, fat pillows bunched behind her. Still, Mrs. Mather rarely complained. She was a Christian lady. Sometimes, to Rydcie's disgust, she shivered in anticipation of sleep, with a nearly sensual abandon; her eyes misted over and her mouth, softened without her dentures, stretched in a wan smile. She gripped her daughter's hand in hers and murmured, "Oh! Rydcie! Thank *you*!—and praise *Him*!"

Rydcie smiled grimly. "Yes Momma!" her lips intoned.

Nights, tangled in damp bedclothes. A mad moon peeking through a window. That cold, slack mouth pressed against hers— sucking, drawing her down. By the intervention of God.

God: in Whom Rydcie did not believe, but of Whom she could not think without feeling a flood of anger.

"Why—it's Rydcie Mather?"

Rydcie, in corduroy trousers, a wool plaid shirt with flap- pockets, scuffed fake-leather boots, was walking hurriedly to her car in the parking lot behind the Hartshill A&P, when she heard a startled, happy voice, and looked up squinting to see, not pretty young Amanda Curle, but the busty, frizzly-haired, coarse-skinned woman Amanda Curle had become. Rydcie stared, blinking. For years she had succeeded in avoiding Amanda Curle—she'd avoided all the Curles, if she saw them in time—and had pushed them out of her mind entirely. (Or had she? Without knowing how she knew, Rydcie knew certain facts about the girl whose life she'd saved: Amanda had had enough sense not to marry that pig-snouted coward who'd grabbed the canoe and left her to drown, instead she'd married another local man, and had begun having her babies, like most of the girls of her generation in Hartshill.) But here was Amanda, thirty pounds heavier, pushy and grinning, walking right up to Rydcie as if they were old friends. How married she looked, how ordinary! There was even a little yellow-haired girl tugging at her arm, staring at Rydcie as if she'd never seen anyone so strange.

How Rydcie endured Amanda Curle's inane chatter—"Why, Rydcie, it's been so long! Where do you keep yourself! How *are* you? And your mother? I was thinking of you—of it—just the other day—" she did not know, afterward; she had to endure the embarrassment of being introduced to the little girl, whose name was Betsey Ann, as "the nice lady who saved your Mommy's life before *you* were born!" The three-year-old Betsey Ann regarded Rydcie with eyes flat as pennies, unimpressed.

Rydcie's face darkened with blood. Now she'd become a public spectacle, for children to gape at.

She muttered something vague and apologetic, said she was late for an appointment, and broke away, leaving mother and daughter to stare after her.

She was forty-two years old.

And You damn You will You leave me alone!

Even in her position of authority behind the wheel of the bus with the letters HARTSHILL JUNIOR HIGH SCHOOL in black on its sides Rydcie Mather was susceptible to spells of self-doubt, self-collapse you might call it. Like the giant glittering icicles, some as long as six feet, the girth of a human torso, hanging from the lower railing of the Post Road Bridge: nothing looks more permanent than those icicles but—where are they, in April?

That thunderclap of a day nine years after she'd run into Amanda Curle and Amanda's daughter in the parking lot—it was one of those days to which Rydcie could assign no name. But she'd known, waking in the morning, that it was a day when, in some way, she would be humiliated, exposed to ridicule; if not in others' eyes, then, yet more mercilessly, in her own.

For this was the day, an October afternoon, when Rydcie

Mather realized that Amanda Curle's daughter Betsey Ann was one of the children riding her bus—had been riding her bus for three weeks, without Rydcie's awareness. (Or had she, seeing, not-seen; knowing, not-known. Such spells of blindness were recurring more frequently.)

So, Rydcie found herself staring horrified through the rearview mirror down the rows of seats: to a seat near the rear: where that giggly, squirmy, bratty yellow-haired girl with the puffy face sat, exchanging wisecracks and profane witticisms with her friends, maroon lipstick smeared on her mouth with a look of something that might glow in the dark. *How had Rydcie failed to see, it was Betsey Ann.*

"Betsey Ann Waller"—that was the name on Rydcie's list of passengers for the term. Amanda Curle had married a man named Waller.

And there was the name "Waller" on the mailbox at 12 Seneca Lane, in the subdivision called Pheasant Hollow, across the river. When, that day, Rydcie stopped to let Betsey Ann and several others off the bus, she stared through near-shut eyes at the yellow-haired girl as, pivoting, no doubt to display her round little buttocks in their snug jeans, Betsey Ann waved and grinned back to her friends on the bus—a red-haired girl whose favorite exclamation was, "Oh, shit!" and the loutish ninth grade boys whose names Rydcie had not yet learned were Bobo, Pete, Sam, Tyke. Rydcie peered at the Wallers' house, what she could see of it at the end of a pretentious curved drive—one of those suburban split-levels popular with Hartshill's younger, affluent families, who scorned living in Hartshill.

Rydcie wrenched her eyes away. Her heart was pounding so violently, she could scarcely breathe. Punching off her flashing red lights, she kicked the gas pedal down to the floor, roused the bus into motion with such urgency that it shuddered and shook like a giant beast coming to life, and leapt forward with a squeal of rubber against pavement. At the rear of the bus the louts cheered, "Go, Miz Mat'er!"

Following that day, that hour, that moment of revelation, until the day of the accident, as it would be called, the following April,

Rydcie Mather was either thinking of Betsey Ann Waller; or, adamantly, not-thinking of her.

Just as, she was forced to acknowledge, you are either thinking of God, or not-thinking of Him.

Whether you believe or not.

She understood that it could not have been by chance—Amanda Curle's daughter, now twelve years old, a seventh grader with Amanda's pretty, debased face, assigned to Rydcie Mather's bus. For the next three years. Every school day, twice daily, for the next three years.

Yet, You will never again bend me to Your will, not even if You set Your foot upon my neck, and grind me into dust.

Observing Betsey Ann and her friends, Rydcie came to see that God had done her one favor, at least: hadn't made her have any children. If she'd had children she would be blind to their true natures, revealed so unmistakably on Rydcie's bus.

Over the years Rydcie had been driving her bus, which seemed, now, to have been most of her lifetime, a change had come upon children of junior high school age. They were no longer "boys" and "girls" but a crude, sly, foul-mouthed, insolent midget-species, somewhere between human and animal. All the Hartshill bus drivers had noticed the change. The casually filthy language, the sense of peril if you dared discipline them. The boys' remarks to the girls—the girls' remarks to the boys. Amid a constant din of voices, laughter, lunging about, commotion. The quieter, smaller children were intimidated, thus "good"—but did it mean that they were *really* "good"? Rydcie had acquired a strong Protestant doubt of inherent goodness, in the face of such evidence of man's fallen nature.

There was a growing problem in the junior high school of beer drinking, and there had long been a problem of smoking—both forbidden activities, of course. Rydcie was shocked to see that twelve-year-old Betsey Ann sometimes smoked, or shared cigarettes with her friends; still more was she shocked, and worried, to see that the child was "high" sometimes, getting on the bus after school. Smoking and drinking were banned from Rydcie's bus, and such was Rydcie's authority, not even the most insolent of the ninth-grade boys had challenged her, thus far.

When, roused from her usual stoic calm, Rydcie Mather braked her bus to a stop and turned to yell, "No monkey business on my bus or you get out and walk—got it?" everyone quieted down, quick. Only once or twice had Rydcie needed to stomp down the aisle, towering over the children, such a look of ferocity in her face, such quivering passion in her being, she intimidated the brats into fearful submission without laying a hand on anyone.

What smirky-sullen faces the children made behind her back, what obscene names they whispered of her, Rydcie did not know and did not wish to know. Enough for her that, at such times, she had triumphed—a part of the sun broken off and flying along in a glaring-yellow chariot, on a road in Hartshill, New York.

That nice lady who saved your Mommy's life. Before you were born.

Mornings, Betsey Ann was invariably late when Rydcie made her Seneca Lane stop, yet, with exasperating slowness, and insolence, she ambled down the driveway to the bus; yawning, puffy-faced, cranky; without a glance at the woman behind the wheel, as if, in her taciturn flush-faced fury, Rydcie Mather did not exist. (Did Betsey Ann know who she was? Certainly not.) Afternoons, Betsey Ann was manic, shrieking-loud, boldly flirtatious as any high school slut. Her jostling and carrying-on with boys made Rydcie's stomach turn. And only twelve years old!

One winter afternoon when the bus was already behind schedule, and Betsey Ann climbed lazily aboard, Rydcie snapped, "Hurry up, or I'm leaving without you!" Betsey Ann slammed past, muttering, "Says who! You don't *dare*, you gotta *wait*, you're the fucking *bus driver*!" In the din of juvenile voices and laughter the girl's words were not fully audible so Rydcie was not required to hear.

Rydcie was whispering, begging. "Momma. I'm afraid something is going to happen. I wish you could help me. Momma?"

How quiet the big old house on Church Street was, without Mrs. Mather! Even Pippa sang grudgingly. He seemed to resent

Rydcie's hopeful whistling into his cage, to spur him into song; though it was mid-winter, and summer long since past, he was still moulting. Tiny yellow pin feathers floated in the air like dust motes and when Rydcie dragged a comb through her snarled, sometimes matted hair, she was likely to find feathers in it.

"Momma, God *damn!*"

Mrs. Mather had died in her sleep the previous spring, a few days before her eighty-second birthday. When, the following morning, Rydcie discovered her, a shocking thing had happened—Rydcie had burst into hoarse, racking sobs, falling over her mother's lifeless body. Rydcie had understood that her mother was failing, she was certain she'd prepared herself for the loss, yet, in the face of it, how she'd collapsed and wept! how she'd raged!

As it would turn out, Mrs. Mather's death would make Rydcie's course of action easier. But, on that May morning, Rydcie hadn't known yet.

Rydcie went to speak with Reverend Cogdon of the distress in her heart, but she took care not to speak of Betsey Ann Waller. Even in beggary she was too proud to utter any mere local, specific *name.*

How astonished Reverend Cogdon looked, as, speaking in a hoarse, rapid voice, Rydcie Mather, whom he scarcely knew, confessed to him that she was fearful of the hatred in her heart; the revulsion she felt for the junior high students who rode her bus. "They are so—impure," Rydcie said slowly. "Their souls, I think. So—" She searched for the right word, her forehead creased, "—unworthy."

Reverend Cogdon, slightly deaf, leaned his good, right ear in Rydcie's direction, composing his face. As, in his youth, he had seemed middle-aged, now, in middle age he seemed youthful, even boyish: he wore his graying hair styled to sweep across his brow, his shirt collars were invariably open and his sleeves briskly rolled up. He coached the Young Christians Softball Team of Hartshill and was a popular local man of God. " 'Unworthy'—?" he echoed.

"Of life."

And then, suddenly, Rydcie Mather was pouring out her heart

in Reverend Cogdon's rectory office. Words tumbled from her mouth as if they had been stored up for decades. She told Reverend Cogdon that "it had all begun" fifteen years ago when she'd saved Amanda Curle from drowning—was forced to save Amanda Curle from drowning, by the hand of God—she'd never had a moment's choice. So much fuss then in this ridiculous town she'd quit her job at the library where she'd been so public—so exposed—and then she'd started driving a bus for the township and she'd done a damned good job and she knew it and they knew it but now, lately—this terrible disgust and hate and sickness almost she was feeling—was He forcing her out of this job too? What was she to do, in self-defense?

"How do you get free of God, Reverend Cogdon?" Rydcie demanded. "You must have plenty of experience with His ways! If I do X, it's God guiding my hand; if I do Y, it's God guiding my hand. Even if you're a sane, rational person—" and here Rydcie discomforted the minister by squinting and grinning at him, "—and don't believe any of this crap for one second, how do you get Him out of the corner of your eye? That's what I want to know!"

Reverend Cogdon, a mild, sweet-natured man who not only accepted his limits but rejoiced in them, as an antidote to pride, was dazed by this torrent of words. For years, Rydcie Mather had been so disdainful of him! In fact, since Mrs. Mather's death nearly a year before, she had not even attended church services.

When the torrent subsided, Reverend Cogdon said briskly, "Miss Mather, I believe in the Here-and-Now." As he always did when making this statement, he rapped his knuckles smartly on his desk. "To prioritize: you say you disapprove of the children who ride your bus? Not *all* the children, surely, Miss Mather?— only, maybe, a *few?*"

Rydcie winced. "The worry of it is, He wants me in His bosom again. I'm determined to go to hell if I have to, instead."

"Oh, but isn't that a bit extreme?" Reverend Cogdon chuckled, blinking in surprise. "I wonder if you aren't missing your mother? Your dear, delightful mother, *I* miss, indeed I do!"

Rydcie said coolly, "Mother has nothing to do with this. She never had a clue as to His deviousness."

"Oh, but isn't that a bit—extreme? 'The ways of God are not the ways of man,' but—"

"My sister was six years younger than me, and she joined the WACs out of high school, and never came back," Rydcie said. "Her name was 'Antigone.' Everyone called her 'Gonne.' *She* ran off, but I can't do that." Rydcie paused, wiping her mouth. "I speak of her in the past tense but she may well be alive, at this moment."

Reverend Cogdon said enthusiastically, "I certainly hope so!"

"Reverend Cogdon, look: I don't believe in any superstition. Call it 'religion'—call it 'faith.' I never have, and I never will. And I refuse to stoop to hatred of my fellow man. It may be vanity—" and here Rydcie squinted and grinned at the minister, narrowing one eye in a wink, "—but, frankly, I believe I am too good for hatred. Even those filthy-mouthed little creatures—I should not hate."

Reverend Cogdon was leaning forward, smiling; a shrewd light had come into his eyes, as it did when he was about to say something unexpected. "Miss Mather, are you absolutely certain it's hatred you feel?—might it be, instead, love?" He paused to let his words sink in. "What if this is God's way of urging you to *love?*"

Rydcie Mather could not have stared at Reverend Cogdon any more incredulously if he'd begun babbling in a foreign language. "Love—?"

"What if this is God's way of urging you to—"

"Love—?"

Rydcie began laughing, loudly. To Reverend Cogdon's chagrin, she stood, dismissing him with a brusque wave of her hand, and walked out of his office. Like that! So rude! Leaving Reverend Cogdon to gape after her, the light dying out of his eyes.

He could hear Rydcie Mather's insulting laughter outside in the parking lot, until, tires squealing, she drove away.

In March, long-delayed construction began on the Post Road Bridge, forcing Rydcie Mather to take a detour (east on the River Road for three miles, to Route 8, over that bridge and then west on the Yewville Pike back into the township of Hartshill, to the suburban area where approximately one-third of her passengers lived) that added twenty minutes to her route. These twenty minutes made the boys and girls still on the bus more difficult than ever to control.

A nightmare, was it?—one afternoon, accompanied by shrieks of monkey laughter and derision, water-filled condoms were tossed about the bus—one splattered the windshield directly in front of Rydcie and fell onto her trousered knees, to her deep mortification.

Another day, plump little Rhonda Piper with her mouthful of braces was so mercilessly teased by bullies (including girls), Rydcie had to stop the bus, threaten the troublemakers with expulsion, and bring the trembling child up to the front of the bus for protection.

In early April, the irrevocable insult: Betsey Ann Waller climbed aboard the bus after school giggling and belching beer, supported from behind by the six-foot-tall thug Bobo who had his hands roughly beneath her arms and the tips of his fingers digging into her breasts, and Rydcie jumped up to interfere, and, instead of being grateful, Betsey Ann Waller screamed, "Ugly old horse-face, keep your hands to yourself! Always looking at me! Go look in the mirror! Damn old fucking horse-face!" Betsey Ann ran to the rear of the bus, and Rydcie shrank back as if she'd laid her hands on an upright column of flame.

Following that, Time passed swiftly. Days and nights in a spin.

Yet shall I defy You. Whether Hell, or oblivion.

Rydcie Mather has prepared for what she must do. So very shrewdly, by not preparing for it in any way that will be detectable, afterward.

For one does not prepare for an accident—not even providing extra food and water for a canary.

The day, April 18, dawns gusty and rain-pelting. The Yewville River, a deep, fast-running river, is swollen several feet above its banks, mud-colored, roiling.

The idea came to Rydcie fully formed as if, already, in her dreams, she has accomplished it: the glaring-yellow bus crashing through the DANGER—BRIDGE OUT—DETOUR signs at the foot of the steep Post Road hill, plunging out onto the skeletal bridge, down into the water. A matter of failed brakes. Slick, slippery, potholed pavement. Accident. Heart pounding, Rydcie tries to peer into the future immediately following the crash. She wonders if the heavy vehicle will float just a bit—if, with its interior pocket of air, it might be carried downstream, and how far. The gas tank is at the rear, yet, when the front hits, and folds like an accordion, might there be an explosion? a fire?—the flames quickly quenched by the river.

Will there be screams? Will Rydcie Mather scream?

Of the twelve persons aboard—eleven children, and the bus driver—will anyone survive?

April 18. Waking to rain pelting against the window, and her heart lifts in exaltation. *See if You can prevent me!*

If Betsey Ann Waller is absent from school today, of course Rydcie must postpone the accident. But Betsey Ann Waller is here.

Sucking on her lower lip, eyes averted, pert little snub nose in the air. Betsey Ann Waller and her friends pushing past giggling and shoving, sidelong glances at the ugly horse-faced woman behind the wheel. The woman who peers at them squinting, a strange dreamy light in her eyes.

In her man's navy blue serge jacket, badge carefully affixed to her breast, fingerless leather gloves. She's gripping the wheel hard, as if prepared for a struggle.

But the morning run goes without incident. The afternoon run is quickened from the start.

Thirty-two passengers aboard, when the bus pulls out of the school driveway at 3:23 P.M. Cautious-seeming at first, head- and taillights on. Down Seventh Street, along Shepherd, to Trumper, to Ferry Street, to the neighborhoods on the east side, then to upper Post Road, the unvarying route, fifteen years of it, stopping, and starting, and stopping, the familiar groan of the brakes, the rattling chassis glaring yellow-orange in the rain.

In the rearview mirror, how oblivious the children. Laughing and chattering as usual. One of the boys has a transistor radio, outlawed on the buses, turned low, but there it is. And there she is, Betsey Ann Waller screwing up her face in happy laughter. The trees, the fields rush by outside, invisible. The Yewville River is invisible to the children, who see only one another. But Rydcie has seen it, Rydcie knows it. Overflowing its banks. A hungry, greedy sound to its rushing waters.

The names of the dead: those children who live on the far side of the river, those still riding the bus when it begins its final plunge down the Post Road hill. *Jimmy Buford. Terri Donovan. Pete Erlicht. Brian Kincaid. Robert Lundt. Shannon Myers. Rhonda Piper. Wayne Schwab, Billy Schwab. Betsey Ann Waller. Holly Zinn.* No survivors.

No one will witness the accident, which will occur at approximately 3:40 P.M. Several motorists, headed in the opposite direction, will report afterward that they'd seen the school bus descending the hill at an accelerated speed, but they'd had no sense that the driver was out of control; no sense that the brakes were failing.

Rydcie Mather, behind the wheel, isn't aware she is being seen, or not-seen. Already, she's beyond that.

Her heart lifts in exaltation—*See if You can prevent me.*

She falls to chatting with the Stearns boy, poor fat kid with the glasses. Now the time remaining to her is so finite, and so swiftly contracting, she feels suddenly generous, gold coins spilling from her pockets!

(These past weeks, long nights when she'd been unable to sleep, Rydcie had read a number of her father's books. Science, natural history. Orren Mather had had a library of many hundreds of books and, as a child, little Eurydice had vowed to read them all. She had not, of course. So this purposeless effort, so close to the end of her life, was precious to her. Amazed, Rydcie read of the Ice Age, the mammoth glaciers covering this part of the world millions of years ago, before God set His hand to interfere. The great fields of ice, the gradual melting. The inland seas. God had had nothing to do with it, it was a perpetual, eternal motion— Rydcie was sure.)

The last child has climbed down, at the last stop, on Post Road.

Gunning the motor, pressing down the gas pedal, descending the long steep hill bordered by straggly trees. Rydcie feels the thrill deep in her bones as the bus accelerates. The rain has lightened and the sky is a glaring white, like something through which, with sufficient force and momentum, one could smash.

The motor's rackety sound. The tires humming and hissing on the pavement. The windshield wipers slap back and forth, back and forth, keeping time with the heavy beat of the transistor's music. The mood of the bus is rowdy, derisive—the DANGER—BRIDGE OUT—DETOUR signs are rapidly approaching, but still some distance away. From somewhere behind Rydcie comes a low, sniggering voice: "Go, Miz Mat'er!"

The Vision

1.

There was no mistaking it now. The shimmering patch of light, which had seemed at first to be an agitation of the air, or an irritation in Floyd Prentiss James's eyes, came into sudden, sharp focus. No mistaking *Her*.

Never had Floyd glimpsed Her living presence, nor had She appeared to him in any dream, in all his sixty-eight years. Yet, there She stood, at the far end of the patio, between the portable Sears barbecue and the weatherworn simulated-redwood fence that divided the Jameses' property from the Houstons' next door—no mistaking Her in Her robin's-egg-blue robe that fell in graceful folds to Her bare feet, Her head uplifted and wimpled like a nun's. In the bright moist light that fell from overhead She stood unmoving, not twenty feet away, her hands clasped in an attitude of prayer against her chest.

Yes it was. Yes it could not be but *was*.

"Holy Mary, Mother of God!"—the familiar prayer escaped Floyd's lips, more a crude exclamation than a prayer. He was frozen in his tracks, the roaring bucking Toro lawnmower throwing up bits of damp grass and earth about his legs; he'd been working in the yard about an hour, first the front, which took about twenty minutes, and now the backyard which was larger, divided in his mind's eye into rectangular sections which he tackled one at a time, pretty well enjoying this first lawn-mowing of the season, his thoughts scattered and drifting like dandelion seed. And he'd pushed the mower around a corner, grunting with the effort, pleased to be working up a mild sweat, and began to notice something in the corner of his eye, and squinted at it—a quivering patch of blue? an outline of a human figure, on the far side of the patio?—baffled, frowning, blinking to get his vision clear. (Floyd needed bifocals for reading, but his eyes for distances were still reliable.) What was it? What could it be? Not a patch of fog, or mist—not in the sunshine. Not Alyce, who was inside the house and who, in any case, would not be standing in such a place, in such a posture. Nor was it a neighbor. Then—*who?*

Floyd stared, dead in his tracks. The figure became more distinct, and appeared now to be beckoning to him. *The Blessed Virgin Mary. On his patio. No mistaking Her!* There is a moment when *seeing* shifts irrevocably to *knowing*, and Floyd Prentiss James felt that moment as a kick in his chest. His heart was poised to hammer despite the pacemaker embedded in his chest to prevent it: he was programmed for the rest of his life for a heartbeat regular as an alarm clock's ticking, never faster. All he could do was exclaim, "Holy Mary, Mother of God, have mercy!"

It was evident that Mary heard him, over the deafening roar of the mower. Her pale hands had opened, and lifted, palms outward, in a gesture of comfort; though Floyd could not see her face very clearly, he seemed to sense its expression, which was one of infinite peace, love, tenderness. *Yes it is I, Floyd, but do not fear: I have always been with you.*

So Floyd was comforted, even as he stood in a paroxysm of astonishment, like that man in the Bible—or was it a woman—who'd turned into a pillar of salt for disobeying God. He would have dropped to his knees in the grass and hid his face except, in the state he was in, he never thought of it!

That day, May 16, 1993, the day the Blessed Virgin Mary appeared on the brick patio at the rear of the three-bedroom ranch house at 188 Myrtle Drive, Manville, New Jersey, showing Herself first to the homeowner Floyd Prentiss James, was a strange blinding-bright windy Sunday exactly one month after Easter Sunday—a fact that would subsequently be noted.

Floyd Prentiss James, a retired machine shop foreman, and his wife Alyce, who lived alone together since their several children were grown and moved away, had attended nine o'clock Mass that morning at Our Lady of Sorrows in Manville, their parish church since 1957; in recent years, since Floyd's retirement, and maybe before that, since his brother Franklin's death, they were pretty faithful churchgoers, and rarely missed a Sunday. Alyce was the one who never skipped Holy Days, and Alyce was the one who almost never failed to take communion. She believed it to be a true sacrament—the body and blood of Christ—truly!—in a way Floyd wanted to believe but couldn't, exactly, if he puzzled over it much. Not that Floyd didn't take communion, ever—of course he did. He'd go at Christmas, and he'd make his Easter duty, and a few other times through the year, depending on his mood. The new way of confession made him uneasy, resentful—there wasn't enough secrecy to it, which meant somehow it wasn't serious. Every change in the Roman Catholic Church made you wonder about the logic of the old way of doing it, which to disobey would have been a mortal sin, but also the newer way of doing it, too. But it was better not to puzzle over this too much. That was the priests' job.

On the morning of May 16, Alyce took communion while Floyd remained in their pew, downlooking, embarrassed, hoping Father O'Callaghan wouldn't take any special notice of him. As the congregation sorted itself in two, some coming forward to the altar rail, others not, it was clear that most who didn't take communion were men; most of those who did were women and young people. In confined quarters like a pew, Floyd tended to perspire. Dressed in a sport coat, white shirt and tie, good shoes, he felt like a trussed turkey. He was a heavyset man with thinning white hair and a pink scalp; his face too was flushed pink, and looked skinned. Much of his weight was in his torso and upper belly, not in his legs or rear end; his shoulders were still fairly muscular, straining the fabric of his beige polyester sport coat. His daughters insisted he was a handsome man, and he liked that, though he knew it wasn't true, just their way of saying they loved him, don't be discouraged, Daddy. After his brother Franklin's death—he and Franklin were twins, though not "identical"—only "fraternal"—he'd been discouraged by life for a while, but that was years ago now, going on six years, and Floyd believed he'd regained his old optimism and his old sense of humor. He was all right. He was fine. The lawsuit his brother's widow got talked into bringing against Johns-Manville Asbestos, where Franklin had worked for thirty years, had been settled out of court, not for the $10 million claimed but for an undisclosed sum even Floyd and Alyce were never told. But that was all right. For now Floyd could stop thinking about it. And he didn't think about it, much, sometimes for days on end. (Unless at night he dreamt about Franklin for how can a man help his dreams, or even know what they *are*?) At the age of sixty-eight Floyd had his own health problems—thank God they were minor—his heart that needed monitoring, and his high blood-pressure he couldn't seem to bring down, and an old injury to his right knee where he'd cracked it unloading a Navy transport truck, back in 1944—this ghost-pain coming back in cold weather—but compared to Franklin he had no cause to complain. Once you're a twin you measure yourself by your twin so when anybody asked Floyd how he was these last few years he'd shake his head marveling, and smile quick like a kid—"Hell, *I* got nothing to complain about." And so it was.

Actually, Floyd worried more these days about Alyce—her "nerves." Her "nerves" that were like a third party in the household, unpredictable and nasty. Her fool doctor prescribed for her a tranquilizer with some name like "Xerox" and Floyd didn't approve of this *mood medicine* you hear about, terrible side effects like dizziness, anemia, paranoia the damned doctors don't seem to know much about nor, if it's senior citizens involved, give much evidence of caring. But nervous and excitable as she was at home, Alyce showed the world a happy-seeming woman with "personality" like a cheerleader's—always smiling, and stylishly dressed, hair permed and tinted the identical butterscotch-red it had been when she'd been a girl of twenty, the prettiest girl Floyd James had had the nerve to ask out, and the sweetest. At least, that was how Floyd remembered it. That was how he told it. And, in company, Alyce referred to Floyd in such a way, too—the handsomest man she'd ever dated, like Jimmy Stewart in his Navy dress uniform. And so polite! And so sweet! And telling this like it was words to a song Alyce would smile over at Floyd who'd be laughing, and winking, and running his fingers through his hair or over his belly, making some good-humored joke about being a little out of condition, him and Jimmy Stewart both.

That morning Alyce went to communion. And Floyd did not. And it was one of those instances where Alyce suddenly flared up, whispering and scolding in Floyd's ear so he muttered, "Hey look, *you* go, Alyce, don't bother about *me*," embarrassed that others might overhear. Alyce regarded him with hurt, angry eyes, the crow's-feet deepening in her powdered skin, whispering, "Aren't you ashamed of yourself, Floyd James!—just plain *lazy*." But Floyd, damn it, wasn't to be bullied. Remaining in the pew arms folded while Alyce marched up to the communion rail alone walking stiffly, her head high, never once glancing back. Sundays she always dressed up. A bright yellow suit with a boxy jacket that disguised the roundness of her shoulders, and a glazed straw hat perched atop her tight butterscotch-red curls. And her spotless white gloves. *Who's that old bag? Why'm I stuck with her?*

Yes and he was deeply insulted by Alyce taking for granted he hadn't any serious mortal sins to prevent him from taking Holy Communion without going to confession first—making out the only reason was, he was *lazy*. Goddamn!

Shows you how much women know about men. How much Alyce knew about *him*, after forty-four years of marriage.

Not twenty feet away the Blessed Virgin stood unmoving. Except the folds of her long silken robe stirred in the wind—*Proof She is real, I am not dreaming.*

Inside the house, Alyce knew nothing of Who had come to them. Which was just like her—watching a rerun of "I Love Lucy" or worse yet chattering over the telephone with one of her women friends.

The Blessed Virgin was regarding Floyd with a look of infinite sweetness and understanding. *Do not fear, Floyd: I have always been with you.* In that instant, Floyd knew this was so. Of course, it was so. Through his eighteen months of wartime combat, other men dying in his presence but never *him*. Floyd swiped at his eyes worried he would begin to bawl like a baby. He was happy that the backyard looked good as it did, like a Mary shrine almost, Alyce's crimson azaleas in full bloom and buds on the rosebushes. Set down in the grass as if the figures had wandered there by themselves were the lawn ornaments Floyd had made with a jigsaw and painted, copying models he'd admired at the K Mart Garden Center—a flame-colored flamingo, an antlered deer the size of a Labrador retriever, a comical dwarf with woolly hair and thick Negroid lips but putty-colored, Caucasian skin. And the grass was rich and green even if only partly mowed.

Hungrily Floyd stared at the Blessed Virgin as, in silence, She stared at him. Time expanded like the ticking of a clock, or the beating of a heart, going slower, and slower, and slower. *I bring you love, I am always here, never doubt Me.* And Floyd knew that this was so. The Blessed Virgin exactly resembled the painted statue at Our Lady of Sorrows he'd seen for many years, and the brightly colored illustration in his first prayer book. She was the Blessed Virgin too of St. Anthony's near Manville General Hospital where in secret he'd gone to pray for Franklin, desperate, angry, and a little drunk fumbling to light a votive candle and kneeling hiding his face half-sobbing *Hail Mary full of grace, the Lord is with Thee* rushing to *Help my brother recover, dear Mary please! There is no one else for me to turn to* but why did Floyd say such a thing since after all there was Jesus Christ, and there was God the Father. Why'd he forget about *them?*

The Blessed Virgin knew of course that Floyd's brother Franklin had died. All that was past. Six years ago. Nothing to do with *now.*

Only then realizing the lawnmower was still on!—all this time, emitting a choking stink of exhaust. Quickly, hands shaking, Floyd switched it off.

Alyce would claim afterward she *knew.* That first sight of Floyd's face and the glassy shine in his eyes—she *knew.*

(Though: confessing to Judy, her older daughter, how her first panicked thought was Dad had had another heart attack, or a stroke. Oh that wild drowning look in the man's eyes!)

Well, she *knew*. She was a devout Catholic and she never missed communion and she prayed to the Blessed Virgin every day of her life and she *knew* this was like nothing that had ever happened to them, Floyd and Alyce, in all of their lives. The way Floyd stumbled panting and desperate into the bedroom, "Alyce! Alyce!" grabbing both her hands like he hadn't done in forty years, "Alyce, come with me!" and Alyce almost fainted, "W-Why? What is it, Floyd?" and Floyd was hauling her into the hall, into the kitchen toward the carport door, saliva gleaming on his lips though he was grinning to reassure her, "There's someone out here, someone you know, Alyce—she's come for us," and Alyce whispered, "But who is it? Please, Floyd, you're scaring me—" knowing whoever it was outside was no one ordinary not even a long-lost relative showing up unannounced. Yes she *knew*.

Then, this: In the midst of her terror they were in the back-yard, and something like sheer sound, wordless sound, was pulsing in her ears, and Floyd was nudging her to look—where?—somewhere on the patio, in the grass *Yes I saw I saw Mary at once and recognized Her* Alyce blinking confused and weak-eyed in the sun her heart hammering as she stared at—what?—what did he want her to see?—Floyd gripping her so tight she almost slipped to her knees in the surprise and pain knowing her husband was mad, it had happened at last, and ir-revocably: an artery burst in his heart, or his brain: but there was such purpose to him urging her to see something, or someone, indicating it with his chin so as not to point, for pointing would be rude, though Alyce could see nothing where Floyd was insist-ing, "There! She's *there*—" where Alyce saw a patch of blown dandelions in the grass, pale filmy seeds lifting in the wind like startled thoughts—and a few yards away—but this could not be it, could it?—the deformed plywood dwarf leering up at her—*this* could not be it could it?—what her husband had dragged her outside to see?

Yes I saw Mary at once. I knew who She was. The look on Her face!—the love and forgiveness She has for us! I knew.

Alyce's voice was faint with terror—"What? What is it? Let me go—" That convulsive shivering inside her, a nerve-attack though she'd taken her second Xanax tablet at noon, wild-eyed she looked from the grassy yet-unmowed space beyond the patio to Floyd's tense face, the skin that was flushed and ashy in patches, the broken capillaries in the nose and cheeks and the staring rapturous eyes of absolute certitude—this triumphant man was not Alyce's husband Floyd was he? *this* man, *her* husband? forced to see him as a stranger might behold him in awe: a barrel-chested white-haired man, going to fat but still muscular in the shoulders and arms, the fabric of his shirt strained across his chest and darkened in sweat, a vein beating at his temple, swirls of steel-wool hair on his arms and the glisten at his lips as roughly, commandingly he pushed Alyce down onto her knees in the grass kneeling beside her himself beginning to pray loudly "Hail Mary, full of grace, the Lord is with Thee! Blessed—" still gripping her tight as he'd gripped her when they'd entered together the sweetly metallic ghastly chill of the intensive care unit after Floyd's brother's surgery—and again in the morgue—and at the funeral home—and Alyce stared blinking at the empty grassy space at which Floyd seemed to be staring, and began suddenly to *see*, uncertain at first what it was, the shape, the quivering figure like moisture illuminated by sunshine, her voice joining her husband's in this prayer filling her with exhilaration and dread, "—Blessed art Thou amongst women, and blessed is the fruit of Thy womb Jesus!" And with no pause for breath beginning again more fiercely than any prayer Alyce had ever uttered, "—Hail Mary, full of grace, the Lord is with Thee! Blessed art Thou amongst women and blessed is the fruit of Thy womb Jesus—" until half-fainting, exhausted, every nerve in her body taut to bursting Alyce suddenly *saw*.

That first Sunday, She remained with them for approximately three hours. Near as Floyd could calculate, from 5 P.M. until dusk.

At dusk, as dusk deepened, lifting from the damp grass Floyd had yet to mow, it seemed that the Blessed Virgin faded into the shadows even as Her worshippers (by this time, there were five) stared helplessly. Yet there was the promise *She will return next Sunday at the same time. Bringing Her message to the world!*

They'd telephoned Father Brendan O'Callaghan, pastor since 1961 of Our Lady of Sorrows, at 6:20 P.M. When Floyd told the priest the news there was a long shocked silence at the other end of the line *I knew what Father was thinking: Omigod Floyd's gone off the deep end, for sure* before the priest said yes of course he'd come over. It was Alyce's fervent wish then and she pleaded so much Floyd had to give in to telephone her closest woman friend in the parish, Betty Gleason who'd lost her husband only a few months ago to lymphatic cancer *I knew it would mean so much to Betty! I couldn't live with myself if I didn't share Her with Betty!* and so Betty Gleason drove over bringing with her her forty-year-old daughter Karin who'd been divorced recently and was under treatment for clinical depression. And in her state of near-delirium Alyce wanted too to telephone their daughters and their son and Floyd tried to calm her agreeing finally to call Ernest himself (for Ernest lived in Trenton, an hour's drive while Judy lived in Fairfield, Connecticut, and Marla in Santa Cruz, California) trying to keep his voice level—"If you can get up here quick enough, Ernie, you and Kitzy, there's a surprise waiting for you"—but the damned fool wasn't in the mood for such secrecy sounding wiseguy-skeptical asking what the big deal was, and Kitzy'd invited some people over for barbecue that evening— And Floyd who'd been squinting out the kitchen window at Her almost losing Her through the glass that needed washing started shouting, "Then don't bother, you little shit! Stay away! Stay *away!*" slamming down the receiver.

Returning then trembling to the patio seeing with relief yes the Blessed Virgin was still there, exactly as She'd been, a look now of infinite pity and compassion on Her face—for of course She knew how Floyd's only son, this evening as always, had disappointed him. The others—Father O'Callaghan, Betty Gleason, Betty's daughter, and Alyce—were kneeling on cushions from the lawn chairs, on the patio, a distance of about fifteen feet from the Blessed Virgin; the old priest, his breath wheezing like a buffalo's, was leading them in prayer. (Brendan O'Callaghan hadn't yet *seen* the Blessed Virgin exactly but he'd *felt* Her presence. Betty Gleason's cheeks were streaming tears of joy and her daughter Karin who had a curiously doughy, battered-looking face was staring fixedly at the space beyond the barbecue at which the others stared. And Alyce—of course, Alyce *saw*.) Floyd sank down onto his knees hiding his face. *Her message is: God loves us. And the world will know peace.*

Though they prayed, the Blessed Virgin Mary began to fade with the sun. By degrees thinning, evaporating. Floyd had a wild idea of switching on the patio lights but by 8:15 P.M. when the western sky was a coarse, mottled gray threaded with suety orange like stained concrete She was gone.

Yet: there was the promise She would return to this same place next Sunday, at the same time. Floyd Prentiss James clearly received this message which then his wife Alyce agreed she had heard, and her friend Betty Gleason—*No not in actual words but we knew. We know. And even when She is not with us—She is with us.*

2.

If only he had sworn them to secrecy!

No: if only he had not shared Her with Alyce!

How many telephone calls in the next several days, how many unexpected visitors ringing their doorbell, or driving by slow and gawking in the street—Floyd and Alyce had never experienced anything like this before in their lives. Each morning, shaken by the gift of their vision, they attended seven o'clock Mass at Our Lady of Sorrows and when they left the church there were many who sought to speak with them, clearly hoping to be invited to their home for next Sunday. Alyce was excitable, talkative and expansive in her "personality" like a balloon into which air is being blown; Floyd stammered and was tongue-tied and had a look— so observers reported—of being "not himself." As word spread in Manville, Father Brendan O'Callaghan too was besieged by the devout, the desperate, and the curious—though the old priest was careful to say he could not claim to have actually *seen* the Blessed Virgin, he had only *felt* Her presence. But yes, he had *felt* it!—of that, there was no doubt.

Early in the week there came a woman columnist for the Manville *Courier* whose popular feature was IN & OF 'OUR TOWN' requesting not only a joint interview with Mr. and Mrs. Floyd James but an invitation to 188 Myrtle Drive for next Sunday—and permission to bring along a photographer! This woman was, Alyce believed, very nice; very sympathetic; trustworthy; not at all mocking, nor even doubting. She pleaded with Floyd to speak with her, but Floyd refused—"*You* talk to her, leave me out of it." Alyce said, sniffing, "Well, maybe I *will*." But both were adamant refusing to speak with the pushy producer of a Newark TV cable channel wanting "exclusive rights" to the "vision of Mary" and arriving at their doorstep with a contract in hand!

Floyd was sick at heart the secret was out and worried the Blessed Virgin would not now return out of disgust with them but Alyce who was clear-minded and purposeful as Floyd had rarely seen her in forty-four years insisted, "Mary is *not* a secret, She is for all the world!" and "Isn't it just like *you*, to be so selfish!" And Floyd was struck by this wondering if Alyce might be right, he *was* being selfish. As people were saying there'd been the famous vision at Lourdes, France, of which all Catholics knew, but also visions of the Blessed Virgin in Italy, Poland, Yugoslavia, Romania— why not northern New Jersey? Such a miracle was a victory, too, if you thought along such lines, for the Roman Catholic faith.

But Floyd had misgivings. But he *was* proud—damned proud.

As his son Ernie kept saying, marveling, in that nasal voice you could interpret as sincere or smart-ass—"Nothing like *this* ever happened to Dad before!"

Floyd kept it to himself how his dreams flew at him like pieces of broken glass, like he was being punished for something; and it was like that in his guts, too. During the day he kept seeing—*almost* seeing—the Blessed Virgin everywhere!— reflected in mirrors, passing a doorway, even, when he was driving his car, out on the street. The way, after their German shepherd Fritzie died years ago the whole family kept imagining they saw him around the house. And Franklin, too, after Franklin's death—Floyd would look into the bathroom mirror unprepared and see the wrong man.

Like your eyes are playing tricks on you. Like they're some kind of enemy not even *you*.

And Floyd's digestion was off, all this excitement. And his

bladder—he'd have to go to the toilet a dozen times a day. Hard for him to sit still for five minutes at a time, self-conscious in church and sweating inside his clothes and, nights, not wanting to sleep and prowling the house and the backyard kneeling near where She'd appeared to him whispering *Thank you Mary, thank you Mary, thank you Mary.* Crying like a kid, his throat choked up, his chest. Because the truth of all this was, this gift to Floyd Prentiss James was undeserved. He'd never been all that religious a man, a pretty lousy Catholic at times in his life. And She'd forgiven him, and gave him the gift of Herself.

Then again, daytime, he'd pace the house jingling keys and coins in his pockets locking himself into the bathroom just to contemplate his face in the mirror—*You? That's you?*—the feverish skin, yellowish cast to the eyeballs, having to laugh with the weird delight of it like winning the $100 million New Jersey Lottery—*The Blessed Virgin singled you out, Floyd? of all living men and women*, you? Because it was pretty hard to believe, he had to admit.

Sure there were skeptics. He'd have been a skeptic himself if it hadn't happened to him. Matt Houston their neighbor who was Floyd's age and retired, too—all but laughed in Floyd's face, like this was some kind of con-game Floyd was putting over on people. Matt liked to identify himself as "Protestant nondenominational" as if that was something to be proud of. Floyd shrugged keeping it affable saying it's fine what people want to believe, he'd never force anybody to believe anything against their will, and Matt Houston sputtered laughing that's for sure, pal, the U.S. of A. is a free country and the Roman Catholic inquisition doesn't play here. And there were other friends, neighbors, even relatives who did not seem to want to believe that the Blessed Virgin Mary had appeared at the Jameses' last Sunday, or was likely to appear next Sunday. Cruelest of all, the Jameses' own children.

Not that Judy, Marla, Ernie came out with it exactly. Not that they called their old man a liar, or a nut. Nor dared to insinuate anything that would upset their mother knowing her "nerves." But there came Judy visiting mid-week to ask many careful questions including how has Dad's health been, and had Father O'Callaghan seen the vision, too—how many people, exactly, had seen Her?—so Floyd smiled hard controlling his temper wanting to ask what the hell difference does it make if one person has seen Her, or one hundred? one thousand? *This isn't prime time TV for God's sake.* And there was Ernie seriously suggesting they hire a lawyer, a friend of his in Trenton—there might be TV or book contracts, or even lawsuits, you never know. And Marla hurt Floyd's feelings like she'd stuck a knife in his guts making the suggestion over the phone, "Has Daddy had his eyes examined lately? Has he had a thorough physical? His heart, his blood pressure—is he okay?"

Before Alyce could answer, Floyd who'd been eavesdropping on this conversation between his daughter in Santa Cruz and his wife in the bedroom interrupted, "You think I'm seeing things, eh? You think I'm crazy, eh? Something so wonderful, an actual living miracle—the Blessed Virgin Mary appearing to mankind—just some delusion in the old bastard's head, eh?" There was a shocked silence on the line Floyd took true pleasure in hanging up on.

But the worst insult, and the most unexpected, came Friday morning after Mass when Floyd and Alyce met with a young priest from the Archbishop's office in the rectory of Our Lady of Sorrows: though the meeting had been described by Father O'Callaghan as a "breakfast conversation," it soon became clear to Floyd that it was more like an interrogation. Father O'Callaghan, chewing his food, kept out of it. Father O'Callaghan who was looking his age, bloated belly like a pregnant woman's and palsied trembling in both hands and hooded evasive eyes while Father Shute did all the talking ignoring the elder priest like he was an embarrassment to the cloth. The most shocking thing about this Father Shute—a young guy, under forty—was his lack of interest in joining Floyd and Alyce and a select number of invited guests this coming Sunday. In fact, he all but winced when Alyce invited him, and the Archbishop, too. Thank you so much, Mrs. James, he said with a cool smile, but that isn't possible. *Like it was beneath this priest and the Archbishop to get involved with Catholics in Manville, New Jersey! Even when the Blessed Virgin Herself was coming!*

The remainder of the breakfast passed by Floyd in a fog. By

this time of the long long week he was feeling the effects of sleep deprivation and a more or less continuous diarrhea. He let Alyce answer Father Shute's questions, didn't seem to notice or care how the poor woman lost her cheery confidence and began to stumble and falter looking to Floyd for corroboration. Like a man pursuing a single fly with a fly swatter the young priest kept pressing it that the vision of the Blessed Virgin Mary of the previous Sunday had to have been some kind of misunderstanding, or worse. Inquiring about the Jameses' neighbors for instance, was there anybody who'd want to play a prank on them? Kids, teenagers? No? Inquiring yet another time exactly how close, in actual feet, had they been to the Blessed Virgin; what did She say to them, in Her exact words; what exactly did She look like; what were Floyd's and Alyce's medical histories; had either of them ever had psychiatric problems, psychotherapy?—so the significance of the interrogation was obvious.

Afterward Alyce said, her eyes reddened as if they'd been rubbed with steel wool, "Wouldn't you think, Floyd, *he'd* be on our side, at least?"

Floyd said bitterly, "Nobody's on our side. Except Her."

3.

Sunday, May 23, dawned gray and drizzling like a day of execution to Floyd's way of thinking but Alyce insisted the weather report called for sun and, sure enough, by early afternoon the overcast sky was high fluffy ribbons of white cloud and a hazy white sun was warming the air. Grudgingly Floyd acknowledged it was to be a beautiful spring day after all, and Alyce's azaleas were still in bloom. And the lawn was now completely mowed and the dandelions dug out (by hand, by Floyd) and on the patio a small fleet of attractive lawn chairs, the upright kind, from K Mart. Since the humiliation of Friday, Floyd and Alyce had stopped answering the doorbell and the telephone and Alyce had cut back on the number of guests they'd invited to join them on their patio, at one time the number was alarmingly high but now it was down to only twenty-three including Ernie and his wife and other relatives which was still a little high for such cramped space but Alyce figured some people could stand on the grass, in a semicircle maybe, observing a certain distance from the Blessed Virgin.

"Assuming She comes back," Floyd said dryly.

Alyce said sharply, "Of course She will. She *promised.*"

On the front page of Wednesday's *Courier* there had been an article headlined MANVILLE COUPLE, OTHERS REPORT "VISION," brief but respectful, and the article had been reprinted in Thursday's Newark *Star-Ledger*, possibly even elsewhere judging from the number of calls the Jameses had been receiving, so they were uneasily aware of the chance of unwanted visitors showing up at their house; but, like people living on an earthquake fault-line, or in a tornado alley, they simply did not think about it. Ernie insisted upon a makeshift barricade of borrowed sawhorses and wire blocking off the backyard from the driveway, and so from the street; but Floyd wouldn't hear of him hiring a security guard. (Which Floyd would have had to pay for, in any case.) As Sunday approached, and anticipation mounted, Floyd kept to himself at home and Alyce seemed to be on the phone constantly chattering to God knows who, distant relatives she hadn't seen or spoken with in thirty years, old high school girlfriends, and of course Judy and Marla with whom she kept in close contact though Floyd declined to speak with his daughters as with anyone else including Father O'Callaghan who he believed in his heart had betrayed them. (Still, O'Callaghan was coming today. Floyd counted that a good sign, that the Archbishop hadn't forbidden him!) It was as if he was setting off on a solitary journey detaching himself from the vanity of the world.

Except: he was filled with a terrible apprehension, mounting almost to terror. The thought that the Blessed Virgin Mary would be coming to his house. Or, the Blessed Virgin Mary would *not* be coming to his house. Blazing like a third eye in Floyd's forehead was this obsession.

How strange it was to him that the first time She had come, only last Sunday—a lifetime ago!—he'd been in utter ignorance of Her coming. He'd simply glanced up from his mowing, and there She was. The way a man lives his life—blindly, in ignorance, but in innocence as well. *If only I could be that man again. But that man is gone.*

Telling Her how when Franklin first got sick, coughing up phlegm like hot brass coins, the doctor diagnosed it as *bronchitis*. But then after a few months, Franklin steadily dropping weight as he was, heavier than Floyd all their lives, and down from two hundred twenty to one hundred eighty, the X ray showed the cluster of tiny tumors in the delicate lining of his lungs—*pleural mesothelioma*. That was the name. Still the hospital didn't give the name *asbestosis* to Franklin's condition until later when the other local cases were being publicized and the lawsuits starting. "Asbes-to-sis" you pronounced it. And it was a death sentence knowing what was known at that point in history, all the recent publicity directed against Johns-Manville Asbestos, Inc. which was being accused of negligence toward its workers, failing to in-form them of the danger of asbestos, failing to provide sufficient safety measures. The terrible thought pierced Floyd's mind like an electric shock *Thank God I never got a job there, thank God it's Franklin not me.* Franklin's salary as a maintenance supervisor in the textile division at Johns-Manville was always higher than Floyd's salary at Ingersoll Tools, Inc., there was that fact between the brothers like a pebble in your shoe so *Thank God, thank you Mary* except the thought came and went so swiftly it was possible to believe it had not come at all.

Franklin, poor bastard built like an ox but the flesh shrank steadily and his chest seemed to cave in except where the stony-hard tumors protruded you could actually feel with your fin-gers!—down finally to one hundred thirty pounds, a wheezing skeleton on a respirator. By then it was brain cancer. "Metas-ta-sis" to the brain. These filthy things the doctors have names for them they rattle off so it seemed to Floyd they were always ex-plaining the names and not the sicknesses. Unless it was all one sickness and that Death. And at that time Floyd was drinking not just ale but hard liquor and blacking out in the car and sleeping his heart kicked and missed its beats and stopped altogether then began again so he felt *he was his own doomed brother and could not escape.* And that night in late spring when poor Franklin was home from the hospital and became disoriented crawling out of the house without his wife realizing and tried to bury himself in the backyard garden where she found him facedown comatose in the mud and screamed and screamed for help. And Floyd in his bed two point six miles away waking choked and panicked believing himself in earth, in muck, trying to bury himself to hide himself from the pitying and horrified eyes of his loved ones. *Holy Mary, Mother of God, have mercy on us now and at the hour of our death Amen.*

Floyd thought of these things, these old memories trimming the lilac bushes he'd already trimmed too nervous to sit inside and wait: desperate for something to do to keep his mind off the time—it was almost 3 P.M.: Alyce had asked their guests please not to come until 4:30 P.M.—which passed more slowly than any time he had ever known.

How many strangers. How many pilgrims. Making their ways on the afternoon of May 23, 1993, to the small city of Manville, New Jersey, in search of a miracle. And when Manville police belatedly cordoned off the subdivision of Pinewood Acres, driving desperately along the curving lanes and into the leafy cul-de-sacs of the adjacent more affluent Oriole Hills, creating traffic congestion, gridlock, confusion, "disorientation." How many, hundreds? a thousand? two thousand? Manville authorities would fix the number at three thousand at the peak of the phenomenon, around 7 P.M. The damage to property, an estimated $6,000–$8,000.

This, Floyd Prentiss James, at whose ranch house in the Pinewood Acres subdivision the Blessed Virgin Mary was said to have appeared for the second time, would not learn until some time later.

By the time Father Brendan O'Callaghan and the other invited guests arrived at 188 Myrtle Drive shortly after 4 P.M. there was already an excited, apprehensive crowd gathering in front of the house, spilling into the street and onto neighboring lawns! The elderly priest in his black vestments, starched white turned-around collar that seemed to be choking his neck stared about with a look of incredulity. An exuberant blond woman, in hair and makeup resembling Hillary Clinton, thrust a microphone into his face and asked him a question he couldn't comprehend. Someone cried, "Father! Bless me, I'm a sinner! Take me to Her!" and when he glanced around, thin lips drawn back from his teeth in a frightened smile, several cameras flashed. A husky middle-aged woman with her white hair in braids, holding a Polaroid camera, was calling to him, "I *am* a Catholic, Father! A lapsed Catholic—" The priest managed to slip inside the front door as Alyce James opened it in agitation. *Who were all these people?*

The majority of the pilgrims were middle-aged and older. Photographs in area newspapers would show many carrying folding chairs and blankets; some were using walkers, and a few were being pushed in wheelchairs. These were not pushy or aggressive people—their mood was anxious and hopeful, but subdued. They were of an age where a miracle would be all that might save them, yet they had not the passion to demand one. There were some younger people, and these were difficult to classify— some of them, with rapt, ecstatic faces, were pilgrims too, but others were clearly curiosity-seekers. Cars, vans, and motorcycles were parked on both sides of narrow Myrtle Drive and more vehicles were approaching. The Jameses' invited guests were having difficulty finding places to park. "Let us through, please! Please let us through, we belong here!" Betty Gleason pleaded shrilly as she and her daughter Karin pushed their way up the Jameses' front walk. The blond woman reporter with a camera crew from New Jersey Cable Channel 59 thrust a microphone at Betty demanding to know why was she here this afternoon? did she believe in miracles? what did she hope to experience? was she a friend of the James family? had she seen the vision of Mary last Sunday? Betty Gleason was tongue-tied but her daughter Karin in a lavender pants suit and frilly white blouse, her eyes glaring with conviction, snatched the microphone and said excitedly, "*I* saw the Virgin Mary last week! Right out back here! I'm a friend of Mr. and Mrs. James! Even if you can't see Her, you can feel Her presence! I can feel it now! She's already here now! You don't even need to *see* Her with your eyes! Let us by now, Mother and I are going *inside*."

*   *   *

They gathered, these select few, on the Jameses' brick patio that Floyd had laid in so painstakingly by hand, their eyes fixed hungrily upon the grassy space beyond the portable barbecue where it was known the Blessed Virgin Mary had appeared the previous Sunday. Father O'Callaghan led them in repeated and fervent Hail Marys, the old priest's voice quickened and his words just perceptibly slurred as if he'd been drinking; this was to be the final year of his fifty-year priesthood and he seemed to know he would not have another. "Hail Mary, full of grace, the Lord is with Thee! Blessed art Thou—" The voices were not quite in unison. Several of the women seemed agitated. Floyd, his old-mannish bony knees aching on bare brick, about twelve feet from the miraculous spot, mumbled his words fiercely without hearing them. He recalled how, as a young boy, he'd raced his prayers with his twin brother, seeing who could finish first without leaving out a single word.

And then, suddenly, he understood: *It was a mistake.*

It was a mistake for the Blessed Virgin to have come to Earth, in Manville, New Jersey, and She must not come again now.

As the others prayed for Her, Floyd Prentiss James, staring with dread at the invisible outline in the air, began to whisper, "—Don't come here, Mary! No! Stay away!" as somewhere in the neighborhood a dog barked frantically as if tormented. Behind him, Alyce's shrill voice rose in a lurching singsong to contend with Floyd's whispered words. "We are not worthy of You, Mary! Stay away!"

But it was too late. To his horror Floyd saw the quivering in the air like molecules of moisture, a bluish-shimmering outline of a female figure, and the uplifted wimpled head. Behind him someone gasped "Oh! *oh!*" and another, "Oh! there She is—!" and others joined in astonished and sibilant as cicadas as Floyd, staring at the Blessed Virgin Mary, felt Her enter his eyes like a stream of liquid fire, and pour into his throat, and into his chest forcing out his breath even as a terrible vise gripped his chest and squeezed as he begged, "No! no! go away!" seeing now unmistakably how the Blessed Virgin's head was a death's head inside the tight white wimple, the eye sockets perfect empty Os and the toothed jaws grinning *Do not fear, Floyd: I have always been with you.*

There were screams as Floyd pitched forward onto his face on the bricks, but Floyd, shrinking rapidly to a pinpoint, heard nothing.

4.

By August 1, a bold yellow *ACE QUALITY REALTORS* FOR SALE sign in the front yard at 188 Myrtle Drive, amid the burnt-out straggly grass. Blinds drawn to the windowsills of the several front windows of the modest three-bedroom ranch house owned by Mr. and Mrs. Floyd Prentiss James. Rumor was, they were selling to move to a retirement village on the Jersey shore.

The rumor was *not* true that Floyd had died of a coronary thrombosis as a vision of the Blessed Virgin Mary "materialized" in his backyard; but it was true that the poor man had never fully recovered from his collapse. His heart had allegedly stopped beating by the time the ambulance delivered him to the emergency room of the Manville General Hospital but within seconds his chest was sliced open, his heart massaged into beating again, he was resuscitated—"To some extent," Floyd joked in his hoarse, cracked voice, squinting upward, "*I* can't complain."

Floyd was not yet sixty-nine years old but he'd become slow and halting in his speech, there was an affable sagging-softness to his face, his eyes were sunk deep as wisdom in their sockets. It was a blessing, people said, that his memory was so poor— mainly, he seemed to remember only pleasant things. For sure, he gave no evidence of remembering *it*.

Nor did Alyce, or any of the family, remind him.

How, the backyard vigil being interrupted by his collapse, and Alyce, their son and daughter-in-law gone to the hospital, strangers swarmed into the backyard and onto the patio, a seemingly ceaseless stream of them from all the corners of the Earth. The Jameses' rightful guests were routed as these pilgrims searched in vain for the Blessed Virgin Mary, trampling the lawn and the flowerbeds and seizing mementos—lawn chairs, cushions, azalea branches, even patio bricks upon which it was believed the Blessed Virgin had stood. The grinning dwarf was carried off in the melee. Handfuls of grass, bits of sod were torn up and carried off. Father O'Callaghan tried to stop the marauding but even the authority of the priesthood was ineffectual. Betty Gleason became hysterical as her daughter Karin got into a fistfight with a woman trespasser who was tearing up handfuls of grass—"You have no right! You weren't invited! She came to us! Damn you, get out of here! She came to *us*!"

It took about forty-five minutes for Manville police to quell the pilfering and vandalism, not only of the Jameses' property but of surrounding properties, and to reroute congested traffic out of the city. There were several arrests. One elderly man, brought to Manville by younger relatives, did in fact die of a heart attack out on Myrtle Drive.

Certain of the Jameses' neighbors, whose lawns were trampled and property damaged, threatened to sue them for having created a "public nuisance"—but the threats came to nothing, for, by late summer, when the ranch house at 188 Myrtle went up for sale, the Jameses had heard nothing further.

Not that Floyd fretted. He was past that. Lying on his lounge chair on the patio, resting, he'd wave and call out "Hello there!" seeing the Houstons next door, or the Ridleys, or imagining he saw them—vague shapes moving beyond the fence. For sure, Floyd harbored no animosity toward *them*.

He understood he'd had a severe heart attack and had nearly died but had *not* died—which was the only significant fact. They explained to him too he'd had a nervous breakdown which he accepted without objection since it explained a lot. Also, the economy of it pleased him: like a two-for-the-price-of-one sale.

One August afternoon Floyd woke startled from a light doze hearing someone call his name. It was a female voice, questioning. He was lying on his lounge chair taking in the heat which comforted the joints of his bones. He was feeling good and rested—he'd left it to Alyce and Ernie to deal with the house sale and the move to Ocean Park Village and whatever else had to be done. What peace, he thought. There'd always been this peace except he hadn't known.

Waking, Floyd glanced up puzzled to see that Alyce wasn't there. Yet he'd heard his name, hadn't he? Awkwardly he turned in the chair, squinting, and saw her, must be her, the vague shape of a woman with reddish hair, coming from the carport and headed in his direction.

Mark of Satan

A woman had come to save his soul and he wasn't sure he was
ready.

It isn't every afternoon in the dead heat of summer, cicadas
screaming out of the trees like lunatics, the sun a soft slow explosion in the sky, a husky young woman comes on foot rapping
shyly at the screen door of a house not even yours, a house in
which you are a begrudged guest, to save your soul. And she'd
brought an angel-child with her, too.

Thelma McCord, or was it McCrae. And Magdalena who was a
wisp of a child, perhaps four years old.

They were Church of the Holy Witness, headquarters Scranton, PA. They were God's own, and proud. Saved souls glowing
like neon out of their identical eye sockets.

Thelma was an "ordained missionary" and this was her "first
season of itinerary" and she apologized for disturbing his privacy
but did he, would he, surrender but a few minutes of his time to
the Teachings of the Holy Witness?

He'd been taken totally by surprise. He'd been dreaming a disagreeable churning-sinking dream and suddenly he'd been wakened, summoned, by a faint but persistent knocking at the front
door. Tugging on wrinkled khaki shorts and yanking up the zip-
per in angry haste—he was already wearing a T-shirt frayed and
tight in the shoulders—he'd padded barefoot to the screen door
blinking the way a mollusk might blink if it had eyes. In a house

unfamiliar to you, it's like waking to somebody else's dream. And there on the front stoop out of a shimmering-hot August afternoon he'd wished to sleep through, this girlish-eager young female missionary. An angel of God sent special delivery to *him*.

Quickly, before he could change his mind, before *no! no* intervened, he invited Thelma and little Magdalena inside. Out of the wicked hot sun—quick.

"Thank you," the young woman said, beaming with surprise and gratitude, "—Isn't he a kind, thoughtful man, Magdalena!"

Mother and daughter were heat-dazed, clearly yearning for some measure of coolness and simple human hospitality. Thelma was carrying a bulky straw purse and a tote bag with a red plastic sheen that appeared to be heavy with books and pamphlets. The child's face was pinkened with sunburn and her gaze so downcast she stumbled on the threshold of the door and her mother murmured *Tsk!* and clutched her hand tighter, as if, already, before their visit had begun, Magdalena had brought them both embarrassment.

He led them inside and shut the door. The living room opened directly off the front door. The house was a small three-bedroom tract ranch with simulated redwood siding; it was sparsely furnished, the front room uncarpeted, with a beige-vinyl sofa, twin butterfly chairs in fluorescent lime, and a coffee table that was a slab of weather-stained granite set atop cinderblocks. (The granite slab was in fact a grave marker, so old and worn by time that its name and dates were unintelligible. His sister Gracie, whose rented house this was, had been given the coffee table–slab by a former boyfriend.) A stain of the color of tea and the shape of an octopus disfigured a corner of the ceiling but the missionaries, seated with self-conscious murmurs of thanks on the sofa, would not see it.

He needed a name to offer to Thelma McCord, or McCrae, who had so freely offered her name to him. "Flash," he said, inspired, "—my name is Flashman."

He was a man no longer young yet by no means old; nor even, to the eye of a compassionate observer, middle-aged. His ravaged looks, his blood-veined eyes, appeared healable. He was a man given, however, to the habit of irony distasteful to him in execution but virtually impossible to resist. (Like masturbation, to which habit he was, out of irony too, given as well.) When he spoke to Thelma he heard a quaver in his voice that was his quickened, erratic pulse but might sound to another's ear like civility.

He indicated they should take the sofa, and he lowered himself into the nearest butterfly chair on shaky legs. When the damned contraption nearly overturned, the angel-child Magdalena, pale fluffy blond hair and delicate features, jammed her thumb into her mouth to keep from giggling. But her eyes were narrowed, alarmed.

"Mr. Flashman, so pleased to make your acquaintance," Thelma said uncertainly. Smiling at him with worried eyes possibly contemplating was he Jewish.

Contemplating the likelihood of a Jew, a descendant of God's chosen people, living in the scraggly foothills of southwestern Pennsylvania, in a derelict ranch house seven miles from Waynesburg with a front yard that looked as if motorcycles had torn it up. Would a Jew be three days' unshaven, jaws like sandpaper, knobbily barefoot and hairy-limbed as a gorilla. Would a Jew so readily welcome a Holy Witness into his house?

Offer them drinks, lemonade but no, he was thinking, *no.*

This, an opportunity for him to confront goodness, to look innocence direct in the eye, should not be violated.

Thelma promised that her visit would not take many minutes of Mr. Flashman's time. For time, she said, smiling breathlessly, is of the utmost—"That is one of the reasons I am here today."

Reaching deep into the tote bag to remove, he saw with a sinking heart, a hefty black Bible with gilt-edged pages and a stack of pamphlets printed on pulp paper—THE WITNESS. Then easing like a brisk mechanical doll into her recitation.

The man who called himself Flash was making every effort to listen. He knew this was important, there are no accidents. Hadn't he wakened in the night to a pounding heart and a taste of bile with the premonition that something, one of *his things*, was to happen soon; whether of his volition and calculation, or seemingly by accident (but there are no accidents), he could not know. Leaning forward gazing at the young woman with an elbow on his bare knee, the pose of Rodin's *Thinker*, listening hard. Except the woman was a dazzlement of sweaty-fragrant female flesh. Speaking passionately of the love of God and the passion of Jesus Christ and the Book of Revelation of St. John the Divine and the Testament of the Witness. Then eagerly opening her Bible on her knees and dipping her head toward it so that her sand-colored limp-curly hair fell into her face and she had to brush it away repeatedly—he was fascinated by the contrapuntal gestures, the authority of the Bible and the meek dipping of the head and the way in which, with childlike unconscious persistence, she pushed her hair out of her face. Unconscious too of her grating singsong voice, an absurd voice in which no profound truth could ever reside, and of her heavy young breasts straining against the filmy material of her lavender print dress, her fattish-muscular calves and good broad feet in what appeared to be white wicker ballerina slippers.

The grimy venetian blinds of the room were drawn against the glaring heat. It was above ninety degrees outside and there had been no soaking rains for weeks and in every visible tree hung ghostly bagworm nests. In his sister's bedroom a single window-unit air conditioner vibrated noisily and it had been in this room, on top of, not in, the bed, he'd been sleeping when the knocking came at the front door; the room that was his had no air conditioner. Hurrying out, he'd left the door to his sister's bedroom open and now a faint trail of cool-metallic air coiled out into the living room and so he fell to thinking that his visitors would notice the cool air and inquire about it and he would say yes there *is* air conditioning in this house, in one of the bedrooms, shall we go into that room and be more comfortable?

Now the Bible verses were concluded. Thelma's fair, fine skin glowed with excitement. Like a girl who has shared her most intimate secret and expects you now to share yours, Thelma lifted her eyes to Flash's and asked, almost boldly, was he aware of the fact that God loves him?—and he squirmed hearing such words, momentarily unable to respond, he laughed embarrassed, shook his head, ran his fingers over his sandpaper jaws, and mumbled no not really, he guessed that he was not aware of that fact, not really.

Thelma said that was why she was here, to bring the good

news to him. That God loved him whether he knew of Him or acknowledged Him. And the Holy Witness their mediator.

Flashman mumbled is that so. A genuine blush darkening his face.

Thelma insisted yes it *is* so. A brimming in her close-set eyes which were the bluest eyes Flash had never glimpsed except in glamor photos of models, movie stars, naked centerfolds. He said apologetically that he wasn't one hundred percent sure how his credit stood with God these days. "God and me," he said, with a boyish tucked-in smile, "have sort of lost contact over the years."

Which was *the* answer the young female missionary was primed to expect. Turning to the little girl and whispering in her ear, "Tell Mr. Flashman the good, good news, Magdalena!" and like a wind-up doll the blond child began to recite in a breathy high-pitched voice, "We can lose God but God never loses *us.* We can despair of God but God never despairs of *us.* The Holy Witness records, 'He that overcometh shall not be hurt by the second death.' " Abruptly as she'd begun the child ceased, her mouth going slack on the word *death.*

It was an impressive performance. Yet there was something chilling about it. Flash grinned and winked at the child in his uneasiness and said, "Second death? Eh? What about the first?" But Magdalena just gaped at him. Her left eye losing its focus as if coming unmoored.

The more practiced Thelma quickly intervened. She took up both her daughter's hands in hers and in a brisk patty-cake rhythm chanted, "As the Witness records, 'God shall wipe away all tears from their eyes; and there *will be* no more death.' "

Maybe it was so? So simple? *No more death.*

Bemused by the simplicity of fate. In this house unknown to him as recently as last week in this rural no-man's-land where his older sister Gracie had wound up a county social worker toiling long grueling hours five days a week and forced to be grateful for the shitty job, he'd heard a rapping like a summons to his secret blood padding barefoot to the dream doorway that's shimmering with light and there she *is.*

"Excuse me, Thelma—would you and Magdalena like some lemonade?"

Thelma immediately demurred out of country-bred politeness as he'd expected so he asked Magdalena who appeared to be parched with thirst, poor exploited child, but, annoyingly, she was too shy to even shake her head yes please. Flash, stimulated by challenge, apologized for not having fresh-squeezed lemonade calculating that Thelma would have to accept to prove she wasn't offended by his offer; adding to that he was about to get some lemonade for himself, icy-cold, and would they please join him so Thelma, lowering her eyes, said yes. As if he'd reached out to touch her and she hadn't dared draw back.

In the kitchen, out of sight, he moved swiftly—which was why his name was Flash. For a man distracted, a giant black-feathered eagle tearing out his liver, he moved with a surprising alacrity. But that had always been his way.

Opening the fridge, nostrils pinching against the stale stink inside, his sister Gracie's depressed housekeeping he tried his best to ignore, taking out the stained Tupperware pitcher of Bird's Eye lemonade—thank God, there was some. Tart chemical taste he'd have to mollify, in his own glass, with an ounce or two of Gordon's gin. For his missionary visitors he ducked into his bedroom and located his stash and returned to the kitchen counter crumbling swiftly between his palms several chalky-white pills, six milligrams each of barbiturate, enough to fell a healthy horse, reducing them to gritty powder to dissolve in the greenish lemonade he poured into two glasses: the taller for Thelma, the smaller for Magdalena. He wondered what the little girl weighed—forty pounds? Thirty? Fifty? He had no idea, children were mysteries to him. His own childhood was a mystery to him. But he wouldn't want Magdalena's heart to stop beating.

He'd seen a full-sized man go glassy-eyed and clutch at his heart and topple over stone dead overdosing on—what? Heroin. It was a clean death so far as deaths go but it came out of the corner of your eye, you couldn't prepare.

Carefully setting the three glasses of lemonade, two tall and slim for the adults, the other roly-poly for sweet little Magdalena, on a laminated tray. Returning then humming cheerfully to the airless living room where his visitors were sitting primly on the battered sofa as if, in his absence, they hadn't moved an inch.

Shyly yet with trembling hands both reached for their glasses—
"Say 'thank you, sir,' " Thelma whispered to Magdalena, who
whispered, "Thank you, sir," and lifted her glass to her lips.

Thelma disappointed him by taking only a ladylike sip, then
dabbing at her lips with a tissue. "Delicious," she murmured. But
setting the glass down as if it was a temptation. Poor Magdalena
was holding her glass in both hands taking quick swallows but at
a sidelong glance from her mother she too set her glass down on
the tray.

Flash said, as if hurt, "There's lots more sugar if it isn't sweet
enough."

But Thelma insisted no, it was fine. Taking up, with the look
of a woman choosing among several rare gems, one of the pulp-
printed pamphlets. Now, Flash guessed, she'd be getting down to
business. Enlisting him to join the Church of the Holy Ghost, or
whatever it was—Holy Witness?

She named names and cited dates that flew past him—except
for the date Easter Sunday 1899 when, apparently, there'd been a
"shower from the heavens" north of Scranton, PA—and he nodded to encourage her though she hardly needed encouraging;
taking deep thirsty sips from his lemonade to encourage her too.
Out of politeness Thelma did lift her glass to take a chaste swallow but no more. Maybe there was a cult prescription against
frozen foods, chemical drinks?—the way the Christian Scientists,
unless it was the Seventh Day Adventists, forbade blood transfu-
sions because such was "eating blood" which was outlawed by
the Bible.

Minutes passed. The faint trickle of metallic-cool air touched
the side of his feverish face. He tried not to show his impatience
with Thelma fixing instead on the amazing fact of her: a woman
not known to him an hour before, now sitting less than a yard
away addressing him as if, out of all of the universe, *he mattered.*
Loving how she sat wide-hipped and settled into the vinyl cushions like a partridge in a nest. Knees and ankles together, chunky
farmgirl feet in the discount-mart wicker flats; half-moons of perspiration darkening the underarms of her floral-print dress. It was
a Sunday school kind of dress, lavender rayon with a wide white
collar and an awkward flared skirt and cloth-covered buttons the

size of half-dollars. Beneath it the woman would be wearing a full slip, no half-slip for her. Damp from her warm pulsing body. No doubt, white brassiere, D-cups, and white cotton panties the waist and legs of which left red rings in her flesh. Undies damp, too. And the crotch of the panties, damp. Just possibly stained. She was bare-legged, no stockings, a concession to the heat: just raw female leg, reddish-blond transparent hairs on the calves for she was not a woman to shave her body hair. Nor did she wear makeup. No such vanity. Her cheeks were flushed as if rouged and her lips were naturally moist and rosy. Her skin would be hot to the touch. She was twenty-eight or -nine years old and probably Magdalena was not her first child, but her youngest. She had the sort of female body mature by early adolescence, beginning to go flaccid by thirty-five. That fair, thin skin that wears out from too much smiling and aiming to please. Suggestion of a double chin. Hips would be spongy and cellulite-puckered. Kneaded like white bread, squeezed banged and bruised. Moist heat of a big bush of curly pubic hair. Secret crevices of pearl-drops of moisture he'd lick away with his tongue.

Another woman would have been aware of Flash's calculating eyes on her like ants swarming over sugar but not this impassioned missionary for the Church of the Holy Witness. Had an adder risen quivering with desire before her she would have taken no heed. She was reading from one of THE WITNESS pamphlets and her gaze was shining and inward as she evoked in a hushed little-girl voice a vision of bearded prophets raving in the deserts of Smyrna and covenants made by Jesus Christ to generations of sinners up to this very hour. Jesus Christ was the most spectacular of the prophets, it seemed, for out of his mouth came a sharp two-edged sword casting terror into all who beheld. Yet he was a poet, his words had undeniable power, here was Flash the man squirming in his butterfly chair as Thelma recited tremulously, " 'And Jesus spake: I am he that liveth, and was dead; and, behold, I am alive for evermore; and have the keys of hell and death.' "

There was a pause. A short distance away a neighbor was running a chainsaw and out on the highway cars, trucks, thunderous diesel vehicles passed in an erratic whooshing stream and on all sides beyond the house's walls the air buzzed, quivered, vibrated, rang with the insects of late summer but otherwise it was quiet, it was silent. Like a vacuum waiting to be filled.

The child Magdalena, unobserved by her mother, had drained her glass of lemonade and licked her lips with a flicking pink tongue and was beginning to be drowsy. She wore a pink rayon dress like a nightie with a machine-stamped lace collar, tiny feet in white socks and shiny white plastic shoes. Flash saw, yes, the child's left eye had a cast in it. The right eye perceived you head-on but the left drifted outward like a sly wayward moon.

A defect in an eye of so beautiful a child would not dampen Flash's ardor. He was certain of that.

Ten minutes, fifteen. By now it was apparent that Thelma did not intend to drink her lemonade though Flash had drained his own glass and wiped his mouth with gusto. Did she suspect? Did she sense something wrong? But she'd taken no notice of Magdalena who had drifted off into a light doze, her angel-head drooping and a thread of saliva shining on her chin. Surely a suspicious Christian mother would not have allowed her little girl to drink spiked lemonade handed her by a barefoot bare-legged pervert possibly a Jew with eyes like the yanked-up roots of thistles—that was encouraging.

"Your lemonade, Thelma," Flash said, with a host's frown, "—it will be getting warm if you don't—"

Thelma seemed not to hear. With a bright smile she was asking, "Have you been baptized, Mr. Flashman?"

For a moment he could not think who Mr. Flashman was. The gin coursing through his veins which ordinarily buoyed him up like debris riding the crest of a flood and provided him with an acute clarity of mind had had a dulling, downward sort of effect. He was frightened of the possibility of one of *his things* veering out of his control for in the past when this had happened the consequences were always very bad. For him as for others.

His face burned. "I'm afraid that's my private business, Thelma. I don't bare my heart to any stranger who walks in off the road."

Thelma blinked, startled. Yet was immediately repentant.

"Oh, I know! I have overstepped myself, please forgive me, Mr. Flashman!"

Such passion quickened the air between them. Flash felt a stab of excitement. But ducking his head, boyish-repentant too, murmuring, "No, it's okay, I'm just embarrassed I guess. I don't truly *know* if I was baptized. I was an orphan discarded at birth, set out with the trash. There's a multitude of us scorned by man and God. What happened to me before the age of twelve is lost to me. Just a whirlwind. A whirlpool of oblivion."

Should have left his sister's bedroom door shut, though. To keep the room cool. If he had to carry or drag this woman any distance—the child wouldn't be much trouble—he'd be miserable by the time he got to where he wanted to go.

Thelma all but exploded with solicitude, leaning forward as if about to gather him up in her arms.

"Oh that's the saddest thing I have ever heard, Mr. Flashman! I wish one of our elders was here right now to counsel you as I cannot! 'Set out with the trash'—can it be? Can any human mother have been so cruel?"

"If it was a cruel mother, which I don't contest, it was a cruel God guiding her hand, Thelma—wasn't it?"

Thelma blinked rapidly. This was a proposition not entirely new to her, Flash surmised, but one which required a moment's careful and conscious recollection. She said, uncertainly at first and then with gathering momentum, "The wickedness of the world is Satan's hand, and the ways of Satan as of the ways of God are not to be comprehended by man."

"What's Satan got to do with this? I thought we were talking about the good guys."

"Our Savior Jesus Christ—"

"*Our* Savior? Who says? On my trash heap I looked up, and He looked down, and He said, 'Fuck you, kid. Life *is* unfair.' "

Thelma's expression was one of absolute astonishment. Like a cow, Flash thought ungallantly, in the instant the sledgehammer comes crashing down on her head.

Flash added, quick to make amends, "I thought this was about me, Thelma, about my soul. I thought the Holy Witness or whoever had something special to say to *me*."

Thelma was sitting stiff, her hands clasping her knees. One of THE WITNESS pamphlets had fallen to the floor and the hefty Bible too would have slipped had she not caught it. Her eyes now were alert and wary and she knew herself in the presence of an enemy yet did not know that more than theology was at stake. "The Holy Witness does have something special to say to you, Mr. Flashman. Which is why I am here. There is a growing pestilence in the land, flooding the Midwest with the waters of the wrathful Mississippi, last year razing the Sodom and Gomorrah of Florida, everywhere there are droughts and famines and earthquakes and volcanic eruptions and plagues—all signs that the old world is nearing its end. As the Witness proclaimed in the Book of Revelation that is our sacred scripture, 'There will be a new heaven and a new earth, as the first heaven and the first earth pass away. And the Father on His throne declaring, Behold I make all things new—' "

Flash interrupted, "None of this *is* new! It's been around for how many millennia, Thelma, and what good's it done for anybody?"

" '—I am Alpha and Omega, the beginning and the end,' " Thelma continued, unheeding, rising from the sofa like a fleshy angel of wrath in her lavender dress that stuck to her belly and legs, fumbling to gather up her Bible, her pamphlets, her dazed child, " '—I will give unto him that is athirst of the fountain of life freely but the fearful, and unbelieving, and the abominable, and murderers, and all liars, shall sink into the lake which burneth with fire and brimstone: which is the second death.' " Her voice rose jubilantly on the word *death*.

Flash struggled to disentangle himself from the butterfly chair. The gin had done something weird to his legs—they were numb, and rubbery. Cursing, he fell to the floor, the rock-hard carpetless floor, as Thelma roused Magdalena and lifted her to her feet and half-carried her to the door. Flash tried to raise himself by gripping the granite marker coffee table but this too collapsed, the cinderblocks gave way and the heavy slab came crashing down on his right hand. Three fingers were broken at once but in the excitement he seemed not to notice. "Wait! You can't leave me now! I need you!"

At the door Thelma called back, panting, "Help *is* needed here. There is Satan in this house."

Flash stumbled to his feet, followed the woman to the door, calling after, "What do you mean, 'Satan in this house'—there is no Satan, there is no Devil, it's all in the heads of people like you. You're religious maniacs! You're mad! Wait—"

He could not believe the woman was escaping so easily. That *his thing* was nothing of *his* at all.

Hauling purse, bulky tote bag, sleep-dazed daughter on her hip, Thelma was striding in her white-wicker ballerina flats swiftly yet without apparent haste or panic out to the gravel driveway. There was a terrible quivering of the sun-struck air. Cicadas screamed like fire sirens. Flash tried to follow after, propelling himself on his rubbery legs which were remote from his head which was too small for his body and at the end of a swaying stalk. He was laughing, crying, "You're a joke, people like you! You're tragic victims of ignorance and superstition! You don't belong in the twentieth century with the rest of us! You're the losers of the world! You can't cope! *You* need salvation!"

Staring amazed at the rapidly departing young woman—the dignity in her body, the high-held head and the very arch of the backbone; her indignation that was not fear, an indignation possibly too primitive to concede to fear, like nothing in his experience nor even in his imagination. If this was a movie, he was thinking, panicked, the missionary would be *walking out of the frame* leaving him behind—just him.

"Help! Wait! Don't leave me here alone!"

He was screaming, terrified. He perceived that his life was of no more substance than a cicada's shriek. He'd stumbled as far as the driveway when a blinding light struck him like a sword piercing his eyes and brain.

Fallen to his knees then in the driveway amid sharp gravel and broken glass and bawling like a child beyond all pride, beyond all human shame. His head was bowed, sun beating down on the balding crown of his head. His very soul wept through his eyes for he knew he would die, and nothing would save him not even irony *Don't flatter yourself you matter enough even to grieve! Ass-*

hole!—no, not even his wickedness would save him. Yet seeing him stricken the young Christian woman could not walk away. He cried, "Satan *is* here! In me! He speaks through me! It isn't me! Please help me, don't leave me to die!" His limbs shook as if palsied and his teeth chattered despite the heat. Where the young woman stood wavering there was a blurry shimmering figure of light and he pleaded with it, tore open his chest, belly to expose the putrescent tumor of Satan choking his entrails, he begged for mercy for help for Christ's love until at last the young woman cautiously approached him to a distance of about three feet kneeling too though not in the gravel driveway but in the grass and by degrees putting aside her distrust seeing the sickness in this sinner howling to be saved she bowed her head and clasped her hands to her breasts and began to pray loudly, triumphantly, "O Heavenly Father help this tormented sinner to repent of his sins and to be saved by Your Only Begotten Son that he might stand by the throne of Your righteousness, help all sinners to be saved by the Testament of the Holy Witness—"

How many minutes the missionary prayed over the man who had in jest called himself Flashman he would not afterward know. For there seemed to be a fissure in time itself. The two were locked in ecstasy as in the most intimate of embraces in the fierce heat of the sun, and in the impulsive generosity of her spirit the young woman reached out to clasp his trembling hands in hers and to squeeze them tight. Admonishing him, "Pray! Pray to Jesus Christ! Every hour of every day pray to Him in your heart!" She was weeping too and her face was flushed and swollen and shining with tears. He pleaded with her not to leave him for Satan was still with him, he feared Satan's grip in his soul, but there was a car at the end of the driveway toward which the child Magdalena had made her unsteady way and now a man's voice called, "Thelma! Thel-ma!" and at once the young woman rose to her full height brushing her damp hair out of her face and with a final admonition to him to love God and Christ and abhor Satan and all his ways she was gone, vanished into the light out of which she had come.

Alone he remained kneeling, too weak to stand. Rocking and swaying in the sun. His parched lips moved uttering babble. In a frenzy of self-abnegation he ground his bare knees in the gravel and shattered glass, deep and deeper into the pain so that he might bleed more freely bleeding all impurity from him or at least mutilating his flesh so that in the arid stretch of years before him that would constitute the remainder of his life he would possess a living memory of this hour, scars he might touch, read like Braille.

When Gracie Shuttle returned home hours later she found her brother Harvey in the bathroom dabbing at his wounded knees with a blood-soaked towel, picking bits of gravel and glass out of his flesh with a tweezers. And his hand—several fingers of his right hand were swollen as sausages, and grotesquely bruised. Gracie was a tall lank sardonic woman of forty-one with deep-socketed eyes that rarely acknowledged surprise; yet, seeing Harvey in this remarkable posture, sitting hunched on the toilet seat, a sink of blood-tinged water beside him, she let out a long high whistle. "What the hell happened to *you?*" she asked. Harvey raised his eyes to hers. He did not appear to be drunk, or drugged; his eyes were terribly bloodshot, as if he'd had one of his crying jags, but his manner was unnervingly composed. His face was ravaged and sunburnt in uneven splotches as if it had been baked. He said, "I've been on my knees to Gethsemane and back. It's too private to speak of." From years ago when by an accident of birth they'd shared a household with two hapless adults who were their parents, Gracie knew that her younger brother in such a state was probably telling the truth, or a kind of truth; she knew also that he would never reveal it to her. She waved in his face a pulp religious pamphlet she'd found on the living room floor beside the collapsed granite marker. "And what the hell is *this?*" she demanded. But again with that look of maddening calm Harvey said, "It's my private business, Gracie. Please shut the door on your way out."

Gracie slammed the door in Harvey's face and charged through the house to the rear where wild straggly bamboo was choking the yard. Since she'd moved in three years before the damned bamboo had spread everywhere, marching from the marshy part of the property where the cesspool was located too

close to the surface of the soil. Just her luck! And her with a master's degree in social work from the University of Pennsylvania!
She'd hoped, she'd expected more from her education, as from
life. She lit a cigarette and rapidly smoked it exhaling luxuriant
streams of smoke through her nostrils. "Well, fuck you," she said,
laughing. She frequently laughed when she was angry, and she
laughed a good deal these days.

It *was* funny. Whatever it was, it *was* funny—her parolee kid
brother once an honors student now a balding middle-aged man
picking tenderly at his knees that looked as if somebody had
slashed them with a razor. That blasted-sober look in the poor
guy's eyes she hadn't seen in him in twelve years—since one of
his junkie buddies in Philly had dropped over dead mainlining
heroin.

Some of the bamboo stalks were brown and desiccated but
most of the goddamned stuff was still greenly erect, seven feet tall
and healthy. Gracie flicked her cigarette butt out into it. Waiting
bored to see if it caught fire, if there'd be a little excitement out
here on Route 71 tonight, the Waynesburg Volunteer Firemen ex-
ercising their shiny red equipment and every yokel for miles hop-
ping in his pickup to come gape—but it didn't, and there wasn't.

Acknowledgments

The stories included in this volume originally appeared in the following publications, often in different forms.

"Act of Solitude" in *Agni Review*

"You Petted Me, and I Followed You Home" in *TriQuarterly*, reprinted in *Prize Stories: The O. Henry Awards 1995*

"Good to Know You" in *Western Humanities Review*

"The Revenge of the Foot, 1970" in *Salmagundi*

"Politics" in *Cosmopolitan*

"The Missing Person" in *Glimmer Train*

"Will You Always Love Me?" in a limited edition by James Cahill Publishing, Huntington Beach, California, 1994; also in *Story*

"Life After High School" in *Atlantic Monthly*

"The Goose-Girl" in *Fiction*, reprinted in *Prize Stories: The O. Henry Awards 1992*

"American, Abroad" in *North American Review*, reprinted in *The Best American Short Stories 1991*

"The Track" in *Gentlemen's Quarterly*

"The Handclasp" in *Kenyon Review*

"The Girl Who Was to Die" in *Gettysburg Review*

"June Birthing" in *Cosmopolitan*

"The Undesirable Table" in *Raritan*; reprinted in *The Pushcart Prize: 1995–1996: The Best of the Small Presses*

"Is Laughter Contagious?" in *Harper's;* reprinted in *The Best American Short Stories 1992*.

"The Brothers" in *Ellery Queen's Mystery Magazine*; reprinted in *The Year's Best Fantasy and Horror 1995*

"The Lost Child" in *Michigan Quarterly Review*

"Christmas Night 1962" in *TriQuarterly*

"The Passion of Rydcie Mather" in *Southern Review*

"The Vision" in *Michigan Quarterly Review*

"Mark of Satan" in *Antaeus*

• A NOTE ON THE TYPE •

The typeface used in this book is one of many versions of Garamond, a modern homage to—rather than, strictly speaking, a revival of—the celebrated fonts of Claude Garamond (c.1480–1561), the first founder to produce type on a large scale. Garamond's type was inspired by Francesco Griffo's *De Ætna* type (cut in the 1490s for Venetian printer Aldus Manutius and revived in the 1920s as Bembo), but its letter forms were cleaner and the fit between pieces of type improved. It therefore gave text a more harmonious overall appearance than its predecessors had, becoming the basis of all romans created on the continent for the next two hundred years; it was itself still in use through the eighteenth century. Besides the many "Garamonds" in use today, other typefaces derived from his fonts are Granjon and Sabon (despite their being named after other printers).